THE

GOD

STONE

BOOK ONE

G.G. Ross

This book is dedicated to Zoe and our sons, without whom, I would have completed the trilogy by now.

It is also dedicated to my fifteen-year-old self. The boy on the school bus, listening to music on his temperamental Discman. I promised you I would finish this one day.

I hope I've done justice to your dreams.

ACKNOWLEDGMENTS

This book exists thanks to the following people;

Zoe Dummett, James Beaumont, Dave Stanton, Rachel Calder, Sarah Painter, Jonathan Dunn, Emily Butler, Nick Laws, Kim O'Donoghue, J. Burke, Rob D., Daniel Greene, E. M., Joe Shrimpling, Lance Buckley, Irena Hynková, Scott Pack, Joe Pierson.

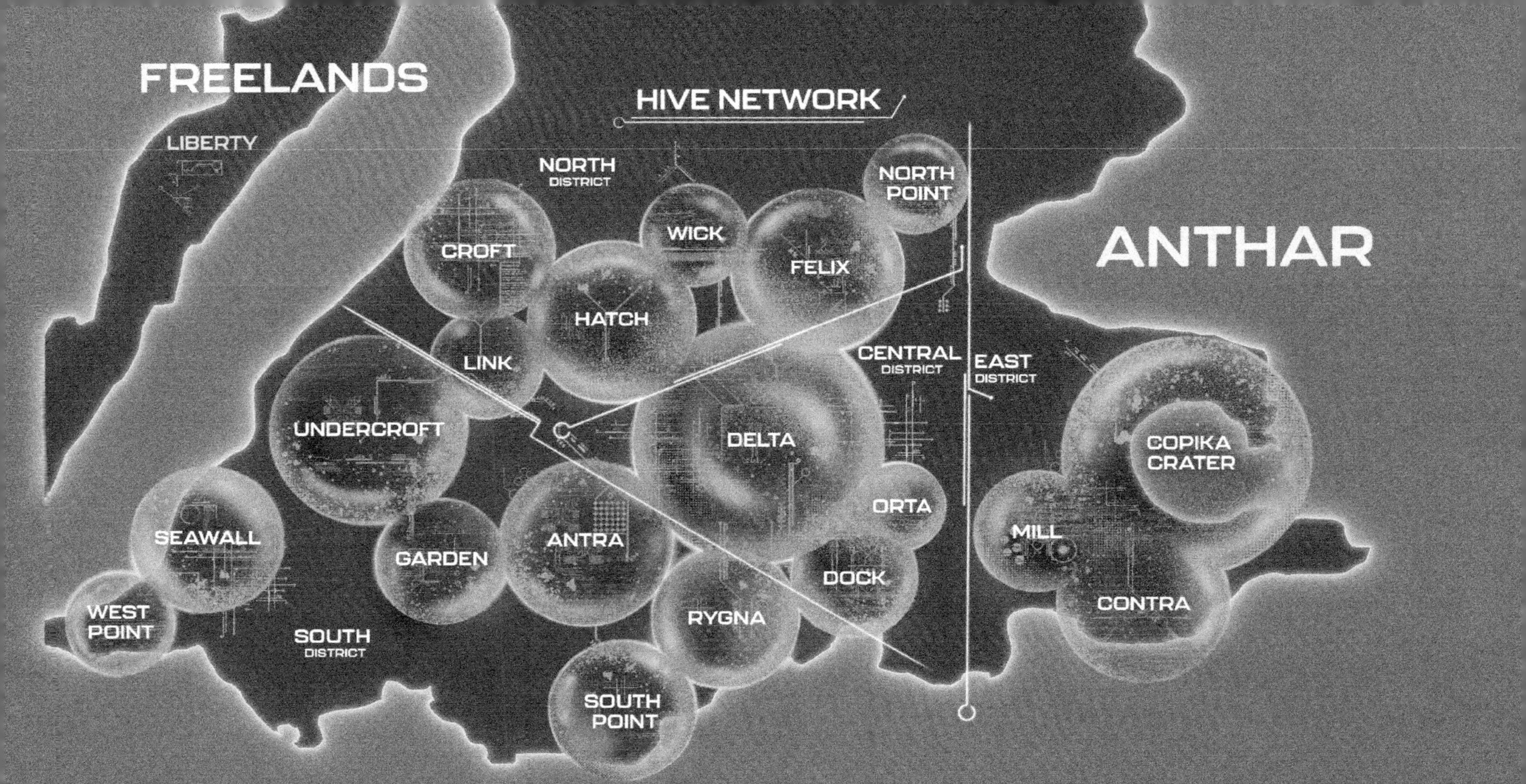
FREELANDS
LIBERTY
HIVE NETWORK
NORTH
DISTRICT
NORTH
POINT
ANTHAR
WICK
CROFT
FELIX
HATCH
LINK
CENTRAL
DISTRICT
EAST
DISTRICT
UNDERCROFT
DELTA
COPIKA
CRATER
ORTA
MILL
SEAWALL
GARDEN
ANTRA
DOCK
WEST
POINT
SOUTH
DISTRICT
RYGNA
CONTRA
SOUTH
POINT

PART I

ANTHAR

CHAPTER 1

The Properties of Inficore

A storm raged in the night.

Gale-force winds drove a continent of black clouds across the sky, lashing sheets of silver rain and lightning through the darkness.

But the storm, for all its fury, had no effect on the city of Felix below. Not a single drop of rain or gust of wind could touch the pristine metropolis. The city's energy dome made quite sure of it. As the storm thrashed impotently against the barrier, the ten million inhabitants of Felix went about their nightly business, undisturbed, confident in their exclusion from nature.

On the western outskirt of the city, a single building shone spectacularly against the night; a tall, sharp crescent of glass, wearing a rooftop garden like a bad haircut. A prominent logo jutted from its curved inner aspect, declaring the building's name.

InfiTech North.

A crowd of journalists from every corner of the Hive Network mingled loosely in the building's forecourt, their attentions split amongst the storm overhead, their superficial conversations, and the dazzling InfiTech building that had invited them to witness history.

Every so often, their heads would turn in unison, drawn by the sudden arrival of another glass, egg-shaped car from the Nexus Portal. The cars popped up from the hole, slid along a curved track, and deposited their occupants at the platform, before disappearing underground.

But further underground, far beneath the deepest reaches of the Nexus Portal, and miles under the InfiTech crescent, through eons of compacted soil, stood three men, waiting in a squat, cramped, industrial bunker.

'Right,' said one. 'Let's go through it one more time. For luck.'

The man who had spoken stood with his arms folded across his chest. He wore a grey T-shirt tucked into black cargo trousers, and an InfiTech

ID card dangled from a lanyard around his neck, displaying his mugshot and credentials; **Adam Maxwell, Senior Blank Programmer**. The photo showed a man with a neat horseshoe of greying reddish hair, wearing round copper glasses.

The real Adam Maxwell puffed out his cheeks in a long exhale.

'Okay …' he said, 'Ford, return to neutral position.'

The man facing Adam straightened to perfect stillness. He wore a full-body kirrion suit, like a slim astronaut, and his expressionless face stared at Adam through the helmet visor, waxlike and completely without hair. He held a crude machine delicately between gloved hands; a metal box covered in dials and exposed wiring.

Genevieve's prototype.

'Ford,' Adam said clearly, 'place the prototype on the floor to your right, with the open side facing *me*.'

Ford obeyed the command, each movement deliberate and smooth. On completion, he remained in a crouch beside the prototype, awaiting Adam's next command.

Good. Absolute control, Adam thought. *No mistakes this time.*

'Okay, Ford, release the machine, stand up, and remove the asset from your harness.'

Ford stood, reached back, and slipped a roughly hewn wooden cup from the holster at his back. Again, he moved with fluid precision.

'He looks nervous,' came a voice from behind Adam.

Adam rolled his eyes at the man slouching in the swivel chair. Gerald smiled up at him, a mug of coffee in one hand.

'He *can't* get nervous,' said Adam. 'He's a blank. That's the whole point.'

Gerald raised his free hand. 'Hey, *you're* the expert,' he said, 'but I know fear when I see it. It's in his eyes.'

'That's *projection*,' said Adam. 'You see fear because you, like most people, are afraid of him. Of blanks, I mean.'

Gerald pursed his lips and gave a so-so rock of his head.

'I wouldn't say I'm afraid of them,' he said, 'but I definitely don't trust them. They're not natural.'

'Oh, and you're *all* about being natural, right? How's that filtered coffee going down? Is the temperature okay?'

Gerald laughed. 'Well, at least I've got the courage to look my age,' he retorted.

This was a fair point. Gerald was in his sixties now and looked the part, with wrinkled skin and all. Meanwhile, Adam, fifty years his senior, looked thirty years his junior.

The perk of opting for Cellular Regeneration Therapy.

'Touché,' Adam said. 'Now shut up and let me get back to work.'

The lift door behind them slid open to reveal Genevieve LePlass. She strode into the bunker, smiling, and a handful of butterflies took flight in Adam's stomach.

'Ah, there you are,' she said, her smile widening.

She had dark hair tied away from her neck in a scruffy ponytail, and thick glasses that magnified her clear, bright-green eyes. She was a head shorter than Adam, blessed with a gymnastic build that belied an astonishing lack of fitness.

She was a little out of breath just crossing the room.

'Sebastian wants us topside to greet the press,' she said. 'He's in a flap about his speech, and, to be honest, I think he's losing the plot.'

'What?' said Gerald, wheeling his chair across the floor. 'You mean Sebastian isn't being cool, calm, and collected?'

'You leave him alone,' Genevieve warned. 'I know he can be difficult, but it's a big night for him, just like us, so I'm giving him a free pass.'

Gerald saluted her with his mug.

'He wants *me* up there?' Adam asked.

Genevieve's eyes darted quickly at Gerald, her cheeks turning slightly pink. 'Well, erm, yes. Unless … unless you're in the middle of something?'

Adam heard the request. The population of butterflies doubled.

'No, that's fine.' He swallowed. 'Yeah, let's go up there.'

Awkwardly, he followed Genevieve into the lift and glanced back at Gerald, who raised an eyebrow over his coffee before the door closed.

Genevieve hit the button, and the lift began to ascend to the surface. They stood facing the door in palpable silence.

Adam's *ears* were sweating.

Say something, he thought as the lift gained momentum. *But what? What should I say? I don't know, why are you asking me? Should I kiss her? Are you joking? You can't even look at her, and your body's made of rubber at the moment. Did you even shower today?*

A horrible minute passed. The atmosphere reached boiling point.

Just say something safe, like, how have you been? *Yeah.* How have you been?

That doesn't sound insane. Say that.

'We should probably talk about last night,' he heard Genevieve say.

'Yeah, probably,' said Adam, his voice higher than usual.

Another silence flourished amid the tension.

'So … what do you think?' said Genevieve.

Adam cleared his throat. 'Well, I think … I think I owe you an apology.'

'Oh?'

'Yeah, I mean, of all the nights it could have happened … maybe … maybe the night before the biggest day of your career wasn't the best idea, you know? I just … You've worked so hard to make this experiment possible, Genevieve. And I would hate to jeopardise it in some way. So … I'm sorry.'

'Ahh, so *that's* why you've been avoiding me today.'

'I haven't been *avoiding* you!' Adam said, looking sideways at her for the first time. But he saw the look on her face. 'Yeah, okay, I've totally been avoiding you.'

'Well, don't,' she said. 'I didn't expect to wake up alone. I thought I'd scared you off.'

Adam felt a weight plummet in the opposite direction to the lift's pull. He turned to look into her green eyes.

'I'm really sorry,' he said. 'I had the best night of my life. Honestly. I only wish it had happened sooner, or forty-eight hours later. Because I know how important today is for you. I just didn't want to be a distraction.'

Genevieve suppressed a smile with difficulty. 'You're not a distraction,' she said. 'Just an idiot.'

Adam nodded, forcing his face to remain earnest. 'Guilty.'

They smiled tentatively at each other, then grinned at their mutual smiling. A second later, Adam felt her hand slip into his, and his whole body tingled. Electricity in his fingertips.

The lift stopped. Adam and Genevieve let their hands part as the delicate atmosphere was sucked out by a cold vacuum.

Sebastian stood framed in the doorway; tall, imposing, wearing a green suit, his jacket buttons undone, tie askew, fists on his hips. All the features of his face seemed oversized to Adam, as though he were slightly less evolved.

'Where have you *been?*' he said to Genevieve. 'They're taking their seats! Is everything in place below?'

'I've completed all my calibrations,' Genevieve replied. 'The prototype is ready.'

'So is Ford,' said Adam. 'And we couldn't ask for a better chamber technician than Gerald. Everything's good to go.'

Sebastian nodded his huge head for a moment, staring inwardly at the floor.

'Okay,' he said finally. He flattened his tie. 'How do I look?'

'Great!'

'Tremendous!'

He narrowed his bulbous eyes at them, then strode into the mass of journalists, heading toward the stage. Rows of chairs, mostly occupied now, stood divided by a central aisle, facing the InfiTech logo on a large screen. Sebastian jogged up a small set of stairs to stand behind a lectern covered with colourful microphones. As he did so, the stragglers took the remaining seats among the field of laptops and notepads, and the general murmur died away.

Genevieve drew a stack of handwritten flashcards from her back pocket and shuffled them nervously into order.

'Good evening,' blared Sebastian's voice through the speakers, 'and welcome to InfiTech North. For those of you who don't recognise me from your cruel, untrue stories, I am Sebastian Fincher, director of InfiTech.'

A perfunctory chuckle swept through the audience.

'Firstly,' Sebastian continued, visibly enjoying his moment, 'I know it's very late, and I'd like to thank you all for coming at such an unsociable hour. Secondly, if you have any complaints about the hour, please remember that this experiment is sanctioned by the Algorithm, and to publish your complaints accordingly.'

Sincere laughter filled the room, making Genevieve glance up from her cards, still mouthing in silent panic. Adam's insides squirmed in sympathy. Brilliant though Genevieve was, the world's spotlight was no place for an introvert.

'We are gathered here tonight to witness something extraordinary,' said Sebastian. 'The next step in our scientific evolution. I could bore you with the details, but I'll leave that to the project leader, whose theories, inventions, and perseverance have made this night possible. Please welcome Doctor Genevieve LePlass.'

'Good luck,' Adam whispered under the applause, as Genevieve marched down the aisle.

She arrived at the lectern as Sebastian stood aside. But he remained at her shoulder, unwilling to relinquish the limelight fully. Genevieve brushed a strand of hair behind her ear as the clapping faded.

'Thank you. Most people know what Inficore is,' she said in a rehearsed tone, eyes on her cards, 'but few understand its properties. While the Hive Network has harnessed Inficore energy for over a thousand years, we have overlooked its most precious quality.'

Heads bobbed in the audience as hasty notes were taken. Genevieve clicked a remote, and the InfiTech logo on the screen was replaced by the image of a glassy, obsidian-black stone glowing faintly purple from within.

'In the Academies,' Genevieve went on, 'we learn what Inficore does; it absorbs energy from starlight, storing an infinite supply within its core – hence its name. But *how*? How does a *stone* contradict the laws of thermodynamics? Well, the answer lies in Inficore's *outer* layer, its surface, which allows photons *in*, but not *out*, generating complex order from chaos, in defiance of entropy. Like a backwards Big Bang. In other words, Inficore can *reverse the arrow of time*.'

A hand shot up in the front row, causing a chain reaction of raised hands and spoken questions from the entire crowd at once. Sebastian leaned smugly across Genevieve.

'Please, *please*!' he said. 'Save your questions for the end. We know time travel is an exciting subject, but you'll all get your turns, I promise.'

Sebastian withdrew, and the hubbub died gradually.

'Erm, actually, no,' Genevieve corrected, looking back at Sebastian. 'We're not aiming for time *travel*, we're aiming for time *emancipation*.'

She clicked the remote, and the Inficore stone on screen was replaced by an image of her prototype. 'This machine is designed to externalise Inficore's time reversal property,' said Genevieve. 'In essence, it will create a controlled point in space where time will flow backwards. We will pass some organic material through this point and test the results. If our models are accurate, the material in question will be subjected to time flowing in both directions simultaneously, which is a paradox, and should be *emancipated* completely from the effects of time. Once we've proven the theory, the implications for all organic material, including ourselves, is staggering.'

The frenzy of questions erupted anew. This time, there was no pacifying the hunger for information. Sebastian pointed to a journalist in the front row. She stood and waited for the cacophony to subside.

'Scarlet Laugherty, Delta One,' she said. 'Doctor LePlass, can you explain, in simpler terms, whatever it is you're talking about?'

Fresh laughter broke out as red blotches rose up Genevieve's neck. Adam winced in anger at the braying journalists. Sebastian quickly blocked Genevieve from view, stepping up to the lectern.

'We're going to drop a piece of wood through a beam of light and see what happens,' he said. 'Is that simple enough?' He pointed to another raised hand.

'What is it you're hoping to find?' asked the journalist.

'We expect the wood to become immune to decay. Permanently.'

'So, this experiment is about immortality?' ventured a third journalist.

'Yes,' said Sebastian, seizing on the word. He leaned closer to the bunch of microphones. 'We're going to make an immortal cup.'

CHAPTER 2

Time Emancipation

Genevieve slouched with her back against the lift wall, face buried in her hands.

'It wasn't that bad,' Adam consoled.

'It was awful,' said Genevieve, muffled. 'He said we're making an *immortal cup*!'

'Yeah, well … They just needed it dumbed down a bit. And maybe you weren't dumb enough to explain it.'

Genevieve revealed her face, her expression one of disapproval. But she smiled.

The lift slowed to a stop.

When the door opened, Adam caught a glimpse of Gerald standing face-to-face with Ford, his nose an inch from the blank's visor, squinting as though trying to locate an animal in a terrarium. He withdrew quickly as Genevieve stormed into the bunker.

'Is the chamber ready?' she demanded.

'Yep,' said Gerald. 'The transfer is idling at one percent power, and the abort system is fully functional. Not that we're going to need it.'

Genevieve inflated herself and whirled to face Adam. 'Is the blank ready? Have you checked the kirrion suit for gaps?'

'Checked and ready,' Adam confirmed. 'But I'd like to run another motion test once Ford's inside the chamber. Even at one percent, the radiation will ionise the kirrion suit rigid, and I want to make sure he maintains optimal motion.'

Genevieve nodded. 'Okay,' she said. 'Let's run through the plan; Gerald, you're at the control desk monitoring the Inficore. I'll watch the prototype. And Adam, you relay my commands to your blank. Everything we do will be broadcast upstairs once Gerald turns the cameras on, so let's get it right. I want clear, constant communication.'

Adam and Gerald high-fived. Genevieve took a deep, steadying breath. 'Let's do it,' she said.

The team walked to a forbidding, cast-iron door with a circular, vault-style handle. Gerald spun the wheel until it clicked. With a practised effort, he leaned back with his full weight and heaved the door slowly open.

The control room inside was a cosy box, just large enough to admit them. Two swivel chairs sat abandoned before a complex control desk covered in levers, switches, and a central readout screen. Behind the desk was a thick blast shield that looked out into the Inficore chamber, which thrummed softly, emanating a warm glow. On the right-hand wall of the control room stood a second heavy door, identical to the first, which led to the airlock antechamber.

Gerald and Genevieve took their positions inside the control room. 'Start the recording,' said Genevieve.

Gerald pushed a sequence of buttons. 'Cameras and mics on. I hope you're receiving us upstairs!'

'Adam, let's get the blank in here so we can close the outer door.'

'Copy that,' said Adam. He turned to address Ford, who remained in neutral stance in the bunker, holding the prototype. 'Ford, turn to face me.'

The blank pivoted smoothly.

'Ford, walk into the control room … that's good. We have the blank and prototype standing by.'

'Copy that,' said Genevieve. 'Gerald, seal the outer door.'

'Sealed.'

'Final checks, please.'

Adam walked around Ford, inspecting each seal on the kirrion suit, tugging randomly at the seams.

'Suit nominal,' he confirmed.

'Prototype also nominal,' said Genevieve. 'Is the test asset in place?'

Adam touched the wooden cup in the holster at Ford's back.

'Cup confirmed.'

'Copy that. Gerald, open the outer airlock door.'

Gerald pushed another button, and the door on the right opened mechanically. Adam ordered Ford inside the tiny airlock, and the door closed behind him. Adam chewed his thumbnail. A moment later, the inner door opened, and the blank stepped into view beyond the blast shield, inside the Inficore chamber.

The chamber was a grey rectangle, roughly three times the size of the control room, with two metal arms protruding from the floor, ten feet apart, like the feet of an enormous crow, buried upside down. And snared tight in the grip of each talon was an Inficore stone, jet- black, each the size of a fist, glowing faintly purple from within.

A solid beam of energy connected the stones across the chamber. Like a handrail made of light. Radiating power.

Adam, now seated in the second chair at the control desk, pulled the microphone closer to his mouth.

'Conducting radio check,' he said. He pushed the talk button. 'Ford, turn your head to the left.'

From behind, Adam saw the blank's helmet rotate to the left in isolation.

'Good,' he said. 'Turn your head to the right.'

Ford obeyed.

'And now, return to neutral stance.'

Adam's heart skipped a beat. The blank did not move.

Adam waited for a second, then swallowed.

'Ford, return to neutral stance,' he said clearly.

Again, Ford remained motionless.

'Shit,' said Gerald.

Adam licked his lips and pressed the talk button more firmly.

'*Ford, return to neutral stance.*'

No reaction.

'*Shit!*' said Gerald.

'All right, let's not panic,' said Genevieve, unable to keep the panic from her voice. 'Tell me what's going on. Adam?'

'Adam, if it touches that transfer beam, we're all dead!' said Gerald. He positioned a shaking hand above the kill switch.

'Wait! I told you, he *cannot* act of his own accord! What does the readout say?'

'Still at one percent.'

'Then his suit shouldn't have hardened much,' said Adam, frowning. 'It must be a problem with the speaker in his helmet. There might be too much interference to hear my commands clearly.'

'What do we need to do?' asked Genevieve.

Adam pressed the talk button again and pronounced each word carefully. '*Ford, return to neutral stance.*'

Slowly, the blank obeyed. Gerald slumped back in his chair and wiped his forehead.

'*Ford, can you hear me?*'

'Yes, Mister Maxwell,' came a toneless voice through the speakers.

Adam felt a hand on his shoulder. 'Get him out of there,' said Genevieve.

A few minutes later, the blank stepped back inside the control room, clutching the prototype, completely undeterred. Adam removed the kirrion helmet to inspect the transmitter, while Ford stared ahead like a statue. Gerald killed the cameras.

'I can't see any obvious problem,' said Adam. 'It must have been static interference from the radiation, like I said.'

'Why would we be getting interference?' asked Genevieve. 'We tested the comms thoroughly.'

Gerald brought up a data page on the readout screen and frowned. He let out a humourless laugh.

'It's the storm,' he said. 'The Felix dome is absorbing the lightning, and the excess energy is feeding back to the chamber, causing these blips.' He pointed at waves on the monitor.

'What can we do?' asked Genevieve.

'Not much,' said Adam. 'Ford should hear most of my commands just fine, but I'm worried he might mishear or misinterpret something in the interference.'

'So, what should we do?' said Gerald. 'Do we scrub?'

'No way,' said Genevieve. 'If we scrub, we lose a whole year. The Algorithm only permitted us *this* date and time because it calculated a dip in the North Quarter's energy consumption. Any other night could be twice as problematic, storm or no storm.'

'But, if Ford can't hear my commands clearly –'

'He won't need to hear your commands,' said Genevieve, unfolding her arms. 'Because *I'm* going in.'

Adam's stomach hollowed. A brief silence filled the control room.

'I don't think that's a good idea,' said Adam.

'I do,' said Genevieve. 'Besides, it's my prototype, my experiment. You would have only relayed *my* commands to Ford anyway. I might not be able to move as easily in the kirrion suit, but I'll be able to react in real-time if anything goes wrong – even if the comms fail.'

'The kirrion suit shouldn't solidify too much at one percent,' said Gerald. 'Mobility only becomes a problem at around seven percent. It'll just feel like you're walking through a vat of honey.'

'And you're confident Genevieve can handle it without training?' asked Adam, willing Gerald to speak sensibly.

'Absolutely,' said Gerald. 'In fact, meaning no disrespect, I'm much more comfortable having a *real* person in there. And if anything gets dicey, I'll just kill the power.'

Genevieve nodded at Gerald before turning to look at Adam. He met their collective gaze.

'I think it's a mistake,' he said. 'Inficore radiation can cause vivid hallucinations. Blanks are immune, but if there's even the smallest leak in that suit –'

'But we know the suit is nominal,' said Genevieve. 'You've checked it, Adam, and we all trust your work.'

Adam bristled. He took a deep breath and attempted not to sound defensive. 'It's not just the suit,' he went on, speaking directly to Genevieve now. 'I've spent two months modifying Ford's musculoskeletal system to peak performance for this, to remove any risk of him making a mistake. Gen … if you slip, sneeze, or make the smallest wrong move in there –'

'I'll kill the power,' said Gerald.

They stared at Adam, awaiting further protests. Gerald lifted his chin in a challenge, and Genevieve tilted her head, her eyes darting between Adam's, reading the truth in his concern. She smiled weakly at his silence.

'Then it's settled,' she said. 'I'll need some help getting into the suit.' She addressed Gerald. 'Could you … give us the room, please?'

Gerald exited into the bunker, leaving Adam and Genevieve alone in the little room. She crossed it in one stride and placed a hand gently on Adam's heart, looking up at him.

'I'll be fine,' she said, 'I promise.'

Adam grabbed the back of her hand with his own but shook his head. His heart pounded under her fingers. 'I don't think you should do this,' he said.

'What, you don't trust me?' Genevieve smiled.

'Of course. I love you.'

The words had spilled from Adam's mouth before he could think, filling the control room like a noxious gas. Adam felt the temperature rise, felt his cheeks burning. He tore his eyes from Genevieve's astonished face and cast them downward, as though looking for the words he had spilled, wishing he could scoop them back into his stupid mouth.

Genevieve lifted his chin. Her lips were softly parted, her eyes wide and glistening behind her glasses. She was about to speak, when the vault door opened a few inches.

Gerald's head poked in through the aperture. 'I just want you to know that, even though we're not broadcasting, the cameras are still recording everything. You know, just FYI.'

Gerald's head departed and the door closed.

For several seconds, Adam seriously considered breaching the Inficore chamber and hurling himself into the transfer beam. He bunched his eyes shut.

'Adam,' Genevieve said a few seconds later, 'you know I –'

'No! Please. Don't say anything. Nothing. Not a word. I … I didn't *mean* to say that. I just … Look, let's just forget about it and move on, okay? *Okay?*'

'Okay,' said Genevieve.

In gruff silence, Adam removed each component of the kirrion suit from Ford and fitted it around Genevieve. He checked the seals methodically, manipulating her limbs roughly in his anger, until he opened the door to the bunker.

'She's ready,' he said.

He and Gerald took up their positions, and the broadcast resumed. Together, the team ran through the same sequence of checks, the atmosphere draining back to normal, until Genevieve appeared inside the Inficore chamber, holding her prototype.

Adam pushed the talk button. 'Radio check,' he said.

'Yeah, picking up a little static,' came Genevieve's voice, 'but receiving clearly enough. Can you hear me?'

'Loud and clear. How does the suit feel in there? Give us a motion update.'

'I can *feel* it hardening, but it's not as bad as I thought. Not enough to worry about, anyway.'

'Good to hear. Stand by.'

Adam turned to Gerald. 'Tell her to place the machine around the stone on the right,' said Gerald. 'That's the one currently *receiving* power from the stone on the left.'

Adam relayed this to Genevieve. She walked deliberately to the rear of the right-hand stone, giving the bright beam a wide berth. Carefully, she lowered her prototype to the floor and aligned it with the locking arm that gripped the Inficore stone in place.

'Okay,' said Genevieve, a little breathless, 'alignment complete.'

'Copy that. Stand by.'

Gerald positioned his hand above the kill switch. He nodded at Adam.

'We're ready when you are,' said Adam into the microphone.

'Copy that. Beginning placement.'

Steadily, Genevieve inched the machine closer and closer to the locking arm, until the arm and Inficore stone were obscured completely, housed inside the machine's open cavity. From Adam's perspective, the beam of light now travelled from the right-hand stone directly inside Genevieve's prototype.

'Placement complete,' she said. 'Stabilisers locked.'

Gerald exhaled sharply and removed his hand from above the switch.

'Copy that,' said Adam. 'Begin calibration.'

Genevieve tinkered with the machine's dials for a moment. 'Calibration complete. We have a signal!' she said. 'Activating Chronosphere Generator.'

She flipped a switch, and four spindles unfurled from the top of the machine, like a mechanical, budding flower.

'Prototype ready,' breathed Genevieve.

Adam looked sideways at Gerald. 'Everything looks good from my end,' he said.

Adam pushed the button. 'Control is green,' he said, his mouth dry.

'Copy that! Initiating Chronosphere test.'

Genevieve crouched to press a final button.

A perfect, electric-blue sphere popped into existence, floating between the machine's spindles, its bizarre, speckled light collapsing inward to its centre. Adam and Gerald leapt to their feet in astonishment. Involuntary noises of surprise and elation filled the cramped space, but none louder than the triumphant voice that blared through the speakers. Genevieve punched the air in slow motion; her theory born into existence.

15

Adam shook his head in disbelief. He imagined the team on the surface. The embraces, the clapping. The frantic journalists. He felt Gerald pat his back.

'Energy has increased to 3.5 percent draw,' said Gerald, retaking his seat.

Adam followed suit.

'Gen, the power has spiked a little. I need you to perform another motion test before we proceed. Please confirm.'

'Confirmed!' said Genevieve, practically dancing with excitement. 'Motion remains nominal. Wow! This is the most beautiful thing I've ever seen!'

'Copy that,' said Adam, grinning. 'Begin test phase two on your mark.'

'Beginning test phase two,' said Genevieve, removing the wooden cup from her harness as though she were under water. She lifted it gracefully, holding it directly above the blue ball of light. 'Test asset in position.'

Cold sweat beaded on Adam's forehead. He pushed the button. 'Make history.'

'Releasing the asset in three … two … one!'

Genevieve opened her hand. The cup fell.

It fell for only a heartbeat, in which Adam, Genevieve, and Gerald, held their breath.

There was a blinding flash of light. The men in the control room were swept into the back wall by the force of the explosion.

Everything plunged into darkness.

A high-pitched ringing filled Adam's ears as he gasped for air in the dark. He scrambled to his knees in dizzy terror and pulled himself up on the control panel. It hissed, and there was a small flame inside it. He coughed in the dusty air.

Above ground, on the surface, a blackout swept across the entire North Quarter of Anthar. In Felix, screams filled the night as the storm rampaged through the defenceless city.

Adam squinted desperately through the fractured blast shield into the pitch-black chamber for Genevieve. But all he could see was the dull afterglow of the two Inficore fragments, staring back at him like the eyes of some otherworldly creature. Someone beside Adam stirred, coughing.

An ominous alarm sounded in the chamber.

Adam pushed the talk button but did not feel its usual powered resistance.

'Gen! *Gen!*' he cried, his ears still ringing. 'Are you all right? Genevieve! Say something!'

But the power was dead.

'Adam,' croaked a voice beside him.

Adam ripped open a drawer under the control panel and fumbled the items around until he felt the cold metal of the torch.

The dusty torchlight cut a small circle on the fractured blast shield and a larger circle inside the chamber, revealing patches of floor and the smouldering remains of Genevieve's machine.

But no sign of Genevieve.

'Is she alive?' asked the voice from somewhere behind him.

'I can't see her!' Adam shrieked, dread rising in his throat.

Gerald pulled himself up beside Adam to help. 'On the left,' he croaked.

Adam flicked the circle of torchlight to the other side of the chamber and found the undersides of two large boots.

Genevieve lay sprawled, face up, completely still. The kirrion suit had tripled in size, encasing her like a cocoon.

The chamber was suddenly bathed in a dull red light. The backup power had kicked in. The whole place was charred and smoking. Blood trickled from Gerald's broken nose. Ford had regained his feet, undamaged.

'Ford!' Adam yelled, gripping the blank by the shoulders. 'We need to get her out of there! Do you understand?'

'Yes, Mister Maxwell,' came the toneless reply.

Without hesitation, Ford stepped through the airlock and sealed the heavy radiation door behind him. He appeared inside the chamber unprotected. Thin lines of blood trickled from the blank's ears, made black by the sinister red light. But Ford marched straight to Genevieve's position. He looked at her for a moment, then lifted his head.

'Is she alive?' Adam cried.

The blank's voice was distant through the cracked shield, but Adam distinguished the words. 'The life support system is detecting a heartbeat.'

Gerald let out a groan. Adam felt his legs buckle. He leaned hard into the smoking control panel, breathing in great gulps.

The worst had not happened.

He tried to calm himself and think. His surroundings kept sliding between ultra-vivid and utterly surreal.

'Good!' he shouted, his voice breaking. 'Pick her up and get her out of there!'

'The kirrion has reached maximum potential,' said Ford. 'I will require assistance to bear her weight.'

'Ford!' Adam shouted. 'Just *drag* her to the airlock!'

'Yes, Mister Maxwell.'

Ford crouched to lift Genevieve's legs. The instant his hand made contact, the blank was blasted across the room as though shot from a cannon. He flew headlong into the opposite wall of the chamber, his head crumpling inside his neck.

A black flower of blood blossomed on the wall at the point of impact.

CHAPTER 3

Awakening

The moment the wooden cup entered the sphere of light, in the tiny, infinitesimal space that separated the moment of non-contact from the moment of contact, a pulse of energy surged outwards from the exact location where the first atom of the cup collided with a photon of blue light. The pulse expanded outward in a perfect sphere, invisible and unstoppable, growing at the speed of light. It sped through the suspended cup, through Genevieve and her machine, through the blast shield and chamber walls, through Adam, Gerald, and Ford, and outwards through the surrounding ground. It engulfed the city of Felix, the continent of Anthar, then all of planet Ithea, and outward still, beyond the planet's atmosphere, beyond the influence of its gravity.

While Adam rummaged blindly for the torch, the intangible supernova met the neighbouring rocky planet and swallowed it instantly, racing outward. It consumed the vast ring of asteroids that encircled the parent star, then ate the star itself, expanding ever further.

Two hours later, as Adam awaited the rescue team, the pulse met the first of the enormous gas planets and swept through it and beyond without hindrance. It found another gas giant, and another, consuming each without slowing, dwarfing them as though they were grains of sand in the path of a tsunami.

Five hours into its expansion, while the emergency team heaved the fossilized kirrion suit encasing Genevieve's body into the transporter, the pulse was passing through the coldest and emptiest reaches of the system. Finally, it met the farthest object held by the star's gravity; a frozen, marble-white planetoid, two-thirds the size of Ithea's moon. The wall of energy devoured the tiny satellite as it had everything else, then disappeared beyond on its eternal journey.

But the planetoid reacted to its passing.

It reacted as though the wave of energy were a signal it had been waiting for.

Suddenly, muted by the vacuum of space, an immense crack exploded from its northern to its southern pole. Canyon-sized and forked like lightning, its emergence blasted giant shards of ice many miles into space, like a fan-shaped geyser of diamonds.

As the ice particles escaped the weak gravity, something unknown began to stir inside the small planet. Something that had lain dormant for a very long time.

A dense black cloud began to pour unendingly from the newly formed chasm. It unfurled higher and higher, like a colossal volcanic plume, until it reached its terminal height and washed backward in a great wave, collapsing to the planetoid's surface, where it spread out, shrouding every inch of white in its darkness.

Slowly, cloaked beneath its new atmosphere, the planetoid stopped rotating. It stopped following its obedient elliptical orbit. It broke free of its enslavement to the distant star and began to move of its own accord.

It began to move inwards. Toward the source of its awakening.

CHAPTER 4

The Fallout

The head prosecutor scowled at the paper in her hands. She examined it thoroughly before slapping it down to underline something with her golden pen. Two colleagues sat on either side of her, both immaculate, staring patiently across the table at Adam, who slouched in his chair, watching the clock on the wall.

They're scanning Genevieve's brain right now, he thought.

Two weeks had passed since the explosion beneath InfiTech. A waking nightmare for Adam. A fortnight of sleep for Genevieve.

A cerebral hypoxia coma, they said.

Adam had stayed by her bedside for five days straight. They kept her on the topmost floor of Felix Primary, pale and skinny with a tube in her mouth. And every day that passed reduced her chances of waking up.

The prosecutor set down her pen and slid the document across the desk. She glared through curtains of sleek black hair until Harold, Adam's lawyer – and brother – who looked like Adam but with a gym membership, picked it up. As Harold read, the prosecutor cleared her throat.

Ironically, her name was Charity.

'Mister Maxwell,' she said, 'the damages from your failed experiment are unprecedented. A quarter of Anthar's power supply destroyed, major infrastructural damage, flooding across Felix, delays to projects across the North and Central Quarters, hundreds of casualties. It's a miracle nobody died!'

'I object to that statement,' said Harold, without looking up from the document. 'I think we can agree this was not my client's experiment.'

'Very well,' Charity replied curtly, 'let me rephrase. The damages from the explosion in which you were *involved* are still being calculated. However, the Algorithm has produced an initial list of reparations that this panel must attribute at our discretion. As such, based on the evidence and testimony received thus far, we have decided on the actions you must take to settle your debts to the Hive. Please see them highlighted on the document before you.'

Harold laid the document on the table and indicated a bullet point with his finger. Adam looked at the words, glassy-eyed, but failed to decipher any meaning. Harold spared him by leaning over to whisper in his ear.

'They want you to train a replacement blank for InfiTech,' he said.

'That's all?' asked Adam, too loudly.

'For now,' said the boy to Charity's right with a smirk.

'You will have one year to satisfy this reparation,' said Charity. 'Failure to deliver will result in your banishment from the Hive Network. Should you refuse, you may face a downgrade in status or banishment from the Hive, pending a trial. Do you agree to satisfy this reparation as set by the Algorithm?'

Harold winked at him.

'Fine,' said Adam. But something else had caught his eye on the document. 'But who are these other reparations attributed to?'

'Your accomplices,' said the girl to Charity's left.

'Let's call them colleagues, shall we?' said Harold. 'This was a sanctioned experiment, not a criminal act.'

The girl blinked deliberately. But Adam didn't care what they thought of him. He was too busy reading the document in detail, alert to its content now.

'Who will have to satisfy *this* reparation?' he asked. 'Who are you expecting to "*secure replacement Inficore*"?'

'That's confidential,' said Charity.

'And impossible,' said Adam. 'You know that, right?'

'It's not your concern,' said the boy.

'Yes, it is,' said Adam. 'Because the other people *involved* are my friends, one of whom is in a coma. And what you're asking of them is impossible.'

'The Algorithm sets the reparations,' said the girl.

'Are you a blank?' said Adam.

The girl's mouth shut tight in scorn. Harold put his hand on Adam's forearm.

'Adam —' he warned, but Adam pressed on.

'I don't care. Gerald has already told me that you charged him with rebuilding the Inficore Chamber. And he also told me that he's accepted banishment instead. So that leaves only Genevieve. You expect *her* to find *replacement* Inficore?'

The boy shifted sideways to whisper something in Charity's ear. Her eyes narrowed. After the boy had finished, she sat forward, laced her fingers together, and rested her elbows on the table.

'If Doctor LePlass accepts her reparation, she will have one year to satisfy her debt to the Hive,' she said.

'She's in a coma!' said Adam, slapping the table, unable to comprehend such obtuse stupidity. But then he realised Charity's meaning. 'Wait … you said, *if* she accepts? What if she *can't* accept her reparation?'

'She will be banished from the Hive,' said the boy coldly.

Adam's stomach dropped by an inch. He removed his glasses to look the prosecutors in the eye.

'But that would be a death sentence,' he said. 'They don't have life-support systems in the Freelands! How can the Algorithm sanction an experiment, thereby accepting its inherent risks, then demand reparations when the experiment backfires? Where's the justice in that?'

'The Algorithm is impartial and infallible, Mister Maxwell,' Charity intoned. 'And as long as we remain citizens of the Hive, we agree to abide by its laws.'

'Well, this particular ruling is bullshit,' said Adam. 'Shouldn't InfiTech absorb some of the blame?'

'InfiTech agreed to the experiment,' said the boy, 'but Doctor LePlass was its architect.'

'And how long does Doctor LePlass have to *accept* her reparation?' asked Harold.

The girl smiled placidly at Adam. 'A week,' she said.

Adam balled his fists. He was about to stand in anger, but Harold kept him pinned to his seat by resting a hand on his shoulder.

'Thank you,' Harold said hastily. 'My client has accepted his reparation, so I will be in touch to arrange the necessary paperwork. Should you need anything from us in the meantime, please, let me know. Come on.'

Harold stood, and Adam followed suit. They trooped from the room without glancing at the prosecutors, emerging into an open-plan office, where grids of grey suits worked in sad, identical cubicles.

'Those *fuckers*,' said Adam. 'How can they sit there and condemn an innocent woman, effectively, to death? We'll have to accept the reparation on her behalf. Buy her some time.'

'Not here,' Harold hissed, regaining his stride.

Many of the office workers had lifted their heads to stare.

Harold led Adam from the building and pulled him around a corner. The adjacent street was a river of pedestrians flowing in both directions. They dived in.

'So, what next?' Adam asked.

'Well, you'll need to train a blank for InfiTech,' said Harold unhelpfully.

'I meant about Genevieve,' said Adam, sidestepping a large group. 'There must be some legal precedent for this. Some way to overrule the Algorithm when its demands are unachievable?'

'Hm. Maybe,' said Harold, frowning.

They walked on for a moment, weaving through the oncoming bodies.

'Go on, what is it?' Adam asked Harold's scowling profile.

'Nothing.'

'You're annoyed because I lost my temper?'

'No, I'm not annoyed.'

'Then what?'

Harold sighed. 'You're not ready to hear it,' he said.

'Hear what? Hal, tell me.'

Harold stopped and looked away at nothing in particular. He checked his watch. 'Let's talk in the morning,' he said. 'Will you go to the hospital?'

It was a request, not a question: Please go away. Adam was too tired to argue. Besides, he needed to know Genevieve's scan results.

'Fine,' he grumbled. 'You want to come?'

Harold was tactful enough to hear the emptiness in this offer. 'No, I'd better get back to the office.'

Adam waited for his brother to meet his gaze. 'Will you look into Genevieve's options for me?'

A muscle in Harold's jaw twitched. 'I'll do some digging,' he said. 'But I'm not promising anything. *You're* my priority. And until you're in the clear, I won't stop for anything.'

Adam was taken aback by this pronouncement. Annoyed and touched in equal measure. 'Thanks,' he mumbled sheepishly.

'Don't get weird about it,' said Harold. 'Go see Genevieve, then get some rest. You look awful.'

They embraced awkwardly until Harold detached himself and disappeared into the swarm.

It seemed much harder to walk without company. Adam dragged his feet to the nearest Portal and put his hand on the summon screen. A green bar of light scanned his hand from his fingertips to the base of his palm. A second later, his account and list of usual destinations appeared. He tapped the top entry: Felix Primary.

As he waited on the busy platform for his NexCar, he absorbed Felix's sounds and sights as though for the first time. Peaceful chatter filled the air as people wandered at ease, picking delicacies from street vendors or relaxing in manicured parkland on laser-cut lawns. White buildings gleamed under a blue sky as the Felix Dome rippled purple somewhere in between.

For all Adam's complaints against the Algorithm, it had truly built a paradise in the Hive. A haven that he had never fully appreciated. He thought about Gerald's decision to accept banishment.

Maybe it wouldn't be so bad. It might even be refreshing to live without power. To read by candlelight and build cooking fires. To work outdoors, barter for goods, and dance the nights away.

The Freelanders must call their city Liberty for a reason, Adam supposed.

But then he thought about bacteria and diseases. What did it feel like to get sick? Would Gerald's Autophage still protect him outside the Hive?

'It's for you!' said a snappy voice beside him, making him jump.

Adam's surroundings came back into focus; a row of impatient faces to his right and the open door of a NexCar before him. He muttered an apology and clambered inside. The car sped him away before it dipped through a Portal into darkness.

No more thinking, he told himself as the car's interior lit up. His back pressed into his seat as the car sped through the tunnel.

'Play the news,' he said with a yawn.

At once, the curved glass frontage of the car came to life, showing a male news anchor with wavy blond hair.

'– expect the power outages to continue across the North as a new, permanent supply is rerouted from InfiTech Central in Delta,' the anchor read solemnly. Next second, his expression suddenly brightened. 'And now, let me ask you a strange question; what's the biggest object you've ever *lost*? Well, the team at the Contra Observatory will likely spare your blushes, having announced this morning that they've lost an entire *planet*!'

He shook his head, smiling at the camera. 'That's right. The planetoid, known as K-71, is believed to have disappeared sometime between three days and three weeks ago, when it was last observed in its usual orbit. Here's lead astrophysicist Yuri Balkov to tell us more. Hello, Yuri.'

The screen split in two as the head and shoulders of a bearded, bespectacled man appeared in a box beside the anchor in lower resolution.

'Good afternoon,' said Yuri Balkov, his name appearing in a banner across his chest.

'Good afternoon,' said the anchor. 'Please, tell us everything about this intriguing development. What do you know?'

'Well,' Yuri chuckled, 'it's been a strange couple of days for us, that's for sure. A planetoid – a large satellite in the depths of our system – has gone missing. Or rather, it's not where it should be, according to our models. And there's no sign of it in the surrounding regions of space, either. It seems to have disappeared without a trace.'

'Do you have any idea what may have happened to it?'

'Yes, it's possible something knocked it off-course. But if that were the case, we would expect to see some kind of signature, like impact debris. It's also improbable that anything could have destroyed it entirely. All our telescopes are currently searching for data. But, so far, we've found nothing. It really is fascinating!'

Yuri's bearded grin filled half the screen.

'Forgive me,' said the anchor, 'this might be an ignorant question, but aren't we talking about a moon-sized object billions of miles away? Why is this disappearance significant?'

'Well, first of all, K-71 is a little smaller than our moon. But its disappearance is highly significant because, in physics, whenever a new phenomenon occurs, it often forces us to rethink our models. And every time we discover new information, it deepens our understanding of the universe.'

Adam snored gently, his head lolling against the headrest, glasses askew. He slept the whole way to Felix Primary until the car surfaced through the Portal and bumped along the track to the platform.

*

Genevieve lay precisely as Adam had left her that morning, her dark hair spread out on the clean white pillow, her thin, bare arms at her sides above the cover, the breathing tube tugging on the left corner of her mouth. The room was a sickly peach colour and somewhat overcrowded by machinery. The only non-medical furniture was the single high-backed chair that had served as Adam's bed, behind which was a large window offering a view of southern Felix. Outside, the setting sun was painting the rooftops orange. The stars and city lights were coming out.

'Well,' sighed Adam, scraping the chair closer to the bed, 'you missed more fun today. Harold and I had our first meeting with the prosecution team. They're a lovely bunch. They want you to replace the destroyed Inficore as a reparation. So, you know, if you could just sort that out. Whenever … How was your scan?'

Genevieve's chest rose and fell in time with the mechanical hiss and ticks that issued from beneath the bed.

She couldn't hear him. Adam knew that. But each day, he spoke to her as though she could. And there was something comforting about addressing her directly. As though he could will her presence in the room.

At times, Adam even felt her watching him.

'I guess I'll wait for Yang to tell me,' he said. 'Hey, did you hear the news? A planet disappeared! Imagine that. It might take some heat off us if we're lucky.'

An orderly in red scrubs walked in carrying a folder. It was Dimple Smile. Adam knew all the faces that came and went but had been too exhausted to learn any names. Only Doctor Yang had stuck.

'Hi,' said Dimple Smile, smiling. 'I didn't see you come in.'

'Oh, I climbed in through the window,' said Adam, deadpan. 'How did the scan go?'

The orderly's dimples disappeared. 'I'm … not sure,' she said. 'Probably best to speak to the doctor.'

'Is she here?'

Dimple Smile tapped her palm with the ridge of the folder. 'I'll go and check,' she said. Then she pivoted and fled from the room.

Adam's gut twisted. Something was wrong. He took a deep breath and quickly buried his concern, smiling without conviction at the inert Genevieve.

'Yeah, I like her too,' he said.

Hiss.

Tick.

Hiss.

Tick.

Several minutes passed before Yang entered the room wearing jeans and a black turtleneck shirt. Evidently, she had been about to leave. Her dark, curly hair fell to her shoulders, and puffy bags clung beneath her eyes. She stopped on the far side of Genevieve's bed. Adam stood.

'What's happened?' he said, eyeing the folder the orderly had carried, now in Yang's hands.

Doctor Yang touched her wrist to her forehead as though wiping away sweat. 'Maybe we should discuss the results outside,' she said.

The room blurred out of focus. But Adam nodded and followed her into the empty hallway.

'Well,' said Yang, closing the door behind them, 'the good news is that there doesn't seem to be any tissue damage from the radiation.'

'Okay,' said Adam, braced.

Yang hesitated. 'I'm not sure how to explain the bad news,' she said. 'I've never seen anything like this before.'

'Tell me,' said Adam, a little shortly. 'Please.'

Yang opened the folder and slid out an X-ray image, a cross-section of a human brain dotted with patches of red.

'This is a scan of a typical comatose patient,' she said. 'It shows low brain function,' she indicated the red areas with her pinkie, 'which is like our auto-pilot. This keeps the basic system going while the patient is unconscious.'

She drew out a second image, almost identical to the first. It had the same red dots, but there were larger yellow, green, and blue patches too, like a topographical map.

'This is a scan of a fully conscious brain,' said Yang. 'You can see the same low brain function but with higher conscious activity too. Again, this is just a sample.'

'Now, let me show you Genevieve's scan.'

Slower than she had done with the others, she withdrew a third X-ray image and handed it to Adam. The difference was apparent at once.

Every inch of Genevieve's brain was vivid red.

Adam frowned at it for a few seconds, then blinked at Doctor Yang. 'What does it mean?'

Yang shrugged uncomfortably. 'I'm afraid I don't know. But, according to that image, Genevieve's unconscious is at maximum capacity. Which makes no sense. You see, our low brain function only regulates our heartbeat, digestion, breathing; the necessary things for survival. But … the sheer amount of brain activity taking place here is astonishing. And the only case of increased low brain function –'

'Is in blanks,' Adam supplied, crestfallen.

Yang jerked back her head in surprise. 'How do you know that?'

'They're my field of study,' said Adam dejectedly.

Yang tilted her head in pity. 'I'm sorry,' she said. 'But there's not much more we can do. If she doesn't wake up in the next few weeks, it's unlikely that she ever will. And even if she does, you need to be prepared. She won't be the person you remember, Adam. Genevieve is gone.'

Adam forced down the lump in his throat. He blinked his searing eyelids.

Absurdly, he heard himself say, 'Thank you' as he handed back the X-ray.

Yang stood there for a moment, uncertain whether to touch his shoulder. Finally, she straightened in a practiced way and said, 'I'm so sorry.' Then she left him standing in the strip-lit hallway.

Adam re-entered the little peach room. He took his seat and stared at Genevieve's motionless eyelids for a long time.

Hiss.

Tick.

Hiss.

Tick.

'I know you're in there,' he said at last, 'and I'm not giving up. I promise, if there's any way to bring you back, I'll do it. Whatever it takes. I promise.'

CHAPTER 5

Reparations

At nine-thirty the next morning, amid the chaotic whirlwind of his life, Adam found himself in a quiet suburb, standing outside Harold's front door.

The midnight message that had summoned him there had been unusually blunt, even for his brother. And Adam didn't think it boded well that Harold wanted to meet at home.

The house was small but perfect, not a thing out of place, except for the scruffy man waiting on its doorstep, who knocked timidly.

Adam's sister-in-law answered the door in a bright jumper. All make-up and perfume and bangles.

'Hi, Wendy.' Adam smiled.

She pulled him into a busty hug, then pushed his face away in cupped hands, smiling up at him. 'Gosh, you look dreadful,' she said. 'Can I get you something to eat?'

'Erm, no thanks,' said Adam, cheeks smushed. 'I've already eaten.'

'Are you sure? I've got leftover turkey and some homemade bread if you like.'

'I'm fine. Honestly.'

She straightened his collar and patted his chest. 'I'll make you a sandwich,' she whispered, then she bustled to the kitchen.

Adam rolled his eyes and kicked off his shoes. 'Where's Hal?' he called after her.

'In the study. But he was up all night, so he might be asleep in there.'

Adam rapped gently on the door to his left.

'Yep,' came Harold's dreary voice from within.

The study was a beige-carpeted rectangle with a double sofa at one end, a desk and computer at the other, and a tropical fish-tank humming from the corner. Harold paced behind the desk, wearing the same clothes as yesterday. The blinds were drawn.

'Everything okay?' asked Adam nervously.

'Ha!' barked Harold, rubbing the back of his head. 'That depends ... What do you want to hear first? The good news, the *weird* news, or the terrible news?'

Adam sank into the soft sofa, palms sweating. 'I dunno. The good news?'

'The good news is, I have formally accepted your reparation. You now have one year to program another blank for InfiTech, and they're sending one to your place as we speak.'

'Great,' said Adam. 'It should only take a few days.'

'The weird news,' Harold continued, scratching his chin, 'is that I've *found a way* to replace the damaged Inficore.'

'What!' Adam's mouth fell open. '*How?*'

'Well ...' Harold began reluctantly. 'How much do you know about *Nephia?*'

Adam frowned. 'The continent on the far side of Ithea?' he said. 'Hardly anything. Why? Are you saying there's unclaimed Inficore in Nephia?'

Harold stopped pacing and slipped his hands into his pockets. 'No. Not unclaimed ... Apparently, the natives worship Inficore. It's sacred to them.'

'You're joking,' said Adam. 'The Nephians have a supply of Inficore?'

'Yep.' Harold shrugged. 'I'm as surprised as you. According to the archive entry I stumbled upon, they call them God Stones.'

Adam let his hands fall into his lap. 'That's ... that's insane! You're telling me that a bunch of savages has access to Inficore stones? And they use them as *ceremonial rocks*! What's the Hive doing about this? Why didn't I know?'

'It's classified,' said Harold. 'There are strict laws that protect Nephian culture from Hive interference. I was only granted access to the archive for reparation research.'

Harold glanced at the door and put a finger to his lips.

Wendy crept in overtly and extended a plate of turkey sandwiches into Adam's lap. Keeping low, her hands splayed in contrition, she mouthed the word *sorry* and retreated from the room.

Adam sat there, clutching the cold plate. 'This is amazing,' he said once the door had closed. 'So, what do I do? How do I get there?'

Harold spun away as though shot in the shoulder. 'Ugh, I knew you'd ask that,' he said, his back turned. 'This is where we're going to disagree, I'm afraid.'

'What do you mean?'

Harold bowed his head, facing away. His shoulders rose and fell. 'Why should *you* go to Nephia?' he said. 'And don't say *because Genevieve's in a coma.*'

'But she *is* in a coma.'

Harold spun back. 'So? That doesn't make her reparation *your* responsibility. Why should *you* shoulder the burden? Because you *love* her?' He made air quotes with his fingers.

Adam put aside the plate and stared up at his brother defiantly. 'Yeah, I do,' he said. 'I'm guessing you saw the recording?'

'I have seen the recording, yeah. And do you know what I noticed?'

'What?'

'She didn't say it back, did she?'

They scowled at each through the bitter silence. A jet of bubbles fizzed through the fishtank. Inwardly, Adam registered the depth of his hurt but forced himself to remain composed. He stood.

'It doesn't matter,' he said. 'I've promised to help, so that's exactly what I'm going to do.'

Harold rolled his eyes. 'Don't get all righteous,' he said. 'The truth is you *barely* know this woman. And you're 112 years old, not a teenager! Why risk your life for someone who's basically dead?'

Adam moved forward threateningly, and Harold, despite being in much better shape, took a step back.

'All right, that was too far,' he admitted. A long moment passed before Harold spoke again. 'How is she?'

'No change,' Adam mumbled. 'And the brain scan wasn't great.'

Harold heaved a sigh. 'I'm sorry to hear that.'

Another silence. Adam watched a yellow fish swim through the eye socket of a fake skull. 'How do I get to Nephia?' he asked.

Harold lowered himself into his chair. 'Well, as luck would have it,' he said begrudgingly, rubbing an eyelid, 'an expedition departs for Nephia from West Point in three weeks. By ship. There's no other way to get there.'

'Thanks,' said Adam, turning to leave.

'Hold on,' Harold called. 'We haven't covered the terrible news yet. Sit down.'

Adam remained on his feet and gestured for Harold to proceed. He looked at Adam soberly.

'I found a glitch in your file,' he said.

'Eh? What do you mean?'

Harold reached back in his chair to tighten the blinds over the window, then stood and resumed pacing.

'I went through your account – back to your graduation – and it doesn't add up. Literally, the numbers are wrong. I added up all the credit for your degrees, your work with blanks, and your every documented achievement or contribution to the Hive … and the figures don't tally. The Algorithm miscalculated your score. You should be a Status Five citizen, not a Seven. And you should never have been assigned to Genevieve's experiment in the first place.'

Adam, who had absently taken a mouthful of turkey sandwich, choked. He forced it down with difficulty.

'You must have miscounted,' he managed.

'I checked my work a dozen times,' Harold persisted, 'and your account is definitely wrong.'

Adam blinked, dumbstruck. 'You think the Algorithm made a *mistake?*' he said.

Harold made panicky pressing motions to silence him.

'I hope not,' he said. 'If the Algorithm is capable of error, then the Hive's integrity is finished. There'd be riots. Pandemonium. No … I'd rather believe that *someone* tampered with your score.'

Slowly, Harold raised a questioning eyebrow. For the first time in weeks, Adam laughed.

'If I could tamper with my Status, do you think I would have stopped at Seven?'

Harold's quizzical expression deepened. 'Anything you tell me will be confidential,' he said. 'You're my brother.'

'Hal, why would I force myself to program a blank for InfiTech? It's ludicrous. No, I didn't *hack* the Algorithm, okay?'

'Okay.' Harold nodded, unconvinced. 'That's a relief. Do you have any friends that might have done it on your *behalf?* Anyone that *really* likes you?'

'I think you know the answer to that.'

Harold smiled but wiped it quickly from his face. 'Well, however it happened,' he said, 'I've caught it and buried it, for now. But, Adam, if you insist on assuming Genevieve's reparation, there's a chance the prosecutors might uncover it. So, I'm formally advising you, as your lawyer, not to do anything stupid.'

'Right,' said Adam reflexively. He took another bite of sandwich, pondering. 'Tell me about this expedition.'

*

When Adam arrived home that afternoon, still reeling from Harold's news, he found two items awaiting him on his front lawn. The first was a copy of the schematics for Genevieve's machine, sent by the Academy at his request. In his delirium after the incident, he had hoped to rebuild the prototype, to better understand why it malfunctioned. It had seemed possible at the time. The second item was a blank human being. Hairless, nondescript, and vacant, like an unfinished waxwork. It had a note around its neck detailing its model type (male), serial number (45225142119), and skill level (basic 2).

Adam ordered the blank to follow him inside.

His house was a mislaid stack of white blocks on a circle of lawn, like a meteor in a grass crater. An architect's notion of style. The interior was a cavern of natural light, with glass surfaces, chrome fittings, and touches of colour in the right places.

Adam detested it.

But it had come with the job at InfiTech, and he would not have to suffer it much longer.

'Can you speak?' he asked the blank once they were inside.

It gave a precise shake of its head.

'But you understand Plain?'

Nod.

'And you can feed yourself and use the toilet?'

Nod.

'Good, an *actual* basic two,' said Adam. 'Well, I'll need to give you a proper name, but for now,' he squinted through his glasses at the serial number again, 'I'll call you *Forty-five*. Do you understand?'

Nod.

Adam decided to test this. He broke eye contact and moved around the kitchen counter. 'Forty-five, stand at the kitchen island.'

The blank obeyed perfectly. It stood at the marble counter facing Adam, awaiting further instruction.

Adam grinned. The irony that he must program a blank from scratch was not lost on him. The same Algorithm that had stopped his work into super-human potential had now gifted him a glorious opportunity to continue his failed experiments. He had a whole year to upgrade this blank for InfiTech. But that task would take him a week at most. In the meantime, he could teach it any manner of things. Whatever occurred to him. They could have some fun.

Silver linings, Adam supposed.

CHAPTER 6

The Expedition Team

Adam and Forty-five walked to the Nexus Portal outside InfiTech. The sweeping crescent stood abandoned and lifeless, as though contaminated. Outwardly, the building displayed minimal damage from the deep explosion, but the Hive engineers had temporarily condemned it as a precaution.

As Adam touched the summon screen, a NexCar appeared through the Portal, with Harold seated inside, poring over a document. He had insisted on coming to West Point to help Adam plead his case with the expedition leader. But Adam suspected his motive was more brotherly than legal.

'Good morning,' said Harold as the circular door pivoted upward like a keyhole cover.

'Morning,' said Adam, climbing in. 'Forty-five, please sit down.'

The blank obeyed, taking a back seat and placing his hands on his knees. Adam threw himself into the available seat next to Harold.

'Forty-five?' said Harold.

'It's what I'm calling him until I can come up with a better name.'

'*Destination?*' inquired the car.

'Academy complex, Shipley Boulevard, West Point Dome,' said Harold.

According to the display, the journey would take around four hours.

'Perfect,' said Harold. 'I've arranged a lunch meeting so you can talk to the whole team. The leader told me to find them in the cafeteria.'

The car descended into the tunnel and launched. Adam had never travelled to West Point before, and much of the route from Felix was above ground. He was pleasantly surprised when, somewhere inside the Hatch dome, they shot through a wall of sunshine from the centre of a blue mountain, the tunnel now a glass tube in the sky. Adam suddenly had a panoramic view of a vibrant city beneath them. Rows of buildings reached up toward the dome roof, the tallest of which passed just beneath Adam's feet. He saw green parks dotted here and there, a glinting lake, complete with boats, and a stadium like the nest of a giant bird. Adam swivelled to point something out to Harold but found his brother asleep, head back and mouth open. Forty-five stared straight ahead, equally oblivious to the splendour.

The tube arced imperceptibly towards the city floor until it levelled out along a central street lined with platforms. The buildings now towered overhead until they suddenly disappeared as the car descended through another Portal underground. Adam checked his phone in the darkness. No messages. No news on Genevieve.

Two uncomfortable hours later, they emerged inside the West Point Academy, a large, glass-roofed concourse packed with people. The NexCar swivelled to a stop at one of the platforms, and as the three men climbed out, the next herd of travellers pushed past them into the car, laughing amongst themselves.

Adam, Harold, and Forty-five made their way through the crowd toward the lone palm tree that dominated the space. Café tables were strewn here and there between surrounding bars and restaurants.

'We need to find the Science Department,' said Harold over the din. 'The expedition leader is a guy called Dimitri Lopek. And just to warn you, he seemed even less keen for you to go to Nephia than I am.'

'Noted,' said Adam.

He spotted a building guide on the far wall where the various departments were listed in colour code. He scanned the list until he found the words 'Science Dept.' next to a purple directional arrow, pointing along a hall.

They quickly discovered that the arrows were essential. The West Point Academy was a maze. The arrows led them along several corridors, up a flight of stairs, and, bizarrely, through a library, which eventually opened out into a bustling cafeteria.

A queue of people slid trays along a waist-height metal shelf while a team of blanks ladled food across the service counter.

Harold touched Adam's shoulder. 'There he is,' he said.

He weaved his way towards a table where four people sat in animated conversation over empty plates. The nearest of the four had her back turned, a blonde woman with pink trainers crossed beneath her chair. The other three were men; the first had a heavy braid down the length of his back; the second was older but solid-looking, with broad arms and a neat, army-style haircut; and a third, shorter man with curly black hair and round glasses, who sat slumped in his seat, arms folded, scowling.

Harold waved to gain their attention as he, Adam, and Forty-five approached. The smaller man sat up in beleaguered acknowledgement. The other faces looked around in unison.

'Good afternoon,' said Harold, looking at each in turn, and then he addressed the smaller man directly. 'Dimitri Lopek?'

The man nodded, pushing his tongue against his back teeth, his pronounced Adam's apple moving up and down under the grey stubble on his neck. The others at his table had adopted polite smiles, but the leader continued to frown.

'Nice to meet you in person,' said Harold. 'I'm Harold, and this is the client I told you about, Adam Maxwell. May we join you?'

The others shifted. The blonde woman made room, the man with the long braid piled the plates on an adjacent table, while Adam and the armyman found additional chairs.

Lopek continued to scowl as the newcomers took their seats.

'Welcome to West Point,' he said, addressing Adam directly, 'though I'm sorry to say you have wasted a journey. I'm Dimitri Lopek, expedition team leader, Nephian culture expert, and former ambassador for the Hive. This is my team.'

He gestured at the woman.

'Oh, erm, my name's Lynn. Lynn Carson,' she said brightly. 'I'm the primary medical officer, also zoologist and botanist, so I'll be collecting flora and fauna samples for study.'

'My name's Kaldor Ugbek,' said the man with the braid, anticipating his turn. He gave Adam a half wave, half salute, grinning earnestly with exceptionally white teeth. 'Call me Kal. I'll be the pilot and navigator while we're on the ship. I'm also an astronomer, tasked with mapping the northern constellations.'

'Bill Conrad,' said the army man, looking squarely at Adam. 'Second in command. My duties are security, safety, and strategy. I'm also the secondary medic. My job is to make sure we all come back alive.'

'Right. Thanks,' said Adam uncomfortably. 'Erm … I'm Adam. I program specialist blanks for the Hive. And I'm sorry to drop in unexpectedly like this.'

Lopek opened his mouth to speak, but Harold cut across him.

'I'll get straight to the point,' he said professionally. 'Adam here has taken on a mandated reparation, against my advice. The Algorithm has now legally tasked him with finding replacement Inficore for the Hive, and he needs a ride to Nephia to accomplish this.'

Lopek laughed overtly, derisively, his face pointed at the ceiling. 'That's completely absurd,' he said once he'd composed himself. 'A *ride* to Nephia? To find replacement *Inficore?* Have you any idea how ridiculous that sounds? Firstly, Nephia is a continent inhabited by protected people. There are stringent laws barring Antharian entry. Nobody is allowed to go there. This expedition, for example, has taken ten years to negotiate, and we've been training as a team for months. Secondly, the notion that you could return with Nephian Inficore is, frankly, insulting and dangerous. You'd be killed before getting anywhere near a God Stone. They're *sacred*, do you understand? Passed down between the Augurs of the Realms, and used to communicate with Ohrak, their God. So, even if you were allowed to go – which you're not – how on Ithea would you go about retrieving one?'

'Well,' said Adam, refusing to be stymied by this pompous little man, 'I guess I would consult a Nephian culture expert, and ask him how *he* would do it.'

The woman, Lynn, covered her mouth with her fingertips to hide a smirk. She had a black ring around her middle finger. Lopek narrowed his eyes at Adam, shaking his head.

'Okay,' he said. 'Well, this Nephian culture expert is telling you that it can't be done. That it shouldn't even be attempted.'

'I've got to try,' said Adam, looking at the other faces for an ally. 'A good friend of mine is in bad shape, and she'll die if I don't satisfy this reparation.'

'I'm sorry to hear that,' said the army man, Bill, earnestly. 'But the Doc's got a point. This mission will be dangerous. And it's too risky to add anyone at this stage.'

'I won't get in the way,' said Adam. 'And I'll do any training required. Just, please, let me come with you. '

'Can you learn an entire language in three weeks?' said Lopek. 'Because you would need to achieve fluency in Phrenaelia.'

'No, he wouldn't,' said Lynn. She picked up a mug of tea and looked over it at Adam. 'I'm still basically rubbish at it.'

'You're not rubbish, Lynn. Your level of understanding is perfectly adequate,' said Lopek. 'Besides, you'll be with me the whole time.'

Lynn sputtered a mouthful of tea back into her mug, laughing. 'Well, that would be true for Adam, too, wouldn't it? I mean, if he came with us, he'd have to stay with us, right?'

'Also, he could learn Phrenaelia on the ship,' said Kal. 'It's gonna take a month or so to get there.'

'It's not just about the language!' said Lopek, confounded by this mutiny. 'That was just an example. There's *so much* he would need to learn. Otherwise, he might end up endangering all of us!'

'How so?' Adam asked benignly.

'Hostile natives,' said Bill before Lopek could retort. 'They're a dangerous breed in Nephia. And our primary mission is to make contact with the Krae. A newly discovered people from the frozen north, who are, by all accounts, even more savage.'

Adam saw a glint in the security officer's eye. The man didn't fear the inherent dangers of this expedition; he relished them. Adam logged the observation as a potential avenue to explore. He addressed Lopek directly, keeping his tone amiable. 'What can I do to win your confidence?' he said. 'How can I assure you that I wouldn't be a burden if I came along? What do you need me to do?'

'I need you to forget this delusion and stop wasting my time,' said Lopek.

'Okay,' said Harold, leaning forward for the first time. 'Adam has tried the diplomatic approach. Now it's my turn.' He stared severely at Lopek. 'Your expedition to Nephia has minimal value to the Hive. The Algorithm doesn't care about your mission; *you* do, hence why it's taken ten years to gain its approval. Restoring the Hive to full power, however, is paramount. In fact, I'd wager that with a little paperwork, I could convince the Algorithm to cancel your expedition, repurpose your ship, and send Adam to Nephia with a unit of soldiers instead.'

Lopek looked momentarily stunned, his face pale and slack. He gulped. 'You … you can't do that,' he said meekly.

'No, he *won't* do that,' said Adam, trying to keep the peace. 'Hal, please don't threaten to tank the expedition.'

A scraping sounded as Lopek stood and stormed from the table through the library. The others watched him in embarrassed silence.

'I'm sorry,' said Harold to the table at large. 'I'd just had enough.'

'We've all had enough,' said Lynn. Kaldor snickered.

'Hey!' said Bill reproachfully. 'The Doc can be annoying, I know, but Nephia is his passion. He's just doing what he thinks is right.'

'What do *you* think is right?' Adam prompted.

'If it were up to me,' said Bill, folding his muscular arms, 'I'd take you with us, no problem. Not to help your friend, though, but because your lawyer's right. Sooner or later, the Hive will need its power restored to full capacity. And the only place to get more Inficore is Nephia. If we can help you fulfil your reparation, we might also neutralise a future war.'

Kal whistled, flashing his eyebrows at Adam, who shifted uncomfortably in his chair.

'Yeah, I'd like to avoid war too, if I can help it,' he said.

'Yeah, that's always nice,' said Lynn.

Bill blew out his lips like a snorting horse. 'All right,' he said. 'From this moment on, let's assume, *quietly*, that you're coming with us. Could you attend a briefing in my office here tomorrow afternoon?'

'Of course,' said Adam at once, delighted.

'Good,' said Bill. 'But we'll still need to convince the Doc. I want you to come prepared with ideas about your reparation. Let's show him what you can bring to the team.'

'I can do that,' said Adam. 'No problem.'

'Great,' said Bill. 'I'll go and make sure he's okay. Lynn, Kal, why don't you show Adam around. He'll also need full medical assessment.'

'Thank you,' said Adam, standing to offer his hand. The security officer got to his feet and grasped it.

'Welcome aboard,' he said. 'Please don't make me regret this.'

'You won't,' said Adam.

Bill looked in both his eyes then took off in the same direction as Lopek.

Harold, Kal, and Lynn got to their feet. 'Well, that's that,' said Harold, adjusting his tie. He looked at Adam. 'Do you need help finding somewhere to stay?'

'Nah, I'll find somewhere,' said Adam. He pulled his brother into an embrace. 'Thanks for all your help, Hal.'

'Be safe,' he said in Adam's ear. 'And stay in touch.'

Harold stood back, aimed a final, curt nod at Lynn and Kal, and departed.

Adam raised his eyebrows sheepishly at his new teammates.

'Genuinely, welcome aboard,' said Kal, grinning. 'And listen, like Bill said, man, don't worry about Lopek. He's an alright guy, really. Usually less … intense.'

'I wouldn't go that far!' said Lynn. 'I mean, let's not lie to the man on his first day. Lopek's a nice bloke, but he's always intense!'

'Yeah, true!' said Kal, his ever-present grin widening. 'But don't take his reaction personally is all I mean. He pulled the same routine when we were forced on him too. Bill included.'

'You guys joined the expedition late as well?' Adam asked, his spirits lifting.

'Yep,' said Lynn. 'Lopek's original plan was a solo mission in a dinghy, I think.'

'Neh, a dinghy wouldn't be authentic enough,' said Kal. 'He'd've floated over naked on a bit of driftwood.'

Lynn screwed up her face, eyes closed.

'Kaldor! Mental images … please.'

Kal laughed. 'Come on, we'll show you around,' he said.

Adam smiled in gratitude and gestured them ahead.

They led him from the dining hall through the rows of books with Forty-five in tow.

'Why is that thing following us?' Lynn asked over her shoulder.

'He's with me,' said Adam. 'I need to program him for a job.'

'Cool,' said Kal.

Lynn's trainers squeaked as they walked, and Kal's braid swung across his back like a pendulum. They pushed through a set of doors into a long hallway. Lynn stopped abruptly and pointed to her name on a door to their left.

'This is my lab, obviously,' she said. 'Bill's got a cupboard next to the lower gymnasium, but he mainly works from Lopek's office on the fifth floor. Do you need somewhere to work with your blank?'

'Um … yeah, if there's somewhere available,' said Adam.

Lynn clucked her tongue, peering down the hall.

'There's a workshop in the tech lab,' she said after a moment. 'It's a bit of a dumping ground, and there's no computer, but it's big, and nobody really uses it. That sound okay?'

'Sounds perfect,' said Adam. He smiled and meant to thank them but said, 'I'm sorry I've intruded like this.'

Kal winked.

'You're saving a friend,' said Lynn. 'We'll help you however we can. Oh, and I'll have to grab you at some point tomorrow morning. I need to scan your Autophage and take a blood sample. Make sure you're not riddled with anything that might wipe out the Nephians.'

'You're in for a treat.' Kal smirked, absently rubbing his forearm.

Lynn frowned at Forty-five. 'Do I need to test the blank?' she asked.

'He won't have any diseases,' said Adam, 'but he should have an Autophage if you want to test it?'

'Okey-dokey,' said Lynn, 'we'll test him too. Now, you've seen the cafeteria, and there are toilets basically everywhere, so … yeah. Any questions?'

'Yes, where's *your* office?' Adam asked Kal.

'Ha! Not here.' Kal grinned. 'I work at the observatory off-site. By the way, where are you staying?'

'I … don't know,' said Adam truthfully. He hadn't considered this. 'We'll probably just get a couple of sleep pods for tonight, then look for somewhere in the morning.'

'Pfff, nah, don't be crazy! Come and stay with me!' said Kal, beaming at him. 'It's not super luxury or anything, but we've got a couple of spare bunk beds if you like.'

Adam groaned inwardly. *Bunk beds?* 'Are you sure?' he heard himself say.

'Yeah, man!' said Kal, putting a hand on his shoulder. 'You're part of the team now. But fair warning, I'm gonna be glued to the scope all night. Been roped in to assist with the K-71 search! Did you hear about it?'

Kal's eyes were orbs of enthusiasm now.

'That's the planet that's gone missing, right?'

'Plane*toid*,' Lynn corrected, but she suddenly looked disgusted. 'Bleurch, Adam, I am so sorry. Kal has etched that detail into my soul over the last two days. It's all he's talked about. And it's not annoying or anything.'

'I'm an astronomer,' Kal shrugged, laughing. 'A massive object in space has just disappeared. And what, I'm supposed to ignore that, am I?'

Lynn rolled her eyes. Kal turned to Adam, palms open, waiting to see where his loyalty landed in the debate. Lynn shifted her weight and considered Adam too. Adam looked from one to the other. He settled his gaze on Lynn.

'I think it's amazing,' he said.

Kaldor clapped his hands so loudly that a passing woman flinched and glowered back at them in fright. He grinned at Adam like a madman. Lynn's smile was one of pity.

'You are going to majorly regret that,' she said sympathetically. And realising he had already agreed to stay at Kal's observatory, Adam suspected she was probably right.

CHAPTER 7

West Point Observatory

Having seen the cluttered workshop that would serve as their office, Adam and Forty-five followed Kal to his observatory, situated outside the dome, beyond the glow of West Point City. They travelled by train, their chosen carriage so packed that Kal and Forty-five had to stand in the aisle for an hour, Kal having insisted that Adam take the only available seat. But as the train rattled along the coast, the passengers dwindled. The sun was setting as they alighted. Only then did Kal disclose that the observatory was a further forty-minute hike.

Adam had never regretted his polite nature more as he trudged through country lanes in the growing darkness, guided only by the swinging red light of Kaldor's torch.

There had been so many moments, thought Adam, clutching a stitch at his side, when he could have insisted on taking a comfortable, warm pod in the city. He had even rehearsed broaching the subject in his head – had formulated the sentences and chosen the right tone – but every time he had opened his mouth, Kal had looked at him with such innocent glee that the words died in his throat. And now he was climbing a mountain in the dark.

A lit window appeared up ahead, surrounded by the dark outline of a building against the twilit sky.

'Welcome to my home,' said Kal, trudging beside him.

Adam squinted like a newborn as they entered the sudden glare. Once his eyes adjusted, he found himself in an open, communal kitchen where a long dining table stood flanked by benches. A squat woman in an orange fleece stirred something at the cooker, and a gorgeous scent filled the room. Adam's stomach groaned. He hadn't eaten since breakfast.

'Evening, Kal,' said the woman. 'Clear sky for the hunt tonight!'

'Brilliant,' said Kal. 'I've brought guests with me. Theresa, this is Adam, the new addition to my expedition team, and erm, this is his blank. Adam, this is my colleague, Theresa.'

'Very nice to meet you,' said Adam. 'Whatever you're cooking smells incredible, by the way.'

'Oh, well, you're welcome to have some,' said Theresa. 'It's chicken Mahkra. Kal's recipe. I've made a batch to see us through the night.'

'Has Yuri called with our coordinates yet?' asked Kal.

'Not yet, but I figure we're quite far down the list.'

'Cool,' said Kal. 'I'll show Adam to his room then. Come on.'

The room was nicer than Adam had expected. There were two bunk beds, a window with a drop-down blind, an empty wardrobe, a single armchair, and a gleaming ensuite bathroom, complete with guest towels. Kal leaned against the doorframe, watching Adam's reaction.

'Have you got any clothes or anything?' he asked.

'I've got a couple of shirts from InfiTech, but everything else I left in Felix. I'll order a couple of stitch boxes tomorrow.'

'No worries,' said Kal, nodding solemnly. Then he smiled. 'Come on, let's eat. Then I'll show you the Nightfinder!'

They sat at the kitchen table for dinner with Theresa, whose cooking tasted even better than it smelled. Adam helped himself to seconds and thirds, while Forty-five consumed his necessary calories before Adam ordered him to bed. Feeling very tired and exceptionally full, Adam followed Kal to the observatory, located a few minutes' walk from the lodgings.

'Why is your torchlight red?' he asked, concentrating on the lit patch of floor in Kaldor's wake.

'Because our eyes take around twenty to thirty minutes to fully adapt to the dark. Which is obviously what you want when stargazing. And red light doesn't interfere with the transition as much. That's why we're so far from the city. Just look at the sky out here!'

Adam looked up at the canopy of starlight. As he stared, more and more subtle lights appeared until he could distinguish the diagonal band of the galaxy across the sky. For an instant, Adam saw the sky for what it truly was; not a ceiling but an endless three-dimensional space that utterly dwarfed him. He shuddered, then half-jogged to catch up with Kal.

After the pleasant surprise of the meal and room, the West Point observatory itself was an utter disappointment. Adam had imagined a huge, grand building with a rotating, domed roof, and a vast telescope jutting into the starry sky. Instead, Kal led him to a medium-sized shed with a flat roof that he slid off manually. In the centre of the shed was a black, stumpy telescope on a concrete plinth built through the wooden floor into the solid ground beneath. The walls were covered in astronomical charts and various images of space things. A hand-held radio and an ancient computer sat on a table against the wall, and leaning against the opposite wall was a stack of folding chairs.

It was colder than deep space.

'Behold … the Nightfinder!' said Kal, switching on weak red lights, which was still more pomp than the stunted telescope deserved.

'Awesome,' said Adam.

Kal opened one of the folding chairs and placed it next to the eyepiece. 'Wanna see some stuff?' he said, tapping the backrest.

Adam sat while Kal booted the computer. A loading bar appeared on the screen.

'So, you'll be mapping the night sky from Nephia, right?' said Adam, tucking his cold hands between his thighs.

'Yup,' said Kal. 'Well, actually, no. It's already been mapped by our satellites. But the Academy wants me to report on the Nephian constellations and any stories and myths behind them.'

'I've never understood constellations,' said Adam.

'What do you mean?'

'Well, they never look like the thing they're named after. Like, I don't get how anyone could see a frog or whatever from two dots. And secondly, I also don't get how there can be fixed constellations at all. I mean, Ithea is constantly revolving, right?'

'Yeah …'

'And it rotates around the sun, which is also moving through space, like all the other stars, right?'

'Right,' said Kal, frowning.

'Well, how can there be fixed constellations with all that movement? Surely the sky should just be a random mess every night!'

Kal doubled over as though someone had punched him, clutching his belly. He laughed so hard that Adam got infected and started laughing too. Every time they tried to stop, they would catch each other's eye and go again. It was some time before they gathered their composure. The computer had been ready for a while.

'Oh, man,' said Kal, wiping an eye, 'that was great. And I know what you mean; it took a long time for the mechanics to click for me, but once it does, it's amazing.'

He typed some numbers on the keyboard, hit 'enter', and the Nightfinder rotated to an exact point.

'Take a look,' said Kal, 'but try not to touch it. It's very sensitive.'

Adam put his right eye to the eyepiece, trying not to touch the rubber circle. Inside, he saw the vivid image of a stunning, pink, cloud-textured wave.

'Wow,' he said earnestly, looking at the Nightfinder with new respect. He suddenly forgot how cold he was.

'That's the Great Wave nebula,' said Kal, looking up at the sky as though able to see it with his naked eye. 'Amazing, isn't it … want to see another one?'

'Yeah!'

Kal punched in another sequence of numbers, and the Nightfinder settled into a new position. Adam peered eagerly into the eyepiece. This time, he saw a spectacular, electric-green shape, like a delicate iris with a dazzling centre. Adam had no words for it. He scanned its beautiful detail.

'That's the afterglow of the Braxton supernova,' said Kal from behind him.

'Unbelievable … show me more!'

They spent a few minutes swivelling through Kal's favourite repertoire of objects. And Adam was well and truly converted to the practice of stargazing. Why had he never done this before? He saw giant finger-shaped plumes of blue gas that were entwined together like a sequence of DNA, something called a pulsar, which looked like a glowing bulb with a spear of light through it, and finally, a pair of stars called the Twins, which was really a cluster of dwarf stars orbiting a supergiant. Adam couldn't remember the last time he had felt such awe. It ended abruptly when they heard Theresa's voice over the radio.

'Theresa to Kal, Theresa to Kal, come in,' she said.

'Send for Kal.'

'You'd better get back here, quick! Yuri's on the phone with our list of coordinates – apparently, we're the only site with a clear sky, so it's pretty extensive!'

'On my way!' said Kal, and he dashed out of the shed clutching the radio.

Suddenly alone, Adam remembered his fatigue and the bitter cold. He got to his feet, shivering, and folded up his chair. He placed it against the others when a noise startled him. He turned and saw the Nightfinder moving slowly to a new position.

He stared at it for a moment.

Kal or Theresa must have typed new coordinates from a computer in the lodge. He checked outside to see whether they were making their way up to him but saw nothing. He moved around the telescope and crouched down to peer into the eyepiece.

At first, he saw nothing but darkness. But then, after a few seconds, his eye found a subtle circle of darkness moving in the centre of the image. He stared hard at the spot, transfixed. The dark shape inched across the viewport. For some reason, the skin on the back of his neck began to prickle. His hairs stood on end. And a shudder passed down his spine that had nothing to do with the cold.

The shed door swung open, and Adam tore himself away from the telescope, his heart pounding.

'If he thinks we can log this many positions in one night, he's going to be disappointed,' Theresa said as she cracked open a chair and placed it at the desk.

'We'll just have to plough through as many as we can,' said Kal, then his eyes found Adam, who had backed against the shed wall. 'You okay?'

His question broke the spell.

'What? Yeah,' said Adam, 'I'm fine.'

'Sorry I left like that, but we've received our search orders – and there's a lot of them!'

Theresa typed in a set of numbers, and the Nightfinder moved once more. Adam stared at it as though it were a coiled snake about to strike.

'Are you sure you're okay?' asked Kal.

'Fine,' said Adam, forcing a smile, 'just tired … I'll, erm … I'll leave you guys to it.'

'Thanks,' said Kal. 'I'll see you in the morning.'

Adam stood in the shed doorway, when the urge to tell Kaldor what he had seen forced him to a halt. Kal and Theresa were poring over the list of numbers, Kal leaning forward while Theresa ran her finger down the screen.

'Wait,' said Adam. They turned to look at him. 'Can you go back to the last position?'

'What?' said Theresa.

'Can you move the telescope back to the last thing it was looking at?'

The two astronomers looked at each other. Theresa looked impatient.

'Yeah, we can,' said Kal. 'What's up?'

'Please move the telescope to its last position. I need to see something.'

Kal turned to Theresa, who sighed and hit a button on the keyboard. The Nightfinder moved slowly to its previous position.

'Take a look,' said Adam.

Kal frowned but checked the viewport. After a second or two, he pulled away to look at Adam.

'The Twins,' he said, 'yeah, pretty amazing. I can print a picture if you like?'

Adam stared at him for a moment, the urge to blurt out what he'd seen conflicting with his instinct to leave them alone.

'No,' he said, finally, 'sorry. I'll leave you to it.'

He left the shed and shut the door quickly as though trying to sever his embarrassment. He froze, clutching the outside door handle, and was grateful to hear Kal and Theresa's voices dive straight into their work.

His sense of unease lifted in the cold night air, and his heart rate slowed to its regular rhythm. He looked up at the cloudless, dome-less sky, which twinkled innocently above. He simply stood there for a moment, the voices, and the tapping of keys from inside eroding his concern. He was overstimulated, that was all. He had seen too many mind-bending things in quick succession. And perhaps the moving circle of darkness, or whatever he had seen last, was simply another natural phenomenon. Maybe a black hole, or dark matter, or something not commonly known by lay people. And why shouldn't such things elicit fear? The pulsar and nebula had sparked wonder, after all. He buried the gnawing unease and returned to the lodge.

The downhill walk was much more manageable. Adam wasted no time and headed straight for his room. He peeled off his clothes, allowing them to fall wherever, and climbed naked into the bottom bunk of the bed not occupied by Forty-five. He curled up in a foetal position under the duvet until his body stopped shivering. Then he drifted into a deep sleep.

His eyes rolled beneath their lids.

Adam sat at the scope of the Nightfinder. He peered inside and saw a sequence of images; Gerald handing him a fragment of Inficore; a faceless man and woman watching him from a floating window; and an indistinct, shadowy figure walking toward him down a long, long corridor.

CHAPTER 8

Autophage

'Are you squeamish?' asked Lynn, wiping Adam's forearm with a wet cotton bud.

'Not really.'

Adam looked away all the same. He felt the sharp scratch and the cold liquid enter his blood and distracted himself with the oddities of Lynn's lab. It was like an exotic pet store. Glass habitats filled the left wall, each containing a specimen, a lizard, spider, or snake. The entire wall to Adam's right housed a vertical cross-section of an ant colony wedged flat behind a pane of glass. He could just make out their tiny network of tunnels, the occasional leaf cutting carried along.

'All done,' said Lynn, pressing a cotton bud against the puncture mark. 'Your Autophage should eliminate the virus within two minutes. And we'll scan it while it works. Just pop your arm in here for me.'

She indicated a white halo. Adam thrust his jabbed arm inside.

'Can you get him to sit down, please?' asked Lynn, eyeing Forty-five.

'Forty-five, please sit down,' said Adam.

The blank obeyed. Lynn knelt, rolled up Forty-five's sleeve, but froze, the needle inches from the blank's skin.

'He's not going to lash out or anything, is he? When I jab him, I mean? I've never treated a blank before.'

'No, they don't have a self-defence reflex,' said Adam, watching a single ant moving resolutely against the current of its co-workers. 'You've got to build that stuff in.'

Lynn inserted the needle.

'So, what kind of things do you program them to do?' she said, wiping a spot of blood from Forty-five's arm.

'All sorts,' said Adam. 'They're mostly used to maintain the domes or expand the Nexus tunnels. Basically, all the high-risk jobs that nobody wants to do. Occasionally, though, I'd teach them something ultra-specific, like how to perform brain surgeries.'

Lynn whipped her head round to gape at him. 'No way!' she said.

'Yeah … and it was a lot easier than you think. It took about six weeks to teach that particular blank.'

'You taught a blank how to perform brain surgery in six weeks?'

Adam shifted to look at her, keeping his arm in the halo.

'It's a lot less impressive than it sounds,' he said. 'All I did was raise her dexterity level off the charts, by forcing her to complete tiny, complex actions all day. Blanks have one big advantage; they're not distracted by anything – doubts, fear, boredom, what they're going to have for dinner … nothing. So, they can concentrate on tasks in a way we can only dream of. Then, I sat her in front of brain surgery footage for a few days, and it was time to put her into practice on a cadaver. She was shown a picture of what the brain should look like, then she just made it look that way.'

'Wow!' said Lynn, shaking her head. 'That's the craziest thing I've ever heard! I guess it won't be long until we doctors are redundant, eh?'

'Oh, don't worry, that'll never happen,' Adam said. 'There's a trade-off, you see. Real doctors have empathy. You can form attachments with your patients. And feel the benefit of your work. So, you commit to a long career filled with empathetic payoff. Whereas the brain surgeon blank burned out after eight months. They put her to work every day, and she performed major surgery on over five hundred people, but the inhuman work rate used up her human body. Yes, her owners could have slowed her down and taught her to look after herself more, but that new knowledge would have chipped away at some of her insane dexterity. Do you see the problem?'

'Sort of,' said Lynn, now sticking a plaster on Forty-five's arm. 'But it's still amazing! What will you teach this one?'

Adam considered Forty-five.

'Ultimately, I've got to train him for InfiTech …' He caught Lynn's eye and smiled. 'But they don't need him back for a year! So, in the meantime, I could teach him whatever I want.'

A red light flashed in the white halo.

'Looks like your Autophage is active,' said Lynn. She moved to the desk and opened her laptop. 'You can take your arm out now.'

Adam rolled up his sleeve and wandered over to the habitats. He peered into the first, where a dark-green snake lay motionless beneath a light bulb.

'So, how did you get involved with this trip to Nephia?' he asked.

'I applied,' said Lynn, frowning at her screen, 'same as most zoologists in the Hive. But my medical background probably swung the Algorithm in my favour. It's a big opportunity to discover something new! Nephian fauna has hardly been studied at all.' She looked over her shoulder at the door and spoke more quietly. 'But that's not why I applied. *My* interest … is in dragons!'

Adam stopped scrutinising a particularly ugly lizard and frowned at her. 'Dragons?'

'Yep,' she beamed, her cheeks turning a shade of pink. 'There are loads of dragon myths in Nephia. But I think they're based on something real. An oral history presumed a story.'

'You think dragons were real?'

'Not *were* real,' she said, '*are* real … fire-breathing and all. I know!' she added, laughing at Adam's expression. 'Everyone thinks I'm mad! But I've got a theory. You see, there's a cluster of islands about a thousand miles off the southern coast of Nephia, which the Nephians call *the dragon's tail*. And, on those islands, we discovered a species of tiny, winged lizards that spit acid. We call them Synkarions.'

Lynn joined Adam at the habitat and nodded at the animal inside. He bent forward to regard the creature within. It was black and slender, roughly the size of a closed fist, its tail hugging its curled body. On closer inspection, Adam saw that what he had mistaken for ridged veins along its flanks were the delicate folds of leathery wings.

'You think that's a dragon?' said Adam, fascinated.

'I do,' said Lynn, gazing in at it lovingly. 'Because the incredible thing about Synkarions is that individuals can merge with others and become bigger. Asexual isogametic fusion, it's called; two adults can bond together inside a cocoon. A few months later, if left undisturbed, they'll emerge as a singular entity – a sort of kitten-sized hybrid. And my theory is, why should it end there? Why couldn't two kitten-sized Synkarions bond into something bigger? And so on. But the problem is evidence. Because there isn't any – except the Nephian legends – and there's the issue of timescale. Yes, two regular Synkarions, like this one, can merge in a matter of months. But merging two kitten-sized hybrids would take exponentially longer, possibly dozens of years. Anything bigger than that, hundreds of years, then thousands, and by the time you get to a full, fifty-foot-long, village-destroying monster, you're talking about millions and millions of years. *But!* Adam … Synkarions have survived on those isolated islands for longer than that. Much longer. What if one – *just one –* ultimate hybrid, built up through a pyramid of pairings, managed to bond together against all the odds? What would you have?'

Adam stared at the tiny sleeping lizard, trying to picture it scaled up. In his mind, he conjured a version too big to fit in the lab. 'You'd have a pretty badass dragon!' he concurred. Lynn put an arm across his shoulders and squeezed.

Privately, Adam thought she was quite mad. But he smiled back at her encouragingly. Lynn's laptop pinged.

'That'll be your data,' she said, moving to her computer. 'Can you ask the blank to put his arm … in … the …'

Lynn trailed off, frowning at her screen, reading. She snorted and covered her mouth.

'When's the last time your Autophage got updated?' she asked.

'Err, three years ago,' said Adam. 'Why?'

'Because it's malfunctioning.'

'What? What do you mean?'

Lynn dipped her head at an angle. 'Well, typically, over three years, you might expect it to eliminate between maybe fifteen and twenty viruses.'

'Okay,' said Adam. 'But, what, mine hasn't eliminated *any*?'

'Oh, no.' Lynn grinned. 'According to the download, your Autophage has destroyed … 5,690.'

Adam blinked over his glasses. 'What does that mean?'

'Nothing.' Lynn shrugged. 'It's just a glitch. I'll put a new one in.'

The word 'glitch' had temporarily rooted Adam to the spot. This was the second time he had heard it in as many days.

Lynn appeared before him, tapping a syringe of luminous green liquid. 'Where do you want it?' she asked. 'Neck, thigh, bum, or shoulder?'

'Definitely shoulder,' he said, twisting side-on.

Lynn pulled down his collar and jabbed him again.

Adam looked over at Forty-five, who was still seated patiently.

'We'd better get going as soon as you're finished,' he said. 'I've got to think of a way I can be useful on the expedition before my briefing with Bill and Lopek.'

'Aah,' said Lynn. 'Can I give you some free advice? Prepare yourself for what you're going to hear in that briefing. For mine, Bill treated me to a little presentation, outlining how I would be raped and enslaved if we got separated.'

'You're joking!' said Adam, stunned.

'Nope,' she said, her mouth a grim line. 'At first, I was angry, but then I realised he was just telling me the truth. It's Bill's job to make sure we take this expedition seriously. And I'm warning you, he's very good at it.'

*

Adam spent the following hours in his workshop, thinking. He paced the wide room, hands in his pockets, repeating the problem in his head, hoping for a flash of brilliance. Harold had all but assured his place on the expedition, yet he wanted to earn it rightfully all the same.

But how could he convince Lopek that he would be an *asset* to the mission? What value could he bring? And what could he possibly offer the Nephians in exchange for a God Stone?

He kicked a loose nail across the floor. 'What do *you* think?' he asked Forty-five.

The blank stared at him like a painting.

Adam pulled his phone from his pocket and absently dialled Doctor Yang. Her voice spoke in his ear. 'Suzie Yang.'

'Doctor Yang, hi, it's Adam Maxwell.'

She sighed into the receiver, so loud that Adam had to move his phone away from his ear. 'Hello, Adam,' she said. 'What can I do for you?'

'I, erm … I just wondered if there was any change in Genevieve's condition?'

'I told you I would contact you with any news.'

'Right,' said Adam. 'I just hadn't heard anything for a while.'

'I'm swamped, Adam. I will call if there's any news.'

She hung up.

Adam brought his phone around to his face to stare at it. *What a bitch,* he thought.

He slid his phone on a workbench and glared at the row of tools. Each implement hung from a hook on a pegboard, their outlines drawn on the wall.

Could he trade a God Stone for a soldering gun or some power tool?

Probably not. They wouldn't be able to power it.

And the flash of brilliance arrived. Power!

He didn't need to rob Nephia of a God Stone, he just needed the power inside! If he could take one of the empty stones from the failed experiment, he could transfer the power from a God Stone into it, and presto, Genevieve's reparation would be fulfilled. The Nephians wouldn't know the difference.

Adam, you genius, he thought.

He snatched up his phone again and dialled Gerald.

CHAPTER 9

The Briefing

Adam arrived at Lopek's office to find the door wedged open. The room appeared dark from the hallway, but when Adam peeked over the threshold, he found Bill and Lopek standing on either side of a table, which shone under a low-hanging light shade. The two men leaned on the table, studying whatever was illuminated on its surface. They looked up as Adam entered.

'Adam,' said Bill, 'right on time.'

Lopek lifted his glasses into his curly hair and strode over to greet Adam at the door, his face remorseful yet stern. He extended a bony hand. Adam took it.

'I'm sorry for how I behaved yesterday,' said Lopek. 'I felt blindsided. But once I'd calmed down, I understood your motive. So … if Bill thinks we can accommodate you safely, and we can honour the original mission parameters, then I'm open to your inclusion.'

'Thank you,' said Adam. 'And look, I'm sorry if I blindsided you. But I promise I won't be a burden. I've actually got an idea how to achieve my reparation *without* robbing the Nephians of a God Stone.'

Lopek pursed his lower lip and bobbed his head politely, without a shred of belief in Adam's conviction. He retracted his hand, kicked the door wedge to seal out the hallway light, then returned to the table.

'Bill was just about to propose an alternative route,' said Lopek.

As Adam got closer to the table, he realised that what he had mistaken for a light shade was actually the lens of a 3-D projector, casting a crystal-clear satellite image of the Nephian continent onto the surface of the table, with ranging topography, vivid coastline, and scattered red dots labelled with the names of its realms, cities, and towns.

'Right,' said Bill, leaning into the projection on his knuckles, triceps rigid. 'The original plan was for Doc, Kal, Lynn and me to sail directly to Berrund in northern Nephia. Our primary mission was to make contact with the Krae and attempt to broker peace in the region. However, Adam, your reparation to the Hive trumps all that, so we need to make finding a God Stone our priority.'

Lopek folded his arms but didn't interrupt.

'Now,' Bill continued, 'we're not sure whether there's a God Stone in Berrund, so it no longer makes sense to land there immediately. Instead, I propose that we sail to Laudria in the south, where the king resides, and where we know there's at least one God Stone.'

Lopek sucked air through his teeth.

'I think that's unwise,' he said.

'Hear me out, Doc,' said Bill, raising a wide hand. 'We can accomplish a whole bunch in one strike if we head to Laudria first; we know there's a God Stone there, so, tick. We can recover at New Antra, the Hive settlement, after the long voyage at sea – tick. And we can deliver supplies to New Antra that they desperately need. If we fail to get a God Stone in Laudria, we sail up the east coast to Ealee and travel inland to Lysk, the religious heart of Nephia, which has two God Stones that we know of. If we fail there, we return to the ship and sail up to Berrund as planned and hope the Doc's contact can help us locate one. It'll be tough going, but we'll hit the two likeliest places to get what we're after.'

Lopek shifted his weight and sighed melodramatically. 'But why not sail to Berrund as planned,' he said, 'and if *that* fails, *then* look elsewhere?'

Bill turned his head to Adam, the underside of his face glowing in the map's luminescence.

'The reason the Doc doesn't want to go to Laudria,' he said, 'is this guy.'

Bill pinched the air above the map and turned an invisible page. The map disappeared, replaced by a hologram of a man, revolving slowly in the centre of the table. He was bulky and broad shouldered, wearing a heavy purple cape that fell below the knees of his ornate gold-and-silver armour, his grimace framed by a helmet.

'You see, in Nephia,' Bill continued, 'they don't have an Algorithm to calculate a person's status. No, sir. Their way is much older and simpler than ours. In Nephia, the more skilled you are in combat, the higher you rank. They duel to the death for power and have done so for thousands of years. And it's shaped them into a race of the toughest warriors you can imagine. Every five years, called a Quintus, the Lords of each Realm may challenge the King or Queen to a duel at a Throne Trial. And this guy,' he pointed at the revolving figure, 'is the current King, Markos Almanfier, who has ruled Nephia for twenty-five years. The longest reign of any monarch in their history.'

Adam looked closer at the revolving figure. Even in holographic form, the King radiated power.

'Now,' said Bill, 'Markos here doesn't like us very much. Antharians, I mean. He doesn't trust our kind.'

'They think we're Elves,' Lopek interjected. 'That's what they call us. And Markos has always believed that we *Elves* are plotting to overthrow him. It's a delusion, of course, but his paranoia makes him mistrustful. And he's easily offended, which is why our training is so important. But it doesn't end with Markos. Any Nephian we insult, whether by accident or design, is likely to challenge the offender to a duel.'

'A duel?' said Adam incredulously.

'Yep. That's why the Doc has taught us so much about Nephian culture. Because the more we know, the less likely we are to cause offence. Worst case, though, if you do get challenged, I will step in on your behalf. But I'm asking you – like I asked the others; please, *please*, never put me in that position. I know I look tough, but here's me next to old Markos.'

Bill clicked his fingers under the projector, and instantly, a Bill Conrad avatar appeared on the table, revolving next to Markos.

Adam sat up involuntarily, staring wide-eyed at the revolving figures. The miniature Bill's head came level with the bottom of Markos's chest. The security officer looked like a skinny adolescent beside the Nephian King.

Adam swallowed.

'I know,' said Bill, 'I wouldn't bet on me either. Especially since I'm not allowed to bring a gun.'

'Why not?' said Adam. 'Sounds like we could all use one!'

Lopek sighed. 'Bill is just poking at an old wound,' he said. 'He and I have discussed this at length. And he knows it's completely out of the question. Not only would it break the Cultural Dilution Act, which requires us to conceal our technology from the Nephian people, but think of the damage introducing a weapon like that could do. Not just to individuals but societally; if a gun suddenly fell into the hands of a Nephian, that person would instantly become the most powerful in the kingdom. The new King or Queen. It would destroy the foundation of their social structure overnight and could plunge the entire continent into chaos.' He peered over his glasses at Bill. 'No. Guns.'

'It's a shame,' said Bill. 'I reckon they might trade us a God Stone for an Elvish weapon.'

'But we don't need to trade anything,' said Adam, seizing his moment. 'I've thought of a way we can satisfy my reparation without acquiring a God Stone. We just need to borrow one for an hour.'

Bill and Lopek frowned at him quizzically.

'If I could bring one of the empty Inficore stones from Felix, we could transfer the power from a God Stone into it. The Nephians don't use the energy inside, right? So, they wouldn't know the difference if we took it.'

Bill raised his eyebrows, impressed. But Lopek's remained knitted together.

'Nephians aren't stupid,' he said. 'They would know the difference, I'm sure. They use God Stones to communicate with Ohrak, their God.'

'How?' asked Adam. 'They don't handle them with bare skin, do they?'

Lopek blinked rapidly but didn't answer, clearly uncomfortable being displaced as the expert in the room.

'Because if they're touching Inficore,' said Adam, 'they're unwittingly activating it, releasing trace amounts of radiation, which damages synapses in the brain. That's probably why they hallucinate this god of theirs. And if we collect the energy, we would actually be doing their brains a favour.'

A fractious silence settled.

'I think you've got him,' said Bill, winking at Adam.

Lopek's expression soured. He sought to regain the upper hand, clutching wildly at straws. 'Well, I still think you'll be challenged to a duel just for asking,' he said. 'So, unless you're secretly an invincible warrior, I would advise against that strategy.'

The idea popped into Adam's mind as though delivered from another reality. 'No, I'm not an invincible warrior,' he said. 'But I could make one.'

Bill and Lopek swapped a look.

'What do you mean?' asked Bill.

'I could program my blank for combat,' said Adam. 'I could train it to fight beyond the skill of any Nephian.'

'What?' said Bill. 'You think you can train a blank to fight at a Nephian standard in a couple of weeks?'

'Sure,' said Adam, enjoying the shock of his casual responses.

'That's ridiculous,' said Lopek, annoyed. 'Even if you could train it to duel skilfully, there's just no way it could match them for strength!'

'It would surpass them,' said Adam. 'It's just a matter of disabling its self-damage regulator and harnessing its twitch fibre potential.'

Bill watched Adam through narrowed eyes but could not conceal his intrigue.

'Let me try.' Adam shrugged at Lopek. 'I'll configure it for defence only, so it won't start any trouble. How do you say 'the protector' in the Nephian language?'

'*De Venus*,' Lopek muttered.

'Then that's what I'll call him,' said Adam. 'DeVenus.'

Lopek glowered, wracking his mind for further arguments. He seemed furious that Adam had quickly solved a problem that had stymied them for months.

And just when he thought the moment seemed brightest, Adam's phone buzzed in his pocket. He opened it to find a message from Doctor Yang, comprising only two words: She's awake.

KININUMBRA

DRAGONEYE
FORTRESS

EDDIS

LEYBRIDGE

BERRUND

FLAT HOME

SALVATION

REON

THE GRASS PLAINS

EMERON

LYSK

FAELUND

MARSH

EALEE

NEW ANTRA

FLORIA

HIGH CASTLE
LAUDRIA

ORBON

BOWHARK

NEPHIA

PART II

NEPHIA

CHAPTER 10

The King, the Elf, and the Augur

Two horse-drawn carriages rattled along the dirt path into the heart of the Kingswood. Six black horses with glossy manes pulled each car, their coats gleaming in the sunshine. The high-mounted drivers kept the horses moving at a brisk trot. The first carriage was a standard black box. Typical in Laudria. But the second was huge. Twice the size of the first, spotless white and covered in vines of ornate, golden ivy.

A sudden thudding sound came from inside the white carriage at a distinct bend in the road above a sloping valley. Both drivers drew on their reins and pulled their horses to a gradual, dusty halt. The doors of the black carriage flew open at once, and three servants leaped out, dressed in dark-green tailcoats. Two ran to the white carriage to open its doors with a bow, while the third began unloading a bundle of spears from the boot of the servant's car.

The tall, slender figure of Rowel Malcifer, the King's Augur, descended gracefully from the royal carriage. He wore a hooded brown hunting cloak over his tailored, silken finery, and his black boots were perfectly polished. His skin was the bronzish colour of all southern Florians. His tightly curled hair was coal black and immaculate, including the goatee that tapered to a point a few inches beneath his chin. Jewelled rings adorned every finger, and a delicate silver collar clung unsupported around his throat, symbolizing his servitude to God.

He surveyed his new surroundings, then nodded once to show his approval.

'This will suffice,' he said. Then he spoke louder into the carriage. 'We have arrived, my liege.'

There came a soft scraping sound, as though several people were getting to their feet in unison. Suddenly, the carriage dipped to one side, threatening to topple into the valley, as a giant figure filled its doorway. The bowing servants stiffened, not daring to look up, and the ground shook under their feet as Markos Almanfier stepped from the carriage.

Taller than his Augur and three times as wide, the King dominated the scene. A solid bulk of muscle in drab hunting garb. He was almost entirely bald, save for the crown of greying hair that circled his head, and his eyes were the voids of a killer.

Rowel exhaled silently, watching his King. To all the servants present, Markos continued to radiate his indomitable power.

None of them could guess the awful truth.

'We shall set off on foot from here, my liege,' said Rowel. 'Ohrak has shown me that a great boar hides in the valley below. You will find him and kill him. I have seen it.'

Markos thrust out a hand expectantly. The servant carrying the leather bundle unfurled his burden on the ground with a clatter. A dozen polished spears with gleaming iron heads were laid out in a row at the King's feet. Markos pointed at the nearest spear, and the servant hastily slid it from its leather loop before placing it in the waiting hand. Markos inspected the barbed point of his chosen spear with indifferent eyes. The servant raised his hands, expecting the spear back, when Rowel spoke again.

'The King will carry his own weapon,' he said, causing the servant to withdraw. 'We will hunt alone and return before nightfall. I will summon you with the horn should we find and kill the beast.'

All three servants bowed. They cleared away the remaining spears and hurried back to their carriage, leaving the King and his Augur alone on the roadside.

'This way, my liege,' said Rowel with a half bow. He turned to begin his careful descent into the valley, and the King followed, using the spear as a walking staff.

When they rounded a thicket of bushes, beyond sight of the servants and drivers, the King dropped to his knee. 'Curse you and your schemes!' he said, breathing heavily.

'How is the pain?' asked Rowel.

Markos grimaced but managed to contort his features into an angry sneer. '*Pain?*' he growled, disgusted. 'I am Markos Almanfier, King of Nephia.' He gripped the spear and pulled himself up to his full height. 'I feel no pain.'

But he knuckled his chest at his heart and gave a slight cough. Rowel watched his face closely for a moment but said nothing.

'This is poison and treachery!' Markos went on in quiet fury. 'An Elvish plot to kill me. I know it!'

'Perhaps ...' said Rowel.

In truth, he understood perfectly that the King's condition had nothing to do with any poison or Elvish intervention. The pain had come on suddenly during a sparring session with Master Ulrich. Thankfully, Markos had managed to conceal his discomfort from all the courtiers, for the King of Nephia must never show any sign of weakness, even for a second, or the news would spread through the kingdom faster than a plague. Their enemies would swarm upon them like flies on a rotting corpse. As the old King's adage warned:

A thousand displays of strength might deter a single enemy.
But a single display of weakness will cost a thousand allies.

Indeed, many such allies kept the King's favour, both near and far. And all of them waited for their chance, waiting to end the Almanfier Dynasty.

'How could you not foresee this plot?' snarled Markos.

'I am uncertain, my liege,' Rowel replied. 'Ohrak did not warn me of this ... *deviation*, I admit. But no matter. We must keep our faith. Never forget that I have seen our ultimate destiny. And while God's intentions in your present suffering are not yet clear to me, it will surely be in service of His greater plan.'

'For Henrik to inherit the throne,' Markos supplied.

'Yes,' Rowel concurred in a forceful whisper, unconsciously checking their surroundings for prying ears. He took a step closer and placed a brave hand on the King's solid shoulder. 'At all costs, we must bequeath the throne to your son and none other. No matter who or what might set itself against us. For it is Henrik and Henrik alone who must lead Nephia through the coming calamity. If we should fail in this purpose, my liege, then all life on Ithea may be wiped from existence. I have seen it.'

Markos set his jaw firmly. He stared at the Augur for several seconds. 'Henrik is a boy,' he said at last. 'He would be slaughtered at the Trial.'

'He is your son,' Rowel reassured. 'His skill already equals your own. You have seen it for yourself. And he will grow strong, my liege. Stronger even than you, perhaps. But we must protect him one more time. You must retain the throne at the Trial for one final Quintus. In five more years, Henrik will be nineteen, the same age as you when you won the throne from your father. He will be ready. But we must give him time.'

Markos twirled the spear, knocking the Augur's hand from his shoulder, then thrust the point deep into the earth between the Augur's feet. Rowel flinched but stood his ground.

'Then tell me,' said Markos, 'how does God expect me to keep the throne when He has allowed the Elves to cripple me? And why can't

Kaiber inherit the throne? She is ready *now*.'

Here it was. The greatest threat to Rowel's plan. Though he had prepared his arguments, his heart beat faster in his chest. *Tread very carefully*, he thought. *The King is blind to what his daughter has become.*

'Lady Kaiber would make an excellent Queen, my liege,' he lied. 'She is probably the greatest warrior alive, save for yourself. And no doubt she would defeat any man foolish enough to stand against her at the Trial. However … you know, as I do … that Queens simply do not last. There have only been six Queens in five thousand years of Nephian history. And not one of them saw a second Quintus. It is not a question of Lady Kaiber's ability, my liege, but of sheer numbers. When a woman sits on the throne, more men will believe they can unseat her. And so more will challenge. One lucky blow could destroy all we have built. And all of Ithea, too, if I have interpreted Ohrak's warnings correctly.'

Rowel waited for his King to respond. He had only shared the most palatable truth about why Kaiber must not be her father's successor. He hoped it was enough. Kaiber Almanfier could not be allowed to rule. She was a twisted soul in an ugly coil. If half the rumours surrounding her were true, she had more than earned her whispered moniker, *Kaiber the Cruel*. The King's wilful blindness to his daughter's growing threat might cost them considerably. Rowel hoped it was not too late to expose her.

'What must I do?' asked Markos bitterly.

Rowel felt a weight dissolve in his stomach. 'Put your faith in Ohrak, my liege,' he said. 'And in *me*. We have overcome greater challenges through His guidance, have we not? And we shall prevail again! Come. It is not much farther to the meeting place.'

They walked on through the dense thicket, the King occasionally stopping to catch his breath until the two men came upon a rocky waterfall cascading into a deep, green pool. A dead boar lay on a slab of rock on the opposite bank, its feet tied together. Beside the boar stood a diminutive, red-headed man in a vivid blue raincoat.

An Elf.

He stood watching the churning, frothy water, hands thrust deep into the pockets of his raincoat. Something white dangled between his lips, and smoke rose from its tip and billowed from the Elf's nose. A leather bag lay between his feet.

The Augur and the King's approach was muffled by the rush of the waterfall. The Elf spotted them as they were almost upon him. He started and threw his white pipe into the pool.

'Rowel,' he said, with a sheepish grin, 'I was beginning to wonder –'

The grin slid from his freckled face as he recognised the Augur's companion. His eyes widened. 'Your Majesty!' he said with a hasty bow, his voice much higher than before. 'I did not expect you.'

The Augur halted their advance.

'*Majesty*?' he said obtusely, looking around. 'You must be mistaken, Doctor Sansil. That word is reserved only for the King or Prince Henrik. And neither is here … are they?'

The Elf blinked rapidly, then grasped the Augur's meaning. 'Of course not,' he said, his voice still high. 'My mistake, my lord. How … how may I help you? Mister Blake said that you wanted to meet *alone*.'

He looked terrified but defiant, like a man at the gallows. The Augur tried to calm him by gesturing vaguely in the direction of the King.

'This man requires your attention, Doctor,' he said pointedly. 'He is experiencing … *irregularities* in his chest.'

The Elf glanced from Rowel to Markos, drowning in panic. Both men towered head-and-shoulders above him. Eventually, he stuttered his head forward, somewhere between a nod and a bow.

'Of course,' he repeated, gesturing with a shaking hand to a large boulder beside the dead boar. 'Would … would you ask your … companion to please be seated?'

Rowel turned to relay the request, and was met by a killer stare.

'You brought me to an Elf?' said Markos in an ominously calm tone.

'Who better to diagnose the poison?' the Augur replied. 'Doctor Sansil is a trusted ally.'

This was another lie. Peter Sansil was the basest form of vermin. A despicable wretch. Possessed by a grotesque fetish for young flesh. He had been captured during a raid of an unlicensed brothel by the City Guard, who brought him to High Castle to face the King's justice. However, when Rowel learned of his medical knowledge, he pounced on the opportunity. He spared the doctor from disembowelment and won his faithful, disgusting service in return.

'He's an Elf,' said the King. But he sat heavily on the rock the doctor had indicated and glowered at him expectantly.

Peter wrung his hands together, looking at Rowel for help. The Augur spoke in Elvish. '*Assess your patient, Doctor,*' he said, eyebrows raised.

The Elf dropped to his knee and opened his medical bag. He fumbled noisily with its contents, eventually drawing out a small metal box with a glass end. He tinkered with the strange object for a moment, hands shaking badly, then shot Rowel a final, reproachful glance before advancing toward the seated Markos.

'W-would you please … remove your shirt?' he muttered.

Without taking his eyes off the doctor, Markos unbuttoned his shirt. His chest and abdomen were covered in greying black hair, his pectoral muscles slabs of fleshy stone. But droplets of sweat beaded on the King's skin, and with his shirt removed, his breathing was perceptibly laboured.

Rowel watched curiously as the Elvish doctor worked. He placed three metal discs on the King's chest, forming a triangle around his heart. Markos sneered whenever the Elf touched him.

His preparations complete, the Elf adjusted the metal box and stared at its glass surface. His eyebrows came together in a frown as he studied the instrument. He looked up at Rowel.

'*Well?*' said the Augur in Elvish. '*Why does he suffer? Speak plainly, in your own tongue, Doctor Sansil. The King will not understand us.*'

The Elf swallowed. '*It's not poison,*' he said. '*The scanner shows that his arteries are badly clogged. Almost blocked. Likely due to poor diet and over-exertion. It's on the brink of attack. Or it's already had one. Or many. I don't know. But there is damage to his cells, suggesting his heart has been in fibrillation at least once. It seems to have recovered naturally this time. But if he suffers another cardiac event, even a small one, he will almost certainly die.*'

Rowel twirled a ringed finger absently through his goatee, forcing his features to remain impassive. He had understood few of the Elf's words, but their meaning was clear. And exactly what he had most feared.

'*I see,*' he said before Markos noticed the hesitation. '*So … what will you do, Doctor? How will you cure him?*'

The Elf's eyes widened. '*Cure him?*' he said. '*Rowel, it's a wonder that he's still alive!*'

Markos rose slowly, causing both men to fall silent at once. He plucked the metal discs from his chest like leeches and tossed them into the pool.

'Another word of Elvish in my presence,' he said, 'and I shall impale you on the ramparts of High Castle.'

'A thousand apologies, my liege,' bowed Rowel swiftly. 'The Elf says it is not poison. And he was about to explain how he would cure you. Were you not, Doctor Sansil?'

The Elf looked stricken. For a mad second, Rowel thought he might attempt to flee. Instead, he remained rooted to the spot, wringing his hands tighter, as though trying to squeeze an answer from them.

'There are medicines …' he said, in his best Phrenaelia. 'Courses of medicine which might … forestall the symptoms. But … it would not be a cure. Not as *you* say, my lord.'

There was a ringing silence.

'What use is a medicine that does not *cure*?' implored Rowel, recovering quickly.

This endeavour must not fail.

'Well … such medicine would act only as a preventative, my Lord. It would merely stop the symptoms from worsening. But even so … your companion must rest and take great precautions from now on.'

'Rest?' growled Markos, as though the word sullied his mouth. 'This year is the Quintus. Every treasonous Lord will soon ride to the Vallichor to challenge me. I must prepare.' He took a step forward and clutched his chest through gritted teeth.

'Your Majesty,' said Peter, 'your heart cannot cope with any added strain. If you fight, you will surely die.'

The Elf had spoken too boldly. Markos's face became a stony mask – a look that Rowel knew well. The Augur acted quickly. He grabbed the Elf by his strange coat and lifted him off his feet, slamming his back against the damp wall of the waterfall.

The Elf let out a pitiful cry. He clawed at the arms that had just saved his life.

'No, Doctor!' said the Augur. 'It is *you* who is risking his life. We are bound by the laws of God and Nephia to host a Throne Trial. Markos Almanfier will fight and defend his throne, as always. And he will be victorious, as always. But he cannot do this while he carries this abnormality! You must find a way to rid him of it! Do you understand?' He pressed the Elf harder into the slimy wall. 'Tell us how to return the King to full strength!'

The Elf's eyes bulged, darting from the Augur to Markos. He kicked feebly at Rowel's knees. The Augur began to sweat too. He had been sure the Elf could cure the problem.

'Kill it,' the King commanded from behind.

'Wait!' rasped the Elf. 'Please! … There is a way!'

Rowel released the Elf, who slid to the ground, red-faced, heaving on all fours.

'Speak,' Rowel commanded.

The Elf propped himself against the wall, breathing heavily. 'There is … a procedure …' he said, his hands splayed before him defensively, 'but it's dangerous.'

'What kind of procedure?' said Rowel, his confidence rekindling.

'A surgical procedure,' said Peter. 'A way to return the Ki – to return your *companion* to full strength … But I would have to open his chest. Clean out the clogged arteries and repair any damaged cells. It's a risky procedure, my lord. And the recovery would take a long time.'

'How long?' demanded the Augur.

The Elf searched the floor for the correct answer. He lifted his ginger head. 'Six months?' he ventured.

Markos and Rowel shared a glance, permission for the Augur to continue.

'Tell me how you would open a man's chest without killing him,' he said.

'Well …' said the Elf, looking slightly more hopeful that he might survive this encounter, 'we would use medicines to render your companion unconscious. It's called anaesthetic.' Something crossed the Elf's face. 'A dangerous medicine that only *I* could administer correctly,' he added. 'Under the influence of such medicine, a patient would sleep peacefully for several hours, without feeling the intrusion of the surgery. I would make an incision along the chest bone, then cut through the plate with a surgical laser to expose the heart, which we would temporarily stop to –'

'That's enough,' said Rowel, once again twisting the point of his goatee with his ringed finger. 'Tell me. Is this procedure common among Elvish doctors? Do you have enough experience with it? Are you confident that it would work?'

The Elf placed his hands on the wall at his back and lifted himself to standing. 'Yes,' he said. 'If I had all the tools and medicine at my disposal, I am confident I could do it.'

Praise Ohrak, thought Rowel.

'Can you get everything you need?' he asked.

'Yes,' said the Elf, finally understanding his role in this exchange. 'Everything we need is at the field hospital in New Antra.'

'New Antra?' Markos spat. 'I will not set foot in an Elvish settlement.'

The Elf nodded vigorously. 'Of course not,' he said, though he looked troubled. 'I will bring the equipment wherever you command, my lords.'

Rowel looked over at Markos. Unconsciously, his eyes found the only scar that marred the King's body, a thin red line above his left hip. A blow that had almost ruined everything. Then their eyes met, and an understanding passed between the two men. The King nodded.

'Do it,' he said.

The Augur reached inside his robe and withdrew a glowing purple stone. He closed his eyes and held it gently to his forehead, searching for that inner place where his thoughts connected to Ohrak.

The familiar pain and flashes swirled through his mind. But he let the sensations pass through him. Once his thoughts had cleared, he spoke silently inside his head. 'Ohrak, my guide, show me the path I must take.'

He waited. The sound of the waterfall became louder and less distinct. Then it came to him. Unbidden. Crystal clear, then blurred, then clear once again as the connection wavered. An image; the head of a wolf-like creature.

It was enough.

At last, Rowel understood Ohrak's intention. And he marvelled at it. The simplicity of it. In a single move, he could distract the Lords of the Realms, occupy Lady Kaiber, neutralise the Elves, cure the King's illness, and secure the throne for Prince Henrik. All the Augur had to do was find the courage to act.

'What did you see?' asked Markos, with a hint of reverence in his voice. Even the greatest King in Nephian history understood his place compared to God's grace.

'Are you familiar with the story of the Warrior and the Wolves, my liege?' said Rowel.

'No,' said Markos, utterly captivated.

'It's an old tale from the Third Scrawl of Jevah. And I confess that it eluded my thoughts completely. The story goes like this. A warrior was walking across a desert on his way home from a great and victorious battle. But he was severely wounded, his left arm broken and lame.

'One day, the warrior was surrounded by a pack of starving wolves. And the warrior knew that he had no strength to fight. So instead, he used the greatest gift that Ohrak bestowed upon him: his cunning. He drew his sword, cut off the injured arm, and tossed it to the smallest wolf.

'The other wolves turned on the runt and killed it. Then they fought over the remains of their fallen brother, mauling and killing each other in mindless, animal bloodlust. Finally, a single wolf remained. But it too was now severely injured; hobbling on three of its legs from the fight. And unlike the warrior, it had no cunning to protect itself.

'The warrior cut off its head with his sword and continued on his journey.'

The Augur finished with a flourish of his jewelled hands and awaited a sign of understanding in the King's eyes. But they remained grey and cold. Then the expression soured to anger.

'A child's story,' sneered the King. 'That is all the wisdom that God has to offer?'

'Yes,' the Augur beamed, unfazed. 'And I shall explain its meaning fully on our journey, my liege.'

'Our journey?'

'Yes. I'm afraid you must come with me to Lysk. The Oracle has called a Gathering of the Augurs, and I cannot risk leaving you in Laudria. One misstep might make your condition public. No, Lysk will be far safer. And the travel may do you some good.' He turned to the Elf and pointed at his chest. He was filled with God's purpose now. 'You will come to High Castle at midnight, two weeks hence. There is a concealed entrance on the northeast corner of the curtain wall, where a small grate covers a drain. My informant, Mister Blake, can show you. Be there in two weeks with everything you need to perform this procedure. I will escort you to the King. Do you understand?'

Peter Sansil gave a watery smile in relief.

Rowel returned the smile warmly.

In his planned adaptation of the Warrior and the Wolves, the Elf would play the runt.

CHAPTER 11

The Gathering

Erik Volsgaard gripped his sodden travelling cloak from inside, as though this would make an ounce of difference to his suffering. But three days of relentless rain had left him wet to the core, and thoroughly miserable.

Not so easily defeated, his horse trudged on valiantly beneath him, its feet squelching in the mud with each stride.

The road, if it could be called a road, was littered with deep hoof-prints and the long trenches of carriage wheels, filled to the brim with brown water, their surfaces alive in the heavy rainfall.

Volsgaard twisted numbly in his saddle. His Obediant, Eurace, lagged some twenty yards behind on his own mare, suffering equally.

This had better be worth it, Volsgaard thought bitterly.

They had left Berrund three weeks ago, but their progress had been hampered by the unseasonal weather, which had stripped their spirits bare. Mercifully, however, they had finally emerged from the Grass Plains of Reon the previous morning and crossed into the Realm of Lysk.

They were close to the Old Capitol now. And a bath, and food, and bed.

No sooner had the comforting thought formed in Volsgaard's mind did he glimpse the familiar cluster of weathered spires peeking above the hedgerow to his right. He heaved a sigh of relief and patted his horse's rain-slicked neck.

A city of thatched houses came into view, their straw roofs almost touching above the labyrinth of narrow, cobbled streets. Taller, more significant buildings sprouted here and there from the canopy of thatch; inns, taverns, halls, and sacred Consels. But all of them were dwarfed by the great stone monuments that loomed atop the city's central hill.

The pillars of civilisation.

Despite the rain, Volsgaard lifted his chin to wonder at their majesty.

The hill at the epicentre of Lysk was broad, squat, and encircled by a wall around its base. Four buildings jutted out from it in opposite directions, like the points of a compass, towering over the city. To the south, hidden from Volsgaard's view, was the great Library of Lysk; a series of white stone buildings that stepped down the hillside in tiers, where the faithful preserved and studied the Book of Scrawls. To the north was the Royal Castle; a collection of imposing black towers and spires reaching into the sky, which had housed the throne of Nephia for more than three and a half thousand years. On the western slope stood the oldest and most magnificent building of all, The First Consel of Ohrak; a round and roofless shrine made of massive, monolithic stones, built by the first Augurs of God. And to the east loomed the scowling statues of notable old Kings, standing guard over the entrance to The Vallichor, the hidden amphitheatre carved inside the hill, where the throne succession was decided in blood.

The rain dripped down Volsgaard's face into his grey beard. Eurace drew alongside him.

His Obediant was an unfortunate soul in almost every regard. Bald and pear-nosed with very few teeth, he wore a tight Collar of Sin around his neck, which rattled with every movement of his head. This, too, was unfortunate because the poor wretch twitched constantly. He was perhaps the worst Obediant alive, but Volsgaard was bound to him by pity. And he liked to encourage the lad.

'Keep close once we enter the city,' said Volsgaard, lifting the hem of his riding cloak to reveal his sword. 'We must keep our wits sharp. And remember to keep the horses ready. If the others prove reluctant to send aid to Berrund, then there is little point in us lingering here.'

Eurace twitched with a rattle of his collar but nodded.

They ambled on horseback through the cobbled streets. Up close, the outer city bore unmistakable scars of neglect; rotting stockades, fallen walls, rusted ironwork, missing cobbles, and derelict public squares. Not a soul stirred. The only sign of life came from the orange glow of an open-fronted smithy, where a stooped blacksmith hammered something forlornly at his anvil.

Generations ago, Lysk had been the beating heart of Nephia. Populous and thriving. A place to which merchants and farmers would travel for many days to peddle their wares. Where circus troupes would compete for the attention of the crowds.

But all that was before the Almanfier Dynasty. Before King Markos's great-great-grandfather, Beauren Almanfier, first won the throne and refused to move from his beloved High Castle in Laudria.

That rebuke of tradition condemned the Old City to its present decay. As all the nobles migrated southward and took their money with them.

Volsgaard kept losing sight of the Royal Castle as they twisted through the maze of streets. Finally, they came upon the circular wall that divided the hill from the peasantry and trudged along it until they found the north gate.

A finely dressed Obediant stood sheltered under the archway, flanked by two armed guards.

'Who approaches the north gate,' asked the Obediant through the tumult.

'Master Erik V-volsgaard. Augur t-t-t-to C-c-c-c-c —'

'Colton Farrow, the Lord of Berrund,' Volsgaard supplied.

The sheltered Obediant glanced between the sodden riders with a smirk, then gave a slight bow.

'Welcome to Lysk, Master Volsgaard,' he said. 'Please, ride into the courtyard, where the groomsmen will relieve your horses. I shall be along shortly to show you to your chambers. I am Wilfried, first Obediant to the Oracle.'

'We thank you for your most gracious welcome,' said Volsgaard, mimicking Wilfried's pompous tone. He heeled his horse gently, and it walked forward. The two guards turned aside in unison.

The inner city of Lysk was alive with activity. Groomsmen led horses into stables. Liveried servants stood poised at every door. And the many glass windows of the castle flickered with candlelight.

A pair of groomsmen descended upon the two riders before they had fully dismounted. True to his word, Wilfried caught up with them and ushered them inside the castle. They handed their dripping cloaks to yet more servants in the foyer, then removed their riding boots, which were taken away for cleaning. Barefoot, they were led through the inner oak door to a musty, dark hallway adorned with cracked paintings, their wrinkled, sodden feet slapping on the flagstone floor.

Wilfried stopped outside a narrow door and bowed for Volsgaard to enter. The room had a small bed, a smouldering fireplace, and little else. It might have disappointed a man of his position. Still, after three weeks in his saddle, Volsgaard could have wept for its deliverance.

*

A timid knocking awoke him the following day. For a moment, Volsgaard struggled to remember who or where he was. It seemed strange to feel so comfortable and dry. The knocking came again.

'Enter,' he said, his voice pinched with sleep.

Eurace rattled in, carrying a bowl of something hot. 'G-good m-morning, Master,' he said. 'I g-got you s-s-s-s-s-'

'Yes, thank you,' Volsgaard interjected, throwing off the bedcovers. He snatched the bowl and began devouring its contents. 'What news?' he asked between mouthfuls. 'When are we expected?'

'S-soon, Master,' said Eurace, collecting Volsgaard's hanging clothes from above the fireplace. 'Some of the o-others are already g-gathered in the Great Hall.'

Volsgaard looked into his Obediant's eyes for the first time and saw that he was frowning.

'What is it?'

'I h-heard the c-cook say that King Markos is here.'

Volsgaard dropped his spoon into the empty bowl.

'The King? Here?'

His Obediant nodded loudly.

'But why? Why would Markos come to Lysk?'

'I d-don't know, Master. The c-cook whispered it to a s-servant girl. I only heard in passing.'

'Are you sure you heard right?'

'Yes, Master.'

'Damn!' exhaled Volsgaard thoughtfully. 'Rowel must have brought him on purpose. He must know we've come to seek allies. Damn, damn, damn!'

He punched his arms into his robe and stamped into his boots, furious that they were already on the back foot. He threw his sword on the bed, changed his mind, wore it, then threw it back on the bed. Once dressed, he clomped behind Eurace through the castle corridors until they reached a polished set of double doors with a bull-ring knocker. Eurace moved to open it, but Volsgaard caught his arm.

'Remember,' he whispered, 'make sure to stand somewhere visible. We may need to make a hasty retreat.'

The Obediant bowed and lifted his hand to the door again, but Volsgaard pulled him back.

'One more thing,' he said. 'Stay silent. Don't announce me, introduce me, or feel duty-bound in any way to say anything. We must be succinct. You understand?'

Volsgaard glimpsed the boy's yellow teeth as his mouth parted in hurt. But there was no time for sentimentality. They had a purpose, and he was determined to achieve it.

Eurace bowed and opened the door for his master, and Volsgaard strode through, chin high, shoulders squared.

The Great Hall was a large, rectangular room with wide stone pillars and several fireplaces. The vaulted ceiling was so high that the morning light shone upward through the painted windows, illuminating rafters that were structured like the rib-cage of a giant. Between the pillars, eleven high-backed chairs had been laid out in a circle, with room enough outside it for the Obediants and servants to perform their duties.

Fifty or so men mingled in clusters around the circle, deep in conversation. Servants scurried between the groups, carrying canapes and goblets of wine. The Augurs scattered among the crowd stood out plainly, dressed like peacocks. A squat black man, whom Volsgaard recognised as the Augur of Bowhark, wore a full-length turquoise gown embroidered with gold and silver flowers. He talked animatedly to a pale, stern-looking man whose blonde hair was scraped back in a ponytail, with a white fox draped over his shoulders. Beyond them, Volsgaard spotted the smug countenance of Rowel Malcifer, the King's Augur. He addressed an avid entourage in his neat, crimson tunic, absently swirling a goblet of wine. A few men surrounding the Royal Augur looked in Volsgaard's direction as he entered and eyed him from head to toe.

Volsgaard almost laughed. He was a warrior, not a wallflower.

A gong sounded softly from the far corner of the hall. At once, the chatter died away, and all heads turned toward the sound. As the note wavered, Wilfried set down the mallet and addressed the room.

'My Lords, masters, and brothers,' he said, sweeping the room with an open hand. 'It is time. Please, take your seats.'

The crowd shifted like an ill-disciplined battalion falling into line. The Augurs strode centrally to their chairs while the Obediants found the walls and the servants melted from the hall. Volsgaard found the nearest chair and sat. Amid the throng, he saw Eurace quietly take up a position near the door.

Good lad, he thought as the room settled into eager silence.

'May I present His Excellency, Master Julius Hepp, the Grand Oracle,' said Wilfried.

The doors behind the Obediant were opened by servants, and the Augurs stood respectfully.

In Volsgaard's opinion, Julius Hepp had aged terribly since their last encounter. He had shrunk by several inches, hunchbacked and frail, his white hair matching his pure white robe. He shuffled slowly over the threshold and across the circle of chairs, supported by an Obediant. The Oracle took a moment to find a comfortable position in his seat, then signalled with a flap of his yellowing hand for the gathering to be seated.

'Welcome, my brothers,' he said, his voice raspy but firm. 'It is wonderful to see you all. I know some of you have travelled a long way, and I extend my gratitude to each of you for your presence here. I am certain you are all curious as to why you have been summoned.'

Rowel Malcifer straightened in his chair.

'This meeting marks the first Gathering of Augurs in over a hundred years,' the Oracle continued. 'Not since the fabled Weeks of Euphoria, when our predecessors met to discuss their sudden, ecstatic visions in this very room.'

The Oracle's wrinkled smile faded.

'It is not with such glad tidings that I have summoned you here today,' he said sadly. 'I am troubled, my brothers. Deeply, deeply troubled. Ohrak has allowed me a glimpse of what lies in our future, and I call upon you to help me understand the breadth of His dire tidings.'

The Oracle paused to wipe the corner of his mouth with a handkerchief.

'Several weeks ago,' he continued, 'Ohrak shared with me a vision, unlike anything I have ever seen before. Something beyond the limits of my understanding. At first, I thought He was warning me that my time had come. That my death was drawing near. For I saw a vast shadow fill the sky above the Vallichor. A black cloud that spread until all light was banished from the world. But then the shadow fell to Ithea. Surrounded me. And from its depths came the figure of a man. And I felt a terror seize my heart. An inhuman fear that I dare not describe. As though God Himself … was afraid.'

The Oracle let his head drop forward as though ashamed.

Nobody moved. Not a strand of hair or fibre of clothing broke the stillness in the hall. Volsgaard, like all present, wrestled privately with the Oracle's echoing words. Eyes fixed on the man who had uttered them. Horrified.

The Augur across from Volsgaard stood up, breaking the spell. It was the blond man with the fox around his neck. 'Master,' he said in a deep voice, 'you must speak with greater care. I do not wish to offend – or accuse – but … to suggest that Ohrak the Eternal could experience *fear* is beyond blasphemy.'

'It is no such thing!' cried the Augur to the Oracle's right, likewise rising to his feet. He was stumpy and rotund, with a gold collar beneath his three chins. 'I too have seen this accursed figure. A man made of shadow, marching towards me from afar!'

'I am not questioning the Oracle's vision,' the blond Augur countered, 'only his interpretation.'

The obese Augur was about to retort, his stubby finger pointed warningly across the circle. But a soft sigh caused him to dam his outburst. He turned to look at the Oracle, whose eyes were closed, facing the ceiling. The two Augurs on their feet glanced at one another, then sat down at once. The Oracle opened his eyes.

'My dear brothers,' he pleaded, suddenly sounding his age, 'you shall all, each of you, have your say on this matter. In fact, I will insist that you do. But before we speak, we must listen to and respect one another. Set aside our mortal politics and speak only the truth. If Ohrak is trying to warn us of an imminent threat, we must heed Him together and prepare. This is our duty as Augurs of God.

'I have shared my vision with you. Now I ask each of you – nay – I beg you to share your insights here. Let us merge our perspectives and piece together Ohrak's message.'

Volsgaard felt sorry for the old man. His speech had been brave and impassioned, but utterly naïve. There was no way on Ithea the men around him would betray their lords and freely share their visions. These were scoundrels. Half of them had no trace of insight whatsoever. They had simply pinned their colours to the correct mast, leeching on the luckiest fighters as they ascended to lordships. And the other half was much worse. These men possessed divine gifts indeed. But not one had used them for the benefit of his people. Instead, they had used them to scheme and plot their way into these esteemed chairs. And Volsgaard was confident they would not risk their positions to pacify a senile old man. Even as he sat there, Volsgaard sensed the thoughts whirling around him. Every man scrambling for an advantage.

Volsgaard glanced at Rowel Malcifer. The Royal Augur looked entirely indifferent to the situation. Even bored. He checked the immaculate fingernails of his left hand before adjusting a sapphire ring. His plan was fully cooked, no doubt. But Volsgaard would make him listen.

He must.

'Let us begin with you, Master Yernen,' said the Oracle kindly, addressing the man seated at his left. 'Please, stand and share with us your latest insights.'

The Augur called Yernen cast around uncomfortably but stood and shook away the sleeves of his robe, bringing his fingertips together at his navel. Volsgaard dismissed him as the talentless type at once.

'I am Petric Yernen, Augur to Lord Costel of Ealee,' he said proudly. 'As a Scriptic, I frequently draw at my lord's behest.'

A *Scriptic*, Volsgaard scoffed internally. *Sit down, you charlatan!* He pictured the man in a frothing trance, his hand scribbling nonsense on a piece of parchment, while his Obediants tried not to laugh.

'My most recent Pictoral,' he continued irrelevantly, 'concerned two faceless entities of enormous power, locked together by lines of action. These entities were evenly matched and drawn in equal scale and weight. The lines between them also flew outward in all directions, signifying change.'

The Oracle nodded politely.

'Indeed,' he said. 'And have you interpreted its meaning? Or do you perhaps have this Pictoral at hand?'

One of Master Yernen's Obediants took a small step forward. But the Augur cocked his head sharply, and the Obediant receded to the wall.

'No, Master,' said Yernen. 'We do not have it … but I have studied it closely and am satisfied with my conclusion. The image depicts my lord, Jado Costel, duelling against King Markos at the Throne Trial and proving himself equal!'

Many of the Augurs, and some of the bolder Obediants, let out howls at this declaration. Rowel Malcifer smirked amid the noise. The Oracle shook his head wearily.

'Furthermore,' Yernen boomed above the derision, his face flushing red, 'the lines of combat clearly show that Lord Costel will be victorious! And that his conquest will bring forth great change to the kingdom! Too long has the noble Realm of Ealee suffered under the rule of a neglectful tyrant! Isolated and forgotten! But we are the menace you feel drawing near! And I shall confess this; that hidden in the Pictoral was a single word … *Ulmar!*'

The howls erupted into guffaws of laughter. One Augur hammered at his knee with a fist.

Lord Jado Costel had once been Volsgaard's enemy, and a fearsome one at that. But he was nothing compared to Markos Almanfier. And certainly no Ulmar. Volsgaard sincerely hoped that Jado had not been duped by the scribblings of this old fraud.

The Oracle raised a hand, and a gradual silence descended. Petric Yernen slumped into his chair, furious and defiant.

One by one, the Augurs stood reluctantly to share their insights. Though none offered any conclusion, having learned from Yernen's mistake. It became apparent that every man had sensed a malevolent shadow in one form or another. Often embodied as one or two indistinct figures. And all sightings had occurred within the last few weeks.

Volsgaard felt a knot tightening in the pit of his stomach. He remembered his own encounter well; a dense black cloud pouring down the slopes of the Bannebar. And a faceless figure standing in its path. He thought he had understood its meaning plainly. But the testimony of his brothers was widening his view.

Suddenly, he became aware that all heads in the hall were turned in his direction, and the Oracle had spoken his name. It was time to decide. Continue the pattern of this shared threat or remain loyal to Lord Farrow and complete his vital mission.

Both paths intersected before him as he stood.

'I am Erik Volsgaard, Augur to Lord Colton Farrow of Berrund,' he said. 'I am a Sensate in possession of a God Stone, and Ohrak has shared much with me of late.'

A ripple of envy swept the room. Nothing on Ithea could bring a man closer to Ohrak than a God Stone. It added credence to Volsgaard's word.

'I too have witnessed a strange shadow,' he said. 'It came from the peaks of the Bannebar Mountains. And when it struck, I saw the Urden Forest in flames.'

He felt a twinge of guilt at this embellishment. But it was necessary to bolster his request.

'I will risk confiding my interpretation of this vision,' he announced. 'And I pray that you will listen. Berrund has been at war with the Kraelings for ten years. Since they emerged from Kininumbra and massacred the villagers of Fairwater –'

A metallic rattling drew the eyes of many in the hall. Eurace spasmed convulsively, staring at the floor.

Volsgaard seized on it.

'Please, forgive my Obediant,' he said. 'He is the sole survivor of the Fairwater attack. And his scars remain with him, plain to see. I believe the shadow I saw referred to the Krae. It symbolised their migration across the mountains. They may be dull-witted animals, but their numbers grow in the Urden each year while our own numbers dwindle. They pour over the mountains, unchecked. And soon, if more Nephian soldiers do not come to our aid, I fear that all of Berrund will fall, as Fairwater did. And if that came to pass, there would be little to stop the Krae army from marching southward on your borders. I am certain this is the mounting threat you have all sensed.'

He turned directly to face Rowel Malcifer, emboldened by the lack of scepticism at his offering.

'Berrund seeks aid from any Realm willing. We require a thousand soldiers to help us raid the depths of the Urden, to drive this menace back over the mountains. I urge you to see the wisdom in this course of action, my lord.'

Volsgaard sat and fixed his attention on the Royal Augur seated to his left. Rowel Malcifer returned the stare, his face inscrutable. He held out his goblet, and an Obediant scuttled forth to claim it.

Rowel stood.

'Wisdom is often a matter of perspective, is it not?' he said with his usual smirk. 'You see, from my perspective, it would be most unwise to send a thousand soldiers to the aid of a known traitor. Especially when his request lands so conveniently on a Quintus!' There were several sycophantic chuckles from his Obediants and loyal Augurs. Volsgaard felt his heartbeat quicken. 'If any Realm supplies soldiers to Berrund, the King will treat it as an act of rebellion. I must also challenge the basis of your central conviction, Master Volsgaard. You believe that Ohrak is warning us of the Krae? Those silver-skinned animals with the bodies of men but the brains of deer? Well, I am sorry to say that I do not share your concern. And I fail to see how Berrund can be at war with such creatures. Unless you are also at war with the bees and the worms?'

Raucous laughter ripped the air. Contorted faces turned to Volsgaard, who felt a hateful bile rising in his throat. He forced himself not to react, but to sit rigidly and let the laughter wash over him. Not one of these fools understood. Across the circle, the Oracle sagged in his chair.

Rowel had the wind in his sails now. 'Or do you confess,' he pressed over the cackles, 'that Lord Scratch is so inept that he is losing the Realm bequeathed him to a tribe of animals?' Volsgaard reached across himself to the hilt of a sword that was not there. Rowel did not see the reflex. He turned instead to Petric Yernen. 'As for your claim, Master Yernen, you are convinced that your lord is the Ulmar reborn? Again, brothers, it amazes me that every five years, as we near a Throne Trial, Ohrak bestows unparalleled fighting skill upon a chosen warrior. Every five years, without fail, a new Ulmar arises. Heralding glorious unity for all the people of Ithea! More amazing still is that each of these unbeatable warriors dies inexplicably at the hands of King Markos Almanfier … except for Lord Scratch, who was allowed to hobble north into obscurity – at which he also failed!' A derisive cheer was directed at Volsgaard and the scowling Augur of Ealee. Rowel shrugged. 'However, if you are convinced, Master Yernen, who am I to dissuade you? King Markos will gladly accept the challenge from Lord Costel!' He pivoted to address the entire circle. 'And any other disloyal lord foolish enough to oppose him! He will fight them all at once, if necessary! I can always make room along the Hall of the Fallen to hang more treasonous ornaments!'

A hearty cheer erupted from the loyalists around the chamber. Volsgaard surreptitiously scanned the faces of his fellow Augurs, making a mental note of any whose cheering seemed false or subdued.

Rowel resumed his seat amid the cheering. He had not mentioned any insight whatsoever. And yet they cheered.

Volsgard dropped his head and rubbed the length of his nose between his thumb and forefinger. In the corner of his eye, through the hubbub, he saw Eurace peel himself from the wall and disappear through the door.

Berrund must continue to face the Krae alone.

CHAPTER 12

The Promised Girl

Elchora kept her feet moving, aiming for the struts. It was important to never break stride inside the crane wheel. If you broke your ankle, you got the whip.

Left, right. Keep. Going. Press. *Down.*

Sweat dripped from her chin. It was stupid to push herself like this so early in the day. But she trudged on regardless, forcing the wheel to turn.

A gap in the planking passed before her eyes with every eighth stride, affording a glimpse of the scene beyond. The six men in her group were sitting shirtless on the floor amongst the scattered white stones, talking together. Elchora could not hear them over the tumble of the wheel, but she saw the warmth and ease in their exchange. One drank from a skin of water. On the following rotation, the skin had jumped to the man beside him. Then the next.

She would get the dregs. If they remembered.

'We got it, Princess!' called a voice from the scaffold above.

Elchora eased her trudging, irritated by the use of her nickname but grateful for the reprieve. The wheel slowed gradually. Her head swam in the new stillness for a moment, and she had to steady herself with a firm grip on the axle. She closed her eyes and waited for the false motion to pass. Beneath her mushy feet, she felt the tension leave the wheel as the limestone block she had lifted was untied from its leather slip by the workers on the parapet.

She climbed out of the wheel, careful not to show her fatigue, and lowered herself into an oblong patch of shade against the castle wall.

One of the Ablemen said something, and the group of men laughed. The speaker peeled away from the others and approached. 'Here,' he said, brandishing the skin of water.

She grunted in thanks and took a swig. The man crouched on his haunches opposite her and peered up at the men laying the stone she had raised.

'You needn't act so tough, you know,' he said. 'Nobody needs you to keep up with us. You'll only hurt yourself and get us all in trouble. So, just … slow down. Go at your own pace.'

The man's name was Jon, a retired soldier, older than her father. Elchora could see that he meant no harm. But the anger flared inside her all the same.

'Thanks,' she said. 'Any more advice?'

Jon let out a humourless chuckle. 'Yes. Try smiling once in a while. A pretty girl like you would make more friends if she smiled.'

He cupped her cheek with a rough hand.

Elchora was about to slap it away when a voice caused Jon to retract his hand as though it was scalded.

'What's this?' said the gruff voice.

Jon leapt to his feet and backed away. The other men were suddenly busy arranging stones, shooting sidelong glances at the barrel-chested man who had appeared beside Elchora and Jon. His head was as round and bald as a cannonball, covered with thick veins. His wiry ginger beard had scratched a crescent of brass discolouration into his silver breastplate.

'Is this man bothering you, Farrow?' growled Victor Maldon, his helmet tucked under his arm.

'No, Commander,' said Elchora, tossing the empty skin to Jon. 'We were just taking a water break.'

Victor surveyed the man coldly.

Had he seen Jon touch her face? Elchora hoped not.

'Back to your work, Ableman,' said Victor, causing Jon to scuttle away without a backward glance. Victor watched him for a moment, then turned to Elchora. 'Get to your feet, Farrow! I have a task for you.'

Elchora stood. She wiped the sweaty strands of hair from her face, grateful that Victor had found her so unkempt. Even the commander could not find her appealing in such a state, surely. Her stomach turned as Victor smiled at her conspiratorially, his slimy lips visible through the thicket of orange hair.

'If any of these maggot cunts ever bothers you,' he whispered, 'come and find me. I would slaughter them all for you.'

She felt a hand on the small of her back and stepped forward tactically into the full view of the workers around them.

Better to keep this public.

'You are most gracious, Commander Maldon,' she replied. 'But I must remind you, sir, that I am promised to Prince Henrik. And until he comes of age, my father, or King Markos himself, will protect me from any … unwanted attention.'

Victor's beard dropped a fraction as the smile beneath it vanished.

In truth, Elchora had no idea whether her betrothal to Henrik remained valid. Not since her father had earned their banishment from Laudria by challenging for the throne. And besides, she had no desire to marry a boy she hadn't seen in ten years. But the ability to conjure the name Markos Almanfier had always been a powerful shield.

'My attentions didn't seem so unwanted at the Spring Harvest,' Victor continued quietly, checking over his shoulder. 'You filthy little slut.'

Elchora shuddered with repulsion.

In hindsight, she saw plainly how the Commander had seduced her. It had felt like the most profound betrayal at the time. But in reality he had simply targeted her loneliness with a series of little performances spread out over many months. Subtle encouragements and kind words deployed gently to erode her resistance. Until, eventually, he came to her in private, in the guise of a friend with a ready ear. Full of questions and sincere interest. And the second she exposed a gap in her armour, he struck, confessing his great love for her, but insisting that he could no longer see her.

Suddenly, it was she who sought him. Cut off from the kindness she had learned to expect. Starved of her only friend. And when he kissed her, then began undressing her, she had no defences left. Nor any suspicion that he was merely enacting the final stage of his cruel plot. Not until he was inside her, with her blood on his cock and her virginity claimed, did she see the mask slip.

It was painful in more ways than one. Gone was the gentle friend. Returned was the rough brute.

'What task must I perform, Commander?' she asked, resolutely meeting his stare.

Victor glanced over her head. One of the other Ablemen had climbed into the crane wheel behind her. The Commander straightened up and resumed his furious but formal tone.

'Lord Farrow believes the Krae are massing for an attack,' he said. 'I'm sending my best scouts to sweep the deeper sections of the forest.'

He took out a parchment scroll, unrolled it, and laid it flat on the ground, using stones to pin its curling corners. It was a detailed map of the Urden.

'I want you to search this section,' he said, scowling up at her and making a vague circle with his finger over the northernmost section of the map. 'There are clearings in this area where an army might assemble. The old river should take you most of the way.'

He had indicated an area almost twenty miles north, deep into Krae territory. A considerable risk.

'When do I set off, sir?' she asked.

'An hour ago,' he growled with a lopsided grin. 'I want you back before sundown.'

'Am I to scout the area alone?'

'Oh, no, Princess!' He laughed. 'I would not risk your precious life so blatantly! Poor Henrik would weep into his wetnurse's bosom if anything should happen to his beloved bride ... oh, no ...' He stood. 'You will go with Almys Fyvern, the New Colour from Eddis. I'm told he has Almanfier blood, and I'd like your opinion on his ability. He may succeed me as Commander when I unseat your father as Lord.'

Elchora clamped her mouth shut. Victor was trying to bait her. Looking for an excuse to whip her at the lashing post.

'As you wish, Commander,' she said.

She strode off, not wishing to remain in his presence a second longer or waste any more daylight.

Almys Fyvern and the New Colours were practicing charge manoeuvres under the watchful eye of Captain Brigg. Elchora leaned against the fencepost and watched as a cluster of thirty riders galloped at full tilt toward a rank of hessian training sacks.

One rider stood out immediately. He had broken away from the pack, galloping fiercely, leading the charge. He was young – possibly younger than Elchora – tall and well proportioned, his dark hair flapping behind him like a flag. She heard the sharp, metallic note as he drew his curved sabre from its scabbard and watched as he brought the sword up high behind his trailing shoulder, ready to slice. He let out a cry of fury as he met the line of bags, forcing his mount to leap through them as he spilled the sand from four of them in a single stroke.

Elchora heard a satisfied chuckle from nearby. Captain Brigg had sidled up to her unknowingly, his focus on the riders.

'Captain Brigg,' she called.

'Ableman Farrow,' said Brigg without turning. 'Why aren't you at the wall?'

'Orders from Commander Maldon, sir. I'm to take one of the New Colours on a scouting mission.'

'Oh, aye? Which one?'

'Almys Fyvern, sir.'

'Hmmph!' Brigg chuckled. 'Of course. Victor is intent on taking the boy under his wing. And no surprise. He's the best New Colour I've trained in years.'

He turned his head to look at her, but she said nothing.

'Well,' he sighed, 'you'd better carry on with your orders … though I doubt even Victor would have the courage to flog *you* at the post.'

Elchora disagreed under her breath as Brigg signalled for Fyvern to join them.

The New Colour brought his steed alongside the pair and dismounted with the agility of a cat. 'Yes, Captain Brigg?' he said.

'A fine ride, lad,' said Brigg. 'But remember to hold the line. A charge is most effective when it strikes as one.'

'Yes, sir.'

Fyvern looked at Elchora. He had a proud triangle of a nose and dark, deep-set eyes. Brigg suddenly seemed to recall why he had summoned the young man.

'Err … this is Ableman Farrow,' he said. 'You are to accompany her on a scouting mission. Follow her orders and keep her safe. You understand?'

'Yes, sir.'

'We must leave at once,' said Elchora. 'But I'll give you a moment to get changed.'

Fyvern tilted his head questioningly.

'We're heading north, twenty miles into the forest,' she said. 'Your armour will be too heavy.'

Fyvern pursed his lips. 'I feel able,' he said.

Elchora was taken aback by this. She turned to Brigg for support. But the captain merely folded his arms and chuckled knowingly at the display of wild confidence. She turned back to the New Colour.

'This is a scouting mission,' she explained. 'You'll draw too much attention if you're rattling around in all that.'

'But if we meet any Krae, I'd like to be armed to fight them,' Fyvern said simply. He strode to his horse and began unfastening the sword tied to its flank.

'We'll be searching for an army of them!' Elchora said incredulously.

Fyvern fastened the sword to his waist, then looked at her, unconcerned. 'I understand,' he said.

Brigg laughed and walked away, patting Fyvern on the shoulder as he passed.

Elchora exhaled in exasperation. *New Colours*, she thought, shaking her head. *He is just another dumb recruit with no concept of his limitations. He had better not slow me down.*

CHAPTER 13

The Stag

The Urden Forest was vast and unbroken. A solid canopy of green propped up by great wooden pillars. It stretched the width of northern Berrund, east to west, and rose halfway up the Bannebar Mountains like a cresting wave.

It was morning.

Deep in the forest, a stag wandered softly, appearing and disappearing among the tree trunks. He walked in silence as patches of dappled light passed quickly up his legs and slowly across his body.

The stag could see his destination through the ranks of dark tree trunks, a bright, flat clearing of short hay-coloured grass where the stream was widest. The stag made his way toward the clearing until his shoulder was level with the last tree. He paused, looking out, uncertain, his ears scanning in all directions, his eyes wide.

A clearing was a dangerous place to linger but the safest place to drink. If anything tried to attack, it would have to outrun him. And he was fast.

He looked out for a long time.

There was nothing. No smell of hunters, no movement beyond the breeze, and no sound beyond the trickle of the stream.

The stag moved into the clearing.

Hidden among the branches of the opposite tree line, Orla Phalhurst was hardly breathing. Something had entered the clearing. And whatever it was, it was big. Its footsteps heavy and confident.

Her wait was almost over.

She couldn't see the creature because she could not see at all. Her eyes were pale grey and blind. Her legs were deformed too, though she did not think of them that way. They were thin and carried no feeling, but they were hers, and she thought of herself as a hunter. She had no need for sight; her remaining senses worked perfectly and served her well, and at that moment, she knew every stride the creature took.

She was lying face down along a thick branch with her right hand stretched out in front, clutching the underside of the branch, with her legs dangling on either side beneath her. She began to feel the tiny vibrations of the creature's footsteps in her fingertips on the tree. *A good spot*, she thought; *downwind, out of sight.*

The creature was getting closer.

Orla tugged the rope in her left hand. After a few seconds, her brother, Gadryon, returned the favour. He was ready with his longbow. But Orla knew the creature was still too far away for an easy shot. So, she waited. Her clammy hand tensed on the rope.

The stag was almost at the water. He paused for a final scan with a foreleg raised, ready to bolt. The wind swept through the trees, flashing the white undersides of the leaves. But nothing else stirred. The stag lowered his head and kissed his reflection, drinking as silently as possible.

With a thump, something crashed into the stag's side. Hot panic flooded his body instantly; signals rushed from his brain to his limbs; *run, run, run*! He moved instinctively, half leaping as he ran for the nearest cover. One of his rear legs fired signals of protest, *pain, damage, danger*! He ran hard through the pain. He was almost inside the trees when a second thump knocked him to the ground. He cried out as he fell, his breath laced with blood and visible in the cold morning air. *Up! Run! Up!* He half rose, but his legs trembled under his weight. He collapsed again, this time into the stream with a splash.

Gadryon whipped his head and shoulder through his longbow and settled it across his chest. His heart raced with excitement, but there was no time to celebrate. The stag's howling would attract the Kraelings, and he didn't like to fight them while Orla was with him. He moved around the tree to stand beneath the spot where she was hidden.

'You got it?' she crowed.

'Twice,' he replied. 'Now fall!'

She could hear the smile in his voice.

Overjoyed, Orla relaxed her aching grip on the branch and let her body roll underneath before letting go. Gadryon caught her. In the same motion, he lifted her over his head and slotted her withered legs into the woven-vine carrier on his back. She gripped his shoulders tightly, and he began to run.

'What is it? A deer?' said Orla, her legs bouncing a little on each stride.

'A stag,' said Gadryon.

'I knew it was big!'

By Gadryon's footsteps, Orla heard the ground change from grass to water. A creature – the stag – rasped for air nearby. Gadryon drew his knife.

The stag felt his whole body growing cold. Unable to move, he looked up and saw his killer. A horrible, two-headed shape silhouetted against the blue sky.

Crouching down behind it, Gadryon took the stag's antlers in one hand and raised his knife above the creature's heart with the other. With conviction, he brought it down hard to the hilt. The stag quivered in the water, and then it was still.

'Can I see it?' Orla whispered.

'Not here. We need to move it to the trees to be safe. This is Krae land – so keep your ears open.'

Gadryon plucked his weapons from the body and washed them in the stream. He gripped the stag's antlers and dragged it in a long, steady heave beyond the treeline. Once sheltered, he lifted his sister above his head and set her down next to their kill.

Orla ran her hands through the short, wet fur. She stroked the pointed face and felt the solid teeth and wet tongue inside its warm mouth. She touched its grainy antlers, rigid backbone, and stiff tail where the fur was different. It smelled of rain and blood.

'It's beautiful,' she said, turning her face in her brother's direction.

'Be quick,' he said. 'Get to work, and don't cut too much.'

Gadryon dropped his knife into the ground next to her. Orla didn't move.

'But … we need to take all of it,' she said.

'No, it's too big,' he said. 'It'll go bad, and you'll get sick again.'

'I won't get sick! I'm only sick of hunting and being hungry! We could make a sack with the skin and carry all the best meat.'

'No.'

'But we wouldn't have to hunt for weeks!'

'I said no, Orla. We cut what we need for the next few days and no more. We bury the head for Ohrak, and the rest we leave for the wolves and the birds.'

Orla gripped a fistful of fur, her face hot. She heard Gadryon turn away from her and drop to his knee. He rested an arrow on his bow to cover her as she worked.

There would be no argument.

Orla snatched up the knife and set to work. She separated the legs from the body and peeled back the skin. She sliced off the best chunks of meat and put them in her satchel, listening resentfully as Gadryon threw the legs into the clearing for the birds. He cut off the head with their father's sword and said a prayer as he buried it. Orla used the time to fill her pockets with more meat. When they were done, Gadryon carried her back to the stream and helped to wash the blood from her forearms and face.

The sun was higher in the sky.

'Time to go home,' he said. But Orla offered no reply. As he lifted her, she went limp to make it harder. But her brother was too strong to notice. When Gadryon was satisfied that they had gathered all their precious belongings, she felt him turn back to look at the offering they had left behind.

'Ohrak, ever watchful,' he whispered, 'we thank you for your bounty. Please accept our gifts, such as they are, and grant us safe passage home.'

*

Gadryon knew it would take the better part of the day to return to Home Cave, especially laden as they were.

Lately, they had been forced to hunt too far south for his liking. But the forest game was disappearing in the war for the Urden, and such risks were becoming necessary.

Orla was silent on his back. She was angry with him, but he knew her anger would ease with a full stomach. Besides, he needed her silence in such dangerous territory.

As he walked, he thought about the stag they had killed, how its blood had mixed so cleanly with the water. His father had taught him how Ohrak communicated through blood, and he understood that God had blessed their kill. Orla had played her part too. *She did well*, he thought. He would tell her so when they were home.

After a time, under the comforting rhythm of her brother's stride, Orla's head became heavy. She thought how easy it would be to rest it on Gadryon's shoulder and sleep like she used to. But she fought the temptation, determined not to feel inferior. Gadryon was her brother and protector, and she would die without him. But she hated feeling like a burden, so she stayed awake as his equal.

She busied herself by twisting the bearskin fur on his shoulder into spikes, humming mindlessly.

Then it happened.

The surrounding forest noises grew louder and louder. They reached a deafening pitch, then united into a single, cacophonous roar. Orla tried to clap her hands over her ears but found that she had no hands, ears, or any physical body at all. She tried to scream for Gadryon but couldn't feel him either. She was alone. Lost in the awful roar coming from all around her. From within her. And she knew nothing but terror. She was screaming for Gadryon to come back, for the world to come back and not abandon her. But she was so small. Small and lost in the endless roar.

Suddenly, she heard a voice from somewhere very deep. It came from everywhere, like the roar, powerful and clear, as though Ohrak Himself were speaking into her mind. And God was immense beyond her comprehension.

'*They are coming,*' it said.

The sound of the roaring changed; it became a hollow rushing, like a strong wind at the mouth of a cave, and Orla began to hear her own scream underneath the sound. Something solid came up to meet her back. The rushing sound grew fainter as more of her feeling returned. She was thrashing wildly, and something was fighting against her. As she fought and screamed, she heard another voice speaking from very close. Gadryon's voice. Her brother gripped her wrists tightly, trying to stop her flailing. Her screaming lessened, and she found that she was lying on the ground, breathing hard, her arms trembling, held by Gadryon at the wrists. Her brother's voice was desperate.

'Orla! What is it? What is it?'

Her thrashing slowed, but her arms were restless and would not stop moving. She swallowed hard. She tried to take deeper breaths and turned her head in all directions as the forest came back to life. She heard birds high above and felt the breeze in the wet hair stuck to her forehead.

'That's right, just breathe,' her brother was saying. 'Breathe.'

Gadryon pulled her into a seated position but did not let go of her wrists. He rested his head against hers. Her face was hot, and she started to cry. She cried for a long time in great sobs that she could not master. Gadryon did not let go of her, and she clutched him and felt him all over as she cried. He stroked her hair and whispered things she could not make out over her crying. Then she swallowed again and followed his breathing until her chest stopped rising of its own accord.

'What happened?' he said, very close.

Gadryon had not heard the awful sound or the voice.

It took Orla a long time to compose herself. 'I heard …' she said, her words far away. 'I heard everything … everything was so loud. Then I lost it.'

'Lost what?'

'Everything.'

Gadryon was brushing the hair out of her face. She was afraid of what she was saying but couldn't stop. Her voice was so weak.

'I heard a voice,' she said.

'A voice? What do you mean, what voice?'

She heard it again in her memory. '*They are coming,*' she said.

Then, something too large rose in her throat, and tears began to roll down her cheeks again, but silently this time. The tears were cold against her hot skin. Gadryon let go of her arms gently and stepped away. Her hands shook badly. It was humiliating to cry, and the shame only made it worse. She wiped away the tears from her cheeks as Gadryon suddenly ran back to her.

'Be quiet!' he hissed, gripping her shoulders tightly. She took a sharp breath in surprise, and in the silence, she heard it; something was moving toward them quickly.

Gadryon lifted her without warning and threw her shoulder against a tree harder than he meant to. He lifted her against the trunk, and instinctively she reached up and grabbed the mossy branch above her head. Her hands were still shaking, but she pulled herself up the tree and found the next branch and the next, her legs dangling beneath her, scraping out wet lines of moss from the trunk.

'Higher!' Gadryon whispered. 'Get as high as you can and be quiet! And don't move 'til I say!'

Once the branches above her became too thin, she put her back to the trunk, tucked away her legs, and made herself as small as she could. She heard Gadryon move around the tree and load his bow. Many footsteps approached at a run, and Orla's stomach dropped away.

Let them not see us, she prayed. *Please! Let them pass by. Blessed Ohrak, father of the world, mother of all, forgive me. If they should find us … give my brother the strength to fight them.*

CHAPTER 14

The Boy

Elchora moved swiftly, crouching low as she darted between trees. This far north, it was vital to stay focussed. To keep her eyes sharp. There was no telling when they might encounter an enemy, even in daylight. She kept the dry riverbed close to her left, a shallow canyon full of rotten leaves and moss-covered stones. Fyvern followed closely behind her. To her surprise, he had thus far managed to keep pace without complaint. But her efforts to go undetected were undermined by the rattling of his armour.

If the Krae heard them coming, they might set a trap.

It was almost midday by the sun's position, and after four hours of tireless advance, they had yet to spot anything. Even a squirrel. And Elchora's annoyance threatened to boil over.

She leant her shoulder into a tree and glowered back, panting hard. Fyvern joined her seconds later, breathing steadily.

'You're making too much noise,' she scorned. 'What hope do we have of passing through unnoticed while you blunder around like a carriage of crockery? This isn't a battle, New Colour. We're scouting! Seeking signs of a large Krae gathering. And if we find any, we mark the position, estimate their numbers, and report back to Leybridge. Got it?'

'Be quiet!' he said.

She gaped at him, astonished. 'How dare you –'

'Shhh!' he hissed, looking around. 'Listen …'

Elchora fell silent at once. She heard only the breeze and was prepared to continue admonishing the New Colour. But then, distant yet unmistakable, she heard it.

Screaming.

The pair locked eyes and cast about for the direction.

Fyvern raised a finger and slowly divined it across the empty river, frowning at Elchora. She cocked her head in the direction he had signalled, then nodded. Fyvern drew his sword, and Elchora followed suit with her dirk knife. She peeled herself from the tree and slid feet-first into the riverbed, hopping on the exposed rocks to the far bank.

Fyvern followed in her wake but overtook her with a burst of speed. Elchora ran to keep up, her feet thudding and crunching on the forest floor.

The screaming became more distinct.

Suddenly, Fyvern dived sideways behind a dense shrub, and instinctively, Elchora mirrored him in the opposite direction, throwing herself behind the nearest tree. She peered around it and saw that Fyvern was adjusting his position, putting his back against the thicket, and looking across at her, a frown creasing his forehead.

What do you see? she signalled.

Fyvern ducked his head out from behind his cover and pulled it back, his frown slightly deeper.

'There's a boy out there,' he said.

Elchora blinked at him. She must have misheard. *Krae?* she signed.

Fyvern shook his head slowly.

She moved in steady increments around the trunk, leading with her right eye, until the forest scene beyond came into view.

There! Around seventy feet away, standing in the open, stood a boy of roughly seventeen. He was wrapped in layers of black bearskin tied with rags, and, from his side-on stance, Elchora could see a strange woven basket on his back, of the kind an apple picker might wear. He held a longbow across his leading thigh, an arrow cocked on the drawstring across his midriff, and the point and pommel of a sword were visible diagonally at either side.

Elchora withdrew her head and looked at Fyvern, who shrugged.

What on Ithea is a boy doing out here? she thought.

From his wild look, he had been out here for some time. Perhaps even lived out here.

But that was impossible. The Krae would have eaten him the first night. Many of the most hardened warriors in Leybridge would not dare venture this far north after sundown. Even Maldon. And while it remained broad daylight, Elchora could not imagine how the boy had arrived here.

Where had he come from?

'I see you!' said the boy, his voice deeper than she had expected. 'Both of you! Go back the way you came!'

Fyvern shifted. 'Who are you?' he called over his shoulder. 'What business have you out here?'

No reply.

'We are soldiers from Leybridge,' Fyvern offered. 'Sent to scout for Kraelings. Now, tell us your purpose … Tell us, or we will attack!'

'Go back the way you came!' the boy commanded.

On instinct, Elchora stepped out into the open with her palms raised.

The boy tautened the bowstring warningly but did not raise the arrow.

'We mean you no harm,' she said. 'I am Elchora Farrow, Ableman in the army of Leybridge. And this is New Colour Almys Fyvern. We are looking for a large host of Krae. Have you seen any gathered in great numbers?'

'Go back the way you came!' the boy repeated.

Fyvern sighed loudly. 'I've had enough of this,' he said. He stepped out brashly and marched at the boy when an arrow slammed into the dirt at his feet. Fyvern bent down and plucked it from the ground to examine it.

'Humph,' he said, 'exactly as I thought. No head. Just a sharpened stick!'

With a snap, he crushed the arrow in his fist, tossed it to the ground, and then proceeded toward the boy, sword in hand.

The boy dropped his bow and drew his own sword. He fell to one knee and thrust it halfway into the ground.

Fyvern stopped short again. 'A formal duel?' he said, surprised. 'Well, if you insist.'

He copied the boy and stabbed the ground, his sword swaying like a sapling under the force. Elchora saw the word 'FYVERN' inscribed vertically along the blade. Few blacksmiths would add such ornamentation. And only if they believed the owner worthy.

'Don't hurt him,' she said in a low voice. 'If you injure him, we'll have to carry him back to Leybridge. Kill him, and he won't be able to answer any questions.'

Fyvern nodded, his eyes on the boy.

'Here are my terms, challenger,' he said. 'Since we have no torches, and you have nobody to act as your second, we will fight until one of us draws blood. If you win, we will go back the way we came, as you ask. But you will come with *us* if *I* win. Do you agree?'

The boy took a deep breath and pulled his sword from the ground.

Fyvern mimicked the action and began his approach. Laterally, he stalked from side to side, watching the boy's footwork. His enemy pivoted on the spot, following the New Colour with the tip of his sword.

'Good,' said Fyvern. 'You move well. Now, let's see if you can defend!'

He lunged forward half-heartedly, and the boy parried the blow. Fyvern used the momentum to change direction. He smiled, then attacked again, aiming a flurry of slashes at the boy's arms. But again, the boy blocked each attempt, rooted to the spot.

The forest resonated with the high-pitched clanging of metal.

Elchora kept a lookout for any signs of movement. This noise would attract any Krae within half a mile. She looked back at the duel and noticed that the boy had remained firmly in the same spot, with his back to the same tree, allowing Fyvern to attack unanswered.

Not the wisest tactic. But the boy was coping well against the onslaught.

Fyvern grinned, nodding in respect. But he was breathing heavily. He launched forward again, slicing with all his might, hammering blows that would have cleaved the boy in half.

But the boy's sword met each effort without any sign of strain or trouble. Even when the blades locked together, with Fyvern pushing forward, his gritted teeth frothing spittle as he glowered down, a full head taller than his opponent. He did not win an inch.

Elchora could not believe it.

There came a moment in all duels when one fighter would realise they were outmatched. Elchora's father had taught her to sense it. To look past the thrusting and cutting and witness the heart of a contest, written in the combatants' eyes. Invariably, a haunting fear would betray the loser's face. Her father called it the collapse of spirit.

She saw it then, in Fyvern's eyes.

He retreated a few paces, spent and enraged, yelling his impotence into the ground. He turned back defiantly, sword held aloft, probing for an opening he might have overlooked.

In his mounting desperation, he stepped further to the boy's left, closer to the tree. And suddenly, a look that Elchora was unfamiliar with altered the boy's expression for the first time.

He unleashed a primal roar that sent shivers up her spine, exploding at Fyvern like a solid bolt of lightning, his sword a blur.

Fyvern had no time to react. He lifted his sword and managed to defend the blow. But the force of it paralysed his left arm to the shoulder. He dropped his sword, clutched his arm like a broken wing, and landed with a clatter on his rear.

The boy's sword was at his throat.

Elchora gaped. The boy had won in a single move.

'Who are you?' Fyvern barked, his voice quavering as he looked along the blade.

'Go back the way you came,' the boy said. He sheathed his sword.

Fyvern's lip curled. Leaning on his good hand, he pushed at the floor and stood up. 'No!' he yelled. 'We agreed the winner must draw *blood*! If you think –'

With a sickening crunch, the boy's fist slammed squarely into the bridge of Fyvern's nose, causing his head to whipcrack.

He dropped like a metal marionette, blood pouring from both nostrils.

The boy crouched at Fyvern's head and wiped the split nose with his fingertips. Then he stood and displayed the blood to Elchora as though concerned she might continue the argument.

Elchora noted that this action was far from a demonstration of triumph. The boy looked – if anything – slightly embarrassed. Unable to meet her eyes.

'Leave,' he said to the ground.

For a long time, she had no idea what to say. Slowly, as sober reality returned, she began to assess her predicament.

She was deep in the Urden Forest, some eight hours before sunset and almost twenty miles from safety, with an unconscious New Colour to drag home. And confronted by a new, unknown enemy.

And perhaps the boy is not alone, she thought. *No, he can't be. We heard a scream …*

She looked up at the tree.

The boy shifted, white knuckles gripping the handle of his sword.

'We will honour the terms of the duel,' she said. 'But you must allow me to revive my companion. I cannot leave him to the Krae.'

The boy nodded.

Elchora kept him in her eye line as she moved to Fyvern's side. She knelt just as he began to gurgle blood from his mouth. She rolled him to his side and watched the blood spill over the dirt. She tilted Fyvern's head upward with one hand, while her other found the bottle of Sacred Water tied at her hip. She unfastened the bottle and poured the water carefully between his lips.

Groggily and with the confusion of a child waking from sleep, Fyvern opened his eyes. He pulled himself to a seated position and looked around, surprised to find himself outdoors.

The boy picked up Fyvern's sword and presented it handle-first to Elchora. Again, without meeting her eye.

She snatched the sword and dug the point in the ground, using the hilt to pull herself and Fyvern to their feet. The New Colour wobbled, clutching her shoulder, the bridge of his nose at an angle, his eyes unfocussed, and a claret goatee around his mouth.

'We'll never make it back before sunset like this,' she said.

'You must go,' said the boy.

'Yes,' she snapped, 'I would like to! But you've made it quite difficult.'

'My sword …' murmured Fyvern, tapping his empty sheath and casting around at the ground, perplexed.

'I've got it,' Elchora said kindly. She drew his arm around her shoulders. 'Come on. It's time to go.'

Without a backward glance but sensing the boy's gaze with her every clumsy stride, she led the New Colour back through the trees toward the riverbed.

CHAPTER 15

The Lord of Berrund

Colton Farrow limped along the narrow dungeon hall as quickly as he could, keeping his head ducked beneath the low, arched ceiling. The torches on the wall bathed the dank brickwork in patches of bronze light, their flames flickering in the wake of his billowing cape. Dirkren, the gaoler, walked a few paces ahead, coughing and retching, a loop of iron keys dangling at his waist. He was a short, stocky man with patches of scruffy hair and yellow-brown teeth. The embodiment of the dungeon's misery.

Dirkren stopped short of the furthest cell and turned to Colton. 'Got 'im in 'ere, milord,' he said, pointing.

Colton stepped past the gaoler and turned to investigate the dark cell. 'I thought we captured two of them?' he said.

'Aye, there *was* two in there, milord,' wheezed Dirkren, 'but thiss'un killed the other and started eatin' 'im. Ripped 'im wide open! So, we dragged out the carcass an' put it on the pikes for the crows.'

A creature stirred in the deepest shadow of the cell, lifting its white-haired head from the floor with a menacing growl before snapping into a defensive crouch. The shape of a man but with inhuman flesh. It was naked, and every inch of skin seemed to glow faintly, ice-white, and so barely opaque that it was almost transparent. Even in the darkness, Colton could make out the creature's purplish, beating heart behind the visible ribs in the white chest. He could see the network of green and blue veins that fed the heart and the razor-thin purple vessels that flowered in the creature's face, hands, and feet. Its permanent war tattoo.

The Kraeling began to shout in its ugly, indiscernible language. Dirkren snorted and spat a viscous globule of phlegm onto the cell floor, which contracted in the filth.

'Thank you, Dirkren,' sighed Colton. 'Please wait outside.'

Dirkren gave a curt bow, then waddled off along the hall, muttering to

105

himself. Colton watched the gaoler leave until his stubby feet disappeared up the stairs. When he could no longer hear the rattle of the man's keys, he returned his attention to the prisoner. *Kraeling*, he thought, sizing up the creature. The name was derived from an old Eddish word for ghost or spirit; *'ka-real'*. *Ghosts from beyond the mountain*. A peculiar thing. The war against them had raged for almost a decade, since they had massacred the village of Fairwater during Colton's first year as the Lord of Berrund. Yet he still understood so little about them. Grendel Farrow, his father and instructor in the art of war, had always taught him to know his enemy. It was the first step in defeating them, he'd said. But Grendel had never encountered the Krae. They were elusive. Ghostly in appearance as well as habit. Able to disappear at will. From the dissection of captives, such as the unfortunate creature before him, Colton had learned that they were not ghosts after all. Their anatomies were almost identical to men – except for their flesh – and they were roughly equal in size and physical strength. Their eyes were different too. Liquid black eyes that saw clearly in the dark but poorly in the daylight. And they were cannibals. Colton had witnessed it during their attack on Leybridge. A young male had plunged its jaws deep inside the chest wound of its twitching brother. Then the eater had lifted its dripping crimson maw and re-joined the assault.

The mere memory made Colton's blood turn cold. *Cannibals*. But it was necessary to know all aspects of an enemy if he wished to destroy them or force them back over the Bannebar.

But *why* had they crossed the Bannebar in the first place? What had driven them over those treacherous peaks to rain death on the poor people of Fairwater ten years ago? Was it simply the bounty of the Urden? Had the Krae overbred in the north and exceeded the resources of Kininumbra? And if so, how many of them would make the journey? How many now infested the Urden? A thousand? *Five* thousand? He knew their number had swollen in the years since their failed assault on Leybridge, though his men were yet to discover their nest and obtain an accurate tally. But more and more of his scouting patrols reported sightings from all over the forest, and lately, some scouts had not returned. The forest itself was beginning to show the strain of bearing this unwelcome parasite; almost all animal populations had dwindled alarmingly, while fewer and fewer of the Leybridge hunting parties dared to venture out and seldom expected to return home with food. The trees themselves were suffering too. A silent, creeping death had permanently stripped every tenth tree of its leaves, leaving them to rot at random intervals throughout the forest. A decay that weighed heavily on the hearts and minds of the people of Berrund. *His* people. Whose sacred Urden he was failing to protect.

And Colton knew the vermin would not remain hidden much longer. If his estimation of their numbers was accurate, they outnumbered his soldiers by ten to one. If the Krae knew this, they could rampage the city and take the Realm.

Colton could not allow that to pass. He would not. If it cost him his life, he would pay the price.

He prayed the Augurs would hear Volsgaard's plea at the Gathering and convince their lords to send aid. It was a desperate hope but not nearly as desperate as his present intention with his prisoner. He would risk being labelled a *jurdah* for this. A traitor to his kind. He peered down the length of the dungeon hall.

If he was going to try this, better to try it in secret.

The Kraeling in the cell had risen by a few inches and taken half a step forward. It stared at Colton with utmost hatred, unblinking, cursing Colton in its alien tongue.

'My name is Lord Farrow,' he said slowly, patting his chest and feeling more than a little foolish. 'What is *your* name?'

The creature ran at him, throttling the bars in fury as it screeched its guttural nonsense. Colton stepped back to let the ghostly, veined arms claw at the air before him.

'*Lord Farrow*,' he repeated over the wailing. '*Do* you *have a name?*'

Spittle frothed from the Kraeling's bared teeth, and its eyes widened. Colton could see the torchlight reflected in their inky blackness.

This was pointless.

He took a deep breath to speak again when he heard footsteps descending the stairs. Dirkren appeared.

'Beg yer pardon, milord,' he said, 'but Master Volsgaard 'as returned.'

Colton nodded in thanks. He gave the Kraeling a final disappointed glance and left it to its caterwauling.

Back above ground, a night breeze swept the southern courtyard. Two men slid wearily from their horses.

'Welcome back, my old friend,' said Colton, beaming at his faithful Augur.

They embraced briefly, clapping each other on the back.

'Well met, my Lord,' said Volsgaard. 'But I'm afraid we do not bear good news.'

Colton read the man's face. 'Markos will not send aid?' he ventured.

'Worse than that.' Volsgaard glanced at Eurace and lowered his voice. 'The King's Augur announced that any Realm who sends soldiers to Berrund will be treated as traitors to the throne.'

Colton spun away. 'Curse him!' he said. 'How can that be his decision? Did you make our position plain?'

'As plain as possible. But Markos – or rather, Rowel Malcifer – understands that many in the Iron Company still hold *you* as their Commander, Colton. And they fear you might inspire their men into rebellion.'

'Absurd!' he replied, waving his hand dismissively. He rounded on the Augur. 'Did any of the Realms seem sympathetic before this announcement?'

'Perhaps,' said Volsgaard. 'But we spoke of our recent insights. And every man had seen a shadow drawing near. This was the reason we had been summoned. And many seemed intrigued by my assertion that this shadow concerned the Krae.'

Colton let out a humourless laugh. 'Yet Markos has ensured that none will send help to the battlefront!'

Volsgaard rocked his head side to side, non-committal. 'Some may yet be persuaded …' he said. 'Either through Ohrak's guidance or by their own consciences. But we would be fools to hope for it, Colton. Rowel Malcifer made it very clear. If any foreign soldiers join our ranks, the Iron Company will march on Berrund.'

'Then we should provoke them to do just that!' said Colton, heat rising up his neck. 'If they come, they will see the truth of our plea with their own eyes, and we will have the Iron Company at our command.'

Colton knew this plan had no merit. But it still irked him to see the derision on the face of his advisor. The Augur's nostrils flared as he stifled a yawn.

'Forgive me, old friend,' said Colton. 'I know you have travelled far to bring me this news, and you are not responsible for its content. You must be weary. Do you have enough strength to seek God's guidance before you retire to your bed? I am in urgent need of His counsel.'

Volsgaard gave a small, earnest smile and bowed. 'Of course, my lord,' he said. 'Eurace, take the horses to the stable and see that they are cared for. Then join us in Lord Farrow's office.'

The Obediant spasmed at this sudden address. Still, he took the reins from Volsgaard and led the horses away at once.

Moments later, Colton took his seat by the smouldering fireside, massaging the old wound along his left thigh – his souvenir from the duel with Markos. He recalled the pain of its creation keenly. The King's sword through his leg. His pride battered. The humiliation of defeat. And his exile to Berrund. Worst of all was the memory in the flesh of his hands. His fingers could still feel the impact of the blow he dealt to Markos's abdomen before he lost the duel. Had he only struck a *little* harder, perhaps everything would have been different.

Volsgaard interrupted his reverie by handing him a glass of red wine and sitting in the chair opposite. 'What is it you wish me to seek?' he asked.

Colton took a draught of his wine. 'I've been thinking in your absence-' he began.

'Most unwise…' chided the Augur.

'– and your news has tipped the balance of my decision.'

He steeled himself. It felt odd to finally speak aloud the thought that had gestated for so long in the recesses of his mind. He felt uncommonly anxious. He forced himself to look into the Augur's eyes.

'I think it's time I retired,' he said.

Volsgaard lurched forward, spluttering a red mist of wine. He wiped his mouth and stared at Colton incredulously.

'*Retire?*' he choked. 'What do you mean, retire? We're at war! On the brink of defeat, no less!'

'Exactly,' Colton pressed on, confused by the euphoria coursing through him.

'But you can't!' Volsgaard exclaimed, hurt. 'You cannot abandon the people of Berrund in their hour of need!'

'Actually, I believe that I *can*,' said Colton. 'Moreover, I *should.*'

Volsgaard hurled himself from his chair and began to pace, glowering at Colton in silent rage. 'If you were any other man,' he said quietly, 'I would call you a coward!'

'Erik, sit down,' said Colton. But the Augur ignored him. 'Listen to my reasons before you pass judgement.'

With visible effort, Volsgaard stopped pacing and clutched the back of his chair, refusing to sit.

'We cannot remain idle,' Colton explained. 'You said yourself that we mustn't pin our hopes on support from the other Realms. And Markos Almanfier will not suffer a sudden change of heart. So, what? Should we wait for the Throne Trial and hope a new, benevolent ruler emerges? Unlikely, I'm sure you'll agree. And even if it *were* guaranteed, the Throne Trial is months away!

'Meanwhile, the Krae grow bolder and bolder. It will not be long before their numbers outweigh their fear of us. Ohrak has shown you this future, time and again.

'If we announce my immediate retirement, however, we shall be bound by law to host a Lordship Trial for Berrund. To determine my replacement. Such a tournament would draw every able warrior in the kingdom right here to Leybridge.' He tapped his armrest with a finger. 'For who could resist the chance to usurp a crippled lord? Especially when his seat offers a gateway to the throne. And the King would be powerless to stop such a migration of soldiers.

'Do you think the Krae would dare attack if our numbers suddenly increased tenfold? Of course not! Erik, I'm certain this is the surest way to buy us some time.'

Volsgaard chewed on his tongue for a while, staring into the fire. 'But what afterwards?' he said. 'Once the time is bought? What then? Those who came would eventually leave, and Berrund would be in the same position. With a *less able* lord at its helm.'

'That,' said Colton, 'is precisely what I seek to understand.'

Volsgaard continued to shake his head. 'And you believe this course of action is best for the *Realm*?' he said. 'Or is it simply what *you* want? And before you answer, don't forget, I know where your heart longs to be.'

'Careful,' Colton warned.

A silence fell between them.

A gentle rattling grew louder in the hallway until a fist hammered on the door.

'Enter,' said Colton.

The door opened, and two men sidled through, Victor Maldon and Lyle Eurace, a comical difference in their sizes. Both wore uncomfortable expressions.

'What is it, Commander?' asked Colton.

'Sorry for the late hour, my lord,' said Maldon with a stiff bow, causing his red beard to fan out from his chest, 'but I wanted to report on the scouting patrols we sent into the Urden.'

'Ah, yes. Did they find anything?'

Maldon hesitated. 'Yes, my lord,' he said. 'One pair reported signs of many cooking fires grouped closely together in a clearing. About eighteen miles due north. The scouts reckoned there might've been two thousand Krae there in the last few days.'

'Two thousand?' asked Volsgaard. 'Any idea where they went?'

'No,' said Maldon. 'The tracks scattered in all directions, they said.'

The Commander cleared his throat.

'Is there something else?' asked Colton.

'Yes, my lord. The scouts I sent farthest to the northeast haven't come back yet.'

Colton sighed and leaned back in his chair. Few soldiers returned after nightfall. This was the third incident in as many months. The Krae had probably killed them for meat.

'Well,' said Colton, 'let us allow them a few days before we declare them dead. What were their names?'

Maldon lifted his head and looked directly at Colton, glassy-eyed. 'Almys Fyvern and Elchora Farrow, my lord.'

An icy fist seized Colton's heart. Volsgaard turned sharply to look at him while Eurace convulsed from the corner.

Show nothing, Colton willed inwardly. *Have faith. Your daughter is a survivor.*

'Thank you, Commander,' he said. 'Let me know if they return.'

Maldon met Colton's eyes with a knowing smile. He turned and marched swiftly from the room, closing the door behind him. Volsgaard waited a few seconds before speaking.

'Colton …' he said.

'I'm not worried,' Colton lied, getting to his feet. 'Both are capable soldiers, and their fate is not certain yet. Besides, you know as well as I do that Elchora would be insulted if I treated her preferentially. She's made that quite clear.'

Volsgaard was about to speak again when Colton cut him off. He could not dwell on the matter further.

'Now,' he said forcefully, 'let us get back to the task at hand! I wish to ask a question of Ohrak.'

Volsgaard stared at him for several seconds but eventually nodded and summoned Eurace to his side.

The Obediant unfastened his shirt with trembling fingers and slipped a hand inside, drawing out the moon-shaped stone that dangled from his necklace. The subtle glow in the stone's depths pulsed in long waves as though it were breathing.

Eurace removed the necklace and placed the stone gently into Volsgaard's open palm. The Augur felt the weight of it for a moment, stared at it in reverence, then took his seat purposefully.

'What do you wish me to ask?' he said.

Colton took a breath. 'I want you to ask whether a warrior exists in Berrund capable of defeating Markos Almanfier,' he said. 'And if so, where might we find them.'

Volsgaard sat up straight. He covered the God Stone with his other palm and brought his clasped hands to his forehead in prayer. Colton watched the Augur avidly. Volsgaard's eyes rolled before shutting. His shoulders dropped as he relaxed, seeking the connection with Ohrak. Sometimes it took minutes, sometimes hours, but Colton knew not to interrupt or make any noise. He had never experienced what the Augurs called *insights* himself, other than typical dreams. But he always felt God's *presence* whenever Volsgaard sought His wisdom. It manifested as a kind of tingling in the crown of his head, which cascaded to a point halfway down his spine. And a sense of calm would wash over him, as though the tingling had cleansed away his concerns.

Presently, however, Colton was firmly grounded by his concern for Elchora. Had she been captured? Killed? Was she being eaten at this very moment? Or was she was hiding somewhere? Waiting out the darkness. He must know. He should wake the city and ride out at once with the full cavalry. Elchora's pride be damned! But there was little he could do. And suddenly, he felt nothing but contempt for the futility of prayer.

His scepticism seemed to infect the Augur, who frowned and shook his head in frustration. Volsgaard dropped his hands to his lap and opened his eyes.

'It's no use,' he said. 'All I see is the Urden. I'm too tired to clear my mind sufficiently. Eurace, sit down. I want you to seek in my stead. We will count it as your training for the day.'

The Obediant swallowed and twitched, rattling the iron collar around his neck. He took Volsgaard's chair beside the fire and looked at Colton like a condemned man at the chopping block. His few teeth were visible in his slackened mouth. Volsgaard handed him the God Stone.

'You heard Lord Farrow's instruction?' asked the Augur. 'You are seeking a champion capable of defeating the King. Do you understand?'

'Yes, M-m-master,' said Eurace.

The Obediant closed his eyes. He adopted Volsgaard's meditative position and held the God Stone to his forehead. At first, his head jerked horribly to the left every few seconds. Then, the involuntary movements gradually became less pronounced until they subsided altogether. Colton began to feel a prickling at the back of his head.

He watched as the Obediant's mouth silently intoned his request.

Suddenly, Eurace's lip quivered. He let out a whimper. His hands shook. His spasms returned more forcefully.

'N-n-n-no!' he pleaded, then again, higher-pitched, 'N-n-no ....'

Colton looked at Volsgaard, aghast. The Augur put his arm around Eurace and gently peeled his hands from his forehead.

The Obediant convulsed so strongly that the God Stone spilled from his grip. It bounced from his lap and skidded across the flagstone toward the hearth.

Colton picked it up but kept his eyes on the Obediant. He had never seen a reaction like this.

'Be still, lad,' said Volsgaard kindly. 'Be still. You're all right. It's over. It's all over. I've got you.'

The Obediant was shivering. 'Sorry – I'm sorry – I'm sorry,' he repeated nonsensically, addressing nobody.

'It's all right, lad,' said Volsgaard. 'Let it pass.'

The Augur looked at Colton in apology. But Colton dropped to his good knee and caught Eurace's eyes.

'What did you see?' he asked.

The Obediant's chest heaved as he struggled to compose himself. 'I s-s-s-saw the U-u-u-rden, m-m-m-m-my l-lord,' he said painfully. 'And th-th-then … th-th-then …'

Eurace's fingers clutched at the collar around his neck as though it had tightened, cutting off his air. He shook his head in protest, tears rolling down his cheeks over the mingled look of horror and disgust on his face.

He collapsed from the chair.

Colton and Volsgaard raised him back up. Eurace's head rolled from side to side over his collar. Colton lifted his wet chin and was relieved to see that the Obediant was still breathing. He looked at Volsgaard, who seemed equally perturbed.

'Forgive me,' said the Augur. 'I shouldn't have pushed him like that. Not when he's so tired. He sometimes relives the Fairwater attack when he seeks. Not as an *insight* but as a … tortured memory. That's likely what he saw, my Lord.'

'Get him to bed,' said Colton, wiping his moist hand on his shirt. 'I have asked too much from both of you after such a long journey.'

Volsgaard lifted a vial of Sacred Water to his Obediant's lips. Eurace clutched at it and drank.

'Is there anything else I can do?' asked Volsgaard.

'Not tonight,' said Colton, pushing himself stiffly to his feet. 'But tomorrow, we will try again. I am determined to find a worthy champion.'

CHAPTER 16

Home Cave

As he pulled his head above the ridge, Gadryon saw the door of Home Cave in the moonlight and knew his rest was near. He gained purchase on the dusty flat side of the cliff with his palms, then, straightening his arms with a final effort, he hauled his body up over the ridge, along with his sister, who was asleep now. He knelt on the rocky cliff edge with his eyes closed. His whole body felt exhausted beyond experience, and, stopping for the first time, the depth of his exhaustion hit him all at once. His fingers hurt the worst. They were palsied and raw from gripping the cliff face, and the tendons in his wrists were strings of pain. He looked at his fingers in disgust and forced his hands into fists, pressing them hard into the rock at his knees.

I must become stronger, he thought.

He got to his feet and walked across the rocky platform to the cave's entrance, to the door that was a crude collection of branches tied like a small raft. The door fitted the cave mouth poorly, but it was their only shelter from the driving winds on the mountain. Their shield from the outside world.

He lifted the door aside quietly with his aching hands and felt the warmer air of the cave on his face. It was dry and smelled of the white flowers that Orla liked best.

It smelled of home.

Gadryon ducked inside the cave without closing the door, allowing the fading light to fall inside. He lifted Orla out of her carrier in the semi-darkness and gently placed her on the bed of palm leaves, suddenly weightless without her. Orla stirred. She adjusted her head against the yellowing leaves, and her grey eyes opened a little.

'I'm sorry,' she said, and her voice was so small that he felt a surge of affection. He knelt beside her and kissed her forehead as their mother would have done.

'Rest,' he said, 'it wasn't your fault.'

'Something took me. From inside. And I couldn't – I couldn't –'

She was trying to get up on her elbows.

'It was only a dream,' said Gadryon, gently holding her down, 'no more than a dream.'

'It wasn't a dream,' said Orla, 'it was real. It felt like … like dying.'

'Hush now. Sleep and tell me tomorrow.'

The leaves crunched beneath her weight as Orla lay down and turned to face the cave wall. Gadryon watched her fall asleep. When the soldiers had finally gone, he had found her shaking from the cold and fear. She could barely speak. And no wonder. It was the first time she had ever encountered other people.

Gadryon wanted nothing more than to collapse into his own bed. But there was work to do. He opened Orla's satchel and was only half angry to see how much meat she had cut from the stag. It had started to smell sickly sweet, and he hoped he was not too late. He would need to cook it right away to keep it good.

He began making a small fire inside the circle of stones on the floor. Once it had caught, he remembered to unplug the wedge from the crack overhead, and he heard the wind whistling far above through the gap. He laid the sweaty meat in strips across a blackened cooking slate, which he propped between the tallest stones over the fire. The meat began to sizzle and spit, while all around him, the shadows danced on the cave walls. He watched them dance, thinking what a welcome comfort they were. How they felt like company.

The girl's name was Elchora Farrow.

No.

He tried not to think. He was too tired, and the smoke was making him drowsy. He turned the meat over with his knife and saw it was cooking well. It spat as he turned it, and the underside was grey. He would cook each side black to make sure.

Elchora's hair was golden.

Stop it, he thought.

He must not think about what had happened. The possible consequences of their discovery were too frightening. He would not think about it. Not while his head was so unclear. He would eat a little, then sleep, and nothing more. Tomorrow he would think.

With difficulty, he cut away a piece of meat that was cooked through and tough, and he said a prayer to Ohrak before touching it to his tongue. It tasted strange and made his tongue tingle, but it was not bitter. He put it in his mouth and chewed it. It was stringy and hard to separate. A poor prize for such a costly endeavour. He wondered what God meant by it. He forced himself to eat a steak and decided not to wake Orla. If the meat had spoiled, they would not both be sick, and if he woke unharmed in the morning, she would have a breakfast fit for a princess. He made sure to cook each piece before covering them for the night.

Curled up in his bed, his eyes closing, he watched the dying red embers of the fire.

Images swam before his half-closed eyes; the face of a woman with golden hair, the flashing of a sword, and a cup of Sacred Water lifted to a mouth.

Sleep washed over him, irresistible, complete, and deeper than the mountain's foundations.

His father handed him the goblet of mead, smiling down at him. It was huge and heavy and warm in his hands.

'And which story would we like to hear tonight?' asked his father.

'Tell the one about Reon, the First King! Or Brør, the Great Bear of the Mountain!'

His father frowned. 'But you've heard those a hundred times!' he said.

'They're my favourites,' said Gadryon with a grin, and he lifted the goblet to his mouth. The mead was warm and sweet.

'Oh, let's hear another one,' said his mother, curled around his back, her pregnant belly huge with life. Gadryon turned to face her. She was dark-haired, like him, and beautiful, her eyes the colour of a storm.

'But I want to hear about Brør!' said Gadryon insistently. He liked the part where his father would pretend to be the giant bear and eat the children. It made him shiver. Brør could swallow a person whole, he would say. They wouldn't even feel it.

'Why don't I tell you the story of God?' said his father.

'Oh, yes, please!' said his mother. 'That's *my* favourite.'

'But there's no fighting in that story!' said Gadryon, looking between them. 'It's so boring!'

'Ah, but the story of God teaches us that there is more to life than fighting, Gadryon,' said his father, his eyebrows raised, head tilted forward. 'And it might help you to understand your lust for fighting too.'

'Fine,' said Gadryon, 'but the story of Brør or King Reon next time!'

His father winked and moved to the far side of the fire. His mother stroked the back of his head.

'In the beginning,' said his father, 'in the Time of Spirits, when our world was nothing more than a lifeless rock, Ohrak, the God of All, made our world His home. He made it a place of eternal peace and great beauty. He made the oceans, the forests, the mountains, the sky, the sun, the moon and all the stars.'

His father paused, his face mystical in the firelight. 'But the world was incomplete,' he said. 'It needed life. And so, God entered the greatest mountain of the Bannebar and touched its heart. The rock turned purple from the light within. It became the first God Stone, full of the wonder of Ohrak.'

He threw a fistful of dust into the flames, which instantly burned green. 'Then, the Spirits came,' he continued. 'Drawn to Ohrak's power. And they knelt before God and listened to His decree.'

His father jumped and looked down at him across the fire. He made his voice deeper, and Gadryon laughed. '*I will grant each of you three gifts*, said Ohrak. *The gifts of Life, Form, and Nature. You must choose your gifts with care, for they cannot be revoked once chosen.*'

His father fell back to his knees. 'The spirits left the mountain and pondered God's decree. When they returned, they entered the cave one by one.

'The first spirit to enter was the spirit known as Bear. She asked this. *Blessed Ohrak, God of All, please grant me life. Give me a form with the greatest strength and the sharpest claws, so I may rule the land. And fill my nature with solitude.*'

His father reared up like a bear. Like Brør, the Great Bear of the mountain.

'As it was asked, so it was done,' he said.

'The next spirit to enter the cave was the spirit known as Eagle. He asked this. *Blessed Ohrak, God of All, please grant me life. Give me a form with the greatest vision and the widest wings so I may rule the sky. And fill my nature with nobility.*'

He stretched his arms out wide.

'As it was asked, so it was done,' said Gadryon.

His father nodded.

'The next spirit to enter the cave was the spirit known as Shark. She asked this. *Blessed Ohrak, God of All, please grant me life. Give me a form with the greatest speed and the sharpest teeth, so I may rule the sea. And fill my nature with hunger.*'

His father brought his fingers together like teeth.

'As it was asked, so it was done,' they said together.

'One by one, each spirit left the cave in its new form, spreading far across the world, to become the animals of Ithea, each with their chosen gifts from God.'

His father's smile faded. 'But one spirit remained … the spirit known as Man. He had lurked in the mountain and listened to all the gifts bestowed upon his sisters and brothers. Until, at last, it was Man's turn to kneel before God. He asked this. *Blessed Ohrak, God of All, please grant me life. Give me a form with the greatest violence and the sharpest mind, so I may rule the world. And fill my nature with greed.*'

With a cry of fury, his face cruel, his father drew his sword and sliced through the fire. The flames swirled in the sword's wake.

'As it was asked, so it was done,' he whispered.

Gadryon saw a deep sadness in the face he remembered. He stood, intending to embrace his father, but found him further away somehow.

He took a step forward, then another, but with each stride, his father and the fire drifted further away. He ran at them desperately until they were nothing more than a faint orange glow on a black horizon.

Something was wrong.

And then he heard it. The terrible sound. A cold, lingering note surrounding him in the night.

The battle horn of the Krae.

They came out of the darkness like ghosts. Many of them. With spears and clubs and swords and voices full of hatred. He saw his father in the distance, sword raised and shouting, holding them back until he was taken. The spears came through his back.

Gadryon turned to his mother, but she was not there. Flames and screaming took the village all around. People and animals were running. He needed his mother. He had to find his mother. Someone lifted him and ran, but he screamed and kicked, and the ground rolled up and hit him. He heard his mother calling him through the smoke and the screaming. Her voice lifted him back to his feet.

She found him.

She came at him and took his hand and crushed his fingers. His mother. Pulling him away, hurting his arm and fingers and dragging him faster than he could run toward the stable, where the roof was ablaze.

The inside was full of smoke and orange light. Horses screaming in their pens. She threw a saddle on one and turned to lift Gadryon. But behind her, a Kraeling charged at them. And Gadryon couldn't speak from choking. Then the point of a knife came through her breast, visible and red, and she fell on him, clutching her soft belly.

The Kraeling rolled her aside, lifting the knife once more above Gadryon. And he was so small, and nobody was left to protect him. But then, his mother rose too. Raging into furious life with her death inside her. Hurling herself with all her strength at the raised arm, she sank her teeth into the marble-white skin.

The Kraeling dropped the knife. It punched at his mother's head with its free hand. Howling. But his mother's will was stronger. She held on until her hand found the knife.

With a bloody shout, she released the arm and drove the knife hard into the Kraeling's eye.

The creature stiffened before collapsing to the floor in a swirl of smoke.

His mother keeled over.

Gadryon reached out. Terrified of her mutilation but desperate for her comfort. She lay there, breathing in spasms. Orla. His mother. Broken and covered in blood. The baby turned inside her.

The doors to the stable crashed open, and God's salvation finally arrived.

The young man with the pear-shaped nose, Eurace, had found them. Wearing his father's God Stone. He had come to save his mother! But when their eyes met, Gadryon understood the truth. And he watched as the man swung himself onto the saddled horse and thundered away into the night.

'Gadryon,' whispered his broken mother.

He bent close to her and took her cold hands in his own.

'Cut it out,' she said.

She put the wet handle of the knife in his hand.

He didn't understand.

'You must be strong,' she said.

He would do it. He would be strong, he said.

He gripped her hand, wanting to go with her.

She left him. The baby rolled in her belly.

Outside the dream, in the cave, Gadryon's hands twitched as he cut her open. Above him, silently, the entire ceiling of Home Cave glowed a deep purple.

CHAPTER 17

Blood

Orla sat propped against the cave wall, her withered legs crossed before her. She held an arrow gently in her hand, tapping the point with her thumb. It did not draw blood. She found her knife and began scraping off thin flakes toward the arrow tip as though trying to get a spark from a flint.

When she tested the point again, she felt a warm trickle down her thumb and across her palm. She put her thumb in her mouth to staunch the bleeding and placed the arrow carefully atop the pile of others. She would blacken their tips in the fire to harden them when Gadryon returned from his hunt.

Five days had passed since their encounter with the soldiers. Five days confined to Home Cave. It was too risky, Gadryon said, to take Orla out with him anymore. Her screaming had brought the soldiers.

He had left her alone each day since.

At first, Orla had cried at this unfairness, but her self-pity had quickly soured into boredom in her confinement.

She missed the routine of hunting. The excitement of it. She missed the noises of the forest and the sensation of living things all around her. Most of all, she missed her brother, who was always so kind to her, and whom she loved more deeply than she could bear.

Home Cave was a cold and lonely place without him.

She was determined to win back his favour by keeping the cave as best she could. She took over all the preparations and the cooking. While Gadryon was out, she swept the floor, gathered firewood, or sharpened their weapons and tools. She also filled the water flasks by crawling into the deepest part of the cave, where she hated going for fear of getting trapped but where fresh water roared noisily into the mountain.

Her isolation dragged her thoughts down into uneasy places when she ran out of tasks.

What if Gadryon didn't come back? What if he got hurt? Or captured? How long could she survive without him?

She often wondered about the people, too. The soldiers who had found them. With their loud, confident voices. She had never heard a Nephian voice that was not her brother's. And their existence was proof of a vast and unknown world. More terrifying than the voice she had heard in her head.

Though that was the thing she pondered most.

What had happened to her before the soldiers came? A voice had spoken inside her, and spoken clearly – *they are coming.*

Had she really heard it? And if so, who – or what – did it belong to? And if it was real, wasn't it possible that it was still in her head at that moment?

She aimed her blind eyes at nothing.

'Who are you, and what do you want?' she asked.

She listened carefully.

A light wind howled softly in the mouth of the cave.

Orla sighed. She picked up the clutch of arrows and tied them into a bundle with a stringy palm frond. She lowered herself sideways to the floor, then pushed herself up slowly until she was standing on her fists, arch-backed, with her legs trailing behind her. She rocked her weight from side to side and walked on her fists, with the clutch of arrows gripped tightly in one hand and her knife in the other. She knew each dip, mark, and detail of the cave floor intimately and navigated the smoothest path to her bed.

When she reached the centre of the cave floor, however, she stopped abruptly, struck by a feeling that she was not alone, like an animal that had stumbled too close to a predator. She could not make sense of the feeling because nothing had happened. There had been no sounds or disturbances or anything. But a peculiar shiver had run through her feeling parts, and she sensed a watching presence close by.

She gripped the knife and the clutch of arrows and swallowed. 'Hello …' she whispered to the silence. 'Gadryon?'

She cocked her head in several directions, trying to catch the presence. A moment passed, and her unease mounted. Beads of sweat formed above her lip.

Summoning all her courage, she suddenly demanded, 'Who's there?'

She was comforted by the power in her voice.

The silence remained unmoved by her demand.

She began to feel the strain of her upright position in her shoulders and knuckles and tried to relax by shifting her weight. Then she straightened her back and twisted to face her legs, the movement causing a dull pain in her lower abdomen.

She waited a few moments longer but eventually concluded that she was alone. No person except she and Gadryon knew the secret entrance to Home Cave. If she had sensed some animal, she doubted any could stay as still, silent, and scentless as this.

She continued on her fists towards her bed.

The dull pain she had felt in her lower abdomen followed her. Absently, she wondered whether she had eaten something rotten. But the sensation didn't feel like stomach pain. It was a strange gripping she had never felt before, as though tiny hands were clenching and unclenching further down. She tried to ignore it and hoisted herself into her bed. But the pain followed her there too.

She began to worry that she had been bitten by something... It was too early in the year for the cave spiders, but their venom was lethal. What if the presence she had sensed was a poisonous spider that had bitten her unfeeling legs? And now she was feeling the effects of its poison for the first time as it spread upwards into her feeling half? The idea of it frightened her. If the poison had spread there from her legs, it might reach her heart and kill her.

But the pain did not spread. Instead, the gripping sensation intensified into cramps. She curled up in her bed and grit her teeth against the pain, rocking for comfort, her arm resting across her abdomen.

She wished Gadryon would come back.

She rested in this position for some time, the pain coming in long waves until she smelled something unusual. A sickly-sweet smell that made her think of raw meat. Nervously, she tried to locate the source of the scent, and, to her horror, her hands found a warm wetness between her legs.

It was blood.

But unlike any blood she had ever known. There was clotting in it, like the blood of a long-dead animal, and it smelled like meat turning bad.

A spider had bitten her, and she was going to die.

Heart hammering in panic, she unwrapped the sodden bearskin from her legs. She ran her hands carefully over each part of her unfeeling half to locate any bumps or puncture marks that might confirm her fear. She found none. Her legs were as skinny, smooth, and numb as always.

The irregular bleeding seeped from her soft folds of flesh. It came out slowly and without end. She found it strange that the pain was further inside and not at the flesh, as it was with most bleeding. Something inside was wrong. If the bleeding carried on like this, she would faint before long. She tried not to panic. She cut out a rough rectangle of bearskin with her knife and held it tight to the soft flesh. It would be saturated within minutes. Orla cut out more pieces in readiness, then began to dress her legs again, holding the first rectangle tightly in place.

She wished Gadryon would hurry back.

No, she thought. *Gadryon must not see it. He will say it's an omen from God, a warning or punishment. He understands the ways of Ohrak, while I do not.* Blind as she was, she had difficulty understanding His signs. For Ohrak spoke in dreams or in visions or with blood. Was God angry that she had screamed and brought the soldiers, as Gadryon was? She didn't know what it meant. But it threatened to undo all her hard work to win back his favour.

She had wrapped one leg successfully when she heard a familiar noise beyond the entrance to the cave. A trilling whistle signalling Gadryon's return. The noise usually lifted her spirits, but with one leg exposed, covered in blood, his whistling sent her into a frenzy. She fumbled to lace up her second leg as quickly as she could. As Gadryon entered, she threw a blanket in guilty desperation across her lower half and froze in an unnatural position.

'I've got food,' he announced. 'Two rabbits. But I missed a third and wasted an arrow on it.'

It seemed he was not looking at her and hadn't seen her toss the blanket.

'You've made more,' he said.

'Yes,' she said breathily. 'Eight of them. But I need to blacken them in the fire.'

'Good,' he said, sounding pleased. 'You get the fire going. I'll cook the rabbits! Where's your skinning knife?'

Orla's heart leapt into her throat. Her knife was beneath the blanket.

'Let me skin them!' she said, holding out her hands to take the rabbits. 'You start the fire. You do it better than me.'

Orla sensed her brother's shrug. She felt the bony fur thrust into her hands, but as she tried to pull the rabbits from his grasp, Gadryon tore them away.

'What have you done to your hand?' he asked. 'Have you cut yourself making arrows again?'

Orla's heart sank. She had forgotten to wash the blood from her hands! Her mind raced for an innocent explanation, but her guilt was plain in the hesitation.

'Orla?' said Gadryon.

'I haven't hurt myself,' she said quickly. 'I don't know what happened! I felt something strange and I … I just … I started bleeding.'

Her words sounded absurd, even to herself.

'What do you mean you started bleeding?' asked Gadryon.

Orla felt a shameful heat on her face. She hid her hands beneath the blanket.

'Show me what you've done,' said Gadryon, both concerned and impatient.

Orla shrank. Perversely, she suddenly hoped that a spider had bitten her. That Gadryon would see a bite mark and know it was not her fault.

'It's … it's coming from …' Orla began, but her voice trailed away.

'Show me,' said Gadryon.

Reluctantly, she peeled back the blanket and the sticky rectangle and awaited his judgement. Her shame peaked in the silence. He was forcing her to show him something she didn't want to share. It violated her dignity, though she had no words for such a feeling. And, most humiliating, here was proof that her insides were just as damaged, flawed, and limited as her crippled exterior.

Gadryon covered her legs with the blanket again and sat beside her.

'What happened?' he asked, trying to sound sympathetic. Orla could hear the discomfort in his voice.

'Nothing!' she said, tilting her blind eyes toward him. 'I finished making arrows, and then I felt a pain inside. Then the blood started coming, and it hasn't stopped, and I don't know what it is!'

She could almost hear him thinking.

'Is the pain still there?' he asked.

'Yes,' she said, the acknowledgement making the pain instantly worse.

'And you're sure you didn't cut yourself with the knife or any of these arrows you made?' he said, examining the bundle.

'No!' she said. 'I'm not useless – I'm not a baby! I can look after myself and didn't do anything wrong!'

'There's blood on this arrow, here,' he said.

'That's from my hand when I tested it!'

'So, you did hurt yourself?'

'No!' she said, thumping her fists into her bed of leaves. 'I was testing the arrows on purpose, and one of them cut me – but it was only a tiny drop, and I stopped it straight away! Then the other bleeding started, but I don't know what did it, and it wasn't my fault!'

There was a silence in which Orla could only hear herself panting. 'You don't believe me,' she said.

'I'm trying to understand.'

'Well, don't!' she hissed, moving away. 'You don't believe anything I say anymore! You don't believe me about the voice, and you don't believe me about this! I haven't hurt myself!'

Orla folded her arms and leaned back against the wall. She felt him rise, and then, a moment later, he handed her one of the water flasks.

'Here,' he said. 'Clean your hands.'

Orla poured the cold water on her hands and used a clean rectangle of cloth to wipe away the blood.

'Is this water from the fall in the cave?' asked Gadryon.

Orla nodded but did not turn to face him.

'You shouldn't go down there when I'm not here,' he said. 'It's too narrow. You could get stuck.'

'Is it gone?' asked Orla miserably, splaying her hands and turning them each way.

'Yes,' said Gadryon, who knelt before her and took her hands in his own. They were warm and calloused. Orla heard him take a deep breath. 'I believe you,' he said.

'Then what is it?' she asked. 'I can't stop the bleeding … Is it a sign from God?'

Another silence.

'I think so,' he said at last, 'but … I'm sorry, Orla … I don't … I'm not sure what it means.'

He exhaled sharply and squeezed her hands. She returned the pressure.

'What will we do?' she asked. 'It hurts, and it won't stop.'

'Let me think,' he said, and she heard the fear in his voice. 'Let's eat and see if it eases. If it doesn't … I'll … I'll think of something … don't worry.'

Orla recognised that this, whatever it was, lay beyond the boundaries of her brother's understanding.

She was more afraid than ever.

*

Orla continued to bleed the next day and the next, and the pain did not abate. Gadryon watched her closely. Kept her fed and watered. He was beginning to panic that something beyond his knowledge was terribly wrong. But he kept himself as calm and composed as possible for Orla's sake. He tried to remember anything that might be helpful from his time in the village as a boy. But nothing came to him except a vague memory of a man who had died from bleeding that the Healer couldn't stem.

Ohrak offered no guidance, despite Gadryon's desperate prayers to the glowing ceiling. He worried that God had abandoned him as punishment for abandoning his sister. That Orla was suffering because of his failure.

On the third day of her suffering, his resolution broke. Orla cried continuously, and he decided he could no longer bear it. It was time to take the risk that had been circling in his thoughts, though he dreaded it.

He would not let Orla die.

He rose early on the fourth day and dressed quietly before Orla woke. He explained his plan when she confirmed that the blood had not ceased.

'You want to go to the town?' she asked, her voice almost breaking.

'Yes,' he said, putting his sword in the sheath at his hip. 'It's dangerous, but they'll have Sacred Water at the Consel. Maybe we can stop your bleeding for good.'

'But you could be gone for days!'

'You're coming with me,' he said, fastening her carrier to his back. She opened her mouth to say something, but he continued, 'I'm not leaving you here to die. But I won't risk taking you into the town either. You'll need to wear your winter coat and pack food and water and all your bravery.'

'Gadryon –'

'My plan is to get you within earshot of Leybridge, then we'll find a safe tree with a good canopy for you to climb. You'll wait for me while I sneak into the town alone and get the Sacred Water.'

'But ... but what if they catch you? They'll kill you. It's not worth it.'

'It's the only way.'

'But I'll die if you're caught, you know it! And I don't want you to die either.'

Gadryon knelt and wrapped Orla's winter coat around her shoulders. She had grown a lot in the past year, and her shoulders felt strong as he held them. Sometimes he forgot that she was so strong.

'I need you to trust me,' he said. 'I won't be caught. Ohrak will protect me. And if not, I will fight my way out through the whole army to get back to you if I must. I promise. I will not fail.'

Gadryon watched the conflict on her face. She sat silently for a moment, then fastened her cloak in resigned assent. Gadryon touched her cheek. He lifted her into the carrier.

Orla embraced him tightly from behind, resting her head on his shoulder. 'Thank you,' she whispered.

They set out from the cave. Gadryon had never found the cliff descent less tiresome.

He aimed for the old stream, which he knew would lead him all the way to the river Ley, which carved Leybridge into two parts.

He knew the town from his childhood and tried to conjure an image of it. In his memory, Leybridge was set back from the trees across a vast field and was fortified by high walls on three sides, with watchtowers, bells, and archers. The war between the Nephians and the Krae had intensified since he had last seen it. And it was likely that extra fortifications had been added.

His first problem would be the field. He had no idea how he would cross it without being seen by the watchtowers. If they saw his approach, they would shoot him dead.

The fourth side of the town was protected by the Ley. He would go by the river. Find a quiet bank within the town's walls where he could emerge unseen. But he was unconfident in the water and would be weighed down by his sword.

His plan and resolve grew weaker with each passing step.

Around four miles into their journey, as the stream began to settle into a silent flow, they crossed the invisible line that Gadryon imagined as the boundary of their territory. Orla gripped him and pushed herself up sharply on his shoulders. He stopped.

'What is it?' he said.

'Smoke,' she replied, sniffing at the air. 'I can smell smoke.'

Gadryon sniffed but caught no trace. The wind blew from the west.

'Can you tell the direction?' he asked. 'It could be more soldiers on patrol.'

'No,' said Orla. 'But I can hear something too, I think. Coming from … that way.' She raised a fist and pointed over his right shoulder. 'It sounds like metal on metal. And shouting,' she said.

Gadryon heard nothing. But he trusted Orla's ears the way she trusted his eyes. 'Let me know if it gets any closer,' he said.

He continued toward the town with a little more haste, leaping over fallen trees, pushing through thickets, and hopping through bogs. It felt essential to avoid the streams. To stick to the harsher terrain where they were less likely to encounter other souls.

After many unrelenting miles, he paused to take a swig of water. When he lifted his chin to drink, he saw a strange wooden hut-like structure floating above in the treetops. His stomach fell away as he realised what it was, and he quickly ducked for cover behind the nearest tree.

The town had erected watchtowers in the forest.

Orla touched his ear with a finger, signalling her desire to speak. He tapped her shoulder twice, purposefully, and she remained silent.

Gadryon peered around the tree trunk. The watchtower loomed above the treeline like some forbidding giant with a square wooden head covered in green moss and dots of pale-blue lichen. The aspect of the box that faced him was half-open, like a balcony, and he could see a large bell hanging from the centre of its ceiling. But there was no sign of any movement inside. *Perhaps the watchers are concealed, or sleeping, or absent,* he thought.

His eyes on the tower, he picked up a stone and threw it away from their position. It struck something hollow in the distance, and the noise carried well in the silence.

Nothing happened. Gadryon kept his eyes on the tower and waited. Orla touched his ear again, and he tapped her shoulder twice.

As silently as he could, he lifted Orla from her carrier and set her down on the floor with her back to the trunk. He looked up at the branches and found them suitable for climbing.

'Be as quiet as you can,' he whispered into her ear.

'What are we hiding from?'

'Watchtower,' he said.

She nodded and rested her head against the tree.

'I need you to climb and hide,' said Gadryon. 'I think the watchtower is empty, but I want to make sure.'

'What will you do?'

'I'm going up there,' he said.

Orla nodded again, more to herself, and she pivoted to face the tree and began climbing with Gadryon's help. She rose smoothly, each arm able to bear her body weight easily.

Once his sister was out of sight, Gadryon turned his attention to the tower. It was wedged between three treetops, swaying innocently with the breeze. He moved toward it, keeping low between tree trunks. There was a hatch on the watchtower's underside, through which the watchers must gain entry. And a rope dangled in a grey line from the hatch to the forest floor.

Gadryon pulled out his knife and held the blade between his teeth. He took his bow from across his chest and nocked an arrow, then moved cautiously to the foot of the rope, keeping his bow half-drawn. The rope prickled his hand. He tugged it to test its strength.

He tied his bow to the bottom of the rope and pulled himself upward, keeping his eyes on the underside of the watchtower, daring the hatch to open.

At the top, he found a knot in the rope that he could use to push himself through the trapdoor. He gave the door a tiny push to test its resistance. It was loose.

Gadryon took a breath, the knife still between his teeth. Then he pushed hard with both feet against the rope knot and launched himself into the tower.

It was empty.

He thanked Ohrak and pulled up his bow.

The tower offered a panoramic view of the forest for miles. To the north, he could see the Bannebar Mountains, blue and hazy in the distance. To the east, he thought he could see the flat grey line of the ocean. And to the west, he saw other towers jutting above the trees but couldn't discern whether they were occupied. Finally, he turned south to look at the town of Leybridge. It stood around a mile away and was laid out almost exactly as he remembered, though perhaps a little smaller. He could see the dots of soldiers patrolling the ramparts. Smoke furled from chimneys. It was a well-armed fortress that forbade welcome to the north. And Gadryon meant to break inside.

He descended from the tower and returned to the tree where Orla was hidden. She dropped into his arms, and he took her to the tower.

'You'll be safe in here,' he told her. 'Pull the rope up once I'm gone so nobody can find you.'

'What will you do?'

'Never mind me, I'll look after myself,' he said. 'All I need is for you to stay here and stay calm. Can you do that?'

'Yes,' she said, and he believed her.

'I need you to do something else,' he said. 'In two hours, the sun will set. Will you be able to feel the difference?'

'Yes.'

'Good. Once the sun has set, I want you to ring this bell as hard as you can for as long as you dare.' Gadryon guided her hand to the short rope beneath the clapper. 'Can you do that?' he asked.

'What will happen?'

'Hopefully, the Leybridge army will come out, expecting a Krae attack. If they do, I'll use them as cover to slip through the gate.'

'But won't someone come looking for me once they realise it's a false signal?' she asked.

'They might,' said Gadryon, 'but by the time they realise there's no attack, we'll be halfway home.'

Orla took a breath to steel herself and nodded, not daring to ask what she should do if he didn't return. 'Two hours,' she confirmed.

They embraced for a moment and squeezed tight.

Gadryon kissed Orla's forehead and disappeared down the rope.

CHAPTER 18

The Bell

Elchora stood atop the northeast tower, sixty feet up, watching the red sunset over the Urden. She drummed her heels and blew into cupped hands. But the cold was deep in her bones.

A month of night watch duty had seemed a lenient punishment for returning late from the forest with Fyvern. But after two weeks of dull, freezing nights, she might have preferred the searing agony of Maldon's whip. At least then, she could have begun her search for the wild boy, whose existence she had kept decidedly secret. Partly because Fyvern had quickly spun his own tale to account for his injuries; a heroic legend concerning a brawl with a wild boar, and partly because Elchora could scarcely believe the boy's existence herself.

She looked out over the darkening treetops.

He was out there at that very moment. Somewhere.

With a great shivering yawn, she turned her attention to the north field, a quarter mile of grass littered with torches like flaming pins on a map. Soon their flickering orange glow would be all that remained in the darkness. And her fellow Ablemen worked hastily in readiness, pushing barrow carts, and driving fresh stakes into the ground.

The daylight was fading.

Elchora watched the furthest pair of Ablemen. It had fascinated her each night, hearing a hammer strike a few seconds after seeing the blow. But soon, the spectacle would be over, and the others could retire to a hot meal and warm beds.

Just then, the distant Ablemen froze, one man holding the hammer, the other bracing the torch. They turned their attention to the line of trees. After a few seconds, the man bracing the torch pulled it from the ground and wandered toward the source of the disturbance. He disappeared among the trees.

131

Suddenly, the torchlight arced quickly, unseen, as though the torchbearer was swatting a fly. The man holding the hammer raced over and vanished into the shadows. Elchora stared at the now-motionless flame, heart racing, all vestiges of cold forgotten.

Nothing happened for several minutes. Then, the torchlight moved, and one of the men stepped out from the forest alone, his face now hooded.

He dug the flame into the ground and strode directly for the barrow cart. He lifted it onto its wheel and steered it toward the city gate.

'Oi!' Elchora yelled, leaning halfway out of the tower. But the hooded figure was too far away to hear. He kept pushing the cart, gathering pace.

Elchora spun and raced down the spiral steps, ricocheting along the outer wall. She had no idea what she had seen, but she would intercept the man and find out. She passed the rampart wall where another guard stood sentry.

'Take my post!' she ordered without stopping.

The watchman leered back, grinning.

'Piss on the floor, princess,' he called. 'Not my fault you ain't got a dick.'

Elchora ignored him and sped down the next flight of stairs. She turned right in the courtyard and pelted for the north gate.

The guards were not at their post. The gate was open. Breathless, she scanned the field for the man pushing the barrow cart, but he was nowhere to be seen. She ducked inside the guard room and saw the feet of a body beneath the table.

Her suspicion compounded into dread.

She had no time to check on her fellow soldier. She had to raise the alarm. Find the intruder.

But there was no need to raise the alarm. Outside the wall, a bell was ringing.

The courtyard burst into life seconds later. Shouts took up from the ramparts above. Men poured from doorways, racing for the armoury.

A louder bell rang in the city.

The Krae were coming.

Elchora knew a second of perfect indecision; follow the bell's command or apprehend the intruder. She made her choice and pushed through the oncoming tide of bodies.

A Kraeling was already inside. She must kill it before it enacted its plan.

She wove through the drilled ranks of soldiers, guessing desperately which way the Kraeling might have gone. She turned one corner and another, and her heart leapt as she spotted an abandoned barrow cart at the entrance to a narrow, fenced alley. She climbed onto the cart and hoisted herself carefully over the spiked fence, as the Kraeling must have done.

But what could it be up to down here?

The alley cut a path between the Consel and the grain store towards the rear of the armoury. A thousand ideas ran through Elchora's head at once.

It was going to burn down the grain store.

It would ignite the dry powder stock while the soldiers donned their armour.

It would rain destruction from within while its brothers attacked from without.

She drew her sword and raced along the alley, all her senses heightened. The bell reverberated relentlessly, and beneath the chimes came the cries of soldiers. Elchora pressed on.

A door to her right was a few inches ajar, its wood splintered at the handle. A crossbow rested neatly at an angle against the outer wall. Elchora frowned through her sweat.

Why would the Kraeling target an empty Consel?

She sheathed her sword, picked up the crossbow, swallowed, and entered the darkness.

The scent of honey candles filled her nose as the chaos outside dimmed. She blinked, holding the crossbow at her shoulder, pivoting in all directions, ready for the creature's ambush. As her senses adjusted, she heard the stream flowing along the sacred ground and saw the branches of the Elder tree against the open sky.

A hooded, armour-clad figure knelt at the base of the tree, its forehead resting against the trunk. Elchora tiptoed forward, eyes alert for any misdirection. She heard the figure's soft whisper, and two facts registered simultaneously. The man's skin was not silver; Elchora could see something clutched in a human hand, and she understood the words the stranger whispered. This was no Kraeling.

'Don't move!' she barked.

The stranger stiffened but obeyed.

'Keep your hands above your head and stand up slowly. I have a bolt aimed at your heart, and that armour won't help you at this range.'

The stranger stood, one hand splayed in the air, the other still clutching the unknown object.

'Turn around,' Elchora ordered.

The stranger obeyed again, turning slowly on the spot.

Two mouths fell open in unison, and four eyes widened as the face that had preoccupied Elchora's thoughts for two weeks stared back at her in equal astonishment.

The boy from the Urden, dressed in the garb of an Ableman.

'You,' she uttered in disbelief. She tightened her grip on the crossbow and took half a step forward. 'You're fighting for the Krae?'

The boy frowned but said nothing.

'You brought them to our gates?' Elchora demanded, cocking her head in the general direction of the war bell.

The boy's posture relaxed a fraction.

'It's not an attack,' he said softly. 'The bell is false.'

'What do you mean!' Elchora snapped, adjusting her aim.

'The Krae are not here! It's not an attack … It's just a distraction.'

'I don't understand! Tell me why you're here!'

The boy swallowed and lowered his arms slowly.

'I needed Ohrak's help,' he said ashamedly, displaying the bottle in his hand. 'Someone is very sick.'

Elchora glanced from the boy to the bottle and back.

'You sounded the war bell so that you could steal *Sacred Water*?'

'Yes,' said the boy, unable to meet her eyes. 'Like you used in the forest.'

Elchora lowered the crossbow but did not slacken her grip. The boy's excuse was so absurd yet sincere that she believed it wholeheartedly at once. And as though to bolster his claim, the war bell chimed its final note.

But as its last note faded, another sound took prominence. A distant horn. And inhuman battle cries.

Elchora cocked her head questioningly. She watched the boy's face as it crumpled into a mask of sheer terror.

'*No!*' he whispered in horror.

And before Elchora could lift the crossbow an inch, the boy had barged her to the ground, thundering toward the door.

The Krae were indeed at the gate.

CHAPTER 19

The Krae

Orla sat rigid with fear, clutching her knife in both hands, an icy coldness pouring down her spine. She was alone and terrified, with no idea what to do.

Somewhere in the distance, a bell had started ringing.

It was not her signal. The two hours had not passed, and she had not dared move since Gadryon had descended the rope. But a bell was ringing, which meant that something had happened.

They had caught Gadryon. She knew it.

She tried to resist the evil thoughts that flooded her mind. She tried to calm herself and to think. Maybe the bell meant something innocent – a call to feast, like in the stories.

But a second bell joined the first, deeper, louder, coming from the town's direction, mingled with the distant whinny of horses. And then suddenly, much closer, Orla heard footsteps. Hundreds of them. Half running, shaking the watchtower. And a horn blew beneath her, standing her hair on end. Then a thousand voices answered the horn's call, a roar of hatred. A sea of footsteps passing underneath her, gathering pace.

The first bell stopped ringing, and Orla heard the whistle of arrows and a distant thud. Then more shouting and the sound of metal hitting metal. A man screamed, and then the screaming stopped abruptly.

Orla felt her tower begin to shake more violently, and her heart plunged into ice-cold water. Inside the noise of footsteps and screaming and the bell clanging, she heard a faint scraping, grunting noise, getting louder. Closer. And she understood that someone, or some*thing*, was making its way up the tower.

She had forgotten to pull up the rope!

She backed herself into the furthest corner from the sound. Her hand found the puddle of warm wetness where she had urinated. The scraping and grunting were very loud now, and she could hear the climber breathing excitedly.

She gripped her knife, begged Ohrak to protect her brother, and, summoning all the bravery in the world, prepared to fight the creature she knew was coming to kill her.

With a *stomp* that shook the boards beneath her, someone jumped over the tower's balcony and landed hard inside.

There was a small silence. Then the terrible, growling voice of a Kraeling spoke. *'Geftoller kra?'* it demanded. *'Mittay ramma ift grissem kra!'*

Orla said nothing. Though she could not have spoken anyway. She clutched the knife in a balled fist behind her back, ready to stab when the creature presented a target.

'Eikhol grissem ramma kolba,' it said, *'ift kra!'*

Orla sensed the creature lean in closer. It sniffed, turned its head toward her urine, and then turned back to inspect her face. By its breath, she tried to calculate where its throat must be and waited for her moment.

Just a little closer.

She felt the Kraeling step away from her and heard it fumbling with something, but she could not determine what it was doing. She kept herself coiled like a snake, ready to strike. And waited.

She jolted as something heavy landed in her lap.

'Wahnei,' said the Kraeling. Then it climbed out from the tower, and its noises disappeared into the sounds of its kind.

Orla remained petrified for a long time, trying to still her pounding heart and release the tension that gripped her, to loosen her hold on the knife.

Tentatively, she felt the item the Kraeling had thrown at her with her free hand. It was coarse and oddly weighted; a sewn leather pouch filled with liquid and stoppered by a wooden plug. She took out the stopper and sniffed.

Water.

A skin of water.

She stoppered it, tossed it aside, and then covered her ears against the horns, bell chimes, and voices. She prayed for Gadryon's life.

Water, she thought.

Wahnei.

*

Gadryon sped through the empty streets toward the north wall, Elchora Farrow on his heels.

'Wait!' she called.

But he paid no heed. He had to get to Orla.

Archers lined the ramparts, their backs facing the courtyard. At the gate, two guards hauled on a vertical chain inside a groove, pulling the portcullis closed until the pointed teeth sank into the cobbled floor.

'Open the gate!' Gadryon called.

The guards looked at each other in spent confusion.

'Open the gate!' Elchora echoed from somewhere behind.

The guards recognised Gadryon's pursuer.

'You're *fucking* late, Farrow!' one chided as the other began hauling the chain in the opposite direction. 'Where's ye bloody armour, girl? An' yours too, lad?'

Gadryon slowed his run as the teeth lifted. He dropped and rolled beneath them once they parted from the floor.

Elchora tossed the crossbow to the idle man and plucked two swords from a barrel before ducking under the portcullis at a run.

Gadryon sprang to his feet to fight her. But she slid to a halt a few feet away and stared at him.

'Tell me you're not with the Krae,' she said, pointing a sword at his chest.

Gadryon spat, ready to charge at her for this delay. But his disgust had won her over. She threw him a sword.

'With me!' she said, running past him.

They crossed the moat bridge together and slipped into the ranks of armoured backs. The Leybridge army stood in organised lines beneath flapping pennants. A shield wall up front, pikemen behind, rows of infantry flanked by cavalry, and archers on the wall. Three men on horseback sat in the epicentre, staring grim-faced over the field of torches.

The horde of Krae outnumbered the trees. A horizon of unbroken white in the darkness, like a solid fog of death. They shrieked and howled and clubbed their crude weapons on wooden shields.

'We should retreat inside the walls,' said the rider on the right. 'There's too many of them.'

'It's too late for that,' said the tall man in the centre, surprisingly calm. 'We make our stand tonight … Archers ready.'

'*Archers ready!*' bellowed the bald man on the left.

The call echoed from above.

'Loose when they charge, Commander,' said the tall man. 'And keep the shield wall at all costs.'

'Yes, milord,' growled the bald man. Then he raised his voice. 'Men of Leybridge, show these cunts your mettle!'

'Oorah!' bellowed the soldiers as one.

In response, the Kraelings charged like an avalanche. They swept the torches underfoot as they ran, bringing a wall of darkness.

'*Loose!*' called the bald man.

A volley of arrows whistled through the night. Gadryon saw many Kraelings spin and fall, trampled by their kin. But it made no difference to the rushing mass.

'*Hold the line!*' called the bald Commander.

The shield wall braced for impact. The pikemen readied their lances. Another volley of arrows flocked overhead.

The Krae smashed into the shields, forcing the line backwards by a whole yard. But the line recovered and held firm under the onslaught as the pikemen skewered the silver bodies from above.

Gadryon searched for a way through the madness. He had to get to Orla. He cursed his stupidity for rushing through the gate. He could have swum upriver and skirted the Krae entirely.

Now he was trapped.

'No!' bellowed a voice over the clattering. And Gadryon was disturbed to see the fear on the tall man's face. He followed his gaze and saw what had unnerved him. The Krae horde had parted to make way for a battering ram. A felled tree sharpened to a point, carried by two rows of huge Kraelings. And the largest Kraeling, wearing a horned skull as a helmet, crouched atop the ram, commanding his creatures forward with a giant club.

The tree smashed through the wall. Shields splintered. Men flew backwards. And the Kraeling king flew across the line.

It was a massacre.

The Kraelings funnelled through the gap and swamped the soldiers holding shields. The mud churned in the chaos, swallowing bodies under feet, drowning screams of terror. The pikemen lasted only a second longer before they too were devoured by the mob of hatred.

'*Second line!*' called the bald man. '*New colours! Form a second line, you useless cunts!*'

Elchora roared forward at the command, and Gadryon followed.

A second line of shields locked together. And the Krae came again, wilder than before. Jubilant in their bloodlust. The white tide smashed into the shields. The ram withdrew for a second assault.

As the Krae hauled the tree backwards, their lines parted to make room, and Gadryon saw his path to the trees.

'*Take them out!*' bellowed the tall man to the archers above. Arrows flew at the Kraelings wielding the tree. Several collapsed under the barrage, and the tree squelched into the ground, crushing legs and feet. But the Krae rallied quickly under the shouts of their huge, bloodied leader. Silver bodies swarmed the tree again, this time covered by shields. They raised their weapon and retreated, ready to batter the Leybridge wall.

Gadryon saw his opening and acted.

He rolled over the locked shields and ran at the gap.

A Kraeling darted to intercept him, snarling hungrily. But Gadryon swivelled and decapitated it. And its body kept running into the wall of shields.

A spear sailed through Gadryon's hair, and the thrower came after it, bone dagger in a white fist. Gadryon lunged to meet the creature. His sword disappeared into the veiny, white chest and emerged crimson-black on the far side.

Many Kraelings converged on him, screeching in rage. The gap to the trees closed. He *must* get to Orla. He ducked, pushed, sliced, stabbed, and roared his lungs raw. He didn't know if he was wounded. He didn't care. He was a mindless beast of adrenaline. A flashing sword of pure survival and hatred. Gutting, cleaving, severing, slaughtering.

Gadryon found himself on a pile of wet, silver corpses in the melee. He had cut a path halfway through the horde. The Krae had backed off to encircle him, many wearing expressions akin to fear.

The larger Kraelings dropped the ram to stampede as a unit. But Gadryon was somewhere else. Somewhere far beyond his human element. On some uncharted plateau of instinct.

He dispatched each new attacker with ease. With venom.

And with each blow, he heard a cheer from the Leybridge army, rising in pitch until their voices screamed in warning.

Gadryon ducked as the massive club whooshed overhead. The Kraeling king, with its horned skull helmet, glared down at him in revulsion. It raised a stomping boot, but Gadryon rolled away before the mud squelched, and in the same motion, his hands found the shaft of a buried pike.

He exaggerated his roll and lifted the submerged spear at an angle.

It skewered the inner thigh of the oncoming Kraeling, who fell to his knee in sharp agony, dropping his club. Its black eyes met Gadryon's for a split second before Gadryon cut off its head.

The circle of fear widened as the Krae backed off in awestruck horror. In their hesitation, the Leybridge army charged.

Caught unawares, some Kraelings swivelled to meet them. But too few to dam the rush of metal. The soldiers pierced the horde through its heart, scattering the Kraeling forces like a snowplough.

Silver streaks raced to the forest in droves, yowling, until the Krae tide retreated like the foam of a wave.

Gadryon joined the jubilant Leybridge pursuit, scanning the line of trees.

He saw the cluster of trees where Orla was hiding. He was thirty feet from the forest.

Twenty.

Ten.

But a hand clapped his shoulder, making him spin. Then another gripped the back of his neck. He turned to face his next opponent, when many hands engulfed him, hoisting him into the air. He thrashed and writhed in their collective grip, but the hands held firm, carrying and tossing him with great, victorious cheers.

No!

He craned his neck toward the forest, reaching out. It receded into darkness as the crowd bore him inside the city wall.

CHAPTER 20

Victory

The air in the Feast Hall trembled with noise. The raucous laughter of victorious soldiers and the scraping of benches across flagstone. Cups hammered tables while serving maids, those less agile – or more agreeable – shrieked as they were taken into arms and groped for sport. Up on the dais, musicians were bent to their instruments, lost in the joy of their art. Those near enough to hear them joined them in drunken song, unintelligible but with absolute abandon.

Victor Maldon pushed through the herd of warm bodies, making his way to his seat at the officers table. In passing, he barged the shoulder of a tall, square-jawed soldier, an archer, causing the man to spill his beer over two others. The man whirled around in a rage, fist drawn back, but he wilted when he saw who had nudged him. Even in his complete intoxication, his face slackened, eyes widened, and his drawn fist fell to his forehead in a clumsy salute. Maldon glowered at him for a moment, then turned his gaze purposefully to stare into the eyes of his drenched companions. Both men swallowed, their cups frozen partway to their mouths. After several seconds, Maldon suddenly barked a laugh, causing all three to flinch. Another second passed before hesitant smiles broke out on their faces, and all three joined Maldon's laughter in relief.

At the officers table, his plate of half-finished chicken and his full goblet of ale sat exactly as he had left them. He tore into both with deep satisfaction, the overspill of ale dampening his beard. Every succulent morsel danced on his palette. A sure sign that Ohrak favoured their victory.

But that idiot New Colour had almost cost them everything. Cost them the city, their lives, the battle, the entire war! Abandoning the shield wall to attack of his own will? Maldon had never witnessed such reckless insubordination. Had one of his own men broken ranks like that, he would have ordered his spearmen to impale the bastard. True, the New

Colour had fought well. Better than well. Lord Farrow must have trained the boy personally.

As though Maldon's thoughts had summoned him, the cripple got to his feet, and an eager silence slowly descended upon the hall. All eyes turned to the lord, who beamed down at his subjects from the high table.

'To victory!' he exclaimed, raising his cup.

A deafening cheer erupted as sloshing cups were thrust aloft. Then another silence followed as each soldier took their drink.

In the quiet, Lord Farrow's expression became stony and sober. 'To our fallen brothers,' he said.

A dull echo of the words went up in broken unison. Maldon heard individual names in the chant, and each man took a longer draught than before. Lord Farrow scanned the hall, taking everyone in.

'To all of you,' he said heartily. 'And the man of the hour!' He raised his goblet in salute to the far corner, where the reckless boy sat surrounded by an entourage of fawning infantrymen.

Fists pounded on tables as all eyes turned to look at the lucky fool who had broken rank and survived his own stupidity. The boy seemed terrified in the glare of such attention. He cast around furtively for an escape, like a cornered rabbit. Maldon began to chuckle, but his mirth died when he saw who was sitting at the boy's shoulder, close enough to be on his lap.

The girl. Elchora.

Maldon's blood boiled in his limbs. Hot bile seared his stomach.

That little slut.

'Commander Maldon?' said Brigg as Lord Farrow resumed his seat and the general hubbub returned. 'Are you all right?'

'What!' Maldon shot back.

Brigg looked at him with a raised eyebrow.

'Are you wounded?' he asked. 'You look pale.'

Maldon wiped his bald pate and flicked his sweat on the floor.

'No,' he said, patting his chest with an angry fist. 'Piece of chicken went down the wrong fucking way.'

Brigg nodded with a grin. 'Imagine that,' he said, eyes clouded with mead. 'You survive a battle against five thousand Krae, only to choke to death on a chicken bone!'

Maldon pointedly refused to laugh. Eventually, Brigg's smile faded. He turned away to resume his conversation with the men to his left. Maldon looked back at Elchora and the boy.

The boy sat with his back to the wall, pinned in place by a group of men who seemed to be re-enacting the boy's beheading of the giant

Kraeling. Elchora was squashed into him so closely that they might have been a single body with two heads. Both looked nervous and distracted, not listening to the men around them. Something conspiratorial between them.

Maldon's eyes swam dangerously as the burning hatred rose from the pit of his stomach. He stood and picked up his dinner knife, the hall blurring around him. He could reach them in three bounds if he dived across the heads and shoulders. He was about to climb onto his table when a figure blocked his path.

'Commander Maldon,' said a distant voice, 'I must speak with you.'

Maldon only had eyes for the evil temptress across the room, who sat there so overtly, mocking him. She sat so close to the boy that he could slit both throats with one slash.

'Commander Maldon!' said the voice, louder this time.

He dragged his eyes away from the pair to see who desired to be his third victim. Another New Colour was staring at him down the length of a crooked nose. It was Almys Fyvern, heir to the Drangonfort of Eddis. His expression was urgent and secretive, and he only half balked when he saw the murder in Maldon's eyes.

'I must speak with you, sir,' he said, 'in private. It's about the soldier who charged the Krae.'

Maldon turned his eyes back to the boy as Fyvern spoke. He was getting to his feet, as was Elchora. They were attempting to leave together.

'What about him?' snarled Maldon, gripping the handle of his knife, his eyes fixed on the departing lovers.

'He's not from Leybridge,' said Fyvern. 'He's not one of us! He came from the forest!'

Maldon surveyed the New Colour from head to toe. 'What are you talking about?' he demanded.

'He's wearing the armour of a New Colour,' said Fyvern. 'But do you recognise him?'

'This might surprise an entitled little shit like you,' said Maldon, 'but I don't tend to memorise the face of every cunt that worms his way into our bottom ranks. Do you hear me? He's not one of mine. I know that much, else he'd be dead. He must be one of the Augur's men.'

Fyvern sucked in his lips apologetically and gave his head a vigorous shake. 'No, sir, he is not!' he whispered. 'I beseech you; that boy is not from Leybridge at all. He lives in the forest. Somewhere far to the northeast in the Urden. I know it. I've seen him before. He is wild, sir. And he wears our colours falsely!'

Maldon frowned, trying to make sense of this. He looked over Fyvern's shoulder to locate the boy, but he and the slut were nowhere to be seen. They had slipped away together. Maldon gripped Fyvern's solid upper arm and dragged him through the singing, swaying crowd toward the high table, where Lord Farrow and Volsgaard were hunched in conversation. They broke apart as Maldon approached.

'Commander Maldon,' said Volsgaard with a smirk. 'Allow me to commend you for your fine work on the battlefield. Your men held the line fearlessly under the circumstances. It was a hellish onslaught, and you faced it with true bravery!'

Maldon let the insult slide. He wanted the truth quickly.

'Thank you, my lord,' he said contemptuously. 'And what did you make of my soldier? The boy who broke the line?'

Volsgaard's smirk faltered. Lord Farrow chimed across him with a watery smile.

'We were just discussing him, Commander,' he said. 'You've done a fine job with his training! Most excellent indeed. I've not seen swordsmanship that proficient since I witnessed King Markos win the throne from his father. The boy is a marvel. What's his name?'

Maldon stepped aside and pulled Fyvern into his position before the high table. A crease appeared between Lord Farrow's eyebrows. 'Tell them,' said Maldon, feeling a cold excitement soothe his anger. His murder of the boy would not only be legal but warranted. 'Tell them what you told me.'

The New Colour took a breath through his long nose and told Lord Farrow the truth.

'Why didn't you report this sighting?' asked Volsgaard when the boy had finished. Fyvern's cheeks turned a faint shade of pink. He was about to answer when Lord Farrow leant forward with a ravenous gleam in his eyes.

'You said he comes from the forest?' he asked.

'Yes, my lord,' said Fyvern.

Lord Farrow and the Augur exchanged a quick glance. They pushed back their chairs and stood together.

'Bring him to me,' said Lord Farrow severely. 'To my chambers. At once.'

'Gladly, my lord,' slurred Maldon.

Still clutching the knife, he turned and ploughed into the heaving crowd, Fyvern following closely at his back.

'With me!' he bellowed into the ears of every sober man he passed.

By the time he threw open the doors of the feast hall, a gang of a dozen confused men marched in his wake.

With a thrill, he wondered what the bitch would think when she found out what this boy was. When she would see him lashed to death by his, Maldon's, hand. She would love him again. He could feel it.

He was going to enjoy this.

CHAPTER 21

The Girl

Orla clutched herself on the floor of the swaying watchtower, shivering. Gadryon was dead. He must be. He would never leave her alone like this. Not ever.

The pains in her abdomen had worsened.

She swallowed the dry ball that inched its way up her throat, determined not to cry. Gadryon wouldn't cry. He would think and form a plan. He would know exactly what to do.

But what could she do?

She could lower herself from this tower, yes, but then, where would she land? Her brother had carried her the whole way here, and she was miles from the safety of Home Cave, with no idea in which direction it lay. And even if she got home safely, evading the predators and Kraelings that would rip her to shreds, what then? How long could she honestly survive on her own?

Her lower belly throbbed.

This had always been her greatest fear. To lose Gadryon and confront the reality of her weak, crippled body. In the past, when she had imagined this moment, she had known so clearly that she would not hesitate. She would not allow herself to die slowly of thirst and hunger. She would decide her own fate. Vaguely, that had always meant throwing herself from the ledge of Home Cave. To feel the final rush of wind on her face before meeting the jagged rocks below. She doubted whether this tree was high enough, and she had no intention of suffering.

With trepidation, she groped for the knife beside her and ran a finger along the flat side of the cold metal blade. It was long. Long enough to reach her brain if she pushed it upward from beneath her chin … or was it? Would it be less painful – quicker – to drag it across her throat?

The thought made the skin on her throat prickle. She threw the knife across the wooden box. It clattered loudly, and Orla backed away from it, pressing herself against the watchtower wall, breathing hard.

Now that the moment had come, she understood that thinking such things was far easier than acting upon them.

Ohrak, help me, she thought.

A strong gust of wind shook the trees bound to the watchtower. Orla slid to the edge of the trapdoor. The wind stopped as abruptly as it had come, and the trees righted themselves, trunks creaking.

She heard a voice.

At first, she wondered whether the noise was simply some trick of the creaking trees. Then she heard it again.

Someone was talking nearby.

She cocked her head, listening hard. The voice was speaking too faintly to hear any words, but she could tell by the rhythm that the speaker was human, not Krae. She tried not to breathe and listened. Her heart pounded in her ears.

'… mber your promise. Not a word,' said the voice in a barely audible whisper.

Silence.

A surging wave of relief shuddered through her as the most beautiful sound in the world rose up from far below – Gadryon's two-tone whistle.

He was alive!

The whistle sounded again, louder, threatening to burst her heart.

Fumbling, Orla ripped open the trapdoor. She poked her head through the gap but withdrew it with a violent jerk.

Wait, she thought. Something wasn't right. If Gadryon was below, who was he talking to?

'Orla!' came a harsh whisper. 'Orla, it's me! I'm back!'

She put her mouth as close to the hole as she dared.

'Gadryon?' she whimpered.

There was a slight pause.

'Yes,' said Gadryon, and she heard her brother's voice plainly.

'Are you … are you alone?' she asked.

Another pause. Longer this time. 'I've brought someone,' he said in a strange voice. 'Someone who can help you.'

Orla didn't move. Gadryon had always said that the townspeople were just as dangerous as the Krae. More so. Because cripples were an abomination to Ohrak. And they would kill Orla on sight. Was someone holding a knife to his throat? Is that why his voice sounded so strange?

'Orla, come down, quickly!' said Gadryon. 'Nobody is going to hurt you, I promise!'

With a deep breath, Orla rolled her body over the gap, holding herself in place with her hands.

'Fall,' said Gadryon.

She huffed, then let herself drop through the square door and swivelled in mid-air so that her back would meet the ground first. A second later, obviously falling from a greater height than she had expected, she felt Gadryon's strong arms catch her with his usual ease. However, he did not swing her around to his back but kept her in his arms like a baby.

'Are you all right?' he asked, touching her head with his own.

'I thought you were dead,' she whispered, uncomfortably aware that another human was nearby, hearing her speak.

It felt wrong. She buried her head into her brother's comforting, hard chest. He held her so tightly that it hurt, but she said nothing.

'This is my sister, Orla,' he said, speaking to the stranger.

Orla waited in silence to gauge how close the stranger was standing.

'Your sister?' asked a voice ten feet away. It was higher than Gadryon's, like her own, and softer.

'Yes,' said Gadryon breathlessly. 'She's hurt, or poisoned, or – I don't know! But I can't stop the bleeding.'

Another silence fell, save for the wind in the trees above.

'Elchora, please,' said Gadryon.

Orla heard a slow intake of breath, followed by a short, sharp exhale.

'Where is she bleeding?' said the voice.

Gadryon shifted his weight uncomfortably, and Orla felt an impulse she had never felt before. It was her blood. She didn't want this stranger to know about it.

'From between her legs,' said Gadryon. 'It's clotted and hasn't stopped since it started three days ago.'

The stranger cleared her throat.

'I know what this is,' she said. 'It … it might be best if Orla and I discuss this alone.'

Orla gripped Gadryon tighter than ever, shielding her face from the stranger. Gadryon's voice was firm.

'No,' he said. 'Whatever medicine you have, you will give it to me.'

'She doesn't need medicine,' said the voice. 'If the blood is coming from the hole between her legs, it's normal. It happens to all women around once a month.'

Orla felt Gadryon's discomfort in his shifting.

'It will go away?' he asked.

'Yes. But it will return. Every few weeks. But it won't do any harm, I promise … she'll just have to endure the discomfort.'

The last words were uttered with a weary resentment.

Gadryon's grip relaxed.

'Thank you,' he said. 'What … what should I do about the blood?'

The voice sighed. 'Let it flow,' she said. 'It can be uncomfortable, but it helps to keep a length of rabbit fur in place … to absorb it. I … I wear them when I bleed.'

Gadryon's heart began to pound harder in his chest. Orla could feel the blood rushing through him. He swallowed.

Abruptly, Gadryon lifted Orla over his head and slotted her into the carrier on his back. She buried her face in the familiar smell of his bearskin.

'Thank you,' he said again.

The stranger said nothing.

Gadryon turned and began to walk away. His feet crunched on the forest floor.

'Gadryon,' called the voice from far behind.

Orla felt her brother freeze.

'It's Gadryon, isn't it? Your name.'

Without another word, Gadryon sprinted into the forest as fast as he had ever moved. Orla clung to him as tightly as she could.

They were going home.

CHAPTER 22

Gadryon

Elchora stayed beneath the watchtower for a long time, staring into the ranks of trees in the direction the boy – Gadryon – had disappeared. A cold drizzle blew at her back and into the forest, stinging her neck and hands.

The night's events seemed like a dream. The battle. Their victory. The return of the boy and his slaughter of the Krae. Elchora had watched him in awe, the sheer spectacle of his ability etched in her memory.

But it had not been a dream. Her injuries attested plainly to that fact. The muscles burned in her shoulder from its efforts in the phalanx. Images from the battle flashed in her mind. Too vivid for any dream. Slick mud swallowing the feet of the front line as the wall was pushed back inch by inch. The barbaric weapons raining fury on the locked shields. And the projectiles tossed over the line; stones, arrows, crude daggers carved from bone, and once, the severed head of a soldier. She could see the Krae battering ram, the blackened trunk of a fallen tree. Blunt but effective. A weapon that none would have credited the animals capable of conceiving. Proof that her father had been right not to underestimate them. She remembered her primal fear as the Krae had pierced through the first wall and stampeded over those poor men, drowning many in the mud.

Then she recalled, once again, Gadryon rolling over the shields, sword drawn, in what had seemed a fit of madness. But she understood now. She knew why he had acted, though she could not believe it. He hadn't crossed the line out of stupidity or for glory. His sister had been in danger beyond, and he had promised to keep her safe.

His sister, she thought, her frown deepening. *It can't be true.*

She turned to look at the field that was still littered with the dead. A dozen Ablemen ushered horse-drawn flatbeds through the quagmire, some collecting the human corpses for burning, others piling up the

Kraelings for the pikes. Suddenly, the Ablemen looked over their shoulders at the Leybridge wall as the drawbridge fell across the moat, and a dozen horsemen wielding torches thundered across it, riding out at a canter.

Elchora's heart skipped a beat.

Even from a quarter-mile distance in the weak morning light, she could distinguish the barrel-like body under the eggshell head of Victor Maldon. He leaned forward as his horse ran, leading the charge. He steered them to the left, avoiding the worst of the scarred ground, then brought them around in a graceful arc until the line aimed straight at Elchora. Victor pointed at her over his mare's neck, kicking it into a gallop.

Elchora stood her ground, puzzled. The scattered Ablemen watched the advance. Victor wouldn't dare do her any harm while there were witnesses around. But as the riders drew closer in the semi-darkness, her urge to run elevated. She glimpsed an arrogant face between bouncing curtains of parted hair, riding close behind the leader.

A shiver ran through Elchora that had nothing to do with the icy drizzle.

Fyvern had told Victor about Gadryon.

She prepared herself for the Commander's wrath, keeping her face defiant as Victor pulled his mare short of running her down. The horse skidded, momentarily lifting its front hooves.

Maldon's forehead was forked with bulging veins. He scowled down at her, nostrils flared, his ginger beard bent in the wind.

'Where is he?' he demanded in a growl as his followers arrived behind him, fanning out at either side. Elchora didn't know their names but recognised them as Maldon's devotees.

'Where's who?' she said, trying to sound innocent.

Maldon tugged on the white mare's reins and drew up alongside her. Elchora had no warning before his boot slammed downward with all his might into her face with a hot, splitting crunch. She crumpled to her knees, gasping for air through the shock, as the intense heat seared outward from her splintered nose and a thick torrent of blood washed down her throat. She keeled over toward her shoulder, hitting the ground sideways while clutching at her face with trembling fingers, coughing dark globules of blood into the wet mud.

Distantly, her head ringing, Elchora heard Maldon dismount with a squelch. He lifted her from the ground by her hair, each strand a piercing needle. Her screaming burned her face more fiercely. She stared up at Maldon's outline through watery eyes.

'Where is he?' he repeated quietly.

Elchora spat a mist of blood into his face, and Maldon dropped her, recoiling half a step. He wiped his eyes calmly with his gloved hand, managing a look of disappointment. He slid the battle hammer from its leather loop at his waist and revolved it in his palm as though deciding which end to use, the solid cube of iron or the sharp claw, like the beak of a raven.

Elchora had no weapon to defend herself. She tried to roll away, but Maldon's boot came down again, pinning her arm to the ground until she could feel her heartbeat in her forearm.

'Commander Maldon!' called an angry voice.

Maldon removed his foot and whirled around, still clutching his hammer.

With relief, Elchora saw the greying figure of Erik Volsgaard riding towards them, a hand resting on the hilt of his sword. His anxious Obediant in tow.

'Lord Volsgaard,' said Maldon with a growl, slipping away his hammer. 'We have yet to find the boy … but I have caught the Ableman who helped him escape.'

Maldon stepped aside to reveal Elchora, gesturing at her with an open palm.

Volsgaard reined his tall black stallion to a walk and slid gracefully from its back. He shot a single glance at Elchora as he closed the gap on Maldon.

'You are not seeking anyone for punishment, you fools!' he bellowed, glowering at the other riders. 'Your orders are to find the boy and bring him back, alive and unharmed, to Lord Farrow. Do you understand? He wishes to question the boy, nothing more.' He strode past Maldon and reached out a hand to Elchora. 'On your feet, Ableman. I apologise for the Commander's stupidity.'

He hoisted Elchora to standing. She swayed, feet shuffling until her balance returned. She wiped the blood from her mouth and felt another sear of heat in her broken nose. Volsgaard's eyes darted around her face, surveying the damage.

'What, by Ohrak, have you done here, Commander?' he said. 'Why were you beating this Ableman?'

'Forgive me, my lord,' said Maldon. 'But Ableman Farrow was seen leaving the feast hall with the boy. We came upon her, and I questioned her as to his whereabouts. She would not comply. I was merely punishing her for insubordination. As is my duty as Commander.'

'Your duty is to protect your soldiers. To lead them,' said Volsgaard, thrusting his face dangerously close to Maldon's. Elchora saw the latter's hand move towards his hammer. 'A true Commander does not brutalise his men, Victor. Not without reason. But you bully for sport, and you go too far! I swear, if I hear one more account against you, just one more complaint, I shall put my sword in the ground at your feet and show your men how tough you really are! Do you hear me?'

Victor's eyes flashed, but his face remained stony. 'Yes, my lord,' he said, bowing without taking his eyes from the Augur. 'I hear you.'

Volsgaard glowered at the men astride their horses, searching for an ally among them. They stared back at him placidly, as though bored, one or two leaning forward in their saddles. Volsgaard turned his attention back to Elchora. 'You were with the boy,' he said. 'Do you know where he is?'

Elchora swallowed metallic blood. 'He fled into the forest, my lord,' she said. 'To the northwest, around half an hour ago … that way,' she added, pointing.

She wasn't sure why she was lying. But she knew nothing good could come from Maldon or his cronies finding Gadryon, no matter what Volsgaard threatened. The boy had saved her life, after all. Had saved all their lives.

'Then he cannot have gone far!' cried Maldon, remounting his horse. He looked at his followers. 'We'll spread out and ride northwest until we catch him.'

Elchora watched Volsgaard deduce the danger.

'No!' he said. 'Commander Maldon, please escort Ableman Farrow back to His Lordship's chambers. I'm sure her father would like to hear her account of the boy's appearance in our midst … Fyvern!' Volsgaard went on before Maldon could intercede. 'You have encountered the boy in the forest before, correct?'

'Yes, my lord,' said Fyvern, shaking back his curtains of rain-slicked hair.

'Good,' said Volsgaard. 'You lead the pursuit. Can you do that?'

Fyvern glanced at Elchora, the leather of his reins cracking in his fist.

'Yes, I recall the *right* direction, sir,' he said. The mounted soldiers beside him shifted in their saddles, swapping irritated looks. Whether they did not like to see their beloved Commander overruled, or whether they did not take kindly to a New Colour leading them, Elchora could not tell. But she was grateful for the Augur's intervention. Maldon would not dare harm her further before escorting her to Lord Farrow. And the horsemen would be less ruthless without their Commander.

'Ride only until midday,' said Volsgaard, 'and turn back if you encounter any large numbers of Krae. They may be beaten, but they are not defeated, and their whereabouts remain our priority. And remember, you are not to harm the boy if you find him.'

'Yes, my lord,' said Fyvern, straightening up in his saddle. 'Riders!' He turned his horse in a circle and raised an arm. 'Forward!'

He tore off toward the trees alone. The other riders glanced at Maldon, who tilted his head. At once, they kicked their mounts and trotted after the New Colour, spreading wide before disappearing into the trees.

At Volsgaard's command, those remaining on the field rode back to the city wall, with Elchora seated behind the Obedient, clutching his waist.

The mud-coated Ablemen saluted lazily as they rode past, having finally cleared the field of the Leybridge dead, with only the scattered Krae left to collect. Inside the walls, the drunken sounds of celebration continued to spill from the feast hall.

Elchora kept the Augur and his Obedient firmly between herself and Maldon as the four climbed the spiral staircase to her father's chamber. She might have been nervous to deliver such strange and incriminating testimony to Colton, whom she rarely saw privately anymore. But she was too tired, bloodied, and beaten to care just now, and she had already resolved to tell the truth. It was out of her hands now. She would accept any punishments so long as she could sleep first.

Moments later, Volsgaard rapped on the heavy oak door.

'Enter,' came her father's voice from within.

Elchora entered last and found the others looking across their shoulders at her expectantly, with her father seated behind his wide desk. A fire crackled in the hearth to her left, spewing mild warmth, while weak dawn light illuminated the painted glass window at the far end of the chamber.

Lord Farrow looked at each of them in turn, his elbows on the table with one fist inside the other palm. His eyes lingered on Elchora, taking in her bloodied visage. His eyebrows came together by the merest of fractions.

'Where is the boy?' he asked.

'Escaped into the forest, my lord,' growled Maldon, his eyes also on Elchora.

'I've sent a dozen horses after him, my lord, with instructions to capture him without harm,' said Volsgaard. 'Ableman Farrow saw which way he went. They'll return with the boy in custody soon enough.'

Elchora gave a tiny, involuntary snort. All heads turned to look at her, each wearing a different expression. Volsgaard raised an eyebrow quizzically. Eurace blinked in rapid surprise. Maldon looked set on murder, while Colton surveyed her with a curious smile.

'Is something amusing, Ableman?' said Volsgaard.

'No, my lord,' she said with a swift bow, growing uncomfortable under the scrutiny. 'I just don't think he'll prove so easy to capture … that's all. He lives in the Urden and has done so for many years. If our scouts have never unearthed him, why should we be able to find him now?'

'How is it that you know so much about him?' said Volsgaard irritably.

'I don't,' she replied. 'But I caught him inside the city before the Krae attacked, and I fought beside him in the battle.'

'The New Colour, Fyvern, told us that he had encountered the boy while on patrol in the forest,' said her father. 'Were you with Fyvern on this patrol?'

Elchora hesitated, heat rising in her swollen cheeks. 'Yes,' she said.

'And why didn't you report this encounter to me, your Commander?' growled Maldon, squaring his shoulders.

'What happened on that first encounter?' asked Volsgaard with a frown. 'Fyvern offered few details.'

Elchora recounted her first encounter with Gadryon but omitted certain specifics. She had promised Gadryon not to mention his sister, and she kept her word.

When she finished describing Gadryon's duel with Fyvern, the atmosphere in the chamber shifted. Volsgaard and Eurace turned to look at her father, who straightened in his chair, looking thoroughly satisfied about something. Maldon stood rigid and perplexed.

'That's a lie,' he said, his face hardening. 'Some unknown boy from the forest beat Almys Fyvern, heir to the Dragonfort, in a duel? How? Who trained him to fight? And where did he come from? Because if your story is true, then the only explanation is that he's a *jurdah*. An adopted Kraeling. Hiding in the Urden with the filth!'

'Think about what you're saying, Commander,' said Lord Farrow calmly. 'We all saw this boy cut down more than forty Krae, single-handed. Young Almys is a good duellist, no question, but this boy … he can fight!'

Colton stabbed his table with a finger, and Elchora suddenly understood his excitement. This year was a Quintus. Markos was bound, by law, to host a Throne Trial before summer's end. He intended to use Gadryon as a champion. From the corner of her eye, she saw Maldon arrive at the same conclusion. His beard twitched as his jaw worked furiously.

'What about the battle?' he grunted. 'How did the boy end up inside the city walls? Wearing our colours and fighting in our ranks?'

'He arrived before the Krae,' said Elchora, wiping a fresh droplet of blood from the end of her nose. 'I was on watch in the east tower when I spotted a figure enter the city gate. I followed, then apprehended the intruder. I recognised him at once.'

'He snuck through the city gate just before an army of Krae attacked?' said Maldon, turning his attention to Lord Farrow. 'Are you still convinced he's not a *jurdah*, my lord? How do we know he wasn't sent ahead by the Krae to infiltrate the walls and open the gates for the enemy?'

'He's not a *jurdah*!' said Elchora forcefully, an idea forming in her head. 'He broke in out of desperation! To steal food … I caught him between the grain store and the bakery. We spoke for several minutes before the Krae attacked. He confessed he was starving – he said the forest game was dwindling thanks to the Krae.'

'If he breached the walls to steal food, then he is a thief, my lord. Plain and simple,' said Maldon. 'Our stores are meagre enough without raids from desperate scavengers! If the boy is found, he must be brought to justice for this crime.'

'Be quiet, Commander!' snapped Volsgaard. 'Your judgement is skewed by your fondness for the lash. Whatever the boy's motive for entering the city, he chose to fight *with* us, and I, for one, am glad that he did. You cannot deny that his efforts turned the tide. The Krae all but fled when he killed their leader.'

'He abandoned a shield wall and left a gap for the enemy!' Maldon thundered. 'He exposed every man beside him to certain death for personal glory. A few lucky blows do not atone for his mistake.'

'If I have to tell you to shut your mouth one more time,' Volsgaard warned, hands poised to draw his sword, 'I'll shut it for you.'

Maldon's smile did not touch his eyes. He puffed his barrel chest at the Augur from across the room, a pudgy, freckled hand resting on the head of his hammer. Eurace backed away until he collided with a chair and stumbled.

Lord Farrow floated soundlessly to his feet. Suddenly very tall and much broader, a tower amid the standoff, radiating a controlled menace. He looked calmly upon both men from his full height.

'You will both hold your tongues until I have finished my interview with the Ableman,' he said. Volsgaard turned away from the Commander at once. He softened his stance and tilted his head toward Elchora's father. Maldon made no such apology. If anything, he looked disappointed. Lord Farrow ignored him and looked at Elchora. 'You said you spoke with the boy for a few minutes before the attack?'

'Yes, my lord.'

'Did you get his name?'

Elchora weighed her decision quickly. 'Gadryon,' she said. 'He told me his name is Gadryon.'

'Gadryon,' Lord Farrow repeated slowly, trying out the name.

A loud rattling of iron made Elchora jump. Eurace had collapsed heavily into a chair, looking lost and pale.

'Master Eurace?' said Lord Farrow. 'Are you unwell?'

The Obediant took several seconds to hear the question. He seemed far away, and when he finally spoke, his features remained anguished. 'N-n-no, my l-l-lord,' he managed. 'J-j-j-j-just t-t-t-'

'Tired?' Colton offered sympathetically. The Obediant nodded with a clinking of his collar, his hands writhing like mating snakes.

Elchora found herself watching the Obediant, frowning. Had he heard Gadryon's name before?

'I'm sure we all need some rest,' said Lord Farrow, interrupting her thoughts. He stamped his right foot several times to rid his wounded thigh of stiffness. 'Get to your beds, all of you. I doubt whether the Krae will dare attack for a long time. Commander Maldon, as soon as your men return from their pursuit, I want the patrol shifts to be sent out as usual. They will report back with any Krae sightings, but if they encounter this Gadryon, they will invite him back to Leybridge at my request. They are not to engage or intimidate him. Is that clear?'

'Yes, my lord,' wheezed Maldon.

'Erik,' Colton continued, 'please escort your Obediant to his chamber and return him to his bed. I shall need you both fit and ready once I've gathered my thoughts on tonight's events.'

Volsgaard gave a curt nod and moved toward his Obediant.

Consumed by some distraction, Eurace allowed his master to guide him to his feet, the shock still written on his face.

Maldon trudged through the door without a backward glance, the sound of his stomping feet receding quickly down the stairs. Elchora took a step, but her father spoke again.

'Elchora,' he said. 'Stay for a moment.'

She felt the familiar agitation inside. Only her father could cut her with such ease. Volsgaard winked at her before shutting the chamber door.

Trapped, she turned to look at Colton, who had moved to the fireplace to warm his back, his palms turned flat towards the flames.

'Did he hurt you?' he asked in a softer tone, his face neutral.

'It's fine,' she lied. It was beginning to sting when she blinked.

Colton let out a long sigh through his nose but nodded. Elchora noticed the bags under his eyes.

'I know you don't like me to interfere in your life,' he said, his eyes downcast. 'So, I won't … unless you ask. But let me offer you some advice; be careful around Victor. Don't let him be alone with you. I mean to set a Lordship Trial soon. And I fear it may embolden him. He will try to humiliate me as publicly as he can and use you to hurt me.'

Elchora's insides squirmed horribly. Did he know? He couldn't. Maldon was surely saving the news of his conquest for the right moment. The thought stirred the memory of his rough hands, the slapping of their skin.

'I can look after myself,' she said.

Her father nodded in thoughtful agreement.

'Tell me more about Gadryon,' he said, changing tack abruptly. 'What did you make of him?'

A new kind of heat blossomed in her face. 'What do you mean?' she asked, holding her breath.

Her father's piercing look was too knowing. 'You fought beside him on the front line,' he explained. 'Tell me, what was he like? I didn't get a good look at him. He seemed very young.'

'He is. My guess is around seventeen, maybe younger. It was hard to tell. He was filthy.'

Colton shook his head in disbelief, his mouth shut tight in a pursed smile. 'Seventeen …' he said to himself. 'And you think he lives alone in the forest?'

'Yes,' she said reflexively, keeping her promise. 'Why do you want to find him?'

Colton thought for a moment. 'I want to meet him,' he said, strolling to the window to peer into the morning. 'And thank him … I've never seen anyone fight the way he did on that field. Especially not at seventeen … not even Markos. Yes. He might be the best fighter I've ever seen.'

Yes, Elchora thought. *And* your *chance at redemption.*

CHAPTER 23

Treason

Kaiber sat with her feet wide apart, one palm resting firmly on the pommel of a vertical sword, its tip on the dungeon floor. With the fingers of her free hand, she pushed idly at the sword's hilt, spinning the blade. The whirr of the revolving sword was the only sound in the crowded, humid prison, except for the witch's footsteps as she paced.

The eyes of every prisoner tracked Varda Subei from behind bars as she glided between the cells. She was tall, with an elegant posture for a Bowharki commoner. Her white eyes emitted pale light in contrast to her flawless black skin. Her face and head were completely hairless, the absence of eyebrows and lashes enhancing her inscrutable expression.

The prisoners stood along the bars at the witch's instruction, emaciated and desperate, allowing her to peer into their eyes, each hoping to be chosen. They were traitors, rapists, murderers, and thieves – criminals all – more than a hundred, left to rot down here in the depths of High Castle, awaiting their appointments with the executioner.

Subei froze mid-stride. She turned to her left with her white eyes fixed upon someone Kaiber could not see. Kaiber stopped spinning her blade, giving the witch the silence she needed. Subei walked toward the cell that had caught her attention. After a moment, she pointed to a prisoner, a broad-shouldered man with a scruffy beard and shaggy hair. He reached through the bars tentatively, placing his wide hand in Subei's elegant fingers.

The witch traced her fingers over the man's knuckles, wrist, and forearm for several minutes without blinking.

Had she been born a man, Varda Subei would have been one of the most celebrated Augurs in Nephia. Able to read the truth in a person's eyes and see the past or future through the careful wielding of objects. A gift called Tracing.

She let the prisoner's hand drop and took a step back.

'This one,' she said softly.

Kaiber nodded at the giant figure standing to her right. Braemond grunted in acknowledgement. The floor shook as he strode toward the chosen prisoner, his solid forearms swinging like hams on a butcher's hook.

The scarred twins, Artan and Elden, on Kaiber's left, chuckled in anticipation. They looked at their mistress like hounds waiting to be fed.

Braemond thrust a key into the cell door and turned it with a click that resonated throughout the dungeon. The nearest prisoners edged toward the door. But when Braemond roared, his stump of a tongue writhing behind square teeth, the prisoners flinched and retreated deeper into the cell. The giant ripped open the door with a squeak.

His eyes on Braemond, the chosen man stepped out, naked, like all the others.

'What is your name?' asked Kaiber, rising to her feet.

The man steadied himself with a deep breath. 'I am Dante Elgado,' he said clearly. 'Captain of the *Foza Mar*. A man of honour, and brother of Andres Elgado, the Bane of Emeron.'

A whooping cheer came from the prisoners behind him.

'A pirate,' said Kaiber, addressing the witch. Subei bowed her gleaming head, her full lips betraying the hint of a smile. Kaiber looked back at her opponent. 'Speak your terms, pirate.'

A prisoner on the opposite side flung himself wildly at the bars, clutching them tightly to his grey chest. 'Captain!' he pleaded hoarsely. 'Please! I beg you! You must demand that we all be freed!'

The prison exploded with shouts and rattling as many other voices bellowed their support of the plea.

Dante held up a hand and waited for silence. 'No,' he said coldly, shaking back his hair. 'Not one man among you deserves his freedom. Dante Elgado included.' He looked across at Kaiber and put a finger to his temple, tapping it with a grin. 'I know why you have come here, Lady Kaiber … Your servant showed me the truth … You have outgrown sparring with sword masters who serve your King father. They hesitate … which stunts your growth. You believe that only men sentenced to die, who will fight you for their lives, can help you surpass your father … and become Queen. Has Dante understood correctly?'

He finished with a tilt of his head, a golden tooth glinting from his grin. Kaiber turned a slow, accusatory look at Subei. The witch stared back with those penetrating eyes, her expression unfaltering. The pirate's grin widened. 'The problem with your plan,' he said, 'is your assumption that I fear death, as you do … But the Elgado brothers fear nothing. So, allow me to set terms that exceed your ambitions and satisfy my honour.

'I vow to destroy you. To attack you with every tooth, nail, and ounce of strength I possess. I will bind myself to this vow. Of you, my lady, I ask for nothing. Win or lose, this dungeon is where I shall die, for my true bargain shall be with God.' He looked up at the ceiling, his shaggy hair falling behind his naked back. 'Ohrak … you miserable, worthless shitdog … Listen to me!

'I see your work in this challenge. And I chose to make the ultimate wager … for my eternal soul and the souls of all my kin!

'If I win, I ask that you pardon the crimes of my brother, my wife, our children, and any that carries my blood upon their deaths. You must cleanse them and welcome them into heaven as your own, oh mighty Ohrak …

'If I lose … I demand only this; that you do your worst unto me and to me alone! Show me the extent of your wrath, my God, if you have the stomach for it … I dare thee!'

The pirate lowered his grizzly head to glare at Kaiber expectantly.

For a moment, she was struck by the plain insanity in the man's eyes. She needed no Trace to see it. The witch had uncovered a madman. Even Braemond had backed away from him.

Kaiber felt a swarm of flies take flight inside her. A sensation she had not felt in years.

At last! A man who would not hold back. The first test of the witch's prophecy. And Kaiber's first hurdle on the path to the throne.

She nodded in respect at the pirate, then crouched to lay her sword on the cobbled floor.

'I accept your terms, Dante Elgado,' she said, unbuttoning her clothes.

If Dante was to fight naked, so would she. Nobody could deny that the fight was fair. The twins clapped their knees excitedly.

The prisoners had fallen silent in the wake of the pirate's wager. Now, all eyes were fixed on Kaiber as she slowly undressed. And all faces dropped as her body was revealed.

Two folds of skin, like sewn-up mouths, stood where her breasts had been. Her abdomen was a lean bar of muscle covered in scars. The handiwork of her beloved Artan and Elden during their lovemaking.

Only Dante's smile remained once she was fully exposed. He regarded her from head to toe with undisguised hunger. Equally surprised to have found such a worthy adversary. In other circumstances, Kaiber would have put him on the rack and taken his seed. She felt the wetness at the thought of it. But she had already accepted the man's terms, and the twins could satisfy her needs when she was done with him. She looked at his member as it unfurled, half-filling with blood.

A fine trophy, she thought.

At a nod from Kaiber, Braemond handed a sword to the naked man, who took it and set his face in a rictus snarl. Kaiber picked up her own blade, letting it slide menacingly across the cobbles.

Their cries resounded from the walls as the two warriors met with furious clangs of steel on steel. Every swipe aimed to sever or kill as they fought at close range. Neither took a backward step or even considered adopting a defensive stance. Dante drew first blood as a glancing thrust sliced a meaty chunk from Kaiber's shoulder. In a counter-move, Kaiber seized the attacking arm before the pain had registered and slammed her elbow into the man's jaw. He fell but used the momentum, turning it into a backward roll, then leapt back to his feet. Lost in his madness, he threw his sword, point-first at Kaiber, like a spear. She narrowly managed to parry it by bringing down her own sword instinctively, sending the missile to clatter through her legs. It gashed her right calf, but she remained standing. Dante advanced as she recovered from the parry, and Kaiber was forced to throw her own sword before the madman was upon her. She threw it while moving backwards, lacking the power she could have delivered, but the point hit its mark, piercing the pirate's abdomen. Dante recoiled from the blow, the sword protruding from his gut. He looked down at the mass of grey tentacles slipping from the wound.

He plucked the sword from himself and charged at Kaiber with the blade held aloft, entrails dragging under his feet. But Kaiber was ready. She lunged forward with the pirate's sword and used his movement to skewer him through the centre of his chest.

For an instant, he stood stunned and quivering, his shocked surprise replaced by horror as his wager manifested in his eyes.

Kaiber let the sword fall with him. He hit the floor with an awful slap, where more of his hot innards slid out. Kaiber looked over at Artan and Elden. Both watched her eagerly.

'Make it quick,' she said. 'And fetch me my prize.'

Jumping with glee, the twins launched into action, uttering, 'Thank you, mistress,' as they passed.

Kaiber turned away to find Subei waiting for her, her clothes draped over an arm. A pitiful scream filled the dungeon, followed by muted gargling. Whispers broke out among the prisoners. One of them vomited.

'You fought well, my lady,' said the witch, proffering her garments. 'As

I knew you would. Against a man of superior strength, equal skill, and greater will … Perhaps now you will believe the truth of my prophecy. "*When the true King falls, his champion shall arise as the Ulmar of Ohrak, and made immortal, for all time.*"'

'But I am not my father's champion,' said Kaiber.

'In time,' smiled the witch.

Kaiber snatched up her clothes. She was about to ask what the witch had seen in the pirate when Subei's gaze settled on the door to the castle, and her mouth split into a broad smile, displaying all the width of her pearly white teeth.

'Ohrak works quickly,' she said, apparently to herself.

'What did you see?' asked Kaiber, her bundle of clothes still gripped in her fist.

'The next step,' said the witch enigmatically. 'A messenger approaches. You will be angry.'

Kaiber's frown had barely formed when a fist hammered on the far side of the door.

'Commander!' came a muffled cry. 'Commander Kaiber, are you there?'

Kaiber stepped beyond the witch.

'Enter,' she said.

The heavy door opened just enough to allow the slim guard entry. He took in Kaiber's nakedness and quickly averted his eyes as though stung.

'It's your father, my lady!' he blurted through his panting. 'He's been attacked!'

'*What?*' Kaiber shrieked, wrenching her neck to glare at Subei.

Had the witch known this would happen?

The guard backed away through the door.

'Who *dared* attack him?' Kaiber continued. 'Who? And *where* are they?' She pulled on her clothes quickly.

'I … I know nothing more, Commander. The Augur said to fetch you right away … he said … he said the King had been attacked and that he may be … dead.'

Kaiber felt a void open within her. A cold calm. At that moment, she knew that nothing would stop her. Wherever blame landed, death would follow.

'Where is the King?' she asked.

'In the old palace stables – on the eastern side!' said the guard.

'Take me to him. Now.'

The guard raced through the door, and Kaiber stormed after him. Her loyal followers made to come along, but she halted them with a look.

'You stay here,' she said, still unsure whether this news was some spell from the witch. This matter was hers alone. Braemond grunted, the others bowed.

Without further delay, Kaiber sped through the door and flew up the winding stairs, taking three at a time, quickly catching up to the guard. He lifted the latch and opened the door for her at the top of the stairs. She marched through it and crossed the antechamber to another set of stairs.

Finally, she reached the eastern foyer of High Castle. Daylight poured through glass windows depicting her ancestors.

Would her father soon join them? Would his sword and armour be nailed along the Hall of the Fallen?

She found two more guards in a state of emergency. She commanded them to lead the way to the King. They spun at once and led her outside to the orchard.

A larger group of people was gathered before the abandoned stables. They scattered at Kaiber's approach, revealing the figure of Rowel Malcifer, propped up on his elbows, a healer tending a deep gash along his midriff. A torn section of his bloodstained, purple robe was cast aside. The Augur gritted his teeth as the healer stitched him. His usually neat beard was scorched on one side, and a cut near his eye wept blood. When he noticed the crowd's parting, he looked up at Kaiber and his pained features morphed into a sneer.

'What happened, Rowel?' Kaiber demanded.

The Augur slapped away the healer's hand and pushed himself to a sitting position, wincing. 'Leave us!' he ordered, glowering at the people above him. They swapped looks before hurrying away through the many doors that opened on the orchard.

Soon, Kaiber and the Augur were alone.

'Where is my father?' she asked, her voice trembling.

'Help me up,' said Rowel, thrusting his uninjured arm across his body.

Kaiber pincered his thin arm in a vicelike grip and yanked him to his feet. The Augur leaned into her and roared in pain.

'In there!' he said, pointing at the stable doors.

Kaiber almost floored the old man as she passed him, but the Augur caught her shoulder in his ringed hand and spun her back to face him. 'Wait!' he said. 'The healers are with him now. There's nothing we can do!'

Kaiber shook the hand from her shoulder and put her nose an inch from the sweating, bronze face. The Augur withdrew his head in alarm.

'What has happened to my father?' she said.

Rowel looked over both shoulders before he spoke. 'An assassin tried to kill him.'

Kaiber's eyes slid over every feature of the untrustworthy face. She gave a tiny nod, allowing him to continue.

'He's alive, my lady, but barely,' he whispered. 'The attacker used a weapon that I've never seen before.'

'Who?'

'The Elf!' Rowel spat. He rubbed at his singed beard. 'He almost got me with it too but missed. I managed to slit his throat before he could use it again.'

'An Elf?' said Kaiber. 'The *Elves* sent an assassin?' She fought against the disorientation, clinging to the Augur's every word. 'Where is this assassin?'

'I told you,' Rowel growled, 'I slit his throat!'

'Tell me exactly what happened, Rowel. All of it.'

Rowel took a step back and peered around once more. The orchard was silent and still, though the air was charged with excitement. Kaiber could hear the urgent voices of the healers inside the stable. It cost her every ounce of self-restraint not to barge in there, to confirm it with her own eyes. But she would hear the Augur's account before releasing him. She needed to know exactly who to blame for this. She required a target for her rage.

'The King and I were discussing preparations for the Throne Trial in the gardens when I heard a strange noise from the vineyard,' said Rowel.

'What noise?' said Kaiber, seizing on the pause.

'A scratching or thumping, I can't remember … I was about to summon the palace guard when the King went inside to investigate. Naturally, I followed him, and the noise led us here. But moments after your father entered, as I came through the doors myself, an Elf leapt from its hiding place in the shadows, clutching a strange metal tube. A weapon with no blade. Instead, a thin red light flashed from its end! And your father had no time to react. The Elf slashed the light along his chest, gashing him from his collar to his navel.

'I tackled him to the ground, barely evading the second blast of his flash weapon, and I slit his throat from ear to ear. The King was alive when I called for the healers, but he may not live much longer.'

Kaiber stopped. She had been pacing as the Augur spoke.

Markos Almanfier could not be dead.

But dead or alive, the Elves would pay for their treason. She would wipe them from the face of Ithea.

The Augur spat and rubbed at his blind eye. Kaiber saw that the skin around it had indeed blistered raw. Though she detested the Augur, it was clear he had saved her father's life.

A flash weapon, she wondered, staring at his injury.

'Where were *you* during this attack, Commander?' the Augur demanded suddenly, spinning to glare at her with his good eye. He took a step forward. 'Are you not the Commander of the Iron Company, Lady Kaiber?' he prompted sarcastically. 'Is the King not your father? Are you not sworn to protect him?'

Kaiber shrank, suddenly eleven years old again, being admonished by her father's frightening advisor.

'I was in the dungeons,' she countered meekly.

The Augur pounced. 'In the dungeons!' he cried. 'Of course, you were! Where else would the King's Commander and protector be? Unless you were plotting against him, like the Farrow traitor before you?' Kaiber stepped back, and the Augur pressed his advantage. 'Don't believe that you can outsmart me, girl! I know everything that happens in this castle! In this kingdom! *Everything!* I know what you and your disgusting little entourage were up to down there. You ought to be ashamed of yourself! Sullying the Almanfier name in the company of a witch who has poisoned you against your own father! While the Elves plot to kill him! Have you no loyalty? Do you even understand the damage you've done? The Throne Trial is mere weeks away! And you have all but gifted the throne to any treasonous lord who would take it! You stupid girl!'

The doors to the stable swung open, and two healers stepped out, their faces half-covered. They froze, heads swivelling between Kaiber and the Augur, uncertain whom to address.

'The King lives, my lord … and my lady,' said the healer on the left with a nervous bow. 'We have cleansed his body as you requested, Lord Malcifer. He has not yet awoken, but he stirs, and I … *we* … believe that he may yet recover from this attack.'

'Thank you,' mumbled the Augur, turning away from Kaiber in disgust.

Kaiber launched herself into the stable without a word, ready for whatever awaited her inside. The healers held the doors as she stepped over the threshold.

The old stable was dimly lit by torchlight. The pens were clean and empty, save for a handful of crates. Kaiber found a pair of feet pointing at the ceiling behind a dividing wall. She could tell by the odd shoes that the feet belonged to the Elvish assassin. The floor was spattered with dried blood.

In the centre of the aisle stood a long woodworking bench, on which a huge body lay, covered in blankets. Kaiber watched the top of the blankets for a long time, hoping to see them rise and fall.

Here, undeniably, lay the body of her father, Markos Almanfier, the longest-reigning King in Nephian history. She steeled herself and stepped closer.

Standing beside him, she could see that he was breathing. But each rise was a shallow effort, and a faint gargle in his breath clawed at her nerves. His usually hard face was soft and serene, untroubled. He looked enormous under the blankets, bigger than Braemond, and at the same time so fragile that she fought the urge to slap him awake. He was the King. An Almanfier. He had never shown such weakness in his life!

She reached out and carefully peeled back the grey blankets.

As the Augur had described, a vertical red gash marked the length of her father's breastbone along the taut seam of his hairy pectorals. Kaiber had never seen a wound like it. A perfectly straight, shallow canyon that glistened like a burn. Kaiber detected the faint aroma of burnt hair as the air beneath the blankets escaped.

The flash weapon, she thought.

Steadily, she lowered the blankets back over her father's chest, careful not to disturb him. But he did not stir. She walked over to the pen where the Elf lay and scanned the floor for the assassin's weapon.

The would-be killer was an ugly little thing. He had orange hair and skin as pale as a Kraeling. His final look of horror was etched forever on his face, his mouth hanging as wide as his windpipe. There was no sign of the weapon.

The Augur has kept it for himself, she thought.

The noise of footsteps running outside made her spin on the spot. The stable doors burst open, and a tall young man stormed through them wearing a handsome blue coat over gleaming silver armour. The boy's face was set in a grimace so familiar that Kaiber briefly saw her father in the doorway. But then, Henrik Almanfier had always been their father in miniature. He eyed Kaiber for a moment, then strode over to their father's side, turning his back on her, coat swirling behind him.

'Who did this?' he asked, his voice high but steady. 'Uncle Rowel said it was the Elves.'

'This one,' said Kaiber, looking back at the small body. Her brother came to stand beside her. They stared at the Elf for a long time in silence. Henrik's chest heaved beneath his armour.

Kaiber sensed Henrik's gaze on her profile. She looked into his smooth, youthful face and saw fear in the eyes that were so much like their father's.

'What do we do?' he whispered.

Kaiber put a tight hand on her brother's nape as if strangling him from behind. She tilted his face upward. 'I will slaughter them all,' she said, Henrik's eyes darting between hers. She kept her grip firm and did not blink until her brother's fear was gone.

Henrik gave a grim nod.

They broke apart as the Augur entered quietly, casting a blade of sunlight onto the stable floor. He kept his seared eye shut tight, but with the other, he stared directly at Kaiber with an air of dour anticipation.

'Well?' he drawled.

Kaiber straightened up and stepped determinedly into the Augur's challenge.

'Send word to every Realm,' she said. 'Tell all the lords that their King has survived an attempt on his life. And that henceforth, we are at war with the Elves. I want them all dead, on sight!'

Rowel folded his arms. 'But what of the Throne Trial?' he said mirthlessly. 'Those same lords will flock to Laudria like wolves when they hear that the King is lame!'

Kaiber took another step. 'Tell any who dares challenge us that the Throne Trial will proceed,' she said. 'Tell them *I* shall fight in my father's stead, as Queen Regent. If any lord wishes to challenge me for the throne, tell them I will come for them.'

Rowel turned away to look down at the fragile, unconscious form of Markos Almanfier, unable to conceal his glint of pride.

'Henrik,' Kaiber continued, rounding on her brother, 'go to the dungeons and fetch my advisors. Tell Subei, Artan, and Elden to meet me in my chambers, and tell Braemond he is the new Commander of the Iron Company. I want a full battalion assembled and ready to march. The war begins now.'

'What about me?' Henrik pleaded. 'What should I do?'

'You will stay here with our remaining forces,' she said, 'to protect our father. Now go!'

Henrik took off in a whirling of his blue cape. Kaiber strode after him. But Rowel stopped her with a hand.

The Augur gave her a curious examination with his eyes. To Kaiber's astonishment, he lifted the hem of his torn robes and knelt before her, taking her right hand in both his own. He kissed her knuckles with surprising warmth, then lifted his charred face to look at her solemnly.

'May Ohrak guide you and keep you safe, my Queen Regent,' he said. The Augur bowed his head.

CHAPTER 24

The New Moon of Eleppa

In the silent expanses of space, Ithea's furthest gas-planet neighbour, Eleppa, turned silently on its axis, performing its ancient dance with its many icy moons. Several of the satellites were large enough to be considered planets in their own right. Only their subservience to their host denied them the title.

The moons orbited the giant in hard-fought equilibrium, their influence generating tidal bulges that swept Eleppa's equator from west to east like flowing bands.

Miles beneath the outer surface, Eleppa's gas was compressed so tightly that it was almost liquid. An incomprehensibly deep ocean of gas. Inhospitable to life. Not a single cell could exist inside its inferno. And certainly nothing complex enough to have developed sight.

But at that moment, if any creature could have floated on its back in the sea of gas and seen upward through the dense atmosphere, its eyes would have seen something new. A black dot that had never appeared before. Passing imperceptibly across the sky.

The same creature might also have felt the rogue wave that travelled north to south. A tiny ripple compared to the lateral swells, but enough to knock the delicate harmony of Eleppa and its moons a fraction off kilter.

Much later, as the black moon continued on its journey across Eleppa's sky, unseen, a single eye, billions of miles away, was pulled from the eyepiece of a telescope.

Yuri Balkov frowned.

'Hmm,' he said, looking around his untidy desk for a notepad. He spotted one trapped under a congealed bowl of cereal and riffled through it to find any page not covered in his scribblings. When he found a blank space, he smoothed out the page and logged the time and date of his observation, writing two words underneath.

Eleppa.

Wobble.

He tossed the notepad back on his desk with a yawn and stretched his arms toward the domed ceiling.

Bedtime, he thought happily.

PART III

VOYAGE

CHAPTER 25

Farewell

Adam strode purposefully through a corridor of Felix Primary. The daylight was fading outside the windows to his right, and the bright lighting overhead was beginning to take on that surreal quality that only hospitals can achieve.

Genevieve had been moved to a room on a lower floor. It was larger and more comfortable; she had a rectangular sofa at her bedside and a television built into the wall. She was no longer attached to any machines. Adam had gotten lost on his way to see her so many times that he knew the layout of the entire building perfectly. The staff knew him by name and greeted him with sympathetic smiles as he passed. They all knew where he was going. He was the sole visitor of the unfortunate woman in room B-98.

When he opened the door of Genevieve's room, Adam found her staring out the window at the orange-and-pink sunset beyond the dome. He stood in the doorway for a moment and watched. She wore a burgundy woollen jumper over her hospital gown, and her pale legs and feet were bare. She looked slender, reduced. The tendons in her feet were sharply visible, and there was too much room inside her jumper. But moments like this gave Adam hope. He was sure nobody had asked her to stand at the window like that. Which meant somewhere inside, Genevieve had decided to look at the setting sun.

It was not the behaviour of a blank.

Adam moved into the room and closed the door to let her know he was there. She didn't react. He cleared his throat, but she simply stood there, spellbound.

'Gen?' he said, feeling a little foolish.

Nothing.

He moved around the bed and stood beside her at the window. The sun was beneath the horizon, but the rippled clouds were lit pink underneath by its residual light, and the naked sky was a field of darkening orange-red.

'This will be my last visit for a while,' said Adam. 'We set sail for Nephia tomorrow morning, so … I've come to say farewell.'

He turned to look at Genevieve's profile.

Here too were signs of her erosion. Her collar bone was a solid ridge, underlining her neck, which was as thin as Adam's forearm, and her taut skin made the contours of her skull more obvious. Her face, however, was not the dull-eyed mask of a blank. There was still a brightness there. A subtle difference, but Adam felt Genevieve in the room, no matter how indifferently she behaved. This was still the woman he knew. She just needed reminding.

'I've made a lot of progress with DeVenus,' he offered, 'and, erm … most of it is down to your machine.'

He smiled at her, pausing as though she might say something.

'I rebuilt your prototype using your schematics,' he went on. 'I thought it might help understand your condition if I recreated your experiment. Do you remember that, Gen? Do you remember the experiment?'

Nothing.

'Well, it occurred to me that if DeVenus is going to protect us on the expedition, neutralising his fear of damage isn't enough. Yes, it would allow him to punch through a wall, but then his arm would be damaged, and he'd be useless. So, I used your machine to transpose some kirrion and Inficore attributes into him. His skin will now harden like kirrion when struck, and he can unleash his full strength without damage, like Inficore. I've also heightened his threat response. All that remains is to teach him how to duel. If I get it right, he should be able to win any fight. Pretty cool, huh?'

Genevieve continued to gaze at a fixed point in the sky.

'Anyway … I can't take your machine with me. It's too big. So, I'm leaving it in Lopek's office at the West Point Academy, along with all my notes. It'll be safe there. Charity, the prosecutor, has argued that it belongs to the Experimental Department in Copika. But don't worry, it's mine until the reparation deadline. By which time, hopefully, you'll be a lot –'

Adam cut off excitedly. Genevieve had turned silently to face him, and he thought he saw the faintest trace of an expression dawning in her eyes. They were widening as though afraid.

'Yes?' he said, studying her face wildly, willing her to talk. Her chest began to rise and fall. Adam watched as her lips parted, unzipping from the middle outward, as her mouth opened slowly.

'Adam,' said a voice from the doorway. Doctor Yang had breezed in, holding a clipboard. 'I was told you were in here.'

'Suzie, come here, quick! I think she's about to say something!'

Adam whipped his attention back to Genevieve, who had also turned to look at Doctor Yang. To his immense frustration, the fleeting expression, whatever it had been, was gone. Doctor Yang watched Genevieve patiently from the far side of the bed for a moment. The silence became awkward.

'She was about to say something – I know it,' said Adam. 'Come on, Genevieve!'

'I think it's important not to pressure her,' said Yang. 'But, whatever you saw, it's a good sign. We just need to be patient.'

Adam kept his eyes fixed on Genevieve's face. To hear her speak after all these weeks would have been monumental. He could depart for Nephia less burdened. He slumped on the bed.

'I understand that you're leaving soon,' said Yang.

'Tomorrow,' Adam muttered.

'How exciting! When will you be back?'

'Six months … Listen, I need to ask you a favour.'

Yang folded her arms, pinning the clipboard to her chest. She looked both consoling and absolutely set to refuse his request.

'I'm taking a phone with me,' he said, 'Would someone keep me posted on Gen's progress while I'm gone? Just a simple message each day?'

Yang rocked on her heels. 'Adam, I have twenty-five other patients, and I work thirteen-hour days. So, no, I don't have time to write you a daily message. Especially if there's nothing to report. Why not assume that a lack of contact means a lack of progress, and I'll send you a message if I see any substantial change.'

'Please,' said Adam, 'just send me NTR – 'nothing to report', if that's easier. I'll assume the worst if I don't hear anything. And a lack of contact could mean signal failure, equipment malfunction, death … please, just NTR unless there's anything important to say … Please, I really need this.'

There was a pause while Yang and Adam stared at each other, the latter pleading silently. Eventually, Yang sighed. 'Do you still have the same number?' she asked.

'Really? I mean, no, it'll be a special satellite phone. I can write it down for you.'

Adam held out his hands in an offer to take the clipboard. Yang didn't budge.

'Send me the number tonight, and I'll see what I can do,' she said.

It wasn't much of a promise, but he didn't want to push his luck. He didn't expect Yang to keep him posted every day for six months, but he thought setting a high bar and letting her fall short would yield a better average than setting a low one she could ignore. He kept his face as earnest as possible and said, 'Thank you.'

'I need to perform some cognitive tests,' said Yang. Adam recognised the dismissal.

He stood between Genevieve and the window, trying to catch her focus. She looked straight through him for a brief second, then, slowly, as though coming back from somewhere far away, her green eyes locked on to his.

'I'm leaving now,' he said, 'but I promise, I'll be back … So … don't be weird for too much longer, okay?'

He felt the urge to embrace her bony frame, but Yang loitered impatiently. He contented himself by putting a hand on her shoulder, and her eyes followed him from the room. Then she turned back to stare out at the now deep-purple sky.

*

Adam woke the following day to the sound of loud banging. He sat up in an unfamiliar bed, bleary-eyed, and waited for his sleep-addled brain to remind him where he was. A door behind him opened, and a tough, silver-haired man appeared in the doorway.

'Wake-up call,' said Bill. 'High tide's in three hours.'

Adam's left eye refused to open. He gave a weak thumbs-up, and Bill disappeared to bang on another door down the hall. DeVenus sat up smoothly in his bed and looked across at Adam, who yawned and stretched his arms wide, fists shaking, before collapsing into the comfort of his pillow.

'DeVenus, open the curtains,' he said.

The blank slid gracefully out of bed and separated the curtains. The patch of sky that Adam could see was white and featureless. He forced himself to look at it until both his eyes could open, then swung himself out of bed.

The cottage Lopek had secured overlooked the harbour, where rows of small white boats undulated on either side of long wooden jetties. Peering out of his window, Adam could see fishermen loading crab cages and coiled nets into a skiff, which rocked and drifted a little on the murky brown water. Further down the line of boats, closer to the cottage, he saw a large wooden ship with furled sails and complex rigging. He was too far to make out the ship's name, but he knew what the golden lettering across the width of its back spelled out.

The Alliance.

The ship would be his home for the next month.

'Let's go and get some breakfast,' he said.

Downstairs, the smell of bacon and coffee filled the kitchen, where Lopek, Lynn, and Bill, still dressed in their night clothes, sat around a driftwood table while Kal busied himself at the cooker, his braid swaying as he worked.

'Good morning,' said Lopek, buttering some toast. 'Big day today.'

'Yeah, erm … *harma rysa*,' said Adam, in his best Phrenaelia. He guided DeVenus to an available chair and sat next to him.

'How's Genevieve?' asked Lynn, both hands around her coffee.

'No change … but her doctor promised to keep me informed while we're away, so …'

'Well, that's something,' said Kal, tapping the side of the frying pan with his spatula. 'What do you want? I've got bacon, sausages, eggs, beans, toast … whatever you like.'

'Err … just a bacon sandwich, please, if you don't mind?'

'Eat as much as you can,' said Bill. 'This is your last chance for a home-cooked meal in a long time. Thanks for that, Kal.'

'No worries.'

True, thought Adam. 'I'll have a bit of everything, in that case. Same for DeVenus, if that's all right?'

Kal waved the spatula in acknowledgement.

'Adam,' said Lopek, 'you need to confirm that all your possessions have been loaded onto the ship correctly. The rest of us did so last night. Bill, please take Adam to *The Alliance* and show him its features. A delegation of Hive officials is coming to wave us off, and I want to ensure we're ready before they get here.'

Bill stood and jerked his head toward the door. 'Come on, then,' he said. 'You can eat your breakfast when we come back.'

Bill led Adam and DeVenus outside, where a neat front garden of flower beds was boxed in by low stone walls and a white gate. Beyond them, out over the water, Adam could see the hazy purple flicker of the West Point dome. He wondered how cold it would be once they had sailed outside the dome's protection. It was dawning on him how much he had taken the perfect climate of the Hive for granted. The open ocean suddenly looked like a hostile force at the gates of civilisation.

As they walked along the jetty, Adam could hear the faint lapping of water between the boats and under the planks. They were soon at the gangplank of *The Alliance*, which seemed smaller up close. Bill turned to face him.

'Right,' he said, 'let's make this a quick tour. This is our ship, *The Alliance*. She's designed to look like a Nephian trading vessel, but she's got some hidden features if we get into trouble at sea. You can't see them beneath the sediment, but a set of propellers can fold into a cavity in the hull. We've got enough battery power to use them for a full week if we need to. We tried to negotiate for more batteries, but, as you know, available power is hard to come by at the moment, so we'll only use the propellers in an emergency. Otherwise, we're sailing on wind power all the way. Follow me.'

Bill turned and bounded up the steep gangplank with ease. DeVenus followed, equally light on his feet, while Adam had to heave himself up using the rope handrails. He reached the level deck of the ship, cut from fresh wood. There were three levels of decking: a small, raised platform at the front end, which tapered into a point; a much larger, raised platform to the rear, where the squat steering wheel stood; and the lower, middle section where the three men currently stood, with a thick mast jutting into the sky from its centre.

'Unfortunately, she was built before you and your blank joined us,' said Bill, 'so she's a bit … cosy for six people. I'll show you to your quarters.'

He led Adam through a door and down a short flight of steps. Adam had to steady himself on the rough wall of the ship as it swayed gently, the constant motion already making him queasy. They landed in a dark, narrow hall lined with four doors, two on each side. Bill was too broad to walk straight down the passage, so he twisted, leading with his shoulder, and side-stepped his way to the last door on the left, which he opened and stepped through.

To Adam's surprise and great relief, the room was relatively large. It had a double bed nailed firmly to the floor, and a small table and chair were fixed to the opposite wall. An electric light, disguised as an oil lamp, protruded from the bed's headrest, and a little window sat above a set of drawers across from the door. All in all, it was better than Adam had feared. He could picture himself spending the night here quite comfortably. But a whole month … well, that was another matter. And, of course, he would be sharing it with DeVenus.

'It's great,' he said.

'It is pretty good, isn't it?' said Bill, looking around. 'She's been sat here for a week, and there are no leaks or anything. But she's never been out to sea, though.'

Adam could have lived without this information.

'Come on,' said Bill, 'let me show you the rest.'

They squeezed back into the narrow passage and followed it to another set of steps, which led down into the cargo hold. Here, none of the technology had been disguised at all. The hold was huge, taking half of the ship's available space and brightly lit by domestic pin lights in the ceiling. The centre of its floor was sunken, like an empty pond, and a walkway circled its perimeter. A pile of objects filled the pond-like cavity. Laptops, tablets, a microwave, batteries, freeze-dried food, two satellite phones, stuffed rucksacks, tents, a telescope and tripod, and a freezer box with a medical symbol on its lid.

'This is your pile, here,' said Bill, indicating a cluster of objects, the most prominent of which was the briefcase containing the empty Inficore fragment. 'Is there anything missing?'

Adam surveyed the objects more closely. 'I don't think so,' he said.

'Good. Now, all our tech must stay down in this area unless we're using it,' said Bill, moving around the edge of the hold to the far wall. 'This dip, where we've loaded everything, is a sinkbox. We can't risk any of our kit falling into Nephian hands. So, if we're boarded, or the ship is captured by hostiles, one of us will have to come down here and pull this lever.'

Bill flipped a wooden handle on the wall until it poked into the room.

Two things happened at once; the pin-lights were suddenly eclipsed by wooden discs, while the walkway folded inward to hide the items below. Adam now stood in a dim, empty space with much less headroom. His mouth was open.

'When I bring the lever down fully,' said Bill, demonstrating this too, 'the sinkbox detaches and lowers itself to the sea floor.'

Adam heard a brief mechanical whirring, and then his stomach lurched as the ship rose, floating higher without the weight of the kit.

'Cool,' he said, unable to suppress his childlike grin.

'To summon it back, I use this.' Bill pulled up his left sleeve to reveal a wide metal bracelet around his wrist. He held his right fingertip to it for several seconds until a tiny display screen appeared.

Adam felt the sinkbox reattach to the ship's keel. He heard the same mechanical whirring, but this time, it ended with several clicking sounds, and Bill flipped the wooden switch back up. The floor unfolded to its original position, revealing all their kit under the pin lights as though nothing had happened.

But Bill let out a growl.

'Idiots!' he hissed, jumping down into the sinkbox. 'I told them to leave this out.'

He drew out a small black case from beneath one of the rucksacks. As he did so, DeVenus took a step toward the security officer and turned his head like an owl. Something about Bill's tone or sudden movement had triggered the blank's heightened threat reflex. For there was a distinct aggression in the subtle action. Bill had noticed it too. He frowned at DeVenus, and they locked eyes silently.

'So,' said Bill, 'you really think this thing can protect us from unfriendly Nephians?'

Adam chuckled to defuse the tension. 'Well … yes,' he said, 'once I've given him the right combination of directives … DeVenus, step back.'

The blank returned to Adam's side, keeping Bill in his field of vision.

'So, you're happy that all your things have been loaded?' said Bill. 'And you understand the function of the cargo hold?'

'Yes,' said Adam.

'Job done. Now go eat.'

Adam and DeVenus left Bill holding the case and returned to devour their slightly cold breakfasts. Lynn and Kal were dressed and ready, cleaning up the kitchen, a palpable air of excitement in their movements and conversation.

Adam showered quickly, then washed up the last of the plates and cutlery. As he was drying them, Lopek entered from outside, looking angry, followed by a small gathering of smiling, smartly dressed people.

'This is where we slept last night.' He waved vaguely. 'Did you want a picture of us around the table?'

A pretty young woman with red hair and redder lipstick replied. 'No, we'll get a group shot in front of the ship.'

'Fine … would any of you like tea or a coffee?' said Lopek, his tone making it clear they should refuse. There was a polite shaking of heads. 'Right, well, we're ready to set sail. So, if you want your photo, you'd better follow me. You four,' he added to the team, 'let's get aboard the ship. The tide's up. It's time to go.'

An excruciating scene followed, in which a monotonous official read out a long speech to nobody in particular, extolling the virtues of the expedition, throughout which Lopek huffed loudly. Then, a young boy, who had won some competition, threw a bottle of champagne at the ship's hull, which failed to smash and disappeared under the water. Lynn doubled over in a silent fit of giggles. When the team gathered for the photograph, she, Adam, Kal, and even Bill had tears in their eyes, with expressions as though sucking sour sweets.

The mood quickly became serious once they were aboard *The Alliance*. Kaldor unfastened her thick ropes from the jetty, and they began to drift backwards. The boat turned in a graceful circle, then began to cut smoothly through the water as they headed toward one of the arched passageways in the dome. The men in the harbour stopped working to wave up at them as they slid by, and the line of boats tied to the jetty rose and fell as the V-shaped ripples in their wake passed under them.

Adam waved at the fishermen.

The Alliance entered the open sea.

CHAPTER 26

The Blank

The first week at sea was nothing short of torture for Adam. He spent most of it sweating in his bed, feeling very sorry for himself, while the others brought him food and water. If he ventured on deck, he doubled over the gunwale while chunks of wet vomit flew from his mouth. He simply couldn't adjust to the perpetual swaying, rocking, and dipping. Lynn's medication had no effect on his suffering. He had even taken Lopek's share, which Lopek had refused on principle, wanting his experience to be as 'authentic' as possible. And annoyingly, like all the others, he seemed to have found his sea legs quickly, while Adam had never known such misery.

On the ninth day of the voyage, at long last, Adam woke up to discover that the ship's motion no longer affected the contents of his stomach. He paced tentatively across his room, testing his new immunity. With each step, his confidence grew until a sensation washed over him that he would later describe as an orgasm of relief.

He was restored. Seafaring and ravenous.

The others delighted in his transformation too. They had come to think of him as some kind of grouchy monster lurking in the ship's bowels. And they eventually confessed that they had been drawing straws to check on him. Adam laughed at this revelation, apologised to each of them, and concurred wholeheartedly with their actions.

He spent the next few days making up for lost time and threw himself back into the action. After breakfast each day, he sat with Lopek for an hour, diligently polishing his Phrenaelia, which improved steadily with each session. After this, he and Lopek would join the rest of the team in their established fishing ritual. Kal would bait the lines and move between the scattered crew, making minor adjustments to their grips and posture. But he kept his distance if anyone's rod started to bend under the weight of a fish. It was an old rule from the Freelands, he explained to Adam, that a struggle between man and beast should remain an equal contest. Only Lynn abstained from the practice, preferring to sit cross-legged on the bow, using Kal's binoculars to search for whales or dolphin pods. Occasionally, she would keep the men's catches to study them. Her favourite was the gross, pulsating venomous squid that Bill had reeled in after a long fight.

The fishing quickly became Adam's favourite part of the day. The whole team gathered on the deck, laughing, as *The Alliance* carried them gently through the waves of the boundless sea. Gradually, Adam noticed something shifting inside him. A feeling hard to grasp, like catching a scent from some forgotten childhood place. When he recognised it for what it was, the days became brighter still. It was the feeling of belonging.

He had always enjoyed his own company, it was true, and he hadn't exactly felt lonely during his years perfecting blanks. But neither had he felt this. The opposite of loneliness. No ... he had not felt this for a long time. And for a brief instant, he saw how he had tricked himself with a simple conviction; that it was too hard for adults to make new friends. It was the lie he had conceived to callus himself against their absence, and now, that callus was being unmade. He was also beginning to understand Lopek's affinity with the world outside the Hive. But this came as no great epiphany. It was an accumulation of dome-less, natural pleasures. The patter of raindrops on the wooden deck, the heat of unfiltered sunshine browning his skin, the cold spray of the sea on his face, and the chill produced by sudden changes in the wind that carried the ship onwards.

After lunch one afternoon, Adam sat in his room with DeVenus, calibrating orders that would make the blank infallible to attack.

Bill ducked into the room, clutching the brass doorknob. He glanced from Adam, who leaned against the dresser beneath the window, to DeVenus, who stood in the middle of the floor, then closed the door behind him.

'Thanks for ... um ... volunteering,' said Adam, rubbing the back of his head. 'Okay ... this err ... this might be a bit weird – I've never done this before – and it might not work, so please bear with me.'

Bill stood awkwardly, arms folded, as the light from the window behind Adam rose and fell with the listing of the ship.

'Bill,' said Adam, 'I need you to stand facing DeVenus. Close enough to put your hands on his shoulders – but don't touch him!'

Bill unfolded his arms; his eyes narrowed suspiciously. Then he shrugged and moved to stand squarely in front of the blank. DeVenus watched him impassively.

'Right,' said Adam, 'there are several things I want to try. Can you help me for a while?'

'Sure,' said Bill. 'I'm curious to see what this thing can do.'

'Well, we're about to find out!' said Adam, grinning. 'Bill, I need you to follow my instructions as precisely as you can, okay?'

'No problem, chief,' he said, smiling at the expressionless blank.

Adam picked up his notes, took a steadying breath, and spoke slightly deeper. 'DeVenus, this is a core instruction. Don't let anyone hit you. Do you understand?'

DeVenus nodded once. Adam exhaled. This was the moment of truth.

'Bill,' he said, 'I want you to punch DeVenus as hard as you can.'

Bill changed his stance and made a huge fist with his right hand, his knuckles turning white. He glanced back at Adam. 'Are you sure?' he said.

Adam nodded.

'Where?'

'Wherever you like.' Adam shrugged.

Bill eyed the blank for a second, deciding where to aim. He drew back his fist a little more, paused, then swung it full force towards DeVenus's midriff.

Quicker than a flash, the blank caught Bill's wrist, stopping his arm dead. He hadn't blinked or moved another muscle.

Adam scoffed in amazement. Bill was frowning at the hand clutching his own, then he gave Adam a wry smile and retracted his fist.

'Try again,' said Adam.

Bill straightened up. He stared at DeVenus with narrowed eyes for a moment. Then, as though to catch him off-guard, he shot his left hand forward from close range, aiming for the blank's chin. But again, a hand had come up to deaden the blow faster than Adam could see. Bill pursed his lower lip and nodded slowly, impressed. He raised his eyebrows at Adam, who looked back at his notes. He mentally crossed out the first line and moved to the next.

'Okay,' he said, his heart beating fast, 'Bill, try a flurry of blows, as many as you can, as hard as you can.'

Bill clicked his neck from side to side. He stepped back, rolled his shoulders, and found a new stance, lower this time, like a coiled snake. He pulsed on the balls of his feet for a moment, taking hard breaths, his face set in a grimace. Then, without warning, he launched forward in a furious assault, throwing punch after punch at a speed that Adam would not have credited. And it would have been formidable to behold had DeVenus not simply stood there, efficiently neutralising each attempt with his hands.

The blank's movements were not as Adam had imagined; he had pictured the flowing skill of a martial artist. But the spectacle before him was very different. It was bizarre, more like watching a jackhammer play whack-a-mole. And the weirdest thing was the unnatural stillness that DeVenus maintained in the rest of his body throughout his defence. After all, his hands were not only stopping Bill's fists, but the total weight of Bill's body behind each blow, and the blank hadn't leant backwards an inch or moved his feet whatsoever.

It was working. DeVenus was using his twitch fibre muscles without tiring.

Bill suddenly pounced back, looking livid. Then he roared, red-faced, and attacked again, putting everything he had into one ultimate effort.

But the result was exactly the same.

Finally, Bill ceased his wasted assault and retreated, panting heavily, with shiny lines of sweat dripping down his cheek from his temple. He rested his shaking hands on his knees, swallowed between great gulps of air, and turned his head to look incredulously at Adam.

'Fuck!' he said.

'Yeah,' Adam agreed.

They both stared at DeVenus and began to chuckle, Bill still leaning forward to catch his breath. Adam glanced down at his list of experiments.

'You, err … you up for a few more things?' he asked.

Bill laughed but nodded, droplets of sweat now dripping from his silvery chin. Adam's fingers trembled from pure excitement. He read out the following line, careful to pronounce every word clearly.

'Okay. DeVenus, this is a core instruction. For any attack you block, you must repay your attacker with ten per cent greater force. Do you understand?'

DeVenus nodded again. Bill looked at Adam with undisguised trepidation.

'It's going to hit back now?' he said.

Adam sucked air through his teeth.

'Yep,' he said, in an apology, 'if the instruction works right.'

The two men looked at the motionless blank.

'Maybe …' Adam began, as Bill straightened up, 'maybe just try and slap him on the arm or something?'

'Right,' said Bill, looking relieved.

He approached DeVenus again, more cautiously this time. And in fact, he looked so hesitant that Adam almost called an end to the experiment on the spot. But Bill had aimed a quick jab at DeVenus's shoulder, which the blank caught. At the same time, a fist flew hard into Bill's shoulder. The security officer spun slightly under the force of the strike before recovering his balance.

'Yes! You okay?' said Adam, ecstatic and worried in equal measure.

'Yeah, fine,' said Bill, shaking his arm and looking quite abused now. 'Just a dead arm … and ruined pride.'

'Sorry,' said Adam. 'We can stop there if you like?'

Bill glanced uncertainly at the notes in Adam's hand.

'What's left?' he said. 'Adam … this is … he's unbelievable. I never thought I'd feel sorry for potential attackers!'

'Well, actually,' said Adam, 'getting him to protect us is the next step … and I think it's the least likely to work. Are you happy to try?'

Bill blew out his cheeks but nodded. 'What do you need me to do?' he asked.

'Nothing just yet,' said Adam. 'DeVenus, this is a core instruction. Don't let anyone hit *me*. Do you understand?'

There was a brief pause, in which DeVenus blinked before nodding. Adam didn't like the hesitation. But he ploughed on regardless. It was the only way to eliminate any incorrect phrasing.

'Bill,' he said, 'I want you to punch *me* this time.'

Bill glanced sideways at DeVenus. 'What will he do?' he said.

'I'm not sure. Hopefully, he'll just block your hand. But there's a chance he'll do nothing or stop you and hit you back. I can't know how he'll interpret combinations of instructions until we test them. And I think this last one might be tricky to get right.'

'Right, so … where do you want me to punch you?' said Bill uncertainly.

'Maybe the stomach?' said Adam. There were less painful places to be struck, but he wanted to make the attack obvious. 'Aim for gentle but firm, just hard enough to wind me.'

'But there's a good chance DeVenus will hit me back harder?'

'Yeah,' said Adam. 'But just think; if he stops you and retaliates, we'll know that the instructions work, and we'll all be safer when we arrive in Nephia.'

Bill understood. 'You ready?' he said.

It was Adam's turn to feel nervous. The security officer suddenly looked a lot bigger. His relaxed fist was half the size of Adam's head.

'Why not,' said Adam.

Bill leant forward and punched Adam in the stomach.

DeVenus did nothing.

'Ooh! Shit. You all right?' said Bill.

Adam folded over, his breath pinned down by the pain in his middle. He had readied himself to be struck, but the blow had still shocked him. He had to twist to take shallow breaths. Bill put the offending hand on his shoulder to help him straighten up. Then, out of nowhere, DeVenus leant forward and punched Adam again in the same spot, but harder. And this time, Adam was not ready for it.

He keeled over sideways and hit the floor, then vomited, genuinely unable to breathe this time.

'Fuck!' Bill shouted. 'Oh shit! Adam! Are you okay? Shit!'

Adam felt the large, heavy hands of the security officer roll him forward onto his knees. For seconds that felt like an eternity, he was stuck on an out-breath, eyes bulging and neck taut, waiting for the muscles in his abdomen to let him inhale. Finally, they released, and he took a painful heave, coughing, and spluttering, as a gloopy mixture of saliva and sick dripped in long strands from his mouth. Bill rubbed his back, saying something Adam couldn't hear over thundering footsteps. Then the door to his cabin burst open, and Kal, Lynn, and Lopek rushed inside.

'What's going on?' Adam heard Lopek say.

'Adam!' said Lynn. Then he felt a much gentler pair of hands on his back.

'He's all right,' said Bill, 'just badly winded.'

'What happened?' said Lopek.

'We were testing the combat skills of his pet over there … but I think it got a bit confused. Hit him in the stomach.'

'DeVenus hit him?' said Kal.

'It's not his fault,' Adam wheezed, sitting back on his heels and covering his midriff with both arms. His voice was hoarse, but he tried smiling to show them he was fine. 'I gave the wrong instructions, that's all.'

Lynn put a cold hand on his forehead and wiped the sick from his chin with a medical wipe. 'Let's sit you up on the bed,' she said.

Bill helped Adam onto the side of his bed, then stood back to give Lynn some space. She knelt between his legs and put her hand on his chest. Her head cocked to one side as she concentrated on the rhythm of his breathing.

'I knew we shouldn't have brought that thing,' said Lopek.

'No! It was an accident,' said Adam. 'I promise, it was going really well until that last part. And I know I can fix it.'

Lopek continued to consider the blank, unconvinced.

'It was pretty amazing, Doc,' Bill concurred. 'And if Adam thinks he can get it right, that's good enough for me. Besides,' he smiled, 'it was kind of funny!'

Bill laughed, and Lynn turned to glower up at him. Adam looked up at Bill too, then pictured the scene from Bill's point of view. He watched himself getting hit twice before hitting the deck. He laughed but winced when his stomach gave a nasty jolt. He covered it more tightly, but Lynn gently prised apart his arms.

'It hit you here?' she asked, touching the tender spot through his jumper. Adam nodded. He still felt a bit sick.

'I might just take a quick look,' she said, then she looked around at the others. 'Can you give us the room, please?'

Kal, Lopek, and Bill trudged to the door, Bill giving Adam a pat on the shoulder as he passed. Once they had gone, leaving DeVenus standing serenely alone, Lynn rolled up his jumper to look at the injury. There was a large red patch on his pale, hairy belly.

Adam felt acutely vulnerable, with his relatively new friend examining his paunch intimately. Lynn was utterly unabashed, however, and prodded away.

'Does it hurt when I do this?' she asked during a particularly forceful push.

It did.

'Not really,' said Adam.

Suddenly, the door flew open again, and Bill came charging back into the room.

'Gather your things into the sinkbox, quick!' he said. 'There's a Nephian ship coming right at us.'

CHAPTER 27

First Contact

Adam, stomach still hurting, stumbled hastily around his room to gather his tech contraband. All he could find was his laptop and the empty Inficore fragment, which he kept in its kirrion case under his bed. He stood in the doorway and scanned the room for inconsistencies, trying to see it through Nephian eyes. The others dashed about in the hall. Purely for appearance, Adam made his bed and smoothed out the cover. The room was clear.

He pushed out into the narrow hall holding the kirrion case out in front like a torch while the laptop trailed in his other hand like a rudder. Lynn was ahead of him at the steps down to the hold. She was struggling with something that looked like a fridge door, covered in metal instruments, and sweating with the effort of heaving the thing. Adam could see a strand of sun-blonde hair flattened into a sweaty golden streak on her neck. Kal's face appeared at the foot of the steps into the hold, and he promptly took one end of Lynn's burden and helped her carry it down the steps and out of sight.

Inside the hold, Lopek stood in the lower level of the sinkbox while Kal and Lynn passed him objects. Lopek pivoted in a frenzy as he grabbed each item. When Adam offered his own, Lopek took them carelessly and half-tossed them onto the heap. Adam blinked at him.

'Is that everything?' Lopek snapped, looking up at all three of them.

Lynn had her hands on her hips, still out of breath. She frowned and made tiny nodding motions with her head, ticking off a mental list. Kal patted all the pockets on his trousers before giving a double thumbs-up. And Adam nodded vaguely.

'You're absolutely sure that there's nothing left in your rooms? Or on your person?' said Lopek with finality. 'Nothing at all?'

They shook their heads. But as Adam did so, he absently patted his pockets as Kal had done, and a wave of adolescent panic surged through

190

him as he felt the phone in his pocket.

'Ah, whoops,' he said, pulling it out.

Lopek's lips almost disappeared as his mouth shut into a tight sphincter beneath flared nostrils. He snatched at the phone, scratching Adam's palm as he did so, and only just managed to stop himself from slamming it on the pile. He rounded on Adam.

'No mistakes!' he said, pointing a thin finger warningly.

Adam enjoyed a brief vision of himself breaking the little man's nose with a swift kick. But in reality, he simply glowered at Lopek as he climbed onto the walkway.

'Lynn,' said Lopek, 'you stay here and close up the sinkbox. And make sure you release it too, then follow us up to the deck. You two, come with me.'

Adam and Kal followed Lopek from the hold. They heard the mechanical whirring as the floor closed over the sinkbox behind them. Adam brought up the rear, and as he passed his room, he put his head in and told DeVenus to wait there. Then, a few moments later, as Adam walked onto the sun-drenched deck, he felt the ship give a lurch that told him it had parted with the secret weight in its underbelly. Bill stood at the starboard rail, peering through Kal's binoculars at the dark but unmistakable shape of a ship on the horizon. The other men joined him.

'She's raised a red flag,' he said, 'but I can't tell what she is. Kal, come take a look.'

Bill offered Kal his binoculars.

'It's a trade ship, I think,' he said, adjusting the focus. 'Yep, I see the red flag too. They're hailing us, signalling their intent to come closer. If we don't raise our own flag, they might sail by. Or they could chase us down anyway.'

Kal and Bill looked at Lopek, who gripped a rigging section, frowning at the distant ship. He looked like he was chewing something.

'Raise a flag and let them approach,' he said.

Bill looked over at him.

'You disagree?' asked Lopek.

'I think we should send out the dragonfly,' said Bill. 'If you want to invite them over, I want to know who's coming.'

Lynn appeared in their midst. 'What's going on?' she said.

'You're about to meet your first Nephians!' said Kal excitedly. 'Come on, come and help me raise a welcome flag.'

Kal took Lynn to a large box at the other end of the ship, where Adam guessed an assortment of flags must be stored. Bill had moved further along the bow. He ejected an ornate silver object from his wrist com.

'Are you sure you want to risk it?' asked Lopek, fixing it with a look of mistrust.

'I'll send it high enough that they won't hear it,' said Bill. 'The zoom on its camera will let us see their teeth from a quarter mile away.'

Lopek turned back to look across the water, still chewing his tongue. He nodded without turning back.

'Right,' said Bill, handing the item to Adam.

It was cold to the touch and much heavier than it looked. It was a perfect silver dragonfly with delicate legs and a double set of opaque wings, small enough to fit in one hand. Bill fiddled with his wrist com.

'Adam,' he said, 'take it to the port side, away from the mast. I don't want it to get caught in the rigging.'

'Is this a drone?' said Adam, moving as Bill had ordered.

'Yep,' said Bill, winking at him. 'Specially commissioned … right, hold it flat on your palm over the side, and when I tell you, move away!'

Adam stood the heavy dragonfly on its thin legs, which dug like pins into his fingers. Carefully, he held it out over the water, straining at arm's length, a fine sea mist spraying his face and bare arm. A few seconds later, the dragonfly's wings twitched, then fluttered. Soon, they built up enough speed that Adam could feel the tiny disturbances of air on his palm, and then its weight lifted as it hovered in place.

'Okay, Adam,' said Bill.

Adam stepped back, mesmerised by the insect floating at his eye level, which appeared to drift sideways through the air as the ship moved beneath it. Then, it took off in a zigzag, vanishing into the blue sky. Adam turned to Bill, who was staring at the screen on his bracelet, trying to keep its display out of direct sunlight. Lopek strode to peer over Bill's shoulder as Adam arrived on the other side.

The screen displayed an empty blue sky for a long time until Bill manipulated it with his fingertips. Gradually, the screen became a darker, more textured blue, covered in white-tipped waves. Then the expansive deck of a ship and a cream-coloured sail inched across it. Adam saw three figures standing close together and realised they were looking at themselves. Bill glanced up as though able to spot the dragonfly's position, then manipulated the screen once more.

Adam looked out at the approaching ship, which seemed to glide unaffected by the swell. It was much clearer now; he thought he could make out the silhouetted people, Nephians, piloting it.

'Here we go,' said Bill, zooming in on the deck of a very different ship.

It was huge. Wide and imposing. It had a large square hole in the centre of its floor, covered by a wooden grill, and odd shapes were lined along the length of its deck. As Bill zoomed, the shapes became white mounds, and figures moved between them.

'It's a trade ship,' said Bill, sounding relieved. 'On its way to the Freelands of Anthar. But we'd better get Kal to verify.'

Bill flew the dragonfly behind the foreign ship to read the name printed across its stern.

'*De Groda Belvaan*,' said Kal, reading the lettering on Bill's screen, 'The Dragon something.'

'*The Dragon's Quay*,' said Lopek. 'Do you recognise it?'

Kaldor laughed. 'No. Nephian trade ships were rare visitors in Liberty, and they stuck to the Nephian trade port. I never saw them.'

'So, it's definitely a trader?' asked Bill.

'For sure,' said Kal, pointing at the screen. 'You can tell by how low she's sitting in the water. She's fully laden too – you can even see cargo fastened down on the main deck.'

'Excellent,' said Lopek. 'Bill, call the dragonfly back. I'll greet them when they draw aside.'

Bill navigated the dragonfly back to *The Alliance,* where it landed neatly in his waiting hand. He flattened it and tucked it back inside his wrist com.

The Dragon's Quay was very close now, and all three of its thick masts and tall sails were visible from the new angle. It looked scarred and weather-worn next to the clean wood of *The Alliance,* which fell easily inside the shadow of the larger ship as it drew aside. The top of *The Dragon's Quay* hull was at least twenty feet higher than *The Alliance,* and the row of hardened Nephian faces peering over it looked astonished to see Elves at sea.

'Good afternoon,' called Lopek in Phrenaelia, and Adam was pleased that he understood the greeting.

If the men aboard *The Dragon's Quay* had looked astonished before, they positively gawped at Lopek now. Some turned to whisper to one another.

'Well met,' said a booming voice from above, and Adam scanned the row to find the speaker. It was a tall, dark-haired man wearing a long, black coat, standing on the edge of the towering ship, his left arm slung lazily through a gap in the rigging. 'What business have you out here?'

Lopek bowed to the man. 'We are a delegation from The Hive Network of Anthar,' he said. 'We travel to Nephia to sew bonds between our people.'

There was a long pause after Lopek said this, in which the Nephian heads turned to watch the dark-haired man closely. Adam looked at Lopek and noticed that Bill had taken a few steps back, slightly further away from the new ship.

'You are the captain?' asked the man, addressing Lopek.

'Yes.'

The man in the black coat drew out a long knife. Adam swallowed. He heard Bill shift behind him.

'I ask permission to come aboard, Captain,' said the man.

The other Nephians stirred and looked at one another. Lopek bowed again.

'At my pleasure, Captain,' he said.

The man above slid the knife carefully along his thumb, then held his hand out as Adam had with the dragonfly. Three heavy drops of blood splattered on the deck of *The Alliance* from the hand, then a thick rope was thrown down, the heavy knot at its end thudding loudly, and the man descended.

He was big, maybe seven feet tall, and powerfully built, judging by how he carried himself downward with such ease. He landed lightly on the deck of *The Alliance*, on the spot where his blood had fallen, and laid his knife down carefully before stepping away. Lopek moved forward ceremoniously and picked up the knife. He seemed to examine it for a moment, looking closely at the fresh blood along its blade. He nodded theatrically, strode to the Nephian captain, and handed it back, handle-first. The Nephian bowed and sheathed his weapon.

'Welcome aboard *The Alliance*, Captain … ?' Lopek let the last word linger, looking for a reply.

'Dawberry,' said the Nephian in his deep voice.

'Welcome, Captain Dawberry,' said Lopek, bowing once more. 'I am Captain Lopek, and this is my crew.'

He turned and slowly swept his arm through the air in front of the others, who stood awkwardly, looking exceptionally unlike a crew. But Captain Dawberry inclined his head at each of them in turn, his face scornful yet full of respect.

'We mistook you for our sister vessel, *The Waycryer*,' he said. 'We set sail together from Rumnee four weeks ago but separated in a storm. It's a rare pleasure to meet an Elvish ship, however. Your craftsmen are master builders.'

He cast admiring looks at some of the sleek detail around him.

'Would you like a tour, Captain?' said Lopek, sweeping a hand over the ship this time.

Captain Dawberry was about to answer when distracted by a movement behind Lopek.

The captain's rope flailed, causing the knot at its end to skid across the decking as a second Nephian climbed down from *The Dragon's Quay*. Lopek flinched as the man landed heavily on the bloodstained floor beside him. Adam noticed that Bill had taken a silent step forward.

The new arrival was much younger than Captain Dawberry. He was leaner and shorter, roughly the same height as Adam, and black tattoos were visible around the collar and sleeves of his tattered shirt. He looked around at the expedition team apprehensively.

'My son, Gilliad,' said Captain Dawberry, then he said something in rapid Phrenaelia to his son that Adam didn't catch before turning to Lopek. 'His blood is my blood.'

Lopek regained his composure and inclined his head to Gilliad, who nodded imperceptibly, then stared around the smaller ship with his mouth slightly open. It occurred to Adam that the boy must be much younger than his height and tattoos implied. His face was pretty and smooth, with no trace of a beard, and his wide eyes kept glancing at his father for reassurance.

'Allow me to show you both around,' said Lopek.

'No,' said Dawberry firmly. 'I will follow you, Captain Lopek, but my son will remain with your crew, with your permission. It is good for him to learn Elvish ways independently, since he will become captain one day.'

Lopek flashed a glance at Bill before replying. 'Of course,' he said, smiling. 'Follow me, Captain Dawberry.'

Lopek led the Nephian captain slowly around the ship. They walked side-by-side, with Lopek slightly in front, pointing out specific features to the much taller man. Bill kept the pair in his field of view until they climbed onto the steering deck, out of sight.

The novelty of seeing Elves had worn off for the Nephian crew. The number of heads peering down from the ship above had dwindled to a handful. Those who remained looked at Lynn with great interest, talking amongst themselves. Lynn was either oblivious to this attention or she didn't care. She was smiling at the boy, Gilliad, who looked like he wanted to say something but didn't know what to say. Adam felt a rush of pity and decided to test his Phrenaelia.

'Good afternoon, Gilliad,' he said, pronouncing each word carefully, 'I am Adam.'

The boy gave a weak smile and stood up a little straighter. He said something in reply, but his accent was too strong for Adam to decipher. It might have been a question. Adam scrambled for something else to say.

'You have a fine ship,' he said lamely. 'Very … big.'

The heads above laughed loudly, now looking at Adam. The boy was grinning too.

'What did I say?' Adam asked Kal.

'You told them their ship was fat,' said Kal, sniggering. 'But more like, obscene or gross … Not cool, man.'

Lynn snorted.

'Lopek would've had an aneurysm if he heard that!' she said.

Gilliad had stepped forward. 'It's my father's ship,' he said slowly. 'But if I work hard and learn well, it will be mine someday.'

Adam, Kal, and Lynn nodded politely. Bill was too busy listening out for Lopek.

'It's an interesting name, *The Dragon's Quay*,' said Adam. 'Do you believe in them? In dragons?'

Adam thought he had made another linguistic error for a moment because Gilliad stared at him with his eyebrows knitted together in confusion. A second later, however, the boy reached under his shirt, pulled out a curved, triangular pendant on a necklace, and brandished it at Adam. Lynn, Kal, and Adam leant in to look at the object, and Lynn gasped so loud that even Bill turned to look at her.

'Is that a *tooth*?' she said, reaching forward to hold it, but Gilliad stepped back and closed it in a tight fist, looking wary. 'Err, help me out!' Lynn went on to her teammates. 'Tell him … tell him I just want to look at it.'

Adam and Kal exchanged a look. Apparently, Kal was privy to Lynn's dragon mania too.

'Erm … Is that a dragon tooth?' Kal asked Gilliad.

The boy nodded but kept the tooth closed in his fist, frowning.

'Ohh, please! *Please!* If I could just have it for an hour to study it!' said Lynn, eyeing the boy's fist covetously. 'Or even a piece! Ask him if I could cut off a little with my surgical laser.'

'Erm, your laser is probably a mile beneath us,' Adam reminded her. 'Besides, I don't think we're even allowed to mention that kind of thing.'

Gilliad suddenly lifted the necklace over his head and opened his hand slowly before Lynn. The tooth sat curved and polished on his grubby hand, a shade away from purest white, and a hole had been made through its wider end for the brown leather string of the necklace. It was twice the size of Adam's thumb. Lynn was staring at it as though hypnotised, her mouth open, her fingers resting softly on her rosy cheeks.

'You want this?' asked the boy.

It was a few seconds before Lynn lifted her head to look at him, her expression unchanged.

'Yes, she does,' Adam supplied.

The boy shut his hand quickly.

'We make a trade,' he said, smirking. 'What can you offer?'

Kal explained what the boy had said to Lynn, who looked around wildly for anything the boy might desire.

'Err … shoes?' she said, gesturing earnestly to her pink-and-white trainers.

The boy glanced at them, then made a face of utmost disgust and shook his head. He looked around.

'Your ship,' he said. 'I want your ship.'

Kaldor and Adam laughed.

The boy did not.

'We cannot offer the ship,' said Kal.

The boy shrugged and began placing his necklace back over his head. Lynn pivoted from Kal to Adam, pleading with them to come up with something to offer. An idea came to Adam. He happened to be wearing the InfiTech shirt he had taken as a souvenir. It was sun-worn with sweat patches beneath the armpits and collar, but the fabric was laced with kirrion.

'Wait,' he said. The boy froze with the tooth dangling just inside his shirt. Adam turned to Kal. 'How do you say 'armour' in Phrenaelia?' Kal supplied the word. 'I will trade you my armour,' he said, pinching the shirt away from his body. 'Elf made …'

It was the boy's turn to laugh.

Adam pointed at Gilliad's knife.

'Give me your knife,' he said.

The boy's smile faded. He stepped back and looked in the direction his father had gone.

Adam held up his hands in apology, looking at Gilliad as innocently as he could.

'Please,' he said, moving forward cautiously, 'let me demonstrate.'

The boy studied Adam's face for a moment. Then, deciding on something, drew out his long knife.

'Are you sure about this, Adam?' said Lynn nervously.

'What's going on here?' came Bill's voice over the sound of his footsteps.

Adam turned to face them slowly, hands still raised.

'It's all right, Bill,' he said, 'I'm just negotiating something with our new friend here.'

'What are you talking about?' said Bill, keeping his voice neutral. 'Why has he taken out his knife?'

Adam smiled.

'Trust me,' he said, turning back to the boy and holding his shirt away from his body by the hem. 'Try and cut it.'

Gilliad's eyes narrowed. He glanced at Bill, then looked uncertainly at Adam's sloping shirt.

'It's okay,' said Adam, 'try and cut through it.'

The boy cautiously dipped the tip of his knife into the shirt but succeeded only in pushing a pyramid of material downward. Adam felt him press harder, the weight pulling behind his shoulders, but nothing happened. Gilliad withdrew his knife and frowned at the shirt, which had sprung back to its normal shape. He looked into Adam's eyes, one corner of his mouth stretching up in an awed grin, revealing a row of slightly yellow molars. Then, feeling a little braver, he put his own hand beneath the shirt, palm up, until his hand was visible under the fabric, and sliced the knife across his fingers. Nothing happened.

He withdrew his hand and examined it. It was unscathed, as was Adam's shirt.

'Elvish armour,' said Adam, nodding sagely, cementing the boy's astonishment. 'Secret armour … and yours to keep if you give us the dragon tooth.'

There was a pause as the boy rubbed the hem of the shirt between his thumb and finger, thinking. Lynn watched him eagerly, occasionally beaming at Adam, who found himself keeping an eye on the boy's knife, suddenly feeling quite vulnerable. Finally, Gilliad looked up at him and gave a stern nod, looking very much like his father. He sheathed his knife, took off the necklace, and handed it to Lynn with a slight bow. Adam took off his shirt.

A roar of laughter came from the heads above as Adam's naked torso was revealed. His round belly was still pink from DeVenus's blow, and he suddenly felt grotesquely self-conscious and soft-looking in front of the tough Nephian sailors. Kaldor made the moment worse. He grabbed a handful of Adam's stomach fat, grinned up at the Nephian crew, and shouted the word *fat* in Phrenaelia. Some of the heads dropped out of sight with redoubled howls of laughter. Adam whipped around to glare at Kal, who was still pinching his stomach, but the man's infectious grin worked its magic, and the sudden rage turned into a fit of hysteria as

Adam joined in on the joke. He thrust his shirt at Gilliad and opened his arms wide to the men above, proudly displaying all his magnificence. And his confidence was rewarded with applause and a hearty cheer, which went up an octave as Lynn kissed him on the cheek.

The cheering faded quickly, however, as the Nephian captain and Lopek returned, the latter staring at the shirt in Gilliad's hand with quiet fury. And it wasn't until the Nephian ship had sailed away, after dignified farewells, that Lopek exploded in Adam's face.

CHAPTER 28

A New Course

Lopek had vented so intensely at Adam that Bill had to physically restrain him. But Adam didn't feel remotely guilty for conducting the exchange. He simply stood there and took the insults, mildly surprised that Lopek, a strict follower of formal etiquette, knew such profane language. It was Lynn he felt sorry for. She remained quiet throughout Lopek's tirade, absently turning over the tooth Adam had obtained, riddled with guilt.

Having exhausted himself, Lopek stormed off to his room, where he stayed all night.

Breakfast the next day was an icy affair. Lopek had risen early to prepare the food in an attempt, Adam supposed, to gain a moral advantage in the upcoming quarrel. But Adam didn't mind this tactic. He had considered his behaviour and prepared his defences. So, he gave Lopek an earnest 'thank you' as he took his seat among the others and began loading two plates for himself and DeVenus. Bill sagged in his chair and gave him a reproachful look, but Adam also detected a faint smile beneath his scorn.

Lopek sat upright, eating his quarter-filled bowl of yoghurt and berries with quiet dignity, eyes fixed on the table. Adam watched him. He had rehearsed his opening statement. 'Lopek …' he said quietly, the others turning to look at him, 'I've thought about what happened yesterday, and I have three things I would like to say.'

Lopek finished his mouthful, set down his spoon, and looked at him, his face unreadable. Lynn and Kal sat as still as DeVenus, and Bill had an expression as though Adam were about to pull a party popper in his face.

'First,' Adam continued, 'I want to say sorry. I should have checked with you before trading anything with a Nephian. And I'm sorry that I didn't. Second, I think you owe me an apology for your disproportionate response because, thirdly, it was only a shirt.'

Kal nodded slowly in agreement while the corners of Lynn's mouth twitched. Bill's eyes darted between Adam and Lopek.

'But it wasn't just a shirt, was it? It was laced with kirrion,' said Lopek.

Adam had anticipated this, but not Lopek's knowledge of the word *kirrion*. The substance was almost as rare as Inficore, and Adam had never met anyone outside InfiTech who knew the term.

'True,' he said, 'but it's not like they'll be able to produce more kirrion now that they've got some. They can't reverse engineer it. You've got to heat up a very complex mixture of chemicals to about five thousand degrees Kelvin – and I'm sorry – but one shirt isn't going to change Nephian culture!'

Lopek blinked rapidly and shook his head. 'Do you know what your problem is, Adam?' he said. 'You always think you're the cleverest person in the room.'

Adam scoffed. This was precisely his impression of Lopek.

'And sometimes,' Lopek went on, 'in a general sense, you may be right. But you don't respect that other people know much more than you do about specific subjects. Would you claim to know more about the planets than Kaldor? No. Do you think you know more about zoology than Lynn? Or more about safety protocols than Bill? I hope not! And when it comes to Nephia, you must appreciate how little you understand compared to me. You have no idea what it's like there. Suppose word gets around that Elves can produce lightweight, impenetrable armour. Every ambitious warrior might head to New Antra to demand their own – and the lives of everyone stationed there might now be in jeopardy. So too might the life of the boy. That shirt might have put a target on his back. It's possible, maybe even likely, that he'll be killed for it.'

Adam had not considered this. He felt a pang of remorse and deflated in his chair. 'Well, I'm sorry,' he said. 'But I wasn't trying to be cleverer than anyone here, nor do I think I am. I just wanted to do something nice for Lynn.'

'Yes,' said Lopek, nostrils flared, 'and in doing so, you have endangered –'

'That's enough!' said Bill, holding a palm up at each of them. He had spoken so loudly and suddenly that DeVenus turned his head to look at him. 'Adam, you shouldn't have given anything away like that, no matter how innocent you thought it was. Don't do it again. Doc, Adam's right; you should apologise for your behaviour! And Lynn, is it a dragon's tooth?'

Bill had asked the last question in the same tone he had used to scold the men. It took Lynn a moment to realise that she wasn't in trouble, and when she heard the question, a look of suppressed delight dawned on her face.

'I think it is!' she said. 'I won't be able to do a DNA test until we're back in the Hive, but it's the exact shape of a Synkarion tooth, only much bigger! And if its DNA does match … it may prove my hybrid pairing theory!'

Kal gave one of his thunderous claps, beaming at Lynn. DeVenus tracked the noise.

'Wow,' said Adam, grateful for the deflection. 'So, the dragon myths might be true?'

Lynn shrugged. 'Maybe!' she said, her cheeks practically glowing.

Bill winked at her.

'That's wonderful,' said Lopek, still looking stern. And after a silence, he turned back to Adam. 'I'm sorry for the way I shouted at you yesterday. Kaldor said that your Phrenaelia was very impressive.'

'Thanks,' said Adam, biting back the impulse to retort. 'And I promise not to trade with any more Nephians without your consent.'

Lopek smiled briefly. But a second later, his frown returned as he picked up his vibrating phone from the table.

'Everything okay?' asked Bill.

Lopek didn't answer. His eyes darted from side to side behind his glasses.

His frown deepened. 'How long until we reach Nephia?' he asked.

Everyone turned to Kal, who had a mouthful of cereal. He swallowed.

'Well, we're way ahead of schedule,' he said. 'If this wind keeps up, we might get there in ten days, maybe nine.'

Lopek began tapping his phone into the palm of his free hand, surveying it suspiciously.

'What is it, Doc?' said Bill.

'It's strange,' said Lopek. 'I can't get hold of my contact in New Antra. I haven't heard from him since I explained our new parameters, actually. I thought my phone might not be working out here, but I just received a message from the Hive; they haven't heard from anyone in New Antra for two weeks.'

Lopek slid his phone on the table.

'Is that unusual?' asked Bill.

'Not necessarily,' said Lopek slowly. 'Two weeks isn't a long enough silence to warrant concern. The consulate may have switched off their tech … or their batteries aren't recharging correctly … but there's something else too.'

He looked around at the others. 'While I was leading Captain Dawberry around yesterday,' he continued, 'he told me that his ship had turned back towards Nephia to avoid a storm. They didn't get close enough to see the land, but they spotted a great column of smoke rising from the direction of Laudria. Two weeks ago … Of course, it might be nothing, but the two facts together make me nervous.'

Bill folded his arms and considered Lopek for a moment. The others exchanged apprehensive looks.

'What are you thinking?' asked Bill.

'I'm not sure. There could be a rational explanation for both occurrences. But it feels ominous that communication with New Antra ended around the same time a column of smoke appeared near its location.'

'You think it's been attacked?' asked Bill.

Lopek pursed his lips. 'I wouldn't like to speculate without more information.'

'No,' said Bill, suddenly quite menacing, 'you *will* speculate. You're the expert on these people. If you think there's a problem, you tell me. What are you worried about?'

Lopek heaved a great sigh. He took off his glasses and rubbed the bridge of his slender nose.

'Worst case,' he said reluctantly, 'Markos has attacked New Antra and burned it down. But … as neat as that explanation sounds, it's not the only one. The two events might be unrelated; as I said, the battery supply might have died – it's quite common. And the smoke might be from a forest fire or a dozen other things. It's too easy to jump to conclusions.'

Bill looked unconvinced.

'It doesn't sound good to me,' said Lynn, touching the tooth around her neck.

Adam and Kal made noises of agreement. Lopek set his glasses back into position and leaned on the table.

'I agree,' he said, 'and, as a precaution, I suggest we change course now and head directly for Leybridge.'

Bill's eyes narrowed. 'Protocol in my risk assessment is pretty clear, Doc,' he said. 'If we're uncertain about landing … we don't. We scrub the mission.'

Lopek flushed, eyes wide.

'That seems a bit knee-jerk, Bill,' he said. 'We can't abort the whole mission just because –'

'Yes, we can,' Bill cut across. 'It's not worth it. I'm not letting you risk anyone's life just because you're obsessed with getting to Leybridge. I mean, why risk it? I know you want to meet these Krae people, but is there something else you're not telling me?'

The atmosphere around the table shifted. There was a small silence, filled by the ship's creaking.

'I'm not obsessed with getting to Leybridge,' Lopek said. 'And I'm offended at the notion I would put anyone's life at risk. I'm simply asking you to be more dynamic, Bill. Not everything is black and white. We'll be safer from the King in Leybridge than in Lysk. And if there's news of any unrest, Lord Farrow can resupply our ship, and we'll sail home. I promise.'

Bill looked unconvinced.

The idea of an early return had sunk Adam's heart. He couldn't go home yet. This was his one chance to retrieve more Inficore. 'What about the drone?' he offered. 'Could we fly it ahead to scope out the situation?'

'No,' said Bill. 'The dragonfly's range is about a mile, which would take us too close to the coast if things have gone sideways. And I'm not allowed to fly it over land.'

'Is there anything like that we could do?' asked Lynn, who evidently didn't want to end the expedition either. 'Kal, didn't you say we're ahead of schedule?'

'Yeah,' he replied, 'by a couple of days.'

'Well, can't we slow our approach for a few days, then? Buy some time? See if more of the picture emerges? The embassy guys might get in touch if we wait a bit, and then we'll know for sure.'

'I don't think that's a good idea,' said Bill. 'I don't want to spend more days at sea than necessary. The weather has been kind to us so far, but as Kal knows, it can turn cruel in an instant. I know you guys want to keep going. I get it. But, Doc, as your appointed security officer, I'm formally advising you to abort.'

All heads, except DeVenus's, turned to Lopek. His face was ashen, and he wore an odd, sickly expression like a scorned but defiant toddler. He took a deep breath, then looked up at his team. 'No,' he said. 'We change course for Leybridge.'

Bill stood, placed his chair neatly under the table, and left the cabin.

CHAPTER 29

Landing

Once Kaldor had finished putting Adam to work, loosening ropes and tying off others, he stood behind the ship's wheel and spun it down to the right. And that was that.

Their destination was now Leybridge.

The ship's prow moved briefly across the water rather than straight through it, but other than that, Adam felt no geographic difference in this new course. A featureless ocean was a featureless ocean in every direction. Although, it did somehow feel safer.

Once Bill had cooled off, his general mood improved quickly. But his attitude had undergone a subtle change that did not recover. Over the next few days, he issued fewer commands, allowing Lopek to take the lead, and spent more time with Adam, Lynn, and Kal. Adam knew this behaviour had little to do with camaraderie, however. It was petulance. Whenever anyone would ask Bill a question, for example, he would defer to Lopek, tight-lipped, in a gesture that plainly said, 'don't ask me; *he's* in charge.'

Lopek became strained and irritable without a partner to help shoulder his responsibilities. And the rift between the two men only deepened the longer it went unaddressed. On the surface, they were extremely cordial with one another. But they had lost the brotherhood of a shared trench, and Lopek suffered as a result.

'We need to say something,' said Lynn after a few days. 'We can't let Bill shirk his duty anymore. Not when we're so close to landing. He needs to get over it and apologise.'

She, Kal, Adam, and DeVenus were up on the steering deck. Bill was over on the bow, staring out at the blue horizon through the binoculars, and Lopek was somewhere below. Kal was at the helm.

'I wouldn't say he's shirking,' said Adam. 'Just look at him over there. He's been glued to those binoculars for the last two days, waiting to spot

Nephia. And I guarantee he'll snap out of it when we arrive. He'll have to.'

'I hope so,' said Lynn, biting her lip.

She was sitting cross-legged with an open notebook in her lap, staring towards the front of the ship. The tooth, potentially a dragon's, dangled beneath her neck. The late-afternoon sun was behind her.

'Don't worry,' said Kal, 'Adam's right. Bill wouldn't let us get into any real trouble. And if he does, DeVenus is ready to step in.'

Kaldor grinned at Adam, who sat opposite Lynn, massaging his bare, bruised feet.

'Careful,' he said to Kal, 'or I'll command him to attack you.'

'Come on,' said Lynn, tapping the notepad maliciously. 'You ready for the next one? I don't know about you, but I'm having loads of fun!'

'Me too!' said Kal, adjusting the wheel.

Adam looked at his feet. There were pale yellow patches on both bridges and smaller, purple bruises around his toes. He decided the left foot looked the least battered.

'Okay,' he sighed, standing up gingerly, 'what does the next one say?'

Lynn traced a finger on the notepad. 'It just says, *Protect me.*'

'Yeah, why not,' said Adam. 'DeVenus, this is a core instruction; protect me. Do you understand?'

The blank nodded, but Adam couldn't be sure whether he'd hesitated. He sighed, stuck out his left foot, holding the heavy book above it at waist height. DeVenus was sure to grab it this time. Surely.

Adam let go.

The spine of the book flattened all five of his toes at once. He let out a yelp and hobbled away, cursing the inanimate DeVenus, while Lynn and Kal laughed. Lynn crossed out the instruction.

'This is the most fun I've ever had,' she said.

'I'm beginning to think it's not possible,' said Adam, flexing his red toes to ensure they weren't broken. 'Why? He protects himself from everything. But nobody else. It's down to his lack of empathy, I'm sure.'

'Please don't quit,' said Kal, grinning.

'How many commands left?' said Adam.

'Four.'

'Right … either of you fancy taking a turn?'

'Oh, absolutely not,' said Lynn. 'This is your experiment. I wouldn't dream of interfering!'

'Hmm … I'll remember that rule when I stumble across a dragon skeleton.'

A sudden hollering from the front of the ship caught their attention. Bill was staring at his bracelet, his free fist raised triumphantly. He turned to them.

'Land ahoy!' he called over the wind.

Lynn stood up. She, Adam, and Kal looked out beyond the ship's bow at the horizon. It remained a solid and unbroken line of water.

'Take a look,' said Bill, coming over. He was alight with excitement. 'Look here!'

He shuffled back amongst them, holding up his wrist display as though checking the time. The others leant close over his shoulders, Kal still holding the wheel.

The miniature screen displayed the view before them; two shades of blue separated across the middle by an invisible line. But there was something else too. The vague shape of a long cloud, or what appeared to be a cloud, perched on the horizon. Adam could see a subtle green colour in the steel grey, and he appreciated for the first time that Nephia was a continent. Until now, it had occupied the recesses of his mind as a general concept. Somewhere that didn't really exist. But there it was, drifting towards him from behind the horizon. Solid, unending, and very real. He felt a thrill surge through him at the sight of it.

'Wow,' said Kal in breathless wonder. Lynn put her arm around his shoulder.

'I reckon we're about fifty miles off the coast, said Bill, looking up at the glinting silver object hovering way above. 'I'll get the dragonfly down. Lynn or Adam, go and tell Lopek we've spotted it. He should be up here when it rolls into view.'

Adam began hobbling away when Lynn grabbed his arm and insisted that he should sit down. She took off down the stairs and disappeared through the door beneath them.

'Now the real fun begins,' said Bill.

A moment later, Lopek scrambled nervously up on the deck, closely followed by Lynn. The team stood clustered together for a long while, staring out to sea as the ship cut through the waves, the wind billowing in the sails above them. Gradually, the distant line of the horizon began to change. Its line was broken by hazy, washed-out features. Faint ridges and slopes sprouted into tiny, faraway mountains as the mass of land began to devour their entire field of view. Bill punched Lopek in the shoulder. They exchanged a significant look.

'I'll have to slow down or change course soon,' said Kal. 'We don't have much daylight left. It'll be much harder to spot any lurking reef or sand bank by starlight – and the moon won't be around until much later. There might not be any ports along this section for a reason.'

'We should make the ship ready,' said Lopek, his eyes drinking in the mass before them. 'Get everything down into the sinkbox.'

Bill turned to the team and said, 'You heard the man.'

Adam and Lynn hastened to their rooms to gather their contraband. Again, Adam had very few items to conceal. When he had finished loading them into the sinkbox, he scanned Kal's room, which was a mirror image of his own, but littered with astronomical charts, harbouring a slightly musty smell. He helped Lynn with her remaining things, including the fridge door, which he learned was a folding table for dissection. It explained why the odour coming from Lynn's room was most repugnant. Bill and Lopek's room was military-grade neat. It bore no signs of their four-week cohabitation. It actually looked more orderly than when they had set off.

'– much closer do we need to get?' Bill said to Kal as Adam and Lynn arrived on the top deck.

'Well,' said Kal, cupping a hand across his brow and twisting to look at the sun's position. 'I reckon we've got about three hours of clear daylight left, then maybe ninety minutes of fading twilight. But we don't know what kind of shallows we're entering. We could maroon ourselves on underwater rocks. If we use the propellers at full speed, we'll get within range of the coast easily before the light fails. I'll be able to spot any coral heads on the approach and get a feel for the water. If we keep sailing, we might be okay, but it's riskier.'

'You want to use up some battery power?' asked Lopek.

'If it were up to me, yeah,' said Kal. 'Otherwise, we could drop an anchor further offshore and wait 'til morning if you like. But I think we should go for it now.'

Bill rubbed a hand down his face as though trying to drag it off.

'What's your reticence, Bill?' asked Lopek. Bill fixed the land ahead with a stern look.

'I was hoping to reserve the batteries for an emergency,' he said, 'now that we're not going to Lysk. But, if Kaldor thinks it'll be safer to speed up and use the daylight, I agree.'

'Then let's do it,' said Lopek.

Adam kept the helm steady as Kal disappeared to start the propellers. It was more challenging than he had imagined. The extended spokes of the wheel came just beneath his chin. Polished wooden handles that pulled with the listing of the ship.

A second later, Adam felt the floor vibrate as a loud churning roared into life. Kal returned and took the wheel, which seemed less agitated in the sailor's grip. Adam looked out at the line of cloudy white water now trailing behind them. The spot where Kal had turned on the propellers was visible a few dozen yards away in the sea.

Kal ordered the team to raise the sails in case they now acted as a drag. Bill took charge of the detail, pairing them up and dividing the work. By the time the last sail was furled and tied, Adam could now see faint details on the distant rocky cliff that marked the nearest stretch of coastline. He could tell they were closer, but it still seemed very far away.

'Which coast do you reckon we're looking at?' asked Bill.

'Which Realm, you mean?' said Lopek. 'It's difficult to say. We must be five hundred miles north of Laudria, at least. It could be the north of Ealee or maybe the south of Reon. Impossible to tell for certain without any available towns or distinguishable features.'

'You wanna get a bit closer?' asked Kal daringly.

Lopek stroked his stubbled throat. 'What do you recommend?'

Kal lifted his chin and peered overboard at the dark-blue water, his hands resting gently on the wheel. 'It looks deep enough.' He shrugged. 'I think we could risk another half-mile if you wanted to get a closer look.'

Bill nodded at Lopek and smiled. Kal spun the wheel once more.

'I need you guys to spot me,' said Kal. 'Stand in pairs on either side of the fore, and just yell back if you spot any eddies. Can't be too careful in uncharted sea.'

Adam rested his elbows on the starboard rail, looking down at the open water ahead. He wasn't sure how useful he would be at this task. The water was nothing but eddies in his eyes. But the others didn't mention them, so he kept his mouth shut. Instead, he watched the momentary white tips of waves that peaked then folded over into the abundance. The occasional flying fish, neon green, that leapt out like missiles from the ship's hull, gliding low in smooth lines over the inconstant surface until they dipped and melted back into the water. There were birds overhead now. The coast was very close.

'Ship!' called Lopek suddenly. 'There's a ship up ahead! Look!'

Adam looked up and saw the wooden body of a ship drifting out from a hidden cove. The dark figure of a man stood in the half-barrel shape that was skewered atop the ship's mast, and its large sail was angled like a cut toenail in the wind. The man in the crow's nest seemed very animated, and the ship angled slowly toward *The Alliance*.

'She's not raising a flag …' said Kal.

'That's a warship,' said Lopek, a mixture of fear and confusion on his face.

Long wooden poles slid upward from the approaching vessel like wings. They were lowered into the water and began to pull in unison.

'Shit!' said Bill. 'Kal, turn us around! Now!'

Kal gritted his teeth and spun the wheel as fast as he could. Slowly, *The Alliance* turned full circle, but the momentum they had gained from the propellers widened their arc and briefly carried them closer to the advancing warship. Adam heard the triumphant call of voices on the wind. The deep pounding of a drum. He saw flashes of dull silver brandished above the heads lining the bow.

His legs became hollow.

'Elves! It's an Elvish ship!' he heard one of the voices cry.

'Everyone! Look at me!' said Bill.

With a great effort, the team tore their horrified eyes from their pursuers. Bill's face was determined.

'We can't outrun them,' he said. 'They are going to board us. We don't run, and we don't hide. Remember your training and stay calm. Follow my lead, and don't say anything unless I tell you. We cooperate. If they take us hostage, we let them take us. Adam, is DeVenus ready to fight?'

Adam shook his head in despair.

'Fine. Take him to the hold,' said Bill. 'I don't want him to start trouble if he's not ready. Put him in the sinkbox and release it. On your way to the hold, get the black case from beneath my bedside and put it at the back of the hold, *not* in the sinkbox. Do you understand?'

Adam nodded.

'Kal,' Bill continued, 'kill the engine. Lynn, you know what to do.'

Bill locked eyes with Lynn, who was trembling badly. But she clenched her jaw tight and nodded. She reached inside her coat and fumbled out a small circular tin. She twisted it open. Adam saw an opaque, paste-like gel inside. Lynn scooped out a thick wadge with a shaking finger. Hesitating only for a second, she began smearing it around her mouth and chin. She cried muffled sobs as angry red blisters formed instantly on the places she had traced. Her finger became scarlet and swollen.

The dreadful voices of their pursuers got louder.

'Elves! We've got Elvish scum!'

'You all know what to do; now go!' Bill yelled over the synchronised heaving of oars, the drumming, and the taunting laughter. Kal sprinted to the stern.

'DeVenus, follow me!' Adam called, crashing his way through the door into the ship. He heard the blank following him but did not turn to look. He found himself pinballing between the walls of the narrow upper hall as he raced along it. He felt the wood against his hands and the gentle air flow against his face. They were under attack. It all seemed so unreal and yet so vivid. He felt the vibrations of the propellers stop and remembered to collect Bill's case just as he passed the security officer's room. It was heavy and cold and unreal. A moment later, he and DeVenus were inside the hold.

'Climb down there!' said Adam.

The blank lowered himself into the sinkbox and stood amid the equipment.

'Lie down!' Adam commanded as he made his way to the wooden lever. DeVenus created a space and lay on his back, staring face-up like a cadaver. Adam worried briefly about how deep the sinkbox would dive and whether there would be enough air in the tiny space for the blank to survive. It didn't matter now. He pulled the lever. The floor unfolded to entomb DeVenus and the kit. Adam flipped the lever again and felt the separation. He threw Bill's case into a corner and raced back to the top deck. The expedition team was huddled together near the door. They clutched him into the tight diamond around Lynn.

'Lynn stays between us,' Bill called from the front. 'Don't get separated.'

The Nephian ship was twenty feet away. The cruel faces were clear. Those nearest were spinning clawlike hooks at the ends of ropes, while those behind them clattered weapons against their decking and shields, jeering. The claws swung into the air and landed loudly on the deck of *The Alliance*. The ropes were pulled tight, and the claws cut into the soft railing.

They were caught. Trapped. Adam felt his limbs fizzing with blood.

The hostile men heaved on the ropes until the two boats bumped together. As soon as they touched, armed Nephian soldiers cascaded over the railings in a thunderous hail of footfall. They spread out on the deck of *The Alliance* until they surrounded the expedition team in a crescent. Adam saw clubs and hooks and swords and spears in their hands. The faces wore a cold astonishment as though they had discovered a great treasure. Adam gripped his teammates, afraid he might faint.

A wild Nephian with a greasy ginger beard and hair shoved his way forward from the middle of the crescent. His visible skin was pocked and clammy, his left eye missing beneath a blackened scar. He raised a heavy axe one-handed above his head and slammed it partway through the wooden floor, inches from Bill's feet. The team jerked backwards, but the security officer did not flinch. The ginger man spoke in a deep growl.

'Who is captain?' he demanded.

Lopek began to separate himself, but Bill's arm kept him tight into the huddle.

'I am,' said Bill. He drew out a black knife from his belt.

The Nephians roared with laughter. One backed away sardonically into the embrace of his fellows. A horizon of missing teeth. The ginger man's only eye stared at the knife in disgust, and his expression soured even deeper when Bill let it drop to the floor with a clatter. 'I do not accept your challenge,' Bill said in a rehearsed voice. 'We yield. Take whatever you please.'

The bearded man stepped around the angled shaft of his axe and picked up Bill's knife with contempt. It looked comically small in his hands. He leaned down to stare into Bill's face for a moment when, without warning, he thrust the knife hard into Bill's upper chest, just beneath the collarbone of his left shoulder. The team convulsed as one. Bill let out a grunt of pain, and his hands flew up to hold the wrist of the Nephian, but he kept his eyes on his attacker's face, breathing hard through gritted teeth.

'I do not accept your challenge,' Bill repeated, his voice strained. 'We yield. Take whatever you please.'

The Nephian twisted the knife. Bill howled in agony.

'Bill!' Lynn screamed. The ugly eye shifted to look at her.

The Nephian hurled Bill to the floor like a child and yanked Lynn forward by the wrist. Adam made to pull her back, but Bill had rebounded to his feet quickly, clutching the handle sticking out from his upper chest, and deliberately blocked Adam's way. The Nephian turned Lynn's face upward with his free hand and scanned it with interest. He recoiled and pushed her back into the team's arms when his eyes found the blisters around her mouth. He wiped his hands on his filthy shirt and spat on the floor.

'Dirty Elvish scum!' he roared. Then he turned to face his eager men and wrenched his axe from the splintered wood. 'Take them below! But do not kill them! We take their bounty and their ship. And make it ready. We sail for Marsh and the Queen Regent. Kaiber will pay well for Elvish heads!'

A cheer went up at these words, but the noise was drowned beneath the deafening sound of weapons clattering together. The bearded man disappeared through the folds of his men, who now approached the team greedily, forcing them back toward the door to the lower decks.

'Let them take us,' Bill hissed, turning to face the team. 'Adam, move, lead us to the hold!'

Adam turned and found that his legs were trembling badly. Overhead, men climbed into the rigging of *The Alliance* to undress her sails. Adam pushed through the door. Inside, he could hear the panicked breathing of Lynn, Kal, and Lopek close behind him. He tried to look at them, but the light was too dim. He saw Bill's silhouette coming last through the door, followed by many, much larger outlines.

'Move!' said Bill, and there was a rattle in his voice this time. 'The narrow halls will slow them down.'

'Silence, Elf!' came a growling voice from behind, followed by a thud and a pained grunt.

Adam realised that he was holding something. It was Lynn's hand; cold and clammy. He didn't remember taking it. He strode quickly past the bedrooms toward the second set of stairs, which he descended to the lower hall. He heard doors being kicked open above and rooms being ransacked by trailing Nephians.

He entered the hold and walked Lynn to the far side to make room for those behind. The fading daylight filled the empty space. He felt numb. Lynn's cold hand squeezed his tightly as Kal and Lopek entered, looking lost and terrified. Bill joined last, half staggering, his face a pale grimace, his black shirt wet with blood.

The security officer wasted no time. He pulled out the knife with a quick jerk and handed it to Kal. Then he whipped off his shirt and began to twist it into a sling. His chest hair was matted with blood. He spoke in an urgent whisper. 'Doc, when they come in, find out what's happening. Kal, take off your shirt and hold it tight to my wound, now! Lynn, tie this around it,' he handed his wet shirt to Lynn, 'Adam, stay at the back and open my case. The code is one-one-seven-eight. Got it?'

Adam nodded. He retrieved the case from the corner and found the coded lock. He manoeuvred behind Kal, who was pressing his balled-up shirt into Bill's shoulder as Lynn struggled to make a knot in the wet shirt. Adam thumbed the numbers into position, repeating the number in his head. *One. One. Seven. Eight.* Lopek stared at him, lips parted as though about to speak.

Two Nephian men ducked into the hold, scowling. Their heads swivelled in all directions, taking in the lack of plunder, their teeth bared. Both were dressed in rusty chainmail and armed with drawn swords. Their eyes landed on the team.

'Where is your cargo?' the nearest man demanded. His broad nostrils flared, and a vivid red scar fell down his cheek from the corner of his eye like a teardrop. 'What do you carry?'

'N-nothing,' said Lopek taking a timid step forward. He gave a reflexive bow. 'We are a diplomatic delegation, come to Nephia to make contact with the Krae … but your captain spoke of a Queen Regent. I pray you, what did he mean –'

The second Nephian, a thinner, white man with bulging eyes and a twisted jaw, sent Lopek spinning to the floor with a backhand. Lopek clutched the side of his reddened face and scrambled around for his glasses with his free hand. Adam felt the ship change course. Footsteps pounded overhead.

'Stay down,' said Bill, his eyes on the Nephians, who turned to look at him. A bead of sweat rolled down the back of Bill's neck. His right hand was splayed behind his back as though waiting to receive something. Adam turned the final digit on the case slowly and silently. He didn't dare look at it, so he tested the latch by feeling each new number. 'Ask them if the King is dead,' Bill finished.

'Is … is Markos Almanfier dead?' breathed Lopek, dragging himself away from his assailant.

The scarred Nephian laughed. The other leant over Lopek and spat at his retreating feet.

'The King lives!' he sneered triumphantly, bulbous eyes wide. 'Tha's right! Your attempt on 'is life failed, scum! Lady Kaiber 'as took 'is place as Queen Regent, 'til the King 'as got his strength back. And she will reward us for more little Elves to slaughter!'

He straightened up, his lopsided jaw quivering as he laughed. His companion stared at Lynn.

'But she won't mind if we 'ave a little fun with you first,' he said. 'And since you got nothin' for us to take, we'll 'aff ter take somink else. I never 'ad Elf pussy before.'

Lynn did not understand his words but got the gist of his meaning. She held herself. Kal stepped in front of her defiantly, and Adam had to move with him to avoid revealing the case. He was halfway through testing all the digits of the final pin.

'Don' touch that one, Bulwei!' said the thinner man, pointing at Lynn in disgust. 'Looks like she's got the rot.'

'That don't matter to me,' said the man called Bulwei, smiling hungrily at Lynn. 'I got it too.' He handed his sword to his fellow and started undoing his chainmail.

'Keep them talking, Doc,' said Bill urgently. 'Lynn … trust me. Take off your clothes. And do it slow. Adam, hurry up.'

Lynn gave Bill a look of such desperate ruin that Adam felt sick. But Bill kept his eyes on the Nephians, his hand still stretched behind his back. Lynn looked at Bulwei and began to pull her shirt over her head. The Nephians' faces lit up as they gawped excitedly at Lynn's smooth, exposed flesh. Bulwei undressed with greater enthusiasm.

Lopek said something, but Adam didn't hear it. The latch on the case gave way. He opened it and felt inside without looking. It was lined with sponge teeth. His fingers found three metal objects. A cylinder. An L shape. A flat rectangle. The Nephians were staring at Lynn as she undid the clasp of her bra. Adam glanced down at the open case.

His stomach disappeared.

Laid neatly inside the case were the components of a gun.

Bill caught sight of the open case in his peripheral vision.

'Lynn,' he said, 'when I finish talking, shout back at me as if I'm talking to you! Adam, put the magazine in the gun and attach the silencer.'

Lynn sobbed something back at Bill while Bulwei proceeded to undo the belt around his trousers. The nameless Nephian leaned on his two swords, staring at Lynn with a mixture of disgust and fascinated relish. Adam used the distraction to duck down and pull the gun from its cut-out. Shaking, he slid the magazine inside the grip the wrong way. He corrected. It clicked into position. He fumbled out the black cylinder and twisted it onto the barrel. Round and round and round it spun. Finally, he could turn it no more. Everyone was shouting by the time he stood. Lynn was screaming, naked. Bulwei had pulled her to the centre of the room by her hair. The other Nephian had raised both swords, standing between Lynn and the team, laughing maliciously. Adam thrust the gun into Bill's hand.

The sequence was over in an instant. Two flashes and the nameless Nephian's smile slid away. Adam felt an aerosol mist of blood on his face as crimson holes appeared in the man's face and forehead. Bulwei pulled Lynn to his chest, a thick arm around her neck. He stared at the gun in awe. But Lynn's hands were free. She wrenched the dragon's tooth from its necklace and slammed it into Bulwei's thigh. His grip slackened in shock. Lynn wriggled clear. *Putt putt putt.* Two rounds in the chest, one in the head. Bulwei keeled backwards. Lynn collapsed to the floor.

'Keep shouting!' said Bill into the stunned silence. He peered down the hall over the gun barrel, then looked up at the ceiling. The sound of furniture being overturned had not changed. Adam and Kal began shouting nonsensical vowels. Lopek stared at Bill. 'We go through the sink hatch and swim for the shore!' the security officer bellowed. 'Kal, open it up!'

Adam helped Lynn to her feet and moved her to the wall. She did not attempt to resist him or cover herself. She simply stared into an invisible void, panting hard. Bill dragged the nameless man aside as the floor began to unfold. A black oval of water was slowly revealed, churning slightly in the ship's momentum. The team stared at the seething mass, uncertain.

'Go!' Bill hissed. 'More will come!'

Adam heard the unmistakable creaking of footsteps on the stairs.

'Stay calm, stick together,' said Bill. 'I'll hold them off!'

Kal and Lopek gathered on either side of Lynn and Adam in a line. They looked at each other, hands clasped tightly. Adam saw his fear reflected back in each of them. The gun flashed behind them, and angry voices cried from the hall.

They leapt as one into the water.

Adam plunged into freezing liquid darkness. Every inch of his skin was pierced by icicles. A roar of bubbles passed his ears from his mouth and nose. He kicked his burning feet wildly and knew a moment of sheer terror when his head bumped into something solid and huge above, blocking his path to the surface. He released Lynn and Lopek's hands and pushed up against the unknown ceiling. The underside of *The Alliance* was slimy and dotted with sharp barnacles. Adam groped his way blindly along it, desperate, trying to move against the ship's momentum. On and on it went. His lungs were empty. He was going to drown. This was his death. The slimy wood curved suddenly upward, out of reach, and his head broke free of the water. He sprayed out a mouthful of salt and took a sharp breath of bitterly cold air. Other heads breached around him in the twilight, coughing and spluttering. The team thrashed towards each other in the pulling wake of *The Alliance*, which towered above them against the night sky. They formed a ring of bobbing heads.

'Where's the shore?' said Lopek, his head whipping in all directions.

'There!' said Kal, staring over Lynn's shoulder.

Adam looked in the direction Kal was indicating. The dark outline of the coast obscured the lowest stars. It seemed impossibly far away.

'Keep moving!' said Lopek. He began to paddle towards the dark mass. Lynn was still staring at the ship, her naked body a ghostly white and rippling in the black water.

'What about Bill?' she cried, jaw trembling in the cold.

At that instant, they heard more muted gunfire from the ship's direction. They looked up. Dim flashes lit up the undersides of *The Alliance's* rigging and sails. Seconds later, a figure dived over the railing and hit the water with a hard splash. Bill had leapt from the stern. He resurfaced a few yards away and pawed his way one-handed toward the team, grimacing in pain as a spear drove into the water beside him.

'The shore is that way!' said Kal.

'Quiet!' Bill hissed, turning his back on the receding ship. 'Stay close and stay quiet!'

Adam heard angry voices from the ship as dark figures lined its bow.

With a grunt, Bill lifted his left arm from the water and held a right-hand finger against the bracelet on his wrist. It lit up brightly in the darkness, and Bill shielded it like a candle flame. There were shouts from *The Alliance*, but the ship continued to sail away.

'We need to keep moving!' whispered Lopek. 'We'll f-freeze! And they might circle back!'

Bill's face disappeared as his wrist screen went dark. 'No!' he said. 'We stay here! It's coming!'

Adam felt the awful cold draining his very soul. His bones shook. His whole body was on fire. He could not understand why Bill was forcing them to linger. Then, a new horror dawned as a monstrous whale broke the surface beside him. For an awful, primal second, Adam expected its jaw to swallow them. But the whale righted itself and merely bobbed innocently. And with a rush of relief, Adam realised it was the sinkbox.

'Grab hold!' yelled Bill.

But there was little need. The whole team was already thrashing toward it, each clutching at one of the locking arms designed to bind the submersible to the ship.

'Hold tight!' said Bill.

Within seconds, the sinkbox began to race forward like a speedboat, pulling them through the water straight for the land. Adam had to adjust his grip to maintain his hold against the drag. He let his numb body be lifted by the force of passing water. His only thought was to hold on. *Hold on!* He hoped the others were doing the same.

An eternity later, Adam felt the sinkbox slow, and his trailing feet began to sink. He saw a faint line of ethereal grey very close. A pebble beach. He heard the waves crashing against it. His heart beat wildly as his feet found the floor. Bill was already standing in the chest-height water, pushing the sinkbox landward with his uninjured arm. The others joined the struggle until their feet splashed and crunched on the shallow stones. The sinkbox slid up onto the beach and refused to be moved further, the tide receding beneath it. Lynn and Lopek collapsed.

'Up!' called Bill. 'Get up! We can't rest here!'

Numbly, Adam helped Lopek to his feet while Kal assisted Lynn. She was shaking violently, her naked skin almost blue. Kal held her tight to his bare chest to shield her from the breeze. Bill attempted to open the sinkbox manually by forcing each locking arm upward. Adam and Lopek rushed over to help, but their hands were stiff and weak with cold, and they managed to lift only one between them. Once all the arms were angled upward, the mechanised roller covering parted from the centre and revealed their belongings, which were tossed haphazardly.

Adam found DeVenus buried amid the jumble, staring upward, still and grey.

The blank was dead.

Adam had barely registered this when Bill whistled and threw a rucksack at Kal, who caught it behind Lynn's back.

'Everyone, get dressed,' said Bill. 'Get into dry clothes and layer up. We need to stay focused. We're not out of the woods yet.'

Kal began pulling clothes from the bag and handing them to Lynn. Adam peeled off his freezing, sodden clothes.

'What the fuck were you thinking, Bill?' came Lopek's voice. 'You brought a gun? After all my warnings? You brought a *gun!* You have no idea what you've done!'

'I know exactly what I've done,' said Bill coldly, tossing a rucksack at Lopek with added venom. 'I've just saved our lives!'

Lopek slammed the rucksack to the pebbled ground.

'At what cost?' he said. 'You've just revealed what we're capable of! What weapons we possess! No Antharian will ever be safe in Nephia again! And you've as good as killed everyone in New Antra!'

'Weren't you listening?' Bill hissed, moving around the sinkbox to stare down at Lopek. 'They think we're at war! Everyone in New Antra is already dead. Nothing matters now. Not your cultural laws, not our expedition. All those parameters are gone, Doc. We are stranded in a hostile land without means of escape or communication. Our only mission now is survival.'

Lopek stared up at Bill for a long moment, fists clenched. Lynn and Kal had stopped dressing to witness the standoff. Eventually, Bill turned away. He tossed a third rucksack angrily across the sinkbox at Adam.

But it didn't arrive.

A grey hand shot up from the depths of the sinkbox to stop the rucksack in its flight, and in the same motion, it was sent hurtling back at

Bill, who took it squarely in the chest and was knocked over backwards by the force of the throw.

DeVenus rose eerily from the centre of the sinkbox, his deathly grey complexion fading away. He swivelled his head to look at each of them in turn. Adam gaped at him.

It was not possible.

CHAPTER 30

Inland

DeVenus jumped from the half-boat, landing silently on the pebbled floor. He stood beside Adam, who continued to stare at the blank, nonplussed. Bill got to his feet clutching Adam's rucksack.

'Whoa,' said Kal. 'Did he just protect you? Did it just work?'

'I … I think it did,' said Adam, letting out a small laugh. He did not understand what had just happened. He had seen DeVenus dead.

'Well, let's congratulate ourselves later!' said Bill, walking over to Adam and cautiously handing over the rucksack. 'Hurry up and get dressed. We need to hide the sinkbox further up the beach. I want to harvest it for whatever we might need once I've formulated our next move. Then we'll need to find somewhere inland to set up for the night. If those assholes presume we're not dead, they'll scout the shore for us, so we must move quickly.'

Lopek commenced to tear off his wet clothes, slapping them to the ground, seething. Adam and Bill followed suit, Bill removing his impromptu sling with some difficulty, tucking his left arm tight to his chest. The others were dressed, Lynn very withdrawn. Bill was looking at her.

'Doctor Carson,' he said, 'would you take a look at my shoulder?

For a moment, Lynn seemed not to have heard him. Then, she lifted her head.

'Sorry, Bill …' she said, 'of course.' And she strode purposefully to the sinkbox to retrieve a medical bag. She rummaged inside it, selected a handful of items, walked over to Bill, and gently guided him to his knee so she could better look at his wound. It bled in a thin trickle down his chest, the blood pooling in the crook of his arm. She set to work.

'Put your wet clothes in the sinkbox,' came Bill's voice from behind Lynn. 'We can't leave any trace that we landed here.'

Adam, Kal, and Lopek gathered all the discarded clothes and slung them into a sodden pile inside the sinkbox. As he peered over its rim, it suddenly dawned on Adam that much of the kit inside had been destined for people who were almost certainly dead.

'Did I hear them right?' Kal asked Lopek. 'Did those men say that Elves had attacked the King?'

'That's what they said,' Lopek replied gravely, looking back at the dark sea. 'But I don't believe it. It doesn't make any sense.'

'Is anyone else hurt?' said Lynn. She and Bill had come back to the sinkbox. Bill wore a rectangular bandage taped down on his shoulder, his arm in a genuine sling.

'Adam's hit his head,' said Lopek.

Adam touched his forehead.

'You've got some blood, just here,' said Kal, pointing at the back of his own head.

Adam carefully dabbed the area Kal had specified. He winced at the sharp stinging pain, his fingertips red.

'Blimey,' he said, suddenly queasy. 'Must've happened when we came up under the boat.'

'Come here,' said Lynn, and just like she had done with Bill, she directed Adam to his knee, her hands cold and soft. She manipulated his head like a barber, then rummaged inside the medical bag at her hip. Adam braced for the pain as Lynn fiddled with his injury. But she was too good. From his kneeling position, with his head cocked to one side, he could see Bill's face clearly in the dim starlight. He was watching Lynn work with a satisfied expression.

It was a shrewd move to get her working like this, Adam thought. Bill's prompt had both distracted Lynn and reminded her of her power.

Very shrewd indeed.

Adam felt something pressed on the cut as Lynn unrolled a tight bandage around his forehead. She tied it on the opposite side of his head, then put a hand on Adam's shoulder to let him know she was done. Adam stood. He could feel his heartbeat in the wound.

'Come on,' said Bill, his free hand resting on the sinkbox. 'Let's get this thing out of sight.' He looked both ways along the beach. 'There,' he said. 'Let's drag it behind that boulder. It's the best we can do.'

The team flanked the sinkbox on either side, each holding one of the protruding arms as they had done in the water. Their destination seemed close, but by resting his hands on the locking arm, Adam knew the sinkbox would not shift easily through the stones.

'DeVenus,' he said. The blank looked at him. 'Help us drag this ship behind that large rock. Do you understand?'

The blank turned his head in the direction Adam had signalled, then he turned back and saw the team bracing themselves against the sinkbox, ready to push. He nodded, then gripped the stunted bow with both hands.

'On three then,' said Bill. 'One, two, three!'

Adam leaned his weight against the arm. To his great surprise, it moved forward immediately, sliding over the large pebbles, the keel carving its way through them, causing them to rise up and part, avalanching on either side with a pleasant clicking and cracking. Adam missed a step on the treacherous, moving stones. He stopped pushing to catch his balance, and the ship continued steadily on its path without him. Adam looked at the team. Lopek had let go too, and Lynn looked like she was barely pushing at all. Bill looked up, and when he saw that the others had stopped, he let go in confusion, but the ship kept moving.

'Kaldor,' said Adam, and Kal raised his head to see that the others had let go. He stopped in his tracks, and the ship slid by him without change in its speed. Adam's mouth fell open.

DeVenus dragged the half-tonne sinkbox through the rocks on his own.

If the effort of hauling it strained the blank, no trace of exertion marred his face. He strolled backwards steadily, with one arm extended to the bow, as though pulling a kite.

'Did you know it could do that?' said Bill, who had sidled up to Adam.

'No,' he said truthfully.

But as he stared at the display of inhuman strength, a fantastic possibility occurred. The experiments with Kirrion and Inficore had worked better than he'd imagined. DeVenus was using the full potential of his body without harm or fatigue, like Inficore. And when DeVenus had appeared dead inside the sinkbox, it wasn't the lack of oxygen that had caused his grey discolouration. No. The Kirrion in his body had temporarily turned him to stone to protect him from suffocating.

Wow.

The team followed in the wake of DeVenus and the sinkbox. Once they were safely sheltered from view, the group began to sift through its contents for anything useful. They extracted the tents and filled their rucksacks with as much food and water as they could carry. They packed some spare clothes, the dead Inficore, and as many medical instruments as Lynn could squeeze into their bags.

'We need to find somewhere to camp for the night,' said Bill. 'I want to get as far away from the coast as possible before daybreak and test out the tents.'

Kal led the team to a grassy dune nearby. It was steep, and the sand shifted underfoot as they climbed. It levelled out atop the cliff, overlooking the stony beach. From this vantage point, even in the near darkness, Adam could make out the sinkbox behind the boulder and the line it had carved through the rocks. It was obvious that the beach had been disturbed. He hoped a passing ship wouldn't notice.

The landscape above the beach was a rugged patchwork of rocky dunes and stout, shrubby plants. Bill led the team in a single file, with DeVenus at the rear. The darkness seemed more complete away from the sea, and everyone except the blank stumbled to the ground more than once, off-balanced by their rucksacks. Adam lost track of time as they trudged. It felt like hours. He was exhausted, and his head throbbed severely. Then, the ground smoothed out into a large field of knee-high grass where the outline of a dead tree was visible, far to the left. Bill led them toward it and set down his rucksack against the trunk. He turned to the others, all of whom were panting.

'This will do for tonight,' he said. 'Let's get as much sleep as we can before dawn, then set off right away. Tents up.'

Once the three tents were erected, Adam ordered DeVenus to get some sleep. Bill shared with Lopek, and Lynn slept alone while Kal took the first watch at Bill's instruction. They would each take an hour. Adam was third in line, which meant he would get two hours if he was lucky.

The tents were large enough to be comfortable, with sleeping bags sewn into the floor. Adam climbed inside, resting his head against his rucksack, careful not to turn on his injury.

Sleep took him at once. But as soon as he had drifted away, he was startled awake by a kick on his foot. Adam sat up and felt warm drool coating his cheek. Two hours could not have passed already. Kal stood at his tent door, whispering something. It took a moment for his words to register.

'Wake up!' he said. 'Someone's here.'

Blearily, Adam crawled from his tent and shivered in the night air. The rest of the team was also emerging, including DeVenus, who seemed perfectly rested. Bill stood a few dozen yards away, staring at something Adam could not see.

'Up there,' said Kal, cocking his head at the small hill to the left. Adam squinted up, still half-asleep, when his eyes found the dark shape of two figures atop the hill on horseback. They were no more than a hundred feet away and so dark that they might have been invisible had they not been silhouetted against the stars. Even at this distance, it was clear that they were watching the team.

'What do you reckon, Doc?' said Bill.

'I'm not sure,' said Lopek. 'I don't know where we are, so there's no telling who they might be. We should stand our ground and let them approach if they want.'

'You're the boss,' said Bill. But his hand felt for the gun tucked into the back of his belt.

The two horsemen continued to stare for some time. Nobody moved except the horses, who nodded in the cold, tails twitching. Eventually, the smaller stranger peeled away and rode off down the far side of the hill out of sight. The remaining horseman began to descend towards the team.

An old man on a white horse came into view. His short, thinning hair was grey, his face covered in deep lines. He stopped his advance a few yards away, holding a crossbow in both hands. He eyed the tents and took in the faces of the team. Then he spoke.

'Who are you?' he said, his voice clear though quavering. 'What are you Elves doing on my land?'

Lopek stepped forward slowly. He bowed. 'We mean you no harm, good sir,' he said. 'We do not mean to trespass on your land. Our ship ran aground offshore and forced us to make land here. We will be gone in the morning at your leave.'

The old man studied Lopek for a moment as though weighing him. He dismounted with surprising agility and walked towards them, his crossbow poised.

Bill's hand was ready behind his back.

DeVenus took a single step toward the approaching man, who stopped advancing at once, watching the blank warily. Adam sincerely hoped that the old man would not attack. He had no idea how DeVenus would react, but he was certain it would not end well for the stranger. Adam cleared his throat to get the blank's attention. The old man looked in his direction too, and his eyes found the bandage on Adam's head.

'What happened to you?' he asked Adam directly.

'I was hurt in the water,' Adam managed. 'Rocks,' he finished lamely.

The old man lowered his crossbow. 'You are healers?' he said.

Lopek looked at Lynn, who didn't understand the discourse.

'Yes,' said Lopek.

Suddenly, the old man dropped to his knees and let the crossbow fall to the ground. 'Ohrak has sent you!' he gasped. 'He has sent you to save my son!'

Bill shot Lopek a quizzical look. Lopek translated what the man had said.

'Ask him what happened to his son,' said Bill.

Lopek asked the question. The old man shook his head.

'He is very sick,' he said pleadingly. 'He was wounded sparring with Lord Costel. And the cut has brought him a terrible fever. I feared he would not survive the night. But Ohrak has sent you to save him!'

Lopek translated the old man's words for Bill, but Lynn stepped forward and crouched on her haunches to look into his face. 'Take me to him,' she said.

Silent tears rolled down the cheeks of the old man, who seemed to understand. He stared at Lynn as though she were a miracle.

CHAPTER 31

The Healer

Adam lay still for ten whole minutes inside his sleeping bag, willing himself to sleep. But it was no use. His mind kept throwing up jarring images from the day, and he became too aware of his heartbeat, which pounded and disappeared in irregular rhythms.

Giving up, he pulled on extra layers, crawled out of the tent, careful not to rouse DeVenus, and joined Kaldor, who sat facing the dark hill over which Lopek, Lynn, and Bill had followed the old man.

'You okay?' said Kal, as Adam sat beside him, sinking a little into the patch of flattened grass.

'Can't sleep,' he yawned, keeping his voice low. 'You get some rest if you want. I'll keep an eye out.'

'Neh, it's okay,' said Kal, shooting Adam a subdued grin that did not reach his eyes. 'I don't reckon I'd be able to sleep much either.' Kal looked up, his braid wiry and dishevelled in the darkness. 'Besides … it's a clear sky.'

Adam looked up too. The stars were indeed out in force. And yet, somehow, their majesty was lost tonight. There was a long silence as the canvas of the tents flapped in the wind.

'How long since the others left?' Adam asked.

'About half an hour. Do you reckon they're okay?'

Kal's profile betrayed his fear. 'I'm sure they're fine. Bill's with them. And he left his silencer, so we'll hear gunshots if anything happens.'

Kal nodded slowly. 'I can't believe he brought a gun,' he said. 'I'm glad. Obviously. I mean, if he hadn't, then Lynn might –'

'It's not worth thinking about, mate.'

'Yeah …' said Kal. 'But the way he just … dispatched those two men – shot them dead, out of nowhere … I've never seen anyone die before. Have you?'

Adam pondered. 'Not unless you count blanks,' he said. 'You feeling okay?'

'Yeah … yeah, I think so,' said Kal, frowning. 'You?'

Adam performed a quick internal scan of the ordeal. He recalled Lynn's terror, her nakedness, the animalistic glee in the Nephians' eyes, their primal excitement, his own sense of helplessness, and the way the Nephians collapsed and spun as the bullets raced through them. Dead before they hit the floor.

Adam's chest caved inward under the weight of raw memory. So swiftly had his faith in people been swept aside, replaced by the cruel truth of nature. His gut ached from the exposure to it. As though some innocent part of himself had been forced to confront its mortality in the presence of evil.

But then he looked over at Kal, his friend, and sensed a more profound trauma than his own. He had two choices: share his suffering or show stoicism. And his instinct told him that there would be more suffering to come. He made his choice.

'Bill saved our lives,' he said with conviction. 'It was them or us.'

Kal turned to look at him. A weak smile played at the corner of his mouth before he was distracted by something over Adam's shoulder. Adam turned to look.

DeVenus stood like a statue in the darkness, staring at the dark hill. Adam followed his gaze, and a moment later, he saw a dark figure crest the hilltop, running toward them. He and Kaldor shared an anxious look, then stood.

When the figure was a few dozen yards away, the pale face of Dimitri Lopek ran into view. He looked stricken. He caught his breath and swallowed.

'The boy's dying!' he said. 'Lynn needs all of us, quickly!'

He jerked his head in a gesture for them to follow, turned, and ran back the way he had come. Kal glanced at Adam, then took off after him.

'DeVenus, guard the tents!' said Adam. And without waiting for the blank to respond, he sped off up the hill behind the others, leaning forward against the climb.

At the top of the hill, Adam saw a vast expanse of night-covered countryside. Down to his left and further away from the hill, he saw dim lights within a small, dark building. Lopek veered toward it, skipping sideways down the steep hill, Adam and Kal following his lead.

The stone and thatched house grew out of the darkness as they ran. Wails came from within, but Lopek pressed onward, undeterred. He flung the door open, and the three hurried inside.

The room they entered was large, musty, and dimly lit by candlelight. Thick wooden beams ran the ceiling length between the stone walls, and the floor was nothing but tightly compressed earth. A long table sat in the centre of the room while the chairs and scant furniture had been cleared against the walls – by Bill, it seemed, who was wiping the table's surface with his good arm.

'We need to carry him down here where Lynn can work,' he said urgently over the awful wailing. 'Upstairs!'

Adam led the way up the creaky, uneven stairs to the upper floor. Lynn had her back to the staircase. She was kneeling at the low bedside of a tall, bare-chested man. The man's face was very young and drenched with sweat, as was the skin of his torso. He looked delirious and terrified, letting out wails of despair in long notes that churned Adam's stomach into knots. The man's father knelt at his other side, desperately clutching his son's hand and staring intently into his wide eyes.

When Adam moved to the foot of the bed, the man's injury came into view; a deep gash of exposed muscle and bone ran from his shoulder to his elbow along the bicep. Lynn's knee was pinning the man's lower arm to the floor as she wiped the inside of the bright-pink wound with a swab. The boy jerked, and the pitch of his wailing intensified.

Lynn discarded the swab in annoyance and turned to look at the others.

'I need to close the wound with my laser,' she said, surprisingly calm. 'But I can't do it from this position while he's thrashing. We need to carry him downstairs to the table, and you'll each need to pin down one of his limbs. Got it? We don't have much time.'

Adam took in the length and weight of the man's body and suddenly wished that he hadn't commanded DeVenus to remain with the tents. Wasting no time, however, he and Kal grabbed a knee and buttock each while the old man and Bill put all three available hands under the boy's head and shoulders. Lynn gently rested the boy's injured arm across his torso and instructed the others to lift on a count of three.

The boy was immense. The four men lifting him struggled him upward crookedly to waist height and began shuffling towards the stairs. The boy came to life in his delirium, writhing powerfully in their arms as though they were eating him alive.

'Father!' he wailed. 'Father, save me!'

'They are healers!' the father grunted in his effort and anguish. 'They are here to save you!'

Adam barely held on as he and Kal were forced backwards down the stairs. At last, they swung the boy around to the table and laid him on it.

Adam stood away, panting.

'Don't let go!' said Lynn, pulling out a chrome cylinder with a tapered nib.

Adam put all his weight on the boy's left leg while Kaldor mirrored him over the right.

'Wait!' said Lopek. 'We can't use a laser! They mustn't see it!'

Lynn looked up at him in outrage. 'Then take the father outside,' she spat. 'The boy is delirious and will die if I don't close the wound.'

Bill sat on the boy's free arm and pinned his head to the side, glowering at Lopek, who whispered urgently to the father. Adam could only hear fragments of what he was saying. The father seemed reluctant to leave his son's side. But Lopek eventually led him through the door before closing it behind them.

'Father!' the boy sobbed pitifully. And Adam felt him try to kick them off, but the fight was leaving him.

Lynn's face became a mask of concentration as she studied the wound closely. Satisfied she had cleaned it, she twisted the laser to the correct setting and held it to the boy's arm like a tattooist's needle. The boy winced as Lynn's face lit up in red light. Adam turned away from the beam's brightness, but he could feel its heat on the wounded crown of his head.

'Father, please!' sobbed the boy.

The leg beneath Adam relaxed.

'He's unconscious,' said Bill.

'Good,' said Lynn. 'Stay on him, though. This will take a few minutes, and he might wake up again.'

The minutes drew out like hours as Adam lay uncomfortably across the boy's leg. Finally, Lynn asked Bill to let go and bring her some bandages. He obliged, and Lynn allowed Adam and Kal to remove themselves from the boy's limbs.

Bill dressed the wound, which was now a wide and shiny pink scar, while Lynn administered an injection into the boy's good shoulder. She straightened up, wiped her forehead, and exhaled.

Adam put a hand on her back. She smiled.

They looked at the sprawled figure on the table for a moment.

'I'll get Lopek,' said Kal, disappearing through the door.

'Good work, Doctor,' said Bill, shaking Lynn's hand.

'We should take him back upstairs while he's out,' she said. 'We'll need to scrub down the table to be safe.'

'Can't we just leave him there?' said Adam, stretching out his aching back.

He said this sincerely, but Lynn and Bill laughed.

The boy's father entered, followed by Kal and Lopek. He saw his son lying still with his eyes closed and looked around at them in terror.

'He's fine,' said Lynn. 'The wound is closed, and I've neutralised any infection. With enough rest and care, he should make a full recovery.'

Lopek translated, choosing each word cautiously. The old man's face sank in relief as he lowered himself into a nearby chair. He looked at each of them, his gaze lingering on Lynn.

'Thank you,' he said. 'And thank merciful Ohrak for sending you to us … you … you have saved my firstborn son.' He wiped a tear from his lined cheek, suddenly older.

'Tell him we need information and supplies,' Bill said softly to Lopek.

'And some breakfast and a bed,' Adam added. Kal and Lynn made noises of agreement.

The old man watched them conversing in their Elvish language, still wary, until Lopek translated the requests.

'Yes!' said the old man with unexpected enthusiasm, regaining his feet. 'You must stay and eat! All of you! Please. Stay as long as you wish!'

The team smiled. But Bill, Adam noticed, watched the old man thoughtfully.

'Thank you,' said Lopek, inclining his head in a tired bow. 'But first, I think our healer would like us to carry your son back to his bed.'

The old man moved past Lopek to stand near his son's head. He brushed a strand of wet hair from the boy's face. 'I did not know that Elves possessed such magic. Or such kindness,' he said quietly. 'I … I'm sorry.'

Bill's eyes narrowed. He glanced at the crossbow hung on the wall but said nothing.

Adam, Bill, Kal, and Lopek carried the boy back up the stairs while Lynn disappeared to wash up. Somehow the boy was even heavier unconscious. But at least he wasn't thrashing. When he was safely in bed, his bandaged arm resting at his side, the team quietly descended the stairs once more, where they found the old man prodding a fire in the hearth and gathering pots and utensils to make breakfast.

Following Lopek's lead, the team brought chairs from against the wall to sit at the table. Adam found that he could barely summon a thought. He was exhausted. And ravenous. He knew only that he would eat whatever the old man was noisily preparing and, hopefully, sleep for at least a week. Lynn and Kal looked equally worn, while Bill frowned angrily about something, and Lopek smiled benignly at the old man's back as he held a dented pan over the fire. Adam wondered idly whether he should fetch DeVenus to join them.

'You know … in all the excitement,' said Lopek with a fake chuckle, 'we forgot to introduce ourselves! I am Dimitri Lo –'

'Please, no names,' said the old man, turning quickly. 'I … I will only forget them.'

'Of course,' said Lopek, his polite smile faltering. 'Err … then what shall we call you, dear host?'

'Ned,' he said, returning the pan to the fire and tapping its rim with his wooden spoon.

Adam saw what looked like scrambled eggs slide off it. His stomach lurched.

'And your son?' Lopek pressed. 'What is his name?'

'Lannis.'

'Ask him about Kaiber,' said Bill, watching the old man.

Ned's stirring stalled briefly at the sound of the name.

'Err … we heard that King Markos has been attacked,' said Lopek, 'and that his daughter, Lady Kaiber, has become Queen Regent. Is this true, Ned?'

'I heard the same,' said Ned, keeping his back turned. 'The heralds and yeomen say that Queen Kaiber is acting as her father's champion, travelling the Realms in the old way to defend his throne at Trial. She is coming to Marsh to fight Jado Costel, the Lord of Ealee. It was he, Lord Costel, who cut Lannis's arm while sparring.'

Bill touched his own injury and shifted uncomfortably in his chair. Adam could see the gears turning in the security officer's head but could not guess what he was contemplating.

'Your son must be a great warrior to fight against a lord,' said Lopek encouragingly.

Ned gathered some cracked plates from a cupboard and began sliding them in front of the team. He put a thick, flour-coated loaf of bread in the centre of the table on a cutting board and began slicing it with a knife. Adam's mouth filled with saliva. He mustered all the civility he possessed to refrain from grabbing at it.

'Lannis is a damned fool,' said Ned, sawing another slice. 'And he did not fight against Lord Costel. Not in that way. He merely sparred with him for the promise of gold. I warned him not to go. Only a fool would fight such a man and trust him to keep his word, I said. Now look at him. Almost killed, and not a single Gilda to show for it. Foolish boy.'

He finished carving up the bread and bade everyone to take a slice. He lifted the pan from its cradle and began to circle the table, ladling out steaming mounds of golden egg.

'Find out what happened to New Antra,' said Bill, holding Ned's gaze and speaking as though thanking him for the meal.

Lopek waited until the old man was serving at his shoulder.

'What do the rumours say happened to King Markos?' he asked. 'Who attacked him? The story we heard was most troubling.'

Ned did not reply at once. He ladled the final portion of eggs over the bread on Lynn's plate, scraping the bottom of the pan as he scooped the last of it. He picked up the knife and took it with him to sit at the head of the table beneath the spot where his crossbow was pinned to the wall. Everyone except Bill was eating.

'I heard that the attempt on the King's life was carried out by Elves,' said Ned, taking his seat. Everyone slowed down their chewing to look at him. 'It is why I greeted you with such hostility. But there is much suspicion surrounding the story of this attack, and there are many accounts of it. Some say that the attempt was the work of a lone assassin. A rogue Elf. But others claim that the King slew a horde of Elves before they wounded him with ungodly magic. A weapon, they say.' Adam saw Lopek glance at Bill as Ned continued. 'But whatever the truth may be, Kaiber Almanfier is now Queen Regent. She has declared war on your kind, and the King has not been seen for weeks.'

'What happened to the Elves in Laudria?' said Lopek. 'There is a settlement there.'

'I do not know,' said Ned gravely. 'But if Kaiber believes that Elves attacked her father, I do not care to imagine what horror she might have wrought upon those that dwell in Laudria. The tales of her cruelty are too gruesome to speak over breakfast. She is ruthless and hungry for Elvish blood.'

Ned's gaze had drifted to the faint dawning sunlight beyond the small window. He looked haunted.

'Doc,' said Bill, 'ask him how far it is from here to Marsh.'

Lopek frowned but asked the question. Ned turned back to Lopek, his eyelids fluttering involuntarily. There was an odd pause before he answered.

'Twenty miles,' he said.

'Everyone keep eating,' said Bill, hiding his urgency beneath a serene smile. 'I think we're in danger, and we need to leave immediately. But I want to test something first. If I stand up, I want you all to stand at the same time. Doc, as calmly as you can, ask him who we saw with him last night. Who was the second figure on the hill, the one that rode away, and where did they go?'

Lynn and Kal traded covert looks but kept eating, as did Adam. Lopek swallowed, then turned to ask the question. Bill watched the old man closely. It was Ned's turn to shift in his chair. He sat up straighter, and his hands slid into his lap beneath the table.

'That was my second son, Flynt,' he said. 'He … he went to Marsh to witness the Trial and to ask Lord Costel for the Gilda that Lannis was promised.'

'Tell him we're leaving,' said Bill.

'We must leave,' said Lopek.

'No!' said Ned pleadingly. 'Please. You must stay and rest. I beg you! I must repay your kindness for saving my son.'

Bill stood. With a scraping of chairs, Adam and the others followed suit. Ned rose too, looking bewildered and terrified. With panicked indecision, he flung himself towards his crossbow on the wall.

Bang.

The gunshot reverberated deafeningly in the stone-walled room, causing Adam to flinch cartoonishly and cover his head with his arms. A high-pitched ringing sounded in his ears as he regained his composure. The old man was crouching on the floor, backed up against the wall in shock, staring wildly from the gun in Bill's hand to the splintered wreckage around him that used to be the lower half of his crossbow. The other half swayed from its nail on the wall, scraping gently across the powder-white hole where the bullet had struck.

The others rubbed their ears as though trying to rid them of water.

'Doc,' said Bill, still aiming the gun at Ned's chest, 'translate everything I say.'

Lopek nodded. Ned froze, mesmerised by the gun's barrel.

'Our ship was captured in the night,' Bill said slowly as Lopek spoke over him in translation. 'The men who took it intended to offer us to Kaiber for a reward. She will pay gold for Elvish heads, they said. The rider who sped away last night, your other son, so you claim, is heading to Marsh, twenty miles away, where Kaiber is. You sent him to fetch the Queen, didn't you? To claim the reward. Didn't you?'

Ned seemed too petrified to move. Lopek took a step backwards, away from the old man.

'We saved your son,' he said in an injured voice. 'We saved Lannis.'

'That was after,' said Ned quietly. Adam recognised the shame in the old man's face.

'So, you have sent word to Kaiber?' Bill demanded.

There was no need for Lopek's translation. Ned sagged.

'I thought you were my enemy,' he said.

The team looked at each other.

'Shit,' said Kal.

'We need to get out of here right now,' said Bill. 'Kal, Lynn, Adam, go and pack up the tents as quickly as possible. Doc, scan this place for anything useful. We set off in ten minutes.'

'Where will we go?' asked Lynn.

'We'll have to head through –' Lopek began, but Bill cut him off.

'No! Don't say anything in front of this scumbag. He'll sell us out again … We'll have to kill him if he figures out which way we're going. Everyone, get to work.'

Bill remained where he was, arm outstretched, while Adam and the others began to move toward the door. They all stopped in their tracks as the old man cried out in despair.

'Please!' he said, rolling up to his knees. 'You cannot leave! They will kill Flynt if they think he has lied. If Kaiber comes and does not find you here, she will kill us all!'

'You deserve it,' said Bill coldly.

The old man seemed to understand. He swivelled towards Lopek. 'Please,' he said. 'I sent Flynt before I knew that Ohrak had sent you for Lannis. I wish I could call him back, but he is heading for Queen Kaiber. They are only boys. Please.'

Lopek looked at Bill.

'Doc, we're not exposing our presence here to Kaiber Almanfier for the sake of this man's family. We've done enough for him. And you know Kaiber will torture and murder us. We can't linger.'

'Maybe we don't need to,' said Adam with a sudden brainwave. All heads turned to regard him. 'Instead of showing our faces, what if we tie him up, then trash the place and leave something only Elves would carry? Make it obvious we escaped? Ned could send them after us in the wrong direction, and Kaiber won't have any reason to harm him.'

Bill thought for five full seconds before giving a single, grim nod.

'Okay,' he said, 'that's the plan. You three pack up the tents. Doc, help me explain what we're doing. Let's go!'

Lynn, Kal, and Adam raced back over the hill in the weak light of dawn. The landscape around them was green and featureless. Ten minutes later, with help from DeVenus, they had packed their collective belongings and were marching back towards the house, weighed down by many rucksacks.

Bill had upturned all the furniture. As the other three entered, he crouched to tie a confused Ned tightly to a chair. Lopek was kneeling before the old man, explaining what they were up to.

'If Kaiber comes,' Lopek said, 'tell her we fled by ship. Do you understand? We took your food and fled by ship.'

The old man winced as Bill tightened the rope around his wrists but nodded.

'Raid the house for as much food and water as we can carry,' said Bill. 'Only one thing left for me to do.'

He walked around the chair to face Ned and punched him with all his might square in the face. The old man and the chair hit the floor together. Ned was unconscious and bleeding from the mouth.

'Did you have to do that?' said Lopek.

'Authenticity,' said Bill, shaking off his fist.

'You told him we're sailing away,' said Adam. 'So, what are we really doing?'

'Heading north, to Berrund,' said Lopek.

'I don't trust him to keep his word, though,' said Bill. 'I reckon he'll tell Kaiber the truth no matter what. So, we're going to release some of his horses to the south while we head north on foot. With any luck, the tracks will lead Kaiber southward, no matter what he tells her.'

Bill took his rucksack from Kal and began strapping it to his back. Lopek did the same. The team ransacked the cupboards for food, leaving as much mess as possible. Lynn found two loaves of bread, which she stuffed into her bag, while Adam found two stoppered bottles they could use to carry water.

Bill untied three horses from a hitching post and shepherded them into a line facing due south. In a coordinated move, he and Kal slapped the rears of the two outside horses, which darted forward, pulling the mare between them in panic. Bill chased them all for a few dozen yards, then shot his gun into the air, causing all three horses to speed up in their flight. They ran until they were far out of sight. Bill turned to Lopek.

'Before we set off, Doc,' he said, 'I just have to ask; are you sure – one hundred per cent certain – that Lord Farrow will welcome us in Leybridge?'

'Yes, I'm sure,' said Lopek, hitching up his bag. 'Besides, I don't see we have any other choice.'

The team looked at each other once more.

'If we're in Ealee, then Berrund is roughly six hundred miles north from here,' said Lopek, looking out across the sea of swaying grass. 'And our first hurdle … is to cross the Grass Plains of Reon.'

The team followed his gaze.

'Lead the way,' said Bill.

PART IV

BETRAYAL

CHAPTER 32

Reunion

Lyle Eurace felt a cold bead of sweat roll down the small of his back. He wished he had not chosen to wear his ceremonial robes. It was too humid out here, in the Urden. But he was doing Ohrak's work, so he had dressed for the occasion.

Though the forest was dangerous, he walked unburdened by fear. Certain, somehow, that no Kraelings would find him. Not today. For Ohrak had finally shown him his purpose. And nothing would disturb His righteous mission. Even the memories that had haunted him for ten years could not imprison him this day. And he intended to enjoy his newfound freedom, no matter how briefly the enlightenment lasted.

A soft breeze eased his perspiration, and he stood for a moment and closed his eyes.

The wind whispered in the trees while the sun shone brightly above.

As he resumed his gentle stride, he began to wonder whether his absence in Leybridge had been noted yet. He doubted it. Master Volsgaard was the only man who might check on him. But the Augur was busy overseeing preparations for the Lordship Trial and could manage well enough without his sickly Obediant. With a grin, however, Lyle pictured his master's face as he discovered the empty room and his abandoned collar.

Lyle had confined himself to his room since the battle with the Krae. For two weeks, he had hidden on the pretence of a fever. Indeed, he had felt most unwell, but his sickness had been born of cowardice. The revelation that Gadryon had also survived the Fairwater attack had toppled him into selfish oblivion. The boy he had left to die was alive. It was a truth that he could not bear. And the more he dwelt upon it, the worse he felt. He considered fleeing Leybridge and changing his name. For what would become of Lyle Eurace if the boy returned? If Lord Farrow's scouts found him? He could speak the truth about Lyle's unforgivable actions.

Once again, fear had consumed him.

He couldn't recall precisely when the revelation had struck him. He had sought Ohrak's wisdom tirelessly throughout his isolation. Hardly ever releasing his master's God Stone from his grip, seeking for hours at a time. Desperate for any answers. But God's silence became deafening. And after many days, he gave up all hope of redemption. As he had abandoned Gadryon during the massacre, so Ohrak had finally abandoned him.

He stopped in the shade of a pine tree and took in his surroundings. From the slope of the ground, he had begun the steady climb up the mountain's foot. The trees grew closer together this far north, taller and thinner than their broad-leafed counterparts in the heart of the Urden. Lyle looked high over the clustered ranks and saw the permanent white clouds that concealed the snowy peaks of the Bannebar. He took a deep breath, detecting a slight thinning in the air.

He was getting close.

The instant he pushed off to resume the climb, something rushed past his ear and thudded into the tree trunk beside him. Reflexively, he ducked, his arms spasming to protect his head.

When nothing else happened, he lowered his arms slowly and looked around. The shaft of an arrow stuck out from the tree trunk. Its impact had splintered the bark, revealing a wedge of pale wood. His heart beat harder, but he knew to keep his movements slow. As he turned, he spread his hands wide to show that he was unarmed.

A bear rolled out from behind a shrub thirty feet away and charged at him. For the briefest second, he believed Ohrak had lured him to a grizzly death. As he backed painfully into the tree in panic, it occurred to him that bears did not fire arrows, nor did they run on two feet. Then, amid the tangle of furs, he saw the face that had haunted him for ten years. A man's face now. But the dark-blue eyes were as bright and innocent as he remembered.

Gadryon slowed as he approached, a second arrow nocked, ready to draw. Lyle watched him advance, as rooted to the spot as the tree at his back. Gadryon suddenly stopped, eyes widening in disbelieving fury. He drew back his arrow.

'Wait!' Lyle shrieked, hands splayed outward in front of his face. 'Please! Don't kill me!'

Agonising seconds passed. Lyle peered through his trembling fingers. Gadryon held the arrow pulled back to his cheek, teeth bared. The effort to keep the arrow drawn conflicted with an equal desire to release it.

'Please, wait,' Lyle pleaded. 'P-p-please … I know that I d-d-d-don't deserve your mercy. And I would not dare seek your f-forgiveness. I ask only that you l-l-l-let me s-speak before you pass your judgement. Please. I come bearing a v-v-vital message.'

The arrow slammed into the tree above Lyle's head. Shards of bark and needles rained over him. Gadryon looked disgusted but did not load a third arrow. 'You should not have come,' he said quietly. 'Go back before I kill you.'

Lyle felt hot tears forming in his eyes. 'You look s-so much like your m-mother,' he choked. 'Did she … Is she alive?'

'Go!' Gadryon roared, his face contorted with hate.

Lyle whimpered but shook his head. 'I will not go,' he said, the tears rolling down his cheeks. 'N-n-not until you've heard my message.'

Gadryon glowered at him. 'How did you know where to find me?' he asked, his voice thick with venom. He suddenly backed away, peering around. 'Are there others?'

'I'm alone,' Lyle reassured quickly. Gadryon looked doubtful. 'When all the scouts kept failing to f-find you, I deduced where you must be h-hiding. It was something the Ableman said; that you were dressed in the skin of a bear.' His voice broke as the tears fell. 'And I remembered your favourite story as a boy.'

Gadryon's chest began to heave, but his eyes remained level and deadly. Lyle sniffed and wiped his cheeks.

'You slew the Great Bear from your father's stories?' he pressed. 'You slew Brør?'

Gadryon looked away and nodded. 'Speak your message,' he said, 'then go.'

Lyle took a deep breath of the cold mountain air. He chanced a step forward. 'I cannot imagine what you must have endured out here, all alone, these past ten years,' he began. 'How much you must have s-suffered … But please, know that my act of cowardice that day has stayed with me ever since, Gadryon. I want you to know that it stayed with me. That I have suffered too. I have carried the shame of my inaction inside and in more ways than I can tell. The fear that took hold of me when Fairwater fell has never left me. Not ever …

'Until last night.'

Lyle gave an earnest, watery smile. Gadryon changed the grip on his bow, unmoved.

'You see, I remembered something your father taught me when I was your age,' he continued. 'Whenever I had trouble seeking, he would remind me that Ohrak alone guides us into the future. And even when we stumble, we do so divinely, each playing our small part in His greater plan. And I wondered, what if God sowed my cowardice and fear inside me? What if the small part I must play included your abandonment? I'm not trying to absolve myself of blame,' he added in haste at the look on Gadryon's face. 'But I asked myself, what if Ohrak used a coward to bring forth a hero? What if you were meant to live alone in this forest and become the strong, brave warrior you are? And then the truth hit me all at once! Beautiful and staggering … until I cried away all my fear and shame. For a heartbeat, I glimpsed a fragment of Ohrak's plan, and your part is yet to be played.

'I laughed for the first time in years when I finally saw what I had missed. The memory was so mundane that I had almost forgotten. It only happened a few weeks ago when Master Volsgaard asked me to seek at Lord Farrow's behest. He wanted to know if any soldier in Berrund could defeat King Markos in combat. And the image that flashed in my mind, more clearly than anything I had ever sought, was the face of the boy I left to die in Fairwater ten years ago. Your face, Gadryon.

'I thought my mind was merely tormenting itself, as always. After all, I knew you to be dead. So, I dismissed the vision like a fool. And even when you returned and demonstrated your divine gifts in the battle, I did not piece the truth together. But I see it now. All that has transpired has brought us both to this moment. To what end, I do not know. But I understand, at last, my place in this world. I have played my part and am ready for my end.'

Lyle reached inside his silken robes and drew out the crescent-shaped God Stone that had belonged to Gadryon's father. Gadryon stared at it, livid yet transfixed.

'I came here today of my own free will,' Lyle said, laughing as he realised that his stutter had gone. 'The message I bear is this; that you, Gadryon, are the Ulmar. Ohrak's chosen warrior, as prophesied in the Book of Scrawls. Born to unite all the peoples of Ithea.'

Lyle knelt and kissed the God Stone before placing it gently on the floor. Gadryon halved the distance between them, stopping his charge abruptly.

'I am not the Ulmar,' he declared. 'I don't want any part in this plan. I want you to go and never come back.'

Lyle chuckled and shook his head. 'You don't understand,' he said. 'You cannot hide from your destiny, Gadryon. Word of your prowess spread like wildfire throughout the Realm when you disappeared. And when the news followed that you were not a soldier but an untrained boy from the Urden, it fanned the flames like a hurricane. I don't think you realise the impact of your fleeting resurrection. I'll wager there's not a soul in Nephia who does not know your name, or will not, soon enough. Lord Farrow sends daily scouts to hunt for you. He means to take you under his wing and train you for the throne.'

'You're not listening!' Gadryon hissed, tossing aside his bow and drawing his sword. He pointed the tip at Lyle's heart. 'I don't want the throne! I don't want to be King! Go back to Leybridge and tell your lord and everyone who will listen that I want to be left alone! I don't care for any of it. Just leave, or I will kill you.'

Lyle nodded, but his certainty remained untarnished. 'If killing me is what you desire, then I am ready,' he said truthfully. 'I came to deliver God's message. And I have delivered it. My part is done, and I am finally at peace. I lay at your feet and await your judgement.'

Lyle clasped his hands together behind his back and shut his eyes. He felt the breeze tickle the freed skin of his neck and drew in a final breath of cold mountain air. He was closer to Fairwater here than he had been since he fled.

He was home.

Ohrak, he thought, *thank you for releasing me from my fears. Thank you for my life. And for blessing me with the gift of atonement before its end.*

The seconds stretched into minutes as he waited, wondering where the boy's sword would strike. When he could bear the suspense no longer, he opened his eyes.

Gadryon was gone.

The God Stone remained at Lyle's knees.

CHAPTER 33

The Ealee Challenge

Winlow awoke with a jolt. She sat up and threw off her bedcovers, her dream forgotten in an instant, and there was no need to rub her eyes. They were alert with excitement for the day ahead. Today promised to be better than Summerfeast, her birthday, and Leenoc combined.

She strained her ears to hear any movement in the house. It was still dark outside her dusty window, but as her eyes adjusted, she began to make out the faint glow on the stones of the staircase wall. Someone was awake in the kitchen.

Please be Father, she hoped.

Father was excited for the day too, in his own fretful way, while Mother would be nothing but a bundle of nerves. A dangerous mood that Winlow knew she must navigate with caution. She had drawn up battle plans in her mind. The first step was to avoid Mother as much as possible and keep close to her brothers, no matter how badly they teased her. If she could win the men before her Mother did, they would argue in her favour and help tip the scales. For Winlow knew well what her Mother's strategy would be: make fretful comments until the atmosphere was thick with a tension that someone must break. And the men would gawp at Winlow, who would eventually succumb to the combined pressure and volunteer to stay home out of guilt.

But not today, she thought.

She was going to Marsh. She would witness the Throne Trial of Ealee; Lord Costel, against Lady Kaiber Almanfier, the Queen Regent. The first Queen in four hundred years.

Winlow tiptoed from her bed, careful not to tread on the loose floorboards. The pre-dawn air was cold outside her bed, and she shivered in her nightdress as she made her way to the basin in the corner. She lifted cupped palms of water, splashed her face, filled the pitcher, and rinsed her hair as quietly as possible.

Her shivering worsened.

Once she was dry and her hair was tied into a single, heavy braid over her shoulder, she began to dress. She had folded her town clothes the night before. She donned each layer slowly, correctly, fastening each thread and brushing out any creases in the lacework, determined not to give Mother any opening for ridicule. The final layer was her brother's old, grey travelling cloak, which she swept over her shoulders with a flourish. She had rescued it from the attic the week before and stuffed it under her bed. It was patched and too big for her frame, but the statement it made could not be ignored.

She was going.

Fully dressed and ready to leave, she sat on the edge of her bed and waited.

Gradually, the sky brightened outside her window as the long minutes drew out. Heart fluttering in mounting anticipation, she withdrew the single Gilda from the inner pocket of the travelling cloak and turned it over in her hands. The gold coin was heavy and cold. The Castle of Lysk etched on both sides. Worth enough to buy a cloak of her own, with some chippings for change. She had found it on the roadside the day the merchants' wagons had come to town, bearing news of the King's attack, and it had cost all her self-restraint not to spend it at the market. But the reward would be worth it.

A creak from the landing made her jump to her feet and clutch the coin behind her back.

Her middle brother, Jon, stumbled past her doorway in his nightclothes, a fist near his mouth, yawning. He glanced into Winlow's room as he passed, then, a second later, he stepped backwards dramatically to fill her threshold, staring at her with a malicious grin. He folded his arms and leaned against her doorway.

'That's mine,' he said, nodding at the cloak. 'Take it off, now. You're not coming.'

'Yes, I am,' she said matter-of-factly.

Jon let out an amused humph, then raised his voice without taking his eyes from Winlow.

'Here, Arthur!' he called. 'Come and look at this!'

Heavier footsteps pounded on the landing floor. Arthur appeared at Jon's shoulder. He ducked his head below the doorframe to see what had caught his brother's attention, half his chin covered in shaving lather, a razor in his hand. When he took in Winlow's dress, there was pity in his smile.

'Don't even try it, Winnie,' he said. 'You know Mother will need help while we're gone.'

'But I want to come,' she said.

'Well, you can't!' Jon laughed. 'You're twelve years old … and you're a girl!'

Arthur slapped the back of Jon's head. 'That's nothing to do with it,' he said. 'We can't all leave, that's all. The animals don't know there's a Throne Trial today, do they? And they'll all need tending as usual. Mother can't do it on her own.'

'But why do I have to stay?' she said, feeling the heat she had sworn to overcome rising. 'Why can't Jon stay and help?'

Jon gave a convincing laugh but glanced sidelong at their elder brother for support.

'Look,' said Arthur, stooping inside the room, 'it's nothing personal, Winnie. I promise. We all know you can look after yourself. But the travellers say that Kaiber is on the warpath, hunting Elves and marching with a thousand soldiers at her back. Marsh will be packed with all the people of Ealee for the Trial. And more. It could be dangerous. And I don't think Mother will allow it. I'm sorry.'

'She couldn't stop me if you were both on my side,' she said.

Arthur sighed and gave the same pitiful smile. Jon stepped forward. 'And why would we be on your side?' he said.

'I'll wager you might think about it,' said Winlow, overtly slipping the Gilda back inside the pocket of her cloak.

Her brothers' faces fell. They stared at the cloak where the weight bounced against Winlow's leg, their mouths open.

'Where did you come by that?' said Jon jealously.

'It doesn't matter,' said Winlow. 'But if you help me convince Mother to let me come, I'll make a wager with you for it …'

Arthur's eyes narrowed. 'What wager?' he said.

Here goes, thought Winlow. Weeks of enduring all the men in the village laugh at how easily Lord Costel – soon to be King – would defeat a woman, could be used to her advantage.

'I'll wager my Gilda against all the chippings you two can muster,' she said, 'that Queen Kaiber will beat Jado Costel at the trial today.'

Jon threw his head back and laughed. Arthur's pity for her vanished at once. He nodded slowly, his one-sided smile now filled with respect. He raised his shaving knife and drew it across the thumb-tip of his right hand, then handed the blade to Winlow. She copied him, careful not to cut more deeply than necessary, and the two clasped hands tight, their blood sealing the bet. Jon grinned behind Arthur, shaking his head at Winlow's apparent stupidity.

When the three of them trooped into the kitchen a few minutes later, they found the small farm table laid with the finest crockery, ready for a feast. Mother was busy stirring something in a pot, her white apron covered in greasy finger marks, her hair tied up in a bun. She spoke without turning.

'You're all up late,' she admonished, still stirring. 'Boys, your father's out preparing the horses. He means to set off as soon as you're finished. Winnie, the cows need bringin' in for milking. We'll start when yer brothers are gone.'

She turned and froze, pan held out in one hand. She dug her free fist into her hip, her eyebrows lifting red lines into her forehead, and her mouth shut so tightly that her lips disappeared. Winlow stared back defiantly, but the boys took their seats as though nothing were happening.

'And what do you mean by this?' she said.

'I've decided I would like to go to the Throne Trial,' said Winlow calmly.

The lines on Mother's forehead came closer together. 'Have you, now?' she said in a high voice. 'And do you suppose that's your decision to make?'

'Ahh, let her come.' Arthur smiled jovially, reaching across the table and helping himself to some toast. 'It's only one day, Mother! And it wouldn't be right to let her miss it, now, would it?'

Mother turned her gaze on Arthur like an owl. He began scraping butter noisily on his toast. Jon grinned. It faltered when Mother's eyes shifted his way.

'I see,' she said, putting the pan down forcefully. 'You're all inonnit, aren't yeh? You've all decided that I am to be yer slave! Is that right? That I should not only feed yeh but clear up after yeh an' all, like a maid, then take care of all the farm work too, I suppose!'

'Oh, give it a rest,' said Arthur daringly. 'We'll make up for any work when we're back. As I said, it's only one day … and it's a day when Lord Costel might finally put an end te'the Almanfier Dynasty! Think o' that! We could have a new King come sunset!'

'I don't care!' Mother snapped. 'I don't want her to go! She's too young to see the like of it! People killin' each other for no reason, all for the right te rule. When it's not right. And it don't matter who wins! Either way, it'll be us – the poor – that suffers. You mark my words!'

'You can't really stop her if she wants to come,' Jon ventured.

Winlow felt the first twinge of guilt. Facing Mother's fury was expected, but having Jon on her side was not. She did not like him fighting in her corner. It made her cause feel wrong.

'Well, let's just see what yer father has to say about this!' Mother trilled as the front door opened.

'Say about what?' said Father, kicking off his boots at the door, his drooping moustache twitching.

'Look at your daughter!' Mother cried.

Father looked at Winlow, frowning. 'What about her?' he asked.

'Look at how she's dressed!'

Father looked at her again, eyes scanning her clothes. 'Sorry!' he said, shaking his head. 'You look lovely, Winnie.'

'No, Thomas!' Mother yelled as Arthur and Jon chuckled at the table. 'She's dressed to come with ye!'

'Oh! Aye. That she is,' said Father, rubbing the back of his neck. 'And that's the problem … isn't it?'

Mother unfastened her apron angrily. She pulled it over her head, balled it up, and threw it on the floor. She stormed out into the garden without boots, or a coat, slamming the door behind her.

A silence fell over the kitchen in her absence. Arthur shook his head dismissively while Jon chewed his bottom lip. Father sighed at the rear door, then looked at Winlow.

'Well,' he said sadly, 'if you're coming, we best leave now before she comes back. You can eat yer breakfast in the cart.'

Ten minutes later, Father and Arthur were sat shoulder to shoulder on the driving seat of the hay cart, their identical, broad backs curved in the same slouch, with Father on the left, at the reins. Winlow and Jon sat in the corners of the cart, facing backwards, the compacted dirt road to Marsh rushing out between their feet.

The road was busier than Winlow had ever seen it. Wagons, carts, and carriages rumbled along in an unbroken line as far as she could see, with twice as many people walking tight to the verge beside the convoy. Occasionally, a merchant wagon would push through the throng, coming the other way, parting the traffic, the drivers muttering obscenities as they passed. Every quarter of a mile, they would pass a pair of horse-mounted guards in gleaming armour, standing just off the road, there to keep the peace and move the traffic along, so Father said.

'Do you really think Kaiber can win?' Jon suddenly asked Winlow, smirking.

'Course she can,' Father chimed in over his shoulder, a pipe balanced between his teeth. 'Don't go thinkin' she'll be a pushover, Jon! Not even for the likes of Jado Costel. She's an Almanfier. And Markos wouldn't let her defend his crown if he didn't think she were worthy. I certainly wouldn't wager against her!'

He winked at Winlow and returned his attention to the road. Jon looked troubled.

'Do you think what Mother said is true?' asked Arthur. 'Do you think much will change for us if Lord Costel wins? I mean, it will get easier for us if our lord becomes the King, won't it? He'll be able to treat us more fairly and such?'

There was a long silence as the cart rattled along. Father drew several puffs of his pipe.

'Who knows,' he sighed at last. 'There's not been a ruler that weren't an Almanfier in my lifetime. And while Lord Costel taxes us to high heaven to pay his own taxes to the King, there's no reason why his replacement wouldn't have exactly the same problem.'

'His replacement?' asked Jon. 'Won't he stay here as King if he wins?'

Father laughed, and Arthur joined him a split second later.

'Of course not!' Father snorted derisively. 'If Jado wins, do you expect him to stay in Ealee, of all places? Crimony, lad! I forget how young you are sometimes. Not a chance, my son. Marsh may seem like a grand city to the likes of us, but it's a pile o' bricks in a bog compurred to High Castle in Laudria. And even smaller against the Vallichor, or so I've heard. Come to think of it, that's where he'd likely take up. On the old throne, in Lysk. Because there's no chance Markos will let him take High Castle! Either way, we'll have to have another trial, a Lordship Trial, to find a new ruler of Ealee once this is over. And only Ohrak knows who that might be.'

The cart rumbled on in silence for a long time. Winlow noticed that many of the faces walking beside the cart were foreign and strange, coming from all over Nephia. And suddenly, her excitement for the rare occasion trebled. Her feet went fizzy and numb.

A large horse bearing a small rider dashed past the line, galloping toward Marsh. Angry jeers of protest followed it as it sped by.

'That was Bramble!' blurted Winlow, turning to sit up on her knees and peer over the side of the cart up the length of the traffic. Even at a distance, she could see the familiar white cloud amid the brown fur on the horse's left flank.

'Bramble?' said Father, confused, leaning across Arthur for a better look. 'Old Ned's horse? And who's that astride her, then? I didn't see.'

'Looks like 'is son,' said Arthur, 'the younger one. What's his name?'

'Flynt,' said Winlow. 'But it can't be. He's younger than me. What would he be doing riding Bramble? He's too small.'

'I don't know,' said Father, taking out his pipe. 'But it can't mean much good. Wasn't the elder son taken ill last week? I thought I heard somethin' like that only the other day.'

'Lannis?' said Arthur. 'He can't be sick, surely? The last I spoke to him, he'd been invited to spar against Lord Costel as a warm-up! In 'is prime, he said. Wouldn't shut up about it.'

Winlow watched as a mounted guard broke through the traffic to stop Flynt and Bramble. They spoke for a few seconds, and then the guard called something to his companion before leading the boy and his horse onward.

As they drew nearer to Marsh, the traffic intensified. Winlow had never seen so many people packed together. The noise was deafening. Her father kept shouting things over his shoulder, but she couldn't hear a word, and Jon shrugged beside her in equal ignorance. They came upon the city gate, wide enough to admit three wagons, side-by-side, and almost as tall again. But even so, the mass of people and horses trudging toward it overwhelmed the entrance, spreading outward along the city wall, each waiting for their turn to enter. Serving maids and waiters from the city inns wove their way through the stagnant tide, hawking flasks of drink and homemade sandwiches over the din. Arthur collared one but almost fell off the cart when the waiter tried to charge three chippings for a flask of water.

Once through the gate, all feet marched tirelessly toward the city's south. So many people that Winlow couldn't begin to guess their number. It was busier than any market day she could remember, combined, including the year she had helped serve at her father's stall before Summerfeast. She imagined being separated from her father and brothers in such a crowd and shivered at the prospect. Perhaps Mother had been right.

At the southernmost tip of the city was the Bowl, an arena made from the old quarry. A giant hole in the ground, where thick steps of carved stone descended in a wide oval to a craggy, boulder-strewn pit.

A five-foot wall surrounded the upper edge of the Bowl, spaced by entrances wide enough for one person to enter at a time. City guards manned each door, though Winlow noted that some looked older than Father, with white hair and wrinkled faces. But even those men gave off an impression of power, clutching quarterstaffs in their gleaming armour.

The many entrances swallowed the crowd until, eventually, only the trundling carts and wagons continued the relentless migration, moving toward the far side of the arena. Winlow stood up to peer down into the Bowl as they edged around the perimeter. The crowd of people poured downward, filling up the rows of steps quickly. A seething mass of colourful ants in a hole. She shuddered at the sight of it and sat down.

A guard flagged her father down, signalling him to stop behind another hay cart along the wall. Dozens of stablemen ambled among the carriages and wagons, carrying buckets of water and hay bags. When Father called one over to tend their horses, she was not surprised to hear the price. The side of the cart was now tight to the wall of the Bowl. Jon stepped onto it, taking his lead from the carts on either side and, to Winlow's amazement, he held out his hand reflexively to guide her safely across. Father and Arthur followed suit, climbing across from their driving seat.

'Look!' said Jon, bellowing, as trumpets began to blare a fanfare from somewhere unseen. 'There's plenty of space for us down there if we start climbing now!'

He pointed to a gap four or five rows from the arena floor that had been left naturally empty by the vying crowd. Without hesitating, Arthur lowered himself over the wall to the top step of the Bowl and turned to collect Winlow in his arms. Their excitement building, the four climbed downward, muttering swift apologies as they pushed their legs between the shoulders and heads of tightly clustered people. As they neared the gap Jon had indicated, the trumpets ended their salute. An energetic silence befell the huddled onlookers. On either side of the uneven quarry floor were two cave-like entrances facing one another across the oval. As Winlow took her seat, wedged uncomfortably between Jon and Father, six figures strode out from the arena entrance to her right. As one voice, the crowd erupted into cheers, some pumping clenched fists toward the group of men below. Winlow inserted fingers into her ears to block out the noise, but she could still hear the deafening chant. Only when she spotted the gold-plated armour of Lord Costel among the men did she realise that the crowd was chanting his name.

Lord Costel, his helmet clutched beneath his arm, raised his other hand to acknowledge his supporters. Clapping bolstered the cheers. The tall man beside the armoured Lord also raised his hands, flapping them while turning to each side of the Bowl.

'Who's that?' asked Jon, leaning across Winlow to prod Father.

'Lord Costel's Augur,' bellowed Father ceasing his clapping at once.

'Hush now!'

The crowd fell quiet. It seemed so eerie to Winlow that so many people could be gathered together and sit in complete silence. The Augur in the arena unfastened a scroll and began to read, his voice distant but clear, echoing around the quarry Bowl.

'On this day,' he announced, 'we gather here, in the great city of Marsh, the jewel of Ealee, to witness, under Ohrak's ever-watchful eye, a challenge for the Throne of Nephia. Lain down by the finest swordsman this great Realm has ever produced, Lord Jado Olfsun Costel!'

The cheering and clapping took up once more, but Winlow was ready this time. She kept her hands loosely cupped over her ears and found that she could control the volume of the crowd by making tiny adjustments to their positions. Lord Costel donned his helmet and took his sword from a squire. The blade was broad and almost as tall as the man wielding it.

He must be very strong, Winlow thought, astonished at the ease with which he wielded the giant lump of metal.

Lord Costel cut the air, slicing several smooth arcs over both his shoulders, testing his motion. He muttered something to one of the squires nearby, and the young man, no older than Jon by his bearing, rushed forth to reach under one of the shoulder plates to refasten a strap. As the clapping died, the Augur continued his proclamation, pivoting slowly to ensure he addressed each row of spectators.

'Lord Costel's opponent, who has come to meet this challenge in the holy representation of King Markos Almanfier, shall be his daughter, the Queen Regent, Kaiber Almanfier.'

Winlow, at the same time as many others, craned her neck and leaned forward to peer into the second cave-like entrance.

This was it. The moment she had dreamt of for weeks. Kaiber Almanfier, the Queen Regent, come to show everyone what a woman could do.

Four figures emerged slowly from the shadows of the entrance cave to the left. One was the biggest man Winlow had ever seen in her life. It was hard to say exactly how big he was at this range, but Winlow guessed that he was easily twice the size of Arthur. A few paces beside the giant walked hunched, greasy-haired twins. And between them walked the most plainly dressed and wretched-looking woman Winlow had ever seen.

Kaiber Almanfier's dark hair was greasy and unkempt. It swung in lank strands beside wide, prominent cheekbones, further pronounced by beady, close-knit eyes. Her armour was dull with a blackish hue.

The crowd began to mutter. Jon laughed. 'Well, there she is, Winnie,' he whispered conspiratorially. 'Clever tactic is that; wearing a pelvis for a face!' He slapped his own knee, silently guffawing at his joke.

Winlow could not hide her disappointment. She didn't know what she had expected, but certainly not this. There was no beauty. No pageantry. The first Queen in centuries was just another man.

'The terms of the duel,' Lord Costel's Augur continued, 'have been agreed upon by both contestants. Armour shall be adorned. Shields prohibited. Swords have been selected by both contestants as their weapons of choice. No additional weapons shall be allowed. If a contestant is disarmed, they shall be granted a reprieve to retrieve their weapon. Only death shall decide the victor.

'Each contestant has elected a second to carry their Flame of Oath. A contestant may instruct their second to extinguish the flame at any moment, representing their forfeiture of the contest. By the law of Ohrak, the victor shall win claim to the throne of Nephia, and be declared the rightful ruler of all the Realms in the kingdom. Before the eyes of those gathered here today, and in the presence of Ohrak, the Almighty, I ask both contestants to step forth and commit themselves to the terms of this duel!'

Lord Costel and the Queen Regent faced one another, twenty feet apart. At the same time, their followers scurried quickly to the perimeter of the arena floor. Kaiber drew her blade and knelt, thrusting the ugly black sword deep into the ground. Lord Costel gave a slight bow before mirroring the movement with his broadsword. Winlow's eyes were drawn away by the spear-high torches that suddenly burst into life behind each fighter. Lord Costel's was held aloft by his Augur, while Kaiber's was held upright by the giant. Once the Flames of Oath were secured, the two contestants stood in ritual unison, eyes locked together, then pulled their swords from the earth.

Both charged forward. Kaiber let out a low, guttural scream as she advanced. Lord Costel brought his sword down with both hands from high overhead. For a second, Winlow thought the enormous blade had split Kaiber in half, but she had deftly dropped her shoulder and allowed it to slam into the ground. Kaiber brought her blackened sword around in a horizontal arc, aiming for Jado's exposed flank. But the Lord of Ealee stepped into the counterstroke and barged Kaiber off-balance with his armoured shoulder. She stumbled backwards but quickly regained her footing. Lord Costel kept her at a distance with the point of his sword. Both began to circle for an opening. Jado suddenly thrust the tip of his blade forward like a viper, and Kaiber barely managed to parry it aside.

Winlow could see the Queen Regent's frustration building. She knew nothing about combat, but even she could see Lord Costel was controlling the space between them, keeping Kaiber at a distance where her sword was useless. Wearing her down with thrusts that would surely strike home sooner or later. Kaiber could do nothing in reply. She kept backing away from the broadsword, occasionally glancing it aside with her black blade.

A collective gasp issued from the crowd as Kaiber stumbled on a loose stone. Lord Costel pounced on her, aiming a heavy blow at Kaiber's back, but she spun at the last second and met his sword with her own. The crowd cheered emphatically as Lord Costel pushed her away. The Augur held his flame higher amid the cheers.

The contestants reset and began circling again, with the same result; Kaiber in retreat while Jado followed her with the tip of his outstretched weapon.

The slow dance continued for a long time as the tension in the Bowl mounted, all eyes watching every step and thrust.

'She's wearing him down,' came Father's voice.

Winlow frowned at him. 'Wearing *him* down?' she said.

'Look at his sword,' said Father, shaking his head. 'He can't keep it pointed out like that much longer if you ask me.'

Winlow looked back at the tentative duellers. Kaiber was still dancing away from Jado, sure-footed now, drawing him along with her. Winlow noticed that the tip of the lord's sword was beginning to angle slightly toward the floor. Jado kept adjusting his grip to lift it as he advanced, but his snake-like thrusts were becoming more laboured and infrequent.

Suddenly, Kaiber struck like a whiplash. She pushed aside the tip of his sword with her own and brought the black blade around her head to slam it into the side of Lord Costel's helmet.

Jado reeled and fell to the floor in an undignified heap of gold-plated metal. The force of the blow had dented the helmet badly. One of the eye slits had crumpled shut. Lord Costel struggled to wrench it off in a panic. But Kaiber had not rushed to finish him. She was looking around at the crowd, and the cold look in her eyes sent a shiver down Winlow's spine into her toes. The giant waved Kaiber's torch lazily.

Lord Costel, head exposed now, heaved himself to standing and grimaced at the Queen Regent. He launched forwards, and Kaiber was momentarily taken by surprise. The swords clanged together in flurries that resonated through the motionless crowd. At close range, however, the short blade gained the advantage. The broadsword was too heavy to keep up with Kaiber's relentless speed, and Jado was forced to lock the edges together to catch his breath. Kaiber allowed him no such quarter. She threw a gauntleted fist between the locked swords, which crunched loudly into Jado's eye socket. Once again, the Lord of Ealee found himself on the floor, only this time, blood poured from his nose, and Kaiber held both their swords.

She tossed the broadsword at Lord Costel's feet.

'We should leave,' Father said sadly. 'This'll only get uglier. She's toying with him now.'

The crowd made half-hearted attempts to buoy their exhausted lord as he got to his feet.

'But he can still win!' said Jon looking up at Father, stricken. 'He can't give up.'

'His pride won't let him,' said Father sadly. 'But I don't want ye to see what's coming. Come on, let's go.'

Father stood but was rooted to the spot by the spectacle below. Lord Costel flew at Kaiber, mustering all his remaining strength into a single, wild attack. But Kaiber was quicker. She sidestepped the primal swipe but left her sword in place, using Lord Costel's momentum to skewer him through his neck.

Winlow felt a cold wave of sickness rise in her own throat as Jado stumbled around, slashing in the wrong direction with the red-soaked length of Kaiber's sword jutting out from his nape.

Many things happened all at once. A woman screamed far above. Kaiber's giant crossed the arena to bludgeon the petrified Augur with his flaming torch. The crowd shifted in panic as armed regiments of black-clad soldiers flooded the Bowl like spiders from both sides of the arena. People began to scramble over each other, climbing toward the exits higher up. But more soldiers appeared there too, standing with spears on every inch of the wall that enclosed the upper rim.

The spectators were trapped.

Winlow felt Father, Arthur, and Jon form a protective huddle around her in the crush.

A voice thundered out over the panic. 'Traitors of Ealee!' it bellowed. The crowd subdued its seething dread as heads swivelled to locate the speaker.

Through a gap between Arthur and Father's arms, Winlow could see Kaiber's ugly face in the centre of the arena floor, chin thrust out as she spoke. 'Hear me now,' she said.

Winlow could see the bloody, twitching form of Lord Costel lying at her feet. His legs had been stripped bare to the waist, and one of Kaiber's servants knelt over him, with his back to Winlow, doing something she could not see. Arthur covered her eyes.

'Don't look, Winnie,' he said.

People around them were pointing and murmuring in disgust, their faces pale. Kaiber's voice rang over the chaos. 'Fifteen years ago, my father forgave your rebellion,' she roared. 'But now, you have squandered the last of his mercy! Your Realm has prospered under his rule. Your children know nothing but peace! And yet, while your merciful King lies dying, you think of nothing but yourselves! You mount a challenge to usurp his throne instead of hunting down his enemies!

'Filth of Ealee; no longer shall you be allowed to live in ignorance of your shame! You shall be stripped of the mercy you took for granted. Your taxes will be doubled! Your toil will be doubled. And your land will feed the Iron Company that rules over you!

'If any among you has reason to quarrel with this decree, then let this be your moment. Step forth and speak your complaint!'

Not a soul stirred. Winlow clutched Father's hand, and he squeezed it until it throbbed. Lord Costel gargled pitifully in the silence.

'Acknowledge, in your hearts, that your cowardly silence condemns you to this fate,' Kaiber bellowed. 'I shall instruct the tax collectors to visit each of your homes. Do not disappoint them. If any word is spoken against my decree, I shall burn this Realm to ashes! Now leave! Return to the suffering and poverty you have brought upon yourselves!'

The soldiers astride the wall lifted their spears, allowing the highest members of the crowd to dart through the exits unmolested.

Winlow kept her head down as she climbed, clinging tight to her father's hand.

The crowd, which had been so alive before the duel, trudged from the Bowl in heavy silence. Father didn't say a word as he drove the hay cart home, no matter what pained questions Arthur asked of him. Without looking up, Jon slid a heavy pouch of material tied with twine toward Winlow across the cart. She unfastened it and saw the shiny cluster of chippings inside. She had almost forgotten their wager. The idea of it made her uneasy. She pulled the heavy Gilda from her cloak pocket and put it in the pouch. Then she turned to sit on her knees and reached forward to place it in Father's lap.

He turned to look at her questioningly.

She smiled at him and turned back to sit with Jon. Perhaps she only imagined it, but she thought Father's posture eased a little.

When they arrived home an hour later, Winlow went straight to the cowshed and hugged her mother tight.

CHAPTER 34

The Trace of a Lie

Varda Subei heard the distant sounds from the Marsh quarry far behind. She could not tell exactly what was happening, but she knew the duel's outcome. She had seen it.

The Queen Regent would be furious that her Augur had disappeared. But something about the young boy Subei was presently following had lit the familiar, painless burning sensation in her stomach. One of the many signs Ohrak had taught her to heed.

The boy had been brought to her tent on the outskirts of Marsh by a city guard. He told Subei that his father had captured a band of Elves somewhere along the coast, and the witch saw the truth in his eyes.

Moments later, they were on the road with a dozen soldiers riding at their heels.

Subei shuddered with pleasure. Something compelling lay ahead.

The journey to the boy's home took longer than expected. The road was empty the whole way, save for the few people Subei felt nearby on occasion, who had all ducked into the bushes at the roadside as the soldiers galloped by. The boy's home stood alone in a vast, sloping field, and as they approached it, the boy dismounted and bid for Subei and the soldiers to do the same.

'We must be quiet, milady,' said the boy earnestly. 'Me father is old. They could 'urt him if they heard us coming.'

Subei fixed her eyes on the building, which sharpened into vibrant focus. She could not sense many people, but if there were Elves inside, she would Trace the truth from each of them.

She ordered the soldiers to surround it. Once they formed the wide circle, Subei walked over to the captain.

'Take the boy and go inside,' she whispered. 'Let him enter first. If you encounter any Elves, I want them captured alive.'

The captain nodded and did as she bade. He grabbed the boy's shoulder and pushed him toward the house, his sword drawn in readiness. They disappeared over the threshold.

The captain returned and waved her inside, his sword in its sheath.

The ground floor was a single large room in complete disarray. A dining table had been overturned, and the floor was littered with debris. The chairs had been tossed aside, except one, in which an old man was bound and gagged. The boy was consoling him in a whisper, unfastening his bonds.

Something about the scene was wrong. Subei couldn't yet see it, but she knew it was there. Something big.

'Stop him,' she said coldly, pointing at the boy without looking at him. 'I want nothing disturbed.'

The captain yanked the boy from his half-freed father.

'Don't hurt him!' said the old man. But he withered under Subei's white gaze.

'Quiet,' she said, picking up a fork that had intrigued her. An image of it sliding between sets of perfect teeth blossomed in her mind. Elvish teeth. She placed the fork back on the floor and traced her fingertips slowly over the surrounding detritus. No other images came.

'Tell me what happened here,' she said serenely, gently caressing the splintered wood of a chair leg.

'I-I came upon some Elves on me land,' said the old man, swallowing. 'By the shore … Six of 'em. I reckoned that someone had been chasing them – and rightly so, of course! They thought I might be an ally. I played along and offered them to come inside. I kept 'em talking while my son here sent for the Queen Regent in Marsh. Who are these people?' he snapped at the boy.

'I am Varda Subei,' said the witch, running an elegant hand over the stonework, the eyes of every man in the room on her back. Her fingers tingled, and she knew she was close to whatever Ohrak sought through her. 'I am the Augur of the Queen Regent.'

'I thought only men …' the old man began, but his fear overruled his stupidity, and the reply died in his throat.

'What happened to the Elves?' Subei prompted.

'Ain't it obvious!' the old man bleated. 'They bloody turned on me, didn't they? Robbed me! Took off with all they could carry and lashed me to me chair! I heard one of them say something about a ship. They needed supplies before they could sail back to their own land. They went toward the coast not two hours ago. If you hurry, you may catch 'em!'

His lies were bitter in Subei's ears. She stopped Tracing and turned.

Some deception was at work here, she knew it, for she could not yet summon the truth. She carefully righted a chair and placed it directly before the old man. His aged face was a puzzle of emotions as she studied him.

As the old man squirmed under her gaze, something behind him began to take sharp focus in Subei's peripheral vision. A peculiar hole in the wall above the old man's head. Shallow, wide, and dusty, as though something had bitten into the stone. Subei stood and drifted past the old man to examine it, carefully Tracing a single fingertip into the grainy crater.

The second her fingertip probed the deepest nook, an image exploded before her eyes. A metal tube clutched in a hand. A blaze of light and a deafening boom. She wrenched her hand away as though burned.

The flash weapon, she thought.

Her heart began to race with excitement. She needed the truth urgently. She spun and stood over the old man, straddling him. She gripped his chin and lifted his face.

'Which way did they go?' she demanded.

'Southward … on horseback,' he lied.

Subei glanced over her shoulder at the captain. The soldier drew his knife and held it to the young boy's throat.

'No!' said the old man.

Subei lifted his chin higher until his face was aimed at the ceiling.

'Which way did they go?' she repeated, towering over him, her nose an inch from his.

'North,' he croaked. 'They went north. Into the grass plains. On foot. One of them spoke of Leybridge! But that's all I know, I swear!'

The truth at last.

'Did you see the flash weapon?' she asked. 'The metal tube with the red light?'

Confusion diluted the old man's fear, and his eyes flitted to the ceiling beyond her. Subei released him and looked up at the wooden beams, her stomach tingling. Someone was up there.

'Don't move,' she said to the entire room.

She picked up the hem of her robes and climbed the creaking staircase. The lamplit upstairs room was empty, save for a squat bed, where a man lay outstretched beneath the covers. His right arm was bandaged in clean, white material, which shone in Subei's eyes like a beacon, brighter than the flame in the lamp. Delicately, she began to unwind the bandage, her excitement building to some unknown crescendo. A long scar beneath the bandage glistened like a burn. When Subei touched it, the veil of lies lifted.

Bent in a crouch, her fingers resting on the scar, her mouth dropped open in ecstasy as the images swam before her pale eyes, opening vistas of truth in her mind.

The attack on the King was false. The Elf was no assassin. Of course not! He was a healer. Markos was weak. The Elf had saved his life. And Kaiber had been played for a fool. Sent to crusade against her father's enemies while the King regained his strength.

What a brilliant move, Subei thought with a smile.

But now it is my *turn.*

CHAPTER 35

The New Colour

Colton read carefully through the message twice, then handed the parchment to Volsgaard.

'Jado Costel is dead,' he said, sitting back in his chair as the Augur's eyes darted from side to side, sifting through the details.

'She raised the taxes?' said the Augur, lifting his head after a moment. 'She can't do that … just because he challenged for the throne!'

'Well, she has,' Colton sighed. 'And who's to stop her?'

The Augur shook his head in disgust as he continued to read. 'What do you suppose she does with them?' he asked suddenly.

'Does with what?' Colton replied.

'The severed cocks from the men she kills. What does she *do* with them, do you think?'

Colton let out a single, dry laugh. 'I don't know.' He shrugged. 'Maybe she's fashioning a necklace.'

'Hmm …' said the Augur, balling up the note and tossing it into the fireplace between them. 'Well, everyone needs a hobby, I suppose.'

They watched the parchment turn black in the flames.

'What do you make of the Elvish attack on Markos?' asked Volsgaard.

'I don't believe it for a moment,' said Colton. 'I spent much time with the Elves in Laudria, and I know them better than most. They're peaceful folk. To send an assassin would contradict their laws. And if they truly wanted Markos dead, there's not much Nephia could do to stop them. Their magic is more powerful than we can comprehend.'

'Then what do you suppose happened to the King? Why the subterfuge?'

'I'm not sure,' said Colton, swirling his wine. 'Rowel is too cunning to let slip any true weakness. The story must be some design of his. Though I cannot guess why he might have concocted it. Perhaps Markos simply needed an excuse to destroy the Elvish settlements. But then, why feign injury and let Kaiber fight in his stead?'

'Well, she must be in remarkable form to defeat a warrior like Jado,' Volsgaard ventured. When Colton remained silent, lost in his thoughts, the Augur pressed on. 'Do you think it's wise for us to continue with this Lordship Trial?'

Colton looked at him questioningly. The Augur assumed greater caution.

'I mean, the Krae have practically disappeared since their defeat, so we no longer need the reinforcements.'

'What are you saying?' asked Colton through narrowed eyes. 'You don't think *I* could beat her if she came to Berrund.'

'Do *you*?' Volsgaard asked plainly.

Colton took a sip of his wine. His eyes slid down to his stiffened leg. 'Probably not,' he admitted. 'But I know someone who could.'

Volsgaard sighed and sat back in his chair.

'Gadryon doesn't want to be found, Colton,' he said. 'We must accept that. And even if we could find him, we would be expecting a great deal from him in very little time; win the Lordship Trial, take your place as lord of Berrund, and then, when Kaiber arrives, defeat her and be crowned as King of Nephia. Does that sequence of events sound likely to you?'

'No,' Colton agreed. 'But then, I don't believe that anyone who defeats Kaiber will truly win the throne. Not while Markos is still alive. Ultimately, I think Gadryon will need to fight the King.'

Volsgaard scoffed in disbelief.

'What?' Colton demanded. 'You don't think he could do it?'

'I think you're letting this fantasy cloud your reason,' said the Augur. 'And I'm concerned about your motives.'

Colton leaned forward heatedly. 'My motive is to remove Markos Almanfier from power. To end the Almanfier dynasty!'

Volsgaard tilted his head, looking troubled. 'Are you certain?' he asked.

Colton flushed. 'Of course I'm certain,' he barked. 'What other motive could I need?'

Volsgaard sighed, his head still tilted. He looked at Colton balefully. 'Are you certain that this obsession with Gadryon is not founded in desire for redemption? In helping him succeed the throne, will you also absolve yourself of your past failure?'

Colton got to his feet. The Augur withdrew and stood up hastily too. He bowed. 'Forgive me, my lord,' he said. 'That was impertinent.'

Colton barely managed to bite back the retort forming on his wine-loosened tongue. He strode to the window to give himself a moment and looked out into the night.

'I thank you for your wise counsel this evening, Master Volsgaard,' he said. 'You are dismissed.'

He heard the light scraping of feet as the Augur turned to leave. But before Volsgaard reached the door, something outside caught Colton's eye.

'Wait,' he said sharply. 'Come here. Something's happening on the wall.'

A cluster of soldiers had gathered on the ramparts, holding torches. Some leaned through the crenels to look down on the north field. Colton felt Volsgaard arrive at his shoulder as one of the soldiers bearing a torch broke away from the pack, running toward the door at the base of his tower. Colton pushed open the window and leaned out into the cold air. 'Soldier!' he called, unable to identify the man's face. Several men turned to look up, but the running man spun around in confusion. 'Up here!' Colton provided. The man found him and ran closer, holding his torch aloft.

'What's happening?' Volsgaard demanded.

'There's someone out on the field, milords!' the man yelled. 'But all the scouts are back!'

Colton looked at Volsgaard and saw reticent hope mirrored back at him. 'Stay there!' he called, slamming the window shut.

The two men arrived on the ramparts, causing the watchmen to scatter back to their posts. Colton snatched a torch from the nearest man and looked out. A lone figure stood amid the sparse flames on the field, two hundred feet from the gate, long shadows meeting at his feet. He stood eerily still, carrying something on his back that Colton could not make out.

'Is it him?' Volsgaard asked, peering from the next lookout.

'Let's find out,' Colton replied. He turned to the soldiers lined on his right and saw a row of heads watching him avidly, each peeking around another. He pointed at the nearest of them in turn. 'You and you, go and prepare three horses at once and bring them to the north gate. Carmichael, go and wake Ableman Farrow and tell her to report to the north gate. Do it. Now!'

The three men sped off at once.

'Are the horses necessary?' Volsgaard asked as he followed Colton down the wooden steps. 'We might frighten him off.'

'If it's not Gadryon, then good,' said Colton. 'And if it is, then I doubt he would flee even if we sounded the war bell.'

'What is happening, my lords?' asked Elchora as she suddenly caught up with them, shivering, bleary-eyed, and fastening a strap on her leather tunic.

'There's a lone figure out on the field,' Colton said. 'Whoever it is, they're too far away to be hailed without stirring every man in the city. I think it might be Gadryon, and if so, you have the best rapport with him.'

Beneath his growing anticipation, Colton could not help but notice the way his daughter's face lit up at the mention of the boy's name. He wasn't sure how to feel about it.

Three horses trotted noisily around a corner, with jogging soldiers at their reins. Colton, Volsgaard, and Elchora mounted.

'Lower the north bridge and raise the portcullis,' Colton called into the night. He turned his horse toward the gate as the iron teeth lifted and the long bridge rattled out on its chains. Colton led the way, walking his horse slowly. The dark figure had not moved. As the party of three approached, the figure lowered its burden to the ground. Colton could see torchlight through the object, a helmet and armour. He gripped the reins of his horse as the figure came into relief.

Gadryon had returned.

Colton slowed his horse to a stop twenty feet from the boy. He looked much younger than Colton had expected, the skin on his face unblemished and pale. His long, dark hair hung in uneven lengths at his shoulders. Colton met the boy's eye while Elchora and Volsgaard drew up on either side of him, their horses' heads dipping in the cold. Gadryon shifted his weight, displaying the sword tucked into a vine belt at his side.

'Gadryon,' said Colton with an awkward smile, suddenly wishing he'd thought of something to say. 'Welcome back to Leybridge. I am Colton Farrow, lord of Berrund.'

'Why are you hunting me?' he asked.

Colton bristled slightly at the brusque informality but quickly recovered, reminding himself that the boy was wild.

'My scouts have merely sought you as an ally,' he said, 'nothing more. I wanted to meet you in person. To look into the eyes of the man who attacked an army of Kraelings and won. And I wanted to thank you for fighting with us that day.'

Gadryon remained still and said nothing. Volsgaard broke the silence before it soured.

'Ableman Farrow told us that you came here for food that day,' he said, as though addressing someone hard of hearing, gesturing at Elchora. 'Is that so?'

'Yes,' said Gadryon swiftly.

Colton saw relief cross the boy's features. Perhaps he had worried they had marked him for a thief, as Maldon had. Whatever his reason, the boy relaxed his stance.

'If you should ever go hungry again,' said Colton, 'know that you will always be welcome in our halls, and supplied with all the food you can carry, as often as you need. Please, consider Leybridge your home.'

For a heartbeat, the boy's hard expression betrayed a childlike longing. But he backed away and grimaced all the harder, as though distancing himself from temptation.

'The Urden is my home,' he said.

Colton nodded. *Tread carefully*, he thought.

'Why have you returned?' asked Volsgaard.

Gadryon's eyes moved involuntarily toward Elchora before he directed them to the armour at his feet.

'I came to return this,' he said.

'Keep it,' said Colton. 'You have more than earned it. In fact, we would be honoured, Gadryon, if you joined our ranks officially, as *my* apprentice.'

Volsgaard shot Colton a wide-eyed warning.

The boy stepped back and lowered his eyes. 'The Urden is my home,' he repeated.

'What if he could do both?' Elchora interjected, drawing all heads in her direction. She was addressing Colton. 'What if Gadryon could train with you but keep his home in the forest? Allowed to come and go as required?'

Colton raised his eyebrows and turned back to Gadryon, deflecting the question his way. After a moment of inner turmoil, the boy gave a single nod, and Colton felt a thrill on the cold night breeze. An old, forgotten feeling stirred in his soul. One of destiny. Of glory. He would train this boy to the peak of his ability. And whatever schemes King Markos and his Augur had planned would be rendered useless.

They had no idea what was coming.

Colton urged his steed forward. 'Then it is settled,' he commanded, unsure how the boy would respond to such authority. 'You will report for training at sunrise, one day hence.'

Gadryon glanced at Elchora once more before giving a stiff bow. In the same motion, he lifted his armour from the ground.

'Leave that here,' said Colton, smiling. 'And I shall forge you a worthier sword.'

Gadryon placed the armour on the floor. He lifted his chin to face Colton expectantly.

Colton regarded the boy for a moment, then gestured to the trees with his head. Gadryon's mouth curved, for the first time, into something like a smile. He turned and sped across the torchlit field, as silent as a shadow. Colton watched him until he vanished into the trees. He wheeled around to look at Elchora. 'Well done,' he beamed. 'Well done! When he returns, I would like you to meet him out here and bring him straight to me.'

'Yes, my lord,' said Elchora, a fraction too delighted.

The father and daughter returned their attention to the darkened tree line for several long seconds.

'Get back to your bed, Ableman,' said Volsgaard, breaking their trance. 'Your father and I need to speak in private.'

Elchora bowed and wheeled her horse around. She dug her heels into its flanks and rode back to the city wall at a canter. Volsgaard waited until she was out of earshot. He sighed impatiently. 'While I'm pleased that I was wrong about the boy's return,' he said, 'I must again urge caution. We know nothing about him, Colton, except that he has talent. And while I too can see him breaking the Almanfier Dynasty, we don't yet know what *he* wants, and I worry that your insistence may drive him away.'

'My *insistence*?' asked Colton.

'Yes,' said Volsgaard patiently. 'The boy is a great fighter. But that fact alone is not enough. He's as timid as a deer. A recluse. And he almost fled when you suggested that Leybridge might become his home. Does that sound like someone who aspires to sit on the throne? To rule over all the people of Nephia?'

Colton's excitement waned under this truth. 'No,' he agreed bitterly. 'I cannot force the boy to win the throne ... but I *know* he can do it, Erik, and Ohrak has surely sent him here for a reason?'

'*Surely*, my lord,' Volsgaard agreed. 'God has gifted the boy with skill and sent him to us. But we need not *train* him to fight. He is ready. What we must do is give him a *reason* to fight.'

'And how should we do that?'

'By not thrusting him into prominence too quickly, my lord. By being delicate in our approach. If you'll forgive me, it is a mistake, I believe, to make him your apprentice. The implication is too obvious. It could stir jealousy among the men and serve to further isolate the boy. Instead, let him join our ranks as a New Colour. Allow him to rejoin society in his own time, to form bonds of friendship. And once he is accepted, and *feels* accepted, we will have a better chance of convincing him to fight for

Berrund against Kaiber.'

'We don't have time for that,' said Colton. 'Kaiber could be here in a matter of weeks or days, and Gadryon must be in a position to accept her challenge when she arrives. We must convince him to enter the Lordship Trial as soon as possible.'

'Yes, but through subtlety, not force, my lord. Fighting for others may come naturally to you, but the boy, I believe, must be primed for combat.'

Colton surveyed his Augur suspiciously. 'Don't slip compliments into your arguments to soften me,' he said.

'I will if it works,' said Volsgaard unabashedly.

Colton took a deep breath of the cold night air. 'I only ask that you consider this matter from a wider perspective,' the Augur continued. 'Don't scare him off. And understand that while Gadryon is greatly admired among the men, he is not universally loved. Maldon will do his utmost to poison people against him. As he did to you when first we arrived in Berrund. If you train Gadryon for the throne, letting him come and go as he pleases, the men will resent him. After all, we don't allow other soldiers into the Urden after nightfall.'

Colton was too tired to argue. 'You're probably right,' he said, 'and I promise to consider your counsel. But as for allowing him into the forest after nightfall …' Colton looked back at the dark row of trees. 'I more pity the beast or Kraeling that crosses Gadryon's path in there.'

CHAPTER 36

The Scar

Kaiber stared at the severed arm. At the shiny red scar she had seen once before.

Cold oblivion consumed her.

It could not be true.

For it would mean a betrayal she could not bear. And she feared the reckless abandon growing in her heart.

The witch must be the liar, she thought. Her father would not use her as a puppet.

And yet the evidence lay on the table before her, undeniable. Kaiber lifted the limb to her nose and smelt the familiar scorched flesh she had scented on her father's chest. If Subei was lying, how could she have replicated it so perfectly? Kaiber let the arm flop to the table in disgust. She stood and paced the length of her tent, gnawing her thumbnail until it bled.

The Augur, she thought, with a burn of bilious hatred. Rowel. *He* had planted this idea in her father's head. She knew it. Perhaps the King was unaware!

But how could he be? As comforting as the notion might be, the King would not have allowed his Augur to act alone. Markos must have volunteered to let the Elf heal him.

A *healer*. She shook her head at her stupidity as she paced. Not an assassin. Of course it was a lie. It was so clear now. They had played on her loyalty, and she, Kaiber, had fallen in line like a foolish little girl. Just as the Augur had planned, she had lain waste to the Elvish settlements in revenge. Killing off her father's enemies for him. She had declared war on the Elves for nothing. And now she was crusading across the kingdom, wiping out every other threat to her father's throne. A throne that belonged to *her* by all the rights of Ohrak and Nephia.

But why?

Why had her father always dismissed her as his heir? Why had she always been overlooked? Shackled and suppressed. Henrik handed everything denied her. What had she done to deserve such disregard? And why did it cut so deeply?

Henrik was Markos's legacy.

She, Kaiber, was alone.

She felt something disappear inside. She stopped pacing. Yes. Rowel might be the architect of this deception, but her father had allowed its construction. It was a knife in the back, and two in the heart. She felt the blades cut her insides raw as tears formed in her eyes.

'Yes,' said the witch. 'You are nothing!'

Kaiber took a step back as though struck. The witch loomed over her.

'I see the turmoil in your heart, my Queen,' came Subei's melodic voice. She surveyed Kaiber's inner child with those featureless, white eyes. 'This truth has wounded you … but *do not* ease your suffering. *Do not* let this wound heal. Let it sink deep, my Queen. Let it destroy you. Let it be your death so that you may rise anew. Use it to transcend your mortal flesh and be reborn as your true self. The Ulmar of Ohrak, as God foretold! Remember Her prophecy: *When the true King falls, his champion shall be reborn as the Ulmar of Ohrak and made immortal for all time.'*

The witch advanced as she spoke. Kaiber backed away, cornered, like a pathetic, snared animal, clutching her abdomen, tears rolling freely. *She is casting a spell on me,* she thought. But suddenly, the murder in her veins fizzled to nothing. Her every muscle loosened as her body purged itself of feeling. The agony in her gut melted away. The hurt lifted. And all that remained inside was cold neutrality.

She straightened slowly and looked at the witch in her new form.

Her flesh had not changed at the surface, but Subei's eyes widened in awe, seeing her Queen's transformation. A smile of recognition played at the corners of her mouth. The witch kneeled.

'At last, you have come,' she said, bowing her bald head to her knee.

Kaiber looked at her surroundings as though for the first time. Her eyesight had sharpened, and her thoughts were clear. Everything had become so simple. She looked down at her faithful servant.

The witch's prophecy was true. Kaiber was the Ulmar of Ohrak. *Made immortal, for all time,* as the prophecy foretold.

'I want them dead,' she said, detached. 'Rowel, Markos, Henrik. All of them.'

Subei stood, her lip curled in a smile. 'I have an idea how we might achieve that end, my Queen,' she said, 'and much more. In Her wisdom,

Ohrak revealed more to me than the King's deception. A band of Elves is crossing the Plains of Reon as we speak. They carry a true flash weapon of unequalled power. If we can obtain that weapon, your transcendence will be complete. Your enemies will perish at your whim. And all shall hail you as Queen and the Ulmar of God.'

The two women stared at each other for a long moment.

'Take me to this weapon,' said Kaiber.

'We must be patient, my Queen. We must think strategically, lest our enemies catch wind of our designs. The grass plains of Reon are vast. Our quarry would see your army in pursuit from many miles away and could slip into hiding. But fear not. I know where the Elves are heading. We must also be wary of the King's Augur, Malcifer. Do not underestimate him, my Queen. His spies watch our every move, and you have publicly announced that you would remain in Marsh to collect taxes. So, that is what we must do. Suppose we were to suddenly deviate from that agenda. We might draw the Augur's attention and alert him of our true intent. Remember that the Iron Company is sworn to the King. Only ten percent of its force marches with us. If a battle for the throne became necessary, we would be crushed. We must fortify our position and strike when the scales are tipped in our favour. We must be patient, my Queen. Our enemies are not yet aware that we have entered the game.'

Mere minutes earlier, Kaiber would have erupted at this request to stagnate. Now, however, only a calm well of patience resided within.

She nodded.

The new Queen would bide her time.

CHAPTER 37

The Warning

Orla lay face down beneath her bearskin bedcover, listening to the wind howl in the mouth of Home Cave. Her skin itched under the heat of her own breath. Stifled. But Orla could not summon the enthusiasm to throw off the covers. Everything was too heavy. Tainted with the permanent sadness that would not let go.

This was her nineteenth, or perhaps twentieth, day confined to the cave, since her time in the watchtower. Gadryon refused to let her leave, even for fresh air. He said that soldiers were patrolling the forest, looking for him. And she would be in danger if seen.

The sadness had become a solid presence, and she had begun to fear that it might never leave. It had taken hold the day or night when she realised that she had lost all sense of time. Without purpose, the routines of hunting, and the feel of the sun or the cool night air on her skin, the days had blended into an endless stream of lonely, spiralling consciousness, broken only by patches of irregular sleep. Even her dreams had shrunk in her confinement. Only by touching the solid walls of her prison could she confirm whether she was awake. And, awake or not, neither state offered relief from the sadness.

Gadryon continued to come and go. Sometimes he came back with food, sometimes with news. But Orla had lost her appetite for both. She guessed as she lay there, overheating beneath her bearskin, that he had been gone for many hours this time. In truth, she had no idea, for she had barely moved, and her arms were becoming as numb as her legs.

She allowed her mind to drift, thinking that sleep might quicken the passage of endless time. She thought of nothing. Of emptiness. A void.

A void.

Her upper body spasmed as the rushing noise began to swell. It was as though a dry waterfall passed overhead, building in volume, louder and louder. Orla's body became weightless as she lost the feeling of her bed, the bearskin, the heat, and the itching. Then, she heard it again, a voice under the rush.

Orla, it said in the strange, rattling breath. Then louder, *they are coming!*

This time, Orla mastered her fear and kept breathing steadily in the rush. She tried to answer, to speak, but no words would come.

Who is coming? she thought.

Death, rattled the voice.

As her heart raced, the rushing ebbed away, and Orla felt the silence and oppression of the cave return. She threw off the bearskin and spoke into the silence. 'Come back,' she pleaded. 'Please … come back.'

She waited. But nothing happened.

She tried to think urgently; why had the voice come back at that moment? Had she done something to summon it? She recalled her first encounter in the forest. She had been on the verge of sleep, then. And just now too, she had been drifting off! She yanked the covers back over her head and tried to wriggle into the same position she had found. For a long time, she simply lay there, waiting. But still, nothing happened.

Go to sleep, she thought. *Go to sleep. Think of nothing. Of nothing.*

As her mind emptied of thought, the rushing took up once more. Orla's heart leapt with excitement.

The rushing stopped abruptly.

'No!' she said aloud. 'Come back! I'll control it this time! I promise!'

She emptied her mind a third time, achieving the required state much more quickly. As the rushing intensified, she breathed steadily, forcing herself to remain calm. To keep the connection alive.

They are coming, the voice repeated.

Who is coming? she thought.

Death.

What does that mean? Orla asked in her mind, trying to keep her nerve. *The Krae?* She thought slowly, with great effort. *Will the Krae attack again?*

Embrace them, said the voice, suddenly higher, more urgent. *Embrace them as brothers!*

Orla tried to shake her disembodied head. *I don't understand*, she thought, struggling to maintain the connection in her confusion. *Tell me what you mean …*

The rushing remained, but the voice did not reply for a long time. Orla held the connection anyway, waiting. The sensation was uncomfortable and bizarre, and Orla's distant body began to tremble under the effort of keeping it alive. It was like squeezing a weak muscle she had never used before.

The voice returned, louder and more prominent than ever. *See the light,* it said.

I don't understand, she thought.

See the light!

The impossible happened. And Orla's sudden astonishment severed the connection at once. For the most fleeting fraction of a second, the voice carried Orla into the dead, unused part of her brain and lit a spark.

And Orla had *seen* it.

She threw off the bearskin, laughing and yelling all at the same time for sheer joy. A joy that crushed her sadness into non-existence.

So many times … so *many times,* Gadryon had tried to explain to her what light was. And neither of them had ever come close to understanding the perspective of the other. Of course, she had always known the word, but never, not in her wildest fantasies, could she have conceived of the thing that had just passed through her mind. *Light!* The moment the voice had spoken the word. She had seen a light, not before her eyes, but in her mind.

Orla laughed at the cave ceiling as hot tears rolled down her cheeks into her ears. She tried to remember the brief flash of light. Exactly as she had seen it. And as she did so, a sharp, searing pain threatened to split her skull in half. But Orla didn't care. Because there it was again. She was able to bring it back at will.

More! she begged. *Please! Show me more!*

For a long time, perhaps several hours, Orla struggled to regain the connection. But it was no use. She was too thrilled to empty her mind. She replayed the flash of light for the umpteenth time when she heard Gadryon's two-tone whistle outside the cave.

Instinctively, she pulled the bearskin back over her head and pretended to be asleep. She heard Gadryon climb through the cave entrance.

'Orla,' he whispered, standing very near, 'are you awake?'

Orla held her breath and lay still. Gadryon sat on her bed and sighed loudly.

'I know you're awake under there,' he persisted, 'and I know you're angry that you can't go outside … but I really need to speak with you.'

Orla slid the cover off her face and tried to assemble her features into the pout she must have been wearing for the last three weeks. She would not tell him about the voice or the light. If he was going to live a life of his own, so would she.

'The lord of Leybridge has asked me to join his army,' he said. 'I've said yes … to stop them hunting for us. It means you can start leaving Home

Cave again … and we can go into the forest together to hunt … but it also means that I might be away more … and for longer. You understand?'

Orla gave a solemn nod, facing away from him. She had always known this would happen eventually. That the big world, far beyond her experience, would take him away from her. And she also knew that Gadryon had not accepted his place among the people for her sake. She could taste his excitement to return to the town. But she didn't care at that moment. Before the miracle, such news would have devastated her. She would have demanded to go with him. If Gadryon had been accepted by the people, he could surely talk them into accepting a cripple too? But now … now she wanted nothing more than to be left alone. To explore her mind and see as much as the voice could show her. The possibilities were unimaginable.

Gadryon stroked Orla's hair. Her tender head throbbed under his gentle touch.

'Thank you,' he said softly. 'I promise to always bring back as much food as I can. And to take you out as often as possible. It won't be like before, but at least they'll stop hunting for us out here.'

Orla pulled the bearskin back over herself and waited. Gadryon stayed on her bed for a long time. Finally, he moved away, and Orla heard him prepare a fire. She imagined its light and grinned in secret under her cover.

CHAPTER 38

Aim to Maim

As Gadryon arrived at the final row of trees, he began to hear voices in the north field beyond. He twisted his left palm on the pommel of his sword to reassure himself that it was there. He tried to swallow, but his mouth was too dry. All through the night, as he had trudged toward Leybridge, he had fought the urge to turn back. But he had arrived. His stomach felt hollow, and his hands stung with a bloodless cold.

What are you doing? he thought, shaking his head as his heart pounded against his ribs. He took several deep breaths before stepping out from the trees.

The pre-dawn field was awake with activity. Hundreds of orange-lit people were scattered far and wide, working in groups by torchlight. Some were children, or so Gadryon thought, until he realised that the shorter figures were obscured below the waist, standing in freshly dug holes. The holes were laid out in a pattern, and once connected, they would form some kind of massive rectangular trench. On the level ground, inside the rectangle of holes, was a giant dirt pyramid, the base of which widened every time one of the workers upended a new wheelbarrow that the diggers had filled. The air was alive with voices and indistinct chatter, the crunch of shovels slicing into the earth, and the dusty hail of loose heaps as they were tossed into the waiting barrows.

One of the figures from a nearby group suddenly peeled away from the others and headed straight for Gadryon. He gripped the hilt of his sword reflexively but recognised the blonde hair of Elchora Farrow. The hilt suddenly became slippery. She was caked in mud below the knees.

'I wasn't sure you would come,' she said, breathless from her toil.

'Nor was I,' Gadryon replied before he could stop himself. Elchora smiled at him, and Gadryon tore his eyes away as though he had looked directly into the sun. He cocked his head at the activity behind her, hoping she hadn't noticed. 'What's happening?'

'Oh … we're building a battle mound for the Lordship Trial next week,' she said, wiping her forehead with the back of a filthy hand. 'People have been pouring in from all over Berrund and Eddis for days to see it, and there won't be enough room to watch it in the old courtyard.'

The nearest digger lifted and stretched out a heaped shovel of mud, then turned his shovel aside, letting the mound slide off into a wheelbarrow with a wet thud.

'Should I help?' asked Gadryon awkwardly.

She smiled again. 'No, these are full soldiers and Ablemen, like me. Lord Farrow has made you a New Colour, a recruit. We call them New Colours because their armour is supposedly untarnished by battle. It doesn't really make sense, but the name stuck. New Colours train together in the courtyard at daybreak. Come on, I'll show you.'

She set off toward the distant city wall, gesturing for Gadryon to follow. He obliged, keeping two paces behind. The surrounding soldiers began to lift their heads from their work as they passed, some gaping openly, and urgent whispers broke out in their wake.

'What are they staring at?' asked Gadryon, his sweaty hand still clutching his sword.

'At you,' Elchora said plainly, turning to walk backwards for a moment and stare at him like the others. 'You're a legend here, Gadryon. The boy from the Urden. The hero who saved us from the Krae. And your return has people excited.'

Gadryon looked around at the torchlit faces watching him. He saw smiles of respect and heads flicking forward in curt bows. Others gawped openly, lips parted in wonder. Gadryon felt something lurch in his stomach, and he suddenly had no idea where to look. Each set of eyes became a pair of needles, prickling at his instinct to run. He had expected indifference, even disdain.

The adulation was too much. He kept walking behind Elchora with his eyes on her heels.

What are you doing?

The prickling sensation vanished abruptly as the watching soldiers dashed back to their work in hurried unison. Elchora had stopped dead in her march, and Gadryon almost strode into her back.

'Why have you abandoned your chores, Princess?' said a voice like gravel in a sifting pan.

Gadryon saw the speaker approaching them over Elchora's shoulder. The man was short but broad and stocky, his head completely bald save for a wiry ginger beard that fanned out in a dense tangle from the length of his jawline. A heavy pick-hammer dangled at his waist, and something about the man's self-assured stride told Gadryon that he knew how to use it. Gadryon's hand burned as his grip tightened on his sword.

'Forgive me, Commander, but I was instructed to greet the New Colour when he appeared,' said Elchora, her speech quick and sharp. 'I am ordered to take him to the training session and introduce him to the others.'

The bald man's gaze slid from Elchora to Gadryon. Though his face remained impassive as he took Gadryon in, his trunk-like body seemed to swell. Elchora seized on the man's silence. She whipped her head back to face Gadryon.

'This way,' she urged. And she struck off once more toward the wall. But the bald man grabbed her bicep and pulled her up short.

'No,' he growled, his lifeless eyes boring into Gadryon's. 'I will take him. You get back to work.'

Elchora wrenched her arm free of the man's grip and leapt beyond his reach.

'My orders are from Lord Farrow, Commander Maldon,' she said. 'I must take Gadryon to Captain Brigg myself!'

Maldon gave a single grunt, like a bear clearing its nose. He returned his attention to Elchora and bared his yellow teeth in a sour smile.

'Lord Farrow won't be the lord of anything for much longer,' he said. 'Not after the Lordship Trial. And I wonder … who will you hide behind when Daddy's gone, Princess?'

Gadryon shifted purposefully, and Maldon's teeth vanished behind a sudden grimace. The commander turned squarely to face Gadryon, a hand resting on his hammer. The two men looked at each other for a long moment, poised. The sounds of digging amplified.

'This way,' Elchora hissed from Gadryon's periphery. She was backing away from Maldon into the darkness toward the city wall. Gadryon relaxed his stance, gave the man a single nod, and then took off after her. As he passed the Commander, he kept his ears pricked for sounds of a lunge. Elchora strode much faster than before.

'Who was that?' Gadryon asked quietly when he caught up with her.

'Victor Maldon,' she said without looking at him. 'He's the Lord Commander of the Leybridge Army … and he doesn't like me very much.'

'Why?'

In profile, Gadryon saw a muscle twitch in Elchora's jaw, but she remained silent as they walked. When their feet pounded across the wooden bridge of the moat toward the city gate, a languid guardsman ambled out self-importantly from an alcove behind the raised portcullis. He had a faded yellow bruise around his left eye socket. When he spotted Gadryon approaching, his desire to head them off seemed to vanish, and he quickly ducked back inside his hole. Elchora took no notice of the guard and continued straight into the city. She pivoted to face Gadryon once they were further inside.

'We're a bit early,' she said, glancing up at the dark-blue sky. With a sigh of impatience, she dug her fists into her hips. 'Well, I'd show you around, but I got the impression that you know exactly where everything is.'

Gadryon shook his head. 'I came to Leybridge often as a boy, but I have no real memory. I knew the Consel because my father used to take me there … he was the Augur of Fairwater. It seemed much bigger back then. All these buildings did. But there was no curtain wall this side of the river, and there were not so many people.'

Elchora nodded. She peered around the silent courtyard, deciding where to take him first. Candle and firelight poured out from several of the windows and doors of the surrounding buildings. The city was waking up. Elchora led him down a narrow alley that emerged into a wider street, pointing randomly to any structures of consequence. He knew the Consel, of course, but also the armoury and the feast hall. So, she took him first past the smithy, where the forge was already lit, and to the stables, where a pair of boys stopped their sweeping to eye them suspiciously. They turned into a wider, cobbled street, where a fat man was wheeling a handcart covered in vegetables. Elchora pointed to a stout grain silo that stood between two bakeries. She told him that the owners had once been married but were now bitter rivals, and neither was good at baking. Gadryon's head swam in the deluge of information. It seemed wrong that a place of such mundane abundance had continued to exist during his many years in exile. Elchora, unaware that ropes were constricting his chest, continued to pile on the evidence with enthusiasm. Before the Krae, she said, the city's north side had housed the civilians because all threats had come from the south, beyond the Ley. So, the south remained heavily fortified to this day. Gadryon struggled to breathe as she led him down the street lined with taverns. He was about to end her unwitting bombardment when the road suddenly opened into a vast square, washed in the blue light of dawn.

'The courtyard,' said Elchora with the sweep of a hand. 'This is where the New Colours train for combat. And where the Lordship Trial would have been held if the city weren't overrun.'

A substantial wooden platform dominated the middle of the square. It stood three feet off the stone floor, fifty feet wide, with enough room between its perimeter and the surrounding buildings for a crowd to gather, twenty people deep. A thick wooden post stood proudly from the centre of the platform, like a ship's mast. The post was covered in black cuts and scratch marks, and a dark halo encircled its base, where many shifting feet had stood.

Elchora looked at Gadryon in profile and followed his gaze.

'That's the lashing post,' she said. 'Maldon's favourite means of punishment. It was used for public executions before my father's time.'

She leapt onto the platform with the agility of a cat, and Gadryon followed. As he landed, the doors on the far side of the square flew open, and a group of young men came through it, laughing and jostling one another. Each wore a studded leather tunic with black breeches and cloth boots. Some leapt onto the platform as Gadryon and Elchora had, while others made their way quickly up the steps. Most looked younger than the soldiers digging up the north field, and Gadryon was pleased to recognise a few faces from the battle. The two men at the group's rear carried a long bundle between them. They heaved it onto the platform with a clatter, and the nearest soldier knelt down to undo the strings binding the cloth. The other men swarmed around the kneeling man, and wooden swords were quickly handed out. One of the men Gadryon recognised began to stride across the platform, absently swinging his sword as he yawned. He froze, his eyes almost bulging out of their sockets when he spotted Gadryon and Elchora.

'Iss him,' he whispered involuntarily, then he rounded on the others, speaking up. 'Here, lads! Look! He really 'as come back!'

Once again, many faces turned to look at Gadryon in unison, reminding him of a hungry pack of wolves. The men swaggered over and crowded in behind the first man, who had pushed forward and thrust out his hand, which Gadryon took hesitantly in his own.

'Gadryon,' exhaled the man as though casting a spell. He squeezed Gadryon's hand tightly and shook it like a seizure. 'Welcome back, lad. Welcome back! Err … my name is Tom Cloyn, infantryman and an archer. I was only two shields away from you in the battle for Leybridge.'

Gadryon nodded at the man called Tom, whose beam of a grin widened. The other men began to speak their names in turn, but Gadryon lost track. Not since childhood had so many people surrounded him. As a gap formed briefly between the men, Gadryon spotted another face he recognised. The soldier he had fought in the woods, Almys Fyvern. He stood back from the crowd, strangling the handle of his sword. The nostrils of his crooked nose flared. Gadryon tried to keep his eyes on Fyvern through the moving bodies. In his silence, the other soldiers erupted with overlapping questions.

'How did you charge the Krae like that?'

'How did you survive?'

'Where did you learn to fight?'

'Why do you live in the Urden?'

'Is it true that you're a survivor of the Fairwater massacre?'

'Are you the Ulmar of Ohrak?'

Gadryon retracted his hand from Tom's grip and took a step back. It was all too much. He wanted to shout, to make them stop. But he couldn't. Mercifully, at that moment, a louder voice from behind the men shocked them into silence.

'Quiet!' it thundered.

The cluster of New Colours turned and separated, revealing an older man striding toward them across the platform. He had a crown of thick silver hair around a balding pate, and an old scar connected his mouth to his ear across his left cheek. He was scowling around at the men as he advanced, looking for the source of their commotion. When he found Gadryon among them, his grizzled features broke into a kindly smile.

'Well, well, well,' he said as the crowd parted to let him through, 'if it isn't the man of the moment.'

Gadryon blinked. He looked to Elchora for aid.

'I've brought you the new recruit, Captain Brigg,' she said promptly. 'This is Gadryon of Fairwater. Gadryon, this is your captain, Jolyon Brigg.'

'It's an honour to have you with us, Gadryon,' said Brigg earnestly. His eyes wandered down over Gadryon's bearskin. 'Have you been fitted for your armour yet, lad?'

Gadryon shook his head.

'Well, we'll get it after duelling practice. I doubt you'll need it against any o' this lot.' The New Colours laughed. Brigg lowered his voice. 'Silly question, because I bloody well know you can fight, but … have you ever had a formal duel before?'

Fyvern shifted behind the pack.

'No, he hasn't, captain,' Elchora supplied quickly.

'Uh-huh,' said Brigg, nodding, his tongue between his teeth. 'And does she do all your talking for you?'

The New Colours laughed louder this time. In their distraction, Brigg gave Gadryon a swift, conspiratorial wink.

'No,' said Gadryon. 'I've never had a formal duel.'

'Ooh,' said Brigg, squinting as though he had tasted something unpleasant. 'I'll let you off for that, but just this once, mind, because you're new. Next time you speak to me, you address me as *Captain* or *sir*.'

Gadryon saw that it was not a reprimand but a lesson. And he was grateful for Brigg's tact. 'Yes, Captain,' he said, warming quickly to the man.

Brigg's scar bunched up on his cheek as he smiled. He spun around and strode back toward the centre of the platform. 'Right, then,' he said, 'that's enough gawping at wonder-boy. Come on, you useless bunch o' pussies. I want two lines facing each other on either side of me!'

The others began to move as one, but Gadryon remained rooted, watching, wracked with uncertainty.

'I'm going to teach you the correct stances for defensive duelling,' said Brigg. 'First, though, I want to see what you've all got up yer sleeves without any instruction. Those of you on my right will be the attackers. On my command, attackers, I want you to throw any and every combination you like at the man opposite yeh. And remember my rule about practice; aim to maim. Nobody learns shit if you hold back. Five points for anyone who manages to hit their opponent on the limbs. Ten points for anyone that strikes a lethal blow. Those of you on my left,' he gestured to the row that included Gadryon, 'you will be the defenders. Don't let these cunts near yeh. Two points for every parry. Five points if you can disarm them. And defend for your lives because the man opposite yeh is coming to kill.'

Gadryon was the last man on the row of defenders, furthest away from Brigg. He looked across at his opponent and saw Almys Fyvern breathing heavily while glaring at him with unreserved hatred. Though he had already beaten him, Gadryon was on Fyvern's turf this time.

A wooden sword was passed down the line. Gadryon took the unfamiliar weight in both hands and tried to find a natural grip. One corner of Fyvern's mouth was pulled upward in a sneer.

'Captain Brigg?' came Tom Cloyn's voice from the far end of the defending line. 'I've got no one attacking me, sir. The lines are uneven.'

'Yes! Thank you, Master Cloyn,' said Brigg, 'that was a test. Ableman Farrow, would you mind joining the attackers and showing these pricks how to duel, please?'

Elchora, who had climbed down from the platform to watch, unfolded her arms in surprise. She leapt onto the platform and caught the wooden sword thrown at her. 'Right, attackers, make room for Farrow. All of you, shift down to the next man. We don't want Cloyn to escape a beating.'

Fyvern fixed his eyes on Gadryon while he shifted reluctantly to face the next man. Elchora joined the attackers opposite Gadryon. She turned to face Gadryon and flashed her eyebrows at him. By the numbness that crept into his limbs, Gadryon wasn't sure whether his situation had improved or worsened.

'Right then,' said Brigg, 'is everyone ready? Master Cloyn, are you happy that someone will attack you? Yes. Good. Take your position and wait for my signal.'

The fellow defenders to Gadryon's right took up stances, their swords angled across their bodies from left hip to right shoulder. Gadryon was still looking at them when Brigg raised a flaming torch to signal the attack. Elchora ran at Gadryon with a roar, in line with the other attackers to her left. The line charged at the defenders at full pelt, and wood clacking on wood rent the air. Gadryon met Elchora's swipe and counter-riposte with relative ease, given his inexperience with a wooden sword. For some reason, it thrilled him to feel the power in her attack. She was not withholding. Between her fourth and fifth strokes, Gadryon saw Elchora's eyes widen at something behind him. He ducked reflexively as Fyvern's sword sailed over his head. He spun and met the second blow, and the blades splintered under the force of the collision.

'Whoa, whoa, whoa!' said Brigg, dancing through the melee. He slapped their shattered swords down but grinned. He leaned in close to Gadryon. 'You're only supposed to fight one of them, lad!'

Fyvern withdrew while the captain spoke. Elchora came to Gadryon's side.

'Captain,' she began, but Brigg had straightened up, frowning at something behind them, and the sounds of duelling died abruptly.

'Commander present!' roared Brigg over the final clack of swords.

Elchora whipped around on the spot, and Gadryon followed suit reluctantly, not wishing to turn his back on Fyvern. Commander Maldon, the bald man, stood on the platform's far side. His hammer was drawn, gripped in one hand, its heavy head a few inches off the floor.

'What the fuck was that?' he growled, leering at all present. 'I came back here … to see why my Ableman has dared abandon her duty for so long … only to find her locking sticks with the fucking children.'

Brigg pushed to the front and bowed as Maldon spoke. 'Forgive me, Commander,' he said. 'I asked Ableman Farrow to stay. We needed an extra man to make up the numbers.'

Maldon pointed his hammer at Brigg. 'That's not the problem, Captain,' he said. 'No, the problem is, the Ableman, the princess, looked like the only fucking one of you who knew what she was doing! Because what I just witnessed from the rest of you was a fucking travesty!'

The New Colours glanced at one other in dejected confusion. Brigg frowned at the Commander.

'Let me demonstrate how it's done,' Maldon continued. 'Get down from the platform, all of you!' Brigg jerked his head and led the New Colours from the platform, with Gadryon and Elchora bringing up the rear. As Gadryon crouched to leap down, his heart skipped a beat when he heard Maldon speak again.

'Not you, Farrow,' he said.

Gadryon looked back to see Elchora's eyes widen as his feet hit the ground. She had frozen in a crouch but straightened up, her jaw set ominously. She and the Commander were suddenly alone on the platform, towering above Gadryon and the New Colours.

'Turn to face me,' said Maldon.

Elchora took a deep breath before she obeyed. Maldon addressed the men assembled beneath him, still holding his hammer.

'Duelling is not the random carnage of battle,' he announced. 'It's more measured. More … personal.' His eyes found Gadryon's and locked onto them. 'The key to defeating your enemy is to outthink them. To control them. To display your dominance and make them suffer. And then you punish them for their mistakes. Observe.'

A sinister smile played on the corner of his mouth before he turned languidly to face Elchora. Gadryon felt a heat burning inside him while, at the same time, a cold bead of sweat trickled down his cheek from his temple.

'I will attack. You try to defend,' Maldon said to Elchora. She had already taken up a pose in readiness, but she firmed her stance further until she shook with tension. Maldon looked down calmly at the New Colours. 'Watch how the Ableman moves. You may learn something.'

Maldon bowed to Elchora, then took up a stance of his own, the handle of his hammer held across his chest in both of his thick hands. Gadryon's heart raced. The difference in their sizes was stark. And Elchora had nothing but a wooden sword against that black hammer.

After a second of poised stillness, Maldon lunged forward and swung the hammer with a whoosh of air. Elchora dived backwards and let the swing pass, keeping her sword aloft and ready as the hammer circled around in a whirl. This time, Elchora was forced to block. She took her sword in both hands and stood her ground, letting the wood between her hands take the brunt of the blow. But the power behind it knocked her aside, and she stumbled to one knee, her puny sword cracking loudly but not splitting. Maldon made her roll away as he drove at her with lethal intent. The hammer crashed through the platform with a clap like a bolt of lightning striking a tree. Three more times, Maldon advanced, with Elchora dodging each attempt. On the fourth swing, however, she had been boxed into a corner. She met the swing with her sword braced against the length of her wrist, and it shattered. Elchora fell from the platform with a cry, clutching her wrist in agony. The New Colours winced, and Brigg shook his head, his eyes on his feet. Gadryon could not see how Elchora had landed, but he heard the thud and the winded grunt and knew she hadn't been able to cushion her fall. Gadryon's blood boiled. His stomach was a ball of venom. Maldon walked casually back to the edge where the New Colours stood in shock. He focussed his attention on Gadryon once more as he spoke.

'Get back up here, Farrow,' he said. 'Just because you're betrothed to the prince doesn't mean I've finished with you.'

Elchora got to her feet slowly, visible only from the waist behind the platform, her blonde hair muddied sideways across her face. She swept it aside to reveal her defiant scorn. Gingerly, she twisted her left wrist while flexing her fingers to check for damage. Then she climbed back onto the platform using only her right hand.

'We haven't quite finished the lesson,' Maldon went on. 'Someone give her another sword!'

Almost every New Colour lifted their practice swords in hasty offering as Elchora limped toward them across the platform. But the wooden handles were quickly withdrawn when they heard Gadryon draw his real sword from its leather sheath. He walked toward Elchora and proffered it solemnly. She gave a glazed nod of thanks and took it without a word. Then she returned to Maldon's side, trembling.

The Commander didn't look at her as he addressed the New Colours. 'That was a small lesson in aggression,' he said. 'Now we come to the second part … discipline.'

Without warning and with brutal accuracy, Maldon swung the blunt square of his hammer into Elchora's unready midriff. She folded in half over it, chin up and mouth open in silent desperation for air, her face puce, eyes bulging, the veins in her neck standing thick with blood. She keeled over onto her knees, wheezing a death rattle. Gadryon pushed forward, but Brigg held him back. Maldon spoke over Chora's gasping.

'The other important thing to remember when duelling,' he said, 'is that you must never lower your guard. Until the flames are lowered or doused, the duel is not over. Now, would anyone else care to try?'

Gadryon shook free of Brigg and was up on the platform before he knew it. He crouched at Elchora's side and tried to lift her chin. But she remained folded, protecting her abdomen with both forearms, breathing in gulps and fits.

Gadryon heard the hammer coming.

He rose and pivoted in an upward corkscrew, stopping the shaft of the hammer dead with his left hand. He pulled Maldon off balance and, using the momentum of his spin, sent his right fist into the bridge of Maldon's nose with all his body weight behind it. He felt the nose pop between his knuckles. Maldon flew backwards through the air, lifted off his feet, and the crowd of New Colours parted as he fell, letting him crash to the stone floor in a heap. All heads turned to look up at Gadryon in astonishment. Except for Fyvern, who wore a peculiar smile. Even Elchora managed to lift her head to see what had happened.

'Get off me!' roared Maldon, flailing at Brigg's attempts to sit him upright.

The Commander rebounded to his feet with surprising agility and smiled. Blood lined his yellow teeth.

'Very good, boy,' he said thickly. 'But did you forget your role was to defend? Because you've just attacked a commanding officer. That's ten lashes at the post!'

*

Fyvern's insides writhed with glee. The Commander's trap had worked beautifully. And the stupid boy stared back, dumb. A juicy fly in the web of a spider.

Fyvern savoured each little agony as it occurred. The boy turned to fawn over the precious little Farrow girl, who coughed up a mouthful of blood and bile. Maldon ascended the platform, coiled whip in hand.

Oh, do it! Fyvern pleaded. *Cut this pretender to shreds! Let them see him for the boy he is! Make them see!*

'Commander Maldon,' said Brigg, 'I beg permission to speak, sir.'

'You're already speaking, Brigg,' growled Maldon. He snorted in a long rumble, then turned his head aside to spit out a thick globule of blood. 'What do you want?'

'Gadryon is a new recruit, my lord,' Brigg attempted pathetically. 'He doesn't know our rules. Perhaps … perhaps you should reconsider this punishment, sir.'

Maldon revolved slowly to face the captain. He squared his shoulders and puffed out his beard-covered chest.

'Would you care to join him on the post, Captain?' he leered.

Fyvern could barely keep still with excitement. Brigg frowned at the Commander with a mixture of confusion and disappointment. 'No, sir,' he said. But he took half a step closer and lowered his voice to a whisper. 'But I don't think Lord Farrow would approve of this, Commander. The Lordship Trial is less than a week away, and you know what he intends for the boy.'

'Hmmmph,' Maldon grunted, ensuring that all present could hear. 'I don't give a wet fucking shit what that old, paper-lord cunt intends, Brigg! This boy is a *jurdah*! Nothing but a filthy Kraeling spy!' He barged past the captain to address the sheep flocked around him, pointing at their false hero. It was more satisfying than Fyvern could have imagined. He watched his Commander avidly as Maldon restored order to the world. 'Can none of you see it?' he went on. 'Is the truth not plain? This boy claims to live in the forest alone. Think on it! The Urden Forest. Which we know to be riddled with Krae scum! Have none of you considered the possibility that he lives among them? Was raised by them? Look at him! His skin may be human, but his clothing is not! And I see him for what he is! This boy is one of them. He was caught breaching our city walls moments before the Krae attacked, you fucking cretins! Then he charged at an army of them, and they magically scattered before him. But why? Is he the Ulmar? The legend made flesh? He killed so many of them, after all! But what if all that killing was a design? Can't you see it? His plot? Because now he's truly inside these walls, is he not? After that single display of incredible skill, our good Lord Farrow intends to wrap his shoulders with the cape of Berrund! And all of you have been taken in, just the same. But if that day comes to pass, and this boy wins the lordship, then I tell you, the Krae will have taken this Realm by stealth! The seeds of that future are already sewn in your hearts and minds. I see it, plain as day. Find them, you fools. Dig them out for the weeds that they are! If you require the tools for the job, then allow me to supply them. Think of every challenge you have suffered to earn your place in this army … the endless training, the gruelling trials, the years of failure. Do you still think this boy should be gifted our colours so easily? Witness, in this very moment, how he has tricked you into subservience. He strikes your Commander, then your captain protests the lash, and not one of you bats an eye! Tell me, would any other among you be afforded such favour? Never. And so, I urge you to strip him of the protection he has planted for himself inside you. Let us test his resolve and his mettle. Lash him to the post!'

The effect of this speech was glorious. Fyvern could see the cold truth seeping into the minds of those assembled. Most now stared at Gadryon with a bewildered kind of scepticism. Some looked angry. Others lost. Heads turned in agitation to Brigg, who wrestled with the evidence himself, absently shaking his head. In the stillness, Fyvern marched purposefully to the platform. And two or three of the New Colours followed in his wake.

Just as they were about to ascend the platform, the boy took his sword from Elchora's grip and plunged it hard through the wood. He stood behind it, staring over Fyvern's head at the Commander.

'I am not a *jurdah*!' he snarled through gritted teeth, exquisitely incensed. 'I am no spy, and I am not the Ulmar, either. I never claimed to be. But if you think my killing of the Krae filth was an act, climb up here and prove it!'

Maldon grinned up at the boy, chuckling. 'I am the lord Commander, boy,' he said. 'I have nothing to prove because this burden is on you. If you have joined my army, you will obey my command. So, either you hug the post like a good boy and prove that you're one of us, or get the fuck out of our city and run back to the forest, like the cunty little Krae-lover I know you are.'

The boy did nothing but seethe for a long moment. The Farrow girl tried to unfurl herself to speak but failed. The boy glanced at the post. Then, without a word, he began to strip off his top layers of matted bearskin, letting them flop to the platform. When he took off the final wrapping, Fyvern's jaw dropped.

The boy's torso was like nothing he had ever seen before. Every inch of him was covered in taut, defined muscle. But these were not the rounded, heavy slabs that Fyvern associated with strength. These were lean and solid, like additional bones. His abdomen was a patchwork of flattened mounds beneath a set of flagstone pectorals. His shoulders were oversized and perfectly round, and his arms grew from them like slender, iron tree roots.

Nobody moved. The boy turned, walked to the post, and embraced it. As he locked his hands together on the far side, his back flared out like the wings of a moth. He twisted to look over his shoulder impatiently, his vines of dark hair obscuring his eye.

Fyvern shook his head, repulsed by his temporary surprise.

'Tie him down,' Maldon growled.

Fyvern was the only man to move. He joined the Commander on the platform and strode together toward the waiting *jurdah*. Maldon stopped short at whipping distance, and Fyvern picked up a short length of rope. The silly boy watched him with wide, fearful eyes. Fyvern tied the boy's clasped hands, pulling the rope until the hands were red and puffy. The boy continued to watch him around the post.

'This is only the beginning for you, *jurdah*,' Fyvern spat as he tested the lack of movement in the boy's bonds. 'The Commander is right about you. And I swear by Ohrak that I will prove it!' He leaned closer. 'Don't think I've forgotten about the scream I heard in the forest.'

The boy's apprehensive stare hardened dramatically, the muscles in his jawline knotting in hatred, betraying the truth. His arms flexed, but it was too late. The bonds were tied.

'He's all yours, Commander,' said Fyvern, backing away. The boy continued to stare at him with that lethal, trapped glare.

Maldon unfurled the whip. He loosened it with a flick of his wrist, sliding its tip across the floor like a thin snake. He looked up at the boy's exposed back and grinned through his beard of blood. He stood side-on with the whip held tight in his right hand, behind him, away from the boy. He leant out toward the whip for a second and then slashed it forward with complete malignancy. The full might of his weight and strength behind the stroke. The whipcrack resounded in the courtyard, and Fyvern saw the diagonal line of dust explode upwards from the boy's back.

But the boy did not react.

Not a flinch or wince passed through him. He continued to stare at Fyvern as though nothing had happened.

Did the Commander miss? Fyvern thought.

But when he looked at Maldon, he saw furious disbelief and knew that the lash had struck true. Maldon leant back a second time and threw himself forward with an almighty roar, putting every last ounce into the blow.

Again, the whip lacerated the boy's back, and blood mist clouded the air over his shoulder. But again, the boy did nothing. His eyes didn't even blink as they bore into Fyvern's.

Fyvern felt a bubble of fear in the pit of his stomach. His arm shuddered as it recalled the power in the boy's single attack in the forest. He circled to the boy's flank, giving the post a wide berth as he moved. He needed to see the lack of damage for himself. But he found two thin, overlapping welts across the width of the boy's back.

It was not possible.

The boy's eyes had followed Fyvern as he moved. They stared into his soul, unblinking, as Maldon's third stroke also failed to register. Fyvern looked over at Maldon. The Commander's bloodied face was purple with rage and, worse, exhaustion. Once again, he put everything he possessed into a fourth and fifth stroke, panting in fatigue now. The New Colours were climbing onto the platform in awed silence, broken only by the futile crack of Maldon's whip. The Commander paced like a caged lion, visibly unnerved, staring down at his hands. He swapped to his left and struck the boy again. No effect, save for the raw, red lines that blossomed silently across his back. Maldon gave a final, primal scream and threw himself forward again and again. But after a few seconds, Captain Brigg stood on the whip in its recoil, and Maldon crashed to the floor as it slipped from his weakened hand. He rolled over, livid. But Brigg's voice stayed level as he spoke into the reverent quiet.

'That was ten lashes, Commander,' he said.

The Farrow girl stumbled to the far side of the post and untied the boy's bonds. He shook the rope free, then looked at Maldon, who lay in a spent heap, panting. The boy lifted Elchora's arm around his bleeding shoulders and hobbled her over to his discarded bearskins. He steadied her, then began to re-dress. All eyes watching him.

Once covered, he put Elchora's arm back over his shoulders and spoke to Brigg. 'She's hurt,' he said.

'I'll take you to the healer,' Brigg said quietly. He blinked several times then spun to face the gathered New Colours. 'You're all dismissed.'

The bubble of fear in Fyvern's gut burst like lava as he watched the boy assist Elchora from the platform. Brigg led the way as Gadryon helped the girl back inside the castle. But Fyvern knew that the New Colours who followed them were no longer following their captain.

CHAPTER 39

The Fallen Champion

Elchora could barely stand. Whenever she straightened, her abdomen spasmed painfully. It hurt to breathe.

Gadryon clutched her side, matching her step, solid as a boulder. Her right arm lay across his back, fingers hooked over his far shoulder. Elchora could feel the heat of his lacerations through his bearskin.

How is he standing? she wondered.

Tom Cloyn led the hobbling pair slowly to the healer's room. It was little more than a cramped, windowless cupboard lit by candles, and a sturdy table dominated its centre. Floor-to-ceiling cabinets lined each wall, their shelves crammed with objects; leaning ranks of dusty books, pear-shaped potion bottles, tied bunches of dry herbs stacked in browning pyramids, and tiny crystal vials of clear elixir. The far door was shut, but Elchora knew it led to the old barn, which served as an infirmary for wounded soldiers.

Tom and Gadryon eased Elchora into a seated position on the table.

'I'll fetch a healer,' said Tom, promptly rushing to the far door. But he froze to look back at Gadryon with an expression of awed incredulity.

'I can't believe it,' he said. 'You truly are the Ulmar of Ohrak.'

He ducked through the door, shutting it quietly behind him. As soon as he was gone, Gadryon's face crumpled. He was breathing heavily.

'What's wrong?' Elchora asked.

'I wish they would stop saying that,' he mumbled. 'I'm not anything. The Ulmar is just a fable from the Scrawls.'

Elchora's stomach jolted as she laughed. 'It doesn't matter if it's a fable,' she said. 'Because even if it is, there's no denying what you're capable of, Gadryon. You have a gift from Ohrak that nobody has seen before. Including my father, who fought the King in his prime.'

Gadryon spun away clumsily. 'What gift do I have?' he said.

'Your strength!' said Elchora. 'Your skill with a sword! You are the greatest warrior alive.'

Gadryon rounded on her. Beads of sweat dotted his brow. 'If I am strong,' he snarled, 'it's because I have climbed a mountain each day since I was seven years old with my sister on my back! If I seem skilled with a sword, I grew up on a battlefield after my home was taken. I have killed bears, wolves, and Kraelings many times in a constant struggle to survive! Do these sound like gifts to you?'

A tear rolled down his cheek, and his chest heaved worse than ever. He swallowed, then half collapsed, pressing his fists into the tabletop with a grimace. Elchora's pain evaporated. She slid from the table to look at him more closely.

'Did he hurt you?' she asked.

Gadryon mastered his breathing and shook his head. Droplets of sweat flew from his hair.

'Let me see your back,' she said urgently. 'The cuts will need ointment, or they will fester.'

Gadryon shook his head again, his mouth shut firm. 'I must go,' he said. 'I shouldn't have come. I must return to Orla.' He pushed himself from the table as if to leave but swayed horribly. Elchora caught his arm. He was boiling.

'Take this off,' she said, panic rising. 'Most men spend a week in the infirmary after a lashing like that. And you might need stitches. Now take it off.'

'I must go home,' he said, pulling away feebly, his eyes unfocused. 'Orla cannot fend for herself. She cannot. Not without me. She needs me. She needs me.'

His eyes rolled as he collapsed. Elchora lunged to hold him upright. She pivoted his weight toward the table with difficulty, guiding his limp upper body onto its surface. She ran to the far side and grabbed his arms before his legs dragged him to the floor. Her stomach seared in agony, but eventually, he lay stretched out upon the tabletop, face down, his head to one side.

She brushed aside his sweat-soaked hair and put a palm on his forehead. The heat was intense. At that moment, the door to the ward opened, and a healer walked through. When his eyes moved from the panting Elchora to the inert Gadryon, he rushed to the table and gently guided Elchora aside.

'A fever,' he said. 'What happened?'

Elchora told him.

'Get me a knife,' said the healer, rolling up his sleeves. But as Elchora turned to search for one, he pulled her back. 'No! Forget that. This hide may be too thick to cut. Quickly, help me untie the bonds.'

They worked together in a frenzy to unfasten the ropes and vines. The underside of the final wrapping was wet with blood, and when they peeled it from Gadryon's back, they uncovered the crisscross of raw welts and shallow canyons seeping blood. The healer hurried over to one of the cabinets and began piling potions in the crook of his elbow. He brought them back to the table and unstoppered a vial, upending it into a rag.

'Clean the wounds,' he said, tossing the sodden rag to Elchora. She almost gagged at the smell of it. 'Wipe away all the excess blood. And be gentle! This will be a lot easier if he can sleep through it.'

Elchora got to work, gently cleansing the weeping lines. She looked up at the healer and saw him ripping an assortment of leaves from the bundles of herbs. He dropped them into a pumice bowl and ground them into powder, adding drops of liquid every now and then. When Elchora was done, she proffered the rag to the healer, who nodded impatiently to a bucket beneath the table. She tossed it in.

The aroma of spice filled the room, and Elchora fought off a sneeze. She pinched her nose and looked down at Gadryon. She could see the heartbeat in his neck.

What will Orla do without him? she thought.

The healer splashed his hands in a water basin, wiped them dry, and then put his fingers into the pumice bowl, scooping out fingers of loose green paste. He smeared it into the deeper cuts and anywhere the bleeding was fresh. In no time, the red marks on Gadryon's back were coated in stodgy green balm, and the healer nodded at his work in satisfaction. He turned to peruse the shelf of elixirs, running his finger along the tiny labels, muttering to himself. Finally, he drew one out, pulling out the delicate crystalline stopper.

'Could you tilt his head up for me,' he said, frowning at the vial. 'He'll only need a drop or two, I should think.'

Elchora slid her hands beneath Gadryon's downfacing cheek and felt a marked reduction in his fever. His head was heavier than expected, but she tilted it until the healer was satisfied that his precious liquid would not dribble from the open mouth. With great care, the healer poured a single drop of the clear fluid into Gadryon's mouth. After a few seconds of close inspection, he allowed Elchora to gently return Gadryon's head to the table.

The door to the castle opened.

Lord Farrow and his Augur crowded into the small room. The healer bowed.

'What happened?' asked Elchora's father, eyes widening at the sight of Gadryon's unconscious form. 'A New Colour told me that Maldon attacked you.'

Elchora repeated the story.

Lord Farrow's frown deepened as she spoke. Volsgaard moved to stand beside Gadryon. He touched his head and closed his eyes. When Elchora was finished, the Augur let out a grunt of anger.

'Curse Maldon!' he said. 'I cannot see the boy's destiny. I will call upon my Obediant, my lord.'

'There's no need,' said the healer. 'This is a violent case of scorch fever, nothing more. The boy should live, my lords. He just needs a few days' rest.'

'How many days?' Lord Farrow asked the healer.

'Three or four.'

'Then perhaps Victor has done us a favour!' Volsgaard whispered. 'The boy may want vengeance for this suffering. And if he must rest for a few days, my lord, then his presence at the Lordship Trial, four days hence, is all but assured!'

'He cannot stay here for four days,' said Elchora. All three men turned to look at her.

'He has no choice,' said the healer. 'The potion we administered will keep him asleep while the fever burns out. He will not wake until it passes.'

'Will he be able to fight when he wakes?' asked Lord Farrow.

'He has already begun the fight, my lord,' said the healer. 'His survival is likely but not assured. I will do all I can to keep him alive.'

'Damn!' said Lord Farrow, glowering at his Augur. 'I should have trained him alone. We must pray that he recovers quickly.'

Elchora watched her father's anguished profile in discomfort. He had always been so heartless when it came to combat. At that moment, for all his compassion, he could not see Gadryon's humanity. In his eyes, the boy was a weapon to be wielded against the Almanfiers. But Elchora knew the truth. As soon as Gadryon woke up, he would return to the Urden to save his sister. And if Orla died in his absence, they would never see him again.

CHAPTER 40

The Hall of the Fallen

Rowel stood with his ringed hands clasped behind his back, watching patiently. The Hall of the Fallen was long and ornately decorated. The carpet that ran its length was blood red, fringed with gold. The walls were dark green, and between the neat row of tall windows along the left-hand wall, which looked out onto the dreary courtyard of High Castle, hung portraits of Almanfier ancestors. Dead kings, stretching back to Beauren Almanfier, who first took the throne for his bloodline a hundred years ago. On the opposite wall were hung the real treasures of the hallway, the gleaming weapons and armour of the victims who had dared challenge for the throne throughout the Almanfier dynasty. Axes, swords, helmets, and breastplates of renowned fighters were pinned like butterflies by golden loops into the green velvet of the right-hand wall. They were spaced every few feet apart, framed by the light from a window opposite. Twenty-nine trophies in all, each representing its bearer's failure, and each displayed proudly. The names of their deceased owners were embossed into bronze placards above them on the wall. The names of the fallen. Rowel stood beside the newest of the trophies. The placard above the ridiculous broadsword read *Lord Jado Costel of Ealee*. The sword's pommel and tip almost exceeded the boundary of the green velvet. Rowel regarded it with a curl of his lip, then turned his attention to the two men approaching from the far end of the hall at a snail's pace.

'Slowly, Father,' said Henrik, his eyes on the King's feet. Markos took another step, leaning heavily on the shoulder of the prince, his tongue hard between his teeth, his brow beaded with droplets of sweaty concentration.

Rowel strode at the pair, smiling.

'You see, my liege,' he said, brushing a mite of dust from the King's robes, 'You regain more of your strength each day.'

'My *strength*?' growled Markos, almost spitting out his gritted teeth. 'It is agony to breathe! Why did I allow you to mutilate me so? I am the King of Nephia! Reduced to a cripple!'

Markos took several steps as though to charge at the Augur, but he stopped halfway, lifting his face toward the ceiling to catch his breath.

'We must be patient,' said Rowel. 'We have many more weeks of this suffering before you are returned to your glory, my king. You must rest as much as possible.'

'How can I rest when you have allowed my daughter to fight my enemies in my stead? What does that say of my authority? Friends and enemies laugh at me alike! And curse that girl! Why did Kaiber not host the trial here, where I could witness it? Was it your idea to campaign across the Realms?'

'I foresaw it,' said Rowel calmly, 'and I admit that I made no attempt to dissuade Kaiber. The people's attention will be drawn to the trial wherever Kaiber goes, keeping it away from you while you recover, my liege. By the time Kaiber has completed her crusade, you will be fully restored.'

'But what if she loses?' said Markos, swaying on the spot. Henrik strode forward to take his father's arm, scowling at Rowel in perfect replica of the King. Markos went on. 'What then, my wise Augur? What if Kaiber is defeated and my throne is taken by some lowly charlatan?'

'Have no fear of that, my king,' said Rowel placidly. 'We have Ohrak's will on our side, and the evidence of Kaiber's prowess stands behind us upon the wall. The lord of Ealee represented our greatest threat, and it was prudent of Kaiber to dispatch him first. As a result, many other Realms have now withdrawn their challenges, reducing our exposure to the unknown. And even if we were blindsided in some way, and an unknown challenger emerged capable of defeating Kaiber Almanfier, I doubt whether anyone would accept such a monarch while you still live, my king. No. Any such champion would have to beat you also if they desired the throne.

'The only piece I cannot predict is Berrund, but I have sent forth a trusted informant. We know the old traitor is hosting a Lordship Trial, so he cannot challenge Kaiber directly. But his successor could. And that future eludes my insight, for there are too many potential outcomes. My informants say Lord Farrow intends to bequeath his cape to a young boy. A boy from the Urden, who has made a name for himself by killing Kraelings.'

'What is the boy's name?' said Markos. 'What is his lineage?'

'I know very little about him, my liege. Only that he is seventeen, and his name is Gadryon.'

'Gadryon?' the King repeated, looking aside with a frown. 'And only seventeen? That troubles me, Rowel. Why would Colton put his faith in a boy so young? He must have talent. And if Colton succeeds, and the boy wins the lordship of Berrund, Kaiber must not underestimate him. Colton's body may be broken, but he can still teach others to fight.'

'What happens to Kaiber if she loses?' asked Henrik suddenly.

The King and the Augur shared a glance before turning to look at the prince.

'As I said, Your Highness,' said Rowel patiently, 'it is unlikely that Kaiber will be equalled in this Throne Trial, let alone beaten. And if by some miracle she is, I doubt the margin of her loss will be so great as to cost her life, if that is your concern? Anyone who harms Kaiber Almanfier unduly will understand that they risk war with Laudria. And all the lower Realms combined could not muster a force greater than our Iron Company. Rest assured, Prince Henrik, the Queen Regent is well protected.'

'*Queen Regent,*' snarled Markos, glowering at his reflection in the vertical broadsword of Jado Costel. 'There lies the greatest flaw in your clever little game, Augur. What if Kaiber's appetite for power is not satisfied by this crusade? Why would a warrior who has conquered all enemies kneel before a cripple? What if Kaiber drops the word *regent*? I would need all my strength and more to beat her if she turned on us.'

'Kaiber would never turn against us!' bleated Henrik, peering up at his father in hurt confusion. 'Not ever! You didn't see how angry she was when you were attacked, Father. She has gone to defend the throne in your name.'

Markos held Henrik's eyes for a moment and stroked the back of his son's head.

'Kaiber's ultimate fate does not matter, Your Highness,' Rowel interjected. 'The King is right. She is gaining much attention in her quest. But her wrath is merely a storm that will pass as all storms do. If she is lured into darkness by her lust for power and forgets her place upon return, she will find the true King waiting for her, whole and ready. This hall proves your divine right to rule, my king. Think of those you have overcome to keep your throne. If Kaiber betrays you, her sword will find its home among these relics. We must be ready to treat her as an enemy, never forgetting our primary cause, my king. If we can secure your place on the throne one more Quintus, Henrik will ascend to power five years hence, and we will have fulfilled our duty to Ohrak.'

The King took a deep breath and winced. His granite eyes found Rowel's, and he nodded grimly. 'Take me back to my chamber,' he commanded of his son, holding out an arm for the prince.

Rowel watched their backs recede as they hobbled away in stride. He did not loosen his smile until they were out of sight. He turned his head to look at Lord Costel's sword hanging on the wall. Something had bothered him about its delivery to High Castle.

Kaiber had not cleansed the blood from it.

CHAPTER 41

True Colours

Orla upended the skin and took long gulps. She let the cold water dribble over her aching cheeks, down her jawline, sore from the smile she had worn for hours. She laughed as she drank. The pain in her face was a comfort. It meant that the past hours could not be a dream.

She hadn't eaten for a long time. Food and water were distractions from her new gift. Her first hurdle had been colours; how to correctly recognise them. So, she had started simple, with a tree.

Once she had made the connection, which was easy now, she had asked the voice to show her a tree. Barely had the thought formed when the strange object appeared alarmingly in her mind. She held it in place as long as she could, overwhelmed by the avalanche of information. At first, she struggled to associate it with the sounds and touch she knew as trees. The connection broke so often that its re-establishment became second nature. And she conjured the tree again and again.

She didn't know which piece had clicked into place first, but she had slowly assembled sense from the glut of information. From the way the little pieces moved and the familiar sound they made, she understood in a fit of excitement that they were leaves. And in the same instant, she finally understood the majesty and the indescribable beauty of *green*. So much of it, in different pieces, all moving in the wind. But she couldn't see the wind itself. Strange. The trunk was brown, lined with detail, and did not move like the leaves.

She tried to recall any conversations she had had with Gadryon about sight and remembered that he had once tried to explain how the mountains grew smaller as they walked away from them. It had made no sense whatsoever to Orla. How could things get smaller or bigger when they were always the same size to touch? But her curiosity began to wonder whether the same anomaly might occur to the tree if she could figure out how to move away from it. She made the request to the voice, but nothing happened. She tilted her bodily head in all directions, but nothing affected the immovable tree. It remained as beautiful and huge as ever, though she had nothing to compare it with. The invisible wind blew one of the green leaves off a brown branch. The leaf grew as it floated toward Orla's vantage point, and she waved her arms blindly in the cave as it took up the entirety of her mind's eye. It had appeared to grow as it came closer, just as Gadryon had tried to explain. But had it actually grown bigger? Or did vision work differently somehow? She couldn't decide, but she adored her new confusion. And she only wanted more.

Next, she learned about the colour blue by bringing forth an image of the sky. It was very different from the tree, and she couldn't make out its boundaries. But she thought that blue might be her favourite colour yet. It was astonishing. She stared at it in wonder for many long minutes in silence. She conjured clouds to understand the colour white and laughed for joy when she saw the silly tuft drifting across all the blue.

In this manner, she had taught herself every colour she could think of, and every colour would dazzle her with its brilliance each time. When she conjured the grey sea, she finally understood what distance looked like. The cold mass heaved up close but disappeared into a pinched line further away. She wept often and laughed at her weeping. She could not believe that such a miracle could befall her.

The times when she was no longer connected to the voice became harder and harder to tolerate. She felt the depth of her blindness as she had never done before. The absence of the world around her now seemed so cruel and unfair. As she finished the water, she wished that Gadryon would return home so that she could share the miraculous news of her gift.

Gadryon, she thought, tossing the empty skin aside. *I wonder what my brother looks like!*

She opened her inner eye and cleared her mind of all thought, save one. *Show me Gadryon.*

An image so intense swam before her that the connection was severed at once. She had briefly seen many people crowded in a room. Their faces were so strange that Orla unconsciously touched her own to make sense of their odd shapes. Her own face felt normal in her hands, but she couldn't believe what faces actually looked like. Round but flat. Soft but solid. With noses that stuck out so far, bright eyes, and hair of different lengths and shades.

She brought the image back with difficulty and held it firm, forcing herself to remain detached, taking in the strangeness of the many forms.

She tried to pick Gadryon out among them. But each peculiar assembly of skin and hair looked like a possible candidate. Nothing seemed to mark her brother out among them.

Suddenly, as though Ohrak understood her confusion, the people's voices sounded in Orla's ears – a sensation she welcomed with great relief. She listened to each person as they spoke, waiting for recognition. But none came. The people talked over each other, laughed, and sang, and the sound became a jumble that broke the connection. When she found it again, she asked to see her brother alone. The same scene materialised in her head. But then, slowly, some bodies began to fade away like the funny drifting clouds she had seen in the sky. One by one, the figures evaporated until only one remained, sitting at a table in the corner. He had black hair and eyes the colour of the sea.

Gadryon!

The connection wavered but stayed.

Orla drifted closer to the brother she had never seen. He turned his head from side to side irregularly, listening to the people Orla could no longer see. She discovered that she could move around him at will, making him bigger and smaller as she hovered weightlessly, back and forth. The connection broke with a thrill as Gadryon whispered to someone unseen.

'Elchora, I must leave,' said Gadryon's unmistakable voice.

Orla lay panting hard on her bed, grinning with painful glee. She knew how Gadryon looked. She tried to square the image with the brother she knew but found the task impossible. Gadryon had been so solid in her blindness. The figure she had seen looked meek and lonely.

At the thought of him sharing a table with strangers, Orla felt a loneliness of her own. Though Gadryon had seemed lost amid the townspeople, Orla could see how he belonged with them. He belonged plainly, for she hadn't been able to pick him out at first. Her loneliness fed a mounting paranoia. If those strangers had accepted him, he might forget his sister and never return. He would build his own life in the town and abandon her forever. They had stolen him because he had saved them from the Krae.

The Krae …

A slim hope formed in Orla's mind.

What if I could help the people fight the Krae? she thought. Gadryon said the townspeople had been looking for their nest. What if she could use her gift to find it? Might they let her live with Gadryon in Leybridge too? Even as a cripple?

She swallowed and cleared her mind at once. The rushing consumed her, and she willed Ohrak to show her the Krae.

At once, the image of many trees formed in her mind. The forest, complete with scattered brown floor, a dark sky overhead, and dim, pearly mountains made small in the distance. Between the trees walked many figures. Too many for Orla to count. Their skin was whiter than clouds, streaked with beautiful lines of red and purple and green under the surface. Except for their skins, they looked exactly like the people Orla had seen around her brother. Strange that humans and Krae held so much hate for each other when they had so much in common.

The many figures continued to march through the trees, moving in uneven rows. Each one carried wooden or silver objects in their hands, and something about the set of their faces caused a spike of fear in Orla that broke her connection.

She returned to the cave, blind and panicked.

Were the Krae marching on the town again? Was this another attack? Gadryon and the people were not ready!

Sensing an unseen precipice drawing near, she calmed her pounding heart and established the connection with Ohrak. The rushing came reluctantly this time, and Orla demanded quickly that it show her the Krae again, just as before.

The faces lined with colour reappeared. Orla glided ethereally among them, trying to deduce the direction of their march. Her inner eye fell upon the largest of the Krae, a beast wearing a white shape over its head, obscuring its face. The monster led the march at the head of the army. Suddenly, horn blasts filled the air. The Krae began to shout. Their pace quickened. Orla watched the leader point at something in the treetops, screaming in its harsh language. A smaller Kraeling peeled from the cluster and threw himself at a strange line dangling from the trees to the forest floor. From how the creature climbed, Orla guessed the line was a rope. She focussed on the climber, momentarily fixated on its ability to use its legs. The climber sped up the rope, snarling with the effort, a silver blade clutched between its teeth. Orla decided to follow it. She might be able to see where the Krae were headed from above.

The top of the rope was attached to a strange part of the tree. A smooth, flat branch that made a pleasing shape with many sides. The climbing Kraeling leapt inside, and Orla followed it. The climber took the blade from its mouth. It spoke to a smaller Kraeling on the inner floor of the wooden shape.

The smaller Kraeling was propped up against the inside wall, its lined face contorted in a rictus snarl.

The precipice shifted closer as the climber tossed something to the smaller Kraeling and uttered a single word.

'*Wahnei.*'

And Orla realised in horror what she was seeing.

The connection broke as she plunged over the precipice. Her scream followed her back to Home Cave, where she clawed at the silvery, vein-lined skin of her face.

She was a Kraeling.

PART V

ULMAR

CHAPTER 42

The Journey to Leybridge

Adam lifted his rucksack from the ground and swung it onto his burning back. He slid his arms through the straps and tightened them carefully until the weight of his belongings stopped dragging him off balance. His legs trembled in protest under the burden, and the deep ache returned in his hips and knees.

Bill had kept them moving at a merciless pace for ten days straight. He kept them walking at night if they covered less than thirty miles during daylight. Adam had realised quickly, however, that to keep walking was often preferable to making camp. The plains were freezing at night, and nothing, not even their tents, could shelter them from the constant, biting wind. It swept unchecked in all directions, seemingly at once, as though it were circling the beleaguered team like a swarm of vultures. The skin on Adam's face had been burnt numb. His nerves now electric to the touch.

The rest of the team was bearing up reasonably well. Perhaps not physically, but mentally. Bill seemed much calmer now that he was firmly in command, while Lopek had found a new ease in his demotion, laughing with the team and telling stories around the campfire.

Every time they had made camp, Lynn took the opportunity to forage, collecting wildflowers and insects. Her rucksack was so laden with samples now that DeVenus had to carry it for her. Of course, they saddled the blank daily with as much weight as possible. If they had stolen one of the farmer's carts, as Adam had suggested, the blank could have pulled everything, including the team, across the endless field and saved them a lot of pain. But Bill had argued that wagon tracks would make a path through the grass and lead any pursuers straight to them. So, they all suffered without.

Well, almost all of them.

Kaldor Ugbek was in his absolute element on the plains. The night sky over the wilderness was vast and clear. Kal stared up at it each night for hours, making notes and drawings, and often fell asleep outside his tent.

Curiously, DeVenus had taken to staring at the sky too. Whether this behaviour was some fault in Adam's programming or if the blank was simply mimicking Kal's behaviour, Adam couldn't tell. But he had caught the blank gazing at the stars, his eyes fixed on something far away, unblinking, as though his threat response had been activated by the twinkling lights.

In the daytime, the plains were spectacular. An endless rolling sea of green and maize-coloured grass, standing waist-high, dancing in mesmerising patterns beneath the wind. Every time they had crested one of the taller foothills, Adam had paused to look around at the panorama of shifting green and been stunned anew. Who could have known that such a place existed on Ithea? He was beginning to understand why Lopek had fallen in love with it.

One night, Adam, Lynn, and Kal had listened in raptured silence as Lopek told Nephian stories. The Nephian culture was so rich with mythology, he'd said, that their natural history had become lost. Entwined in their legends. Adam's favourite story had been that of King Reon, for whom the Realm and the grass plains were named. Reon had lived over two thousand years ago, when Nephia was divided into many smaller kingdoms. He and the other Kings were invited to a gathering by the Augurs to make peace. But the summons was a trap laid by Reon's rival, King Hraglud of Floria, who desired to rule all Nephia. The assembled Kings were slaughtered, and assassins had been sent to butcher Reon's wife and heirs. Reon escaped and returned home to discover this terrible act. He donned his armour, having signed a peace treaty, and rode alone to claim vengeance. The people of every town he passed flocked to join his cause. But they were still outnumbered heavily by the mighty army of Floria when the two forces clashed. They met on the plains, which were then a vast forest, and Hraglud's army quickly proved too strong for the ragtag militia. Reon watched as his feeble army scattered in retreat, but then, when all seemed lost, he spotted Hraglud across the field.

Reon galloped at the enemy line, filled with a rage that scorched to behold. His retreating soldiers galvanised in his charge, turning to follow their King for a final assault. Reon crashed through the Florian infantry at full speed and came through the other side without his horse. He ran at the second line of infantry and cleaved his way through them, emerging with knives and arrows in his back. But still, he kept running forward.

In a panic, Hraglud sent his cavalry to run Reon down. Three hundred horses stampeded over the wounded King, mangling him into the turf.

But once the dust settled, Reon rose, enraged, spitting blood, unwilling to accept his death. He continued to lope toward the unprotected Hraglud. The King of Floria turned to flee, but it was too late. Reon caught up with him and slit his throat.

His revenge complete, Reon finally succumbed to his injuries. He knelt, thrust his sword into the ground, and keeled over.

Both armies had stopped fighting to watch Reon's final moment. They gathered around his broken body, friend and foe alike, and proclaimed him the true King of all Nephia. King Reon the First, who had ruled for a heartbeat before his death.

Thus began the tradition of Kings battling for the throne and thrusting swords into the earth.

Reon's body was returned to Eddis to be buried with his family. But his sword remained in the ground. A monument to his valour. And so it stood in place for centuries while the forest decayed around it.

'According to legend,' Lopek finished, 'it's still out here somewhere. Hidden amid the tall grass. And anyone who finds it must leave it undisturbed, lest the wrath of Reon fall upon them.'

The following day, despite his cynicism and mounting pain, Adam tried to catch a glint of metal in the swaying grass. But these flights of fancy were cut short by Bill, who had a knack for anchoring everybody to their present, mortal peril.

While Adam adjusted the straps of his rucksack, the safety officer watched the screen on his wrist. The drone whirred high above him. He rotated its camera slowly, scanning the horizon for any signs of danger. A morning ritual that always ended the same way.

'No sign of any danger,' he announced. Then he piloted the drone back into his waiting palm in a series of controlled dips. Kal and Lynn doused the fire. The embers hissed as the water hit them, and a mushroom of white smoke billowed into the air. Bill watched it float up with a frown.

'Okay, team. Is everyone ready?' asked Lopek, fastening his own straps. His bag was no bigger than Adam's, but it stuck above his head like a reverse periscope.

The team gathered around the steaming ashes. All eyes had dark bags beneath them, and the men had stubbled faces.

'Right,' said Bill. 'We'll aim for another thirty miles today. But we must be close to Berrund now, so keep your eyes peeled for signs of people. Remember, if we can see them, they can see us.'

There was a general amount of nodding. Kaldor yawned behind a fist, and Bill shot him a stern look.

'I know we're all tired,' the safety officer said, 'but I don't want anyone to let their guard down or get complacent. We've been lucky so far. The weather's been good, and you've all managed to keep up nicely. But we're in a hostile place. The people here – and the environment – can turn on us at any time. And we've only got two more days' worth of water. So, be on the lookout for any freshwater pools or streams. If we don't refill soon, we'll get in trouble quickly.'

As the day wore on, the team spread into a long, natural line, walking in single file, with Bill way at the front and DeVenus behind Adam at the rear. Adam kept a few paces behind Lopek, watching his lower half flicker in and out of view as the stalks of grass folded back into place behind him.

The sky above was crystal blue, marred only by the long white feather of a cirrus cloud high in the atmosphere. Up ahead, on the crest of a small hill, Adam saw that Bill had stopped, a shadow removing its rucksack against the sky.

Adam and DeVenus were the last to crowd around him.

'Looks like we're almost out,' said Bill, nodding to the northeast. 'There's a town about five, maybe six miles over there, just above the bluff. See it?'

Adam turned to look in the direction Bill had indicated.

The grassy plain stretched away to his left, but a little way to the right, the land turned sharply eastward. Between the plains and the distant cliffs, very low, Adam could just about see the flat grey line of the ocean. He scanned the distant cliff edge, squinting, and found what the security officer had seen. A cluster of small, grey-washed rooftops poking above the ridge.

Kaldor was looking through his binoculars.

'There's boats down there,' he said.

Lopek unfurled his map. 'That must be Salvation,' he said excitedly, eyes flitting between the town and the map. 'That's the border into Berrund!'

'You mean we've made it?' asked Lynn, stepping forward to look over his shoulder. 'No more bastard meadow?'

Adam chuckled. 'I thought you liked the bastard meadow,' he said. 'What kind of biologist are you?'

'One who's used up all her sample containers.'

'I wouldn't celebrate just yet,' said Lopek. 'It's still a long way to Leybridge. Probably four more days, at least.'

Bill frowned. 'You sure we can trust this old friend of yours, Doc? I mean, if Kaiber has declared war on the Elves, how do you know he won't turn us over?'

All heads turned to Lopek.

'Lord Farrow is a good man,' he said assuredly. 'He will give us a ship with enough supplies to get home, I promise. We can trust him with our lives.'

'Hmm,' said Bill, looking back to the distant town. 'I dunno … no offence, Doc, but you haven't seen the guy in, what, ten years? People change. Might be less risky to just steal one of them boats down there. Any decent rig we can get our hands on, so long as Kal can sail it.'

Lopek shifted his weight, considering. 'Well, if that makes you feel better,' he said, 'you must certainly do it. But I am going to Leybridge. If you find a boat here, I'm not coming with you.'

'Ha!' said Bill. 'Oh yes you are! We're in survival mode now, Doc. That means I'm in charge. If we find a seaworthy ship, we're stealing it and going home. Got it? I'll tie you to the mast myself if I have to. Nobody stays behind.'

Lopek blinked several times, shaking his head. The corners of the map cracked both ways in the wind.

'You can't do that, Bill,' he said. 'There's more at stake here than making contact with the Krae people. If Adam doesn't drain a God Stone of its power, the Hive will go to war with Nephia, and thousands may die. I cannot let that happen. If there's Inficore in Berrund, Lord Farrow will know of it. Getting to Leybridge is our only chance to borrow a God Stone.'

Kal stepped forward and prised the map from Lopek.

'If it means anything,' Adam cut in before Bill could reply, 'I'd like to keep going too. I don't want to cause a war if I can help it.'

'Let's do both,' blurted Kal, closing the map. Bill and Lopek frowned at him.

'What, steal their power and start a war?' said Adam.

Lynn grinned, but Kal ignored him.

'Why don't we wait until nightfall,' he said, 'steal a ship, and sail to Leybridge? Boats that size won't carry enough supplies to get the six of us home. But they'll get us to Leybridge, easy. And once we're there, if it's safe, we could ask Lopek's contact for a bigger ship.' Bill worked his jaw from side to side, unconvinced. Kal continued. 'If anything looks suspicious from your drone, we can always turn around and sail away. What do you think?'

*

In the moonless dark, Adam and the team inched along the roaring coastline beneath the town of Salvation. More than half the boats had sailed away, reducing their options to a handful of smaller crafts that bobbed against the ramshackle pier.

Kal and Bill had dumped their bags and ducked out quietly to inspect them. They'd barely reached the far end of the pier when Adam saw the lantern swinging down the steep steps toward them from the town. He tapped Lopek's shoulder frantically, and he and Lynn turned in fright, their faces partially lit by the oncoming light. The three of them looked at each other, unsure of what to do. If they called out for Bill, whoever was approaching would hear their shouts. But there was nowhere to hide. The lantern bearer stopped abruptly on the bottom step.

'Who's there?' came a male voice from behind the pool of light. The lantern was lifted higher. 'Who's out here in the dark?'

Adam looked at DeVenus, hoping the blank would finally jump into action and earn his name. But he was looking up at the sky. Lopek pushed his way toward the stranger with his hands spread wide before him.

'We mean you no harm, good sir,' he said. 'We are simple travellers looking for –'

'Ambassador Lopek?' said the man incredulously, switching to Plain. 'What on Ithea are you doing here?'

The stranger squeaked open the rear shutter of the lantern to illuminate his face. He was short, tanned like leather, with short black hair and silver sideburns. An Antharian.

'Shit, there's a whole bunch of you,' said the man.

'I'm sorry,' said Lopek, squinting into the lamplight, his hands still raised, 'but who are you?'

Adam heard footsteps pounding across the wooden boards of the pier.

'Hey!' came Bill's voice, and the lantern swung out in his direction. Those against the shore were swallowed by darkness.

The security officer slowed down as he approached, blinking, the fist of his right hand in the palm of his left, aiming his gun. Adam felt DeVenus stand before him, shielding him from the security officer. His eyes were fixed on the weapon.

'Whoa, whoa!' said the unknown Antharian as Bill clicked back the hammer. The scene flashed as the lantern shot up into the air. 'Are you crazy? What the fuck are you doing with a gun, you lunatic?'

Bill looked momentarily stunned by the stranger's use of Antharian Plain. But he kept his gun steady. Kal peered into the oscillating light from behind the security officer, wielding a long oar like a club.

'My name is Joe,' said the man deliberately over the surf. 'Joe Blake. I used to work with you in the colony, Ambassador. In New Antra. I don't want any trouble. I just came down to collect my things. I didn't know you were down here.'

'Joe Blake?' said Lopek. 'Yes. Yes, I know that name. You were the technical support officer before I left, is that right? The repairman.'

'That's right,' Joe agreed quickly. 'I fixed your computer once. Had to solder a paperclip cutting to your motherboard?'

'Joe Blake,' Lopek nodded. 'What are you doing out here, Mr Blake?'

'What am I doing out here? I live here, Ambassador! Been here for eight years. What are *you* doing out here? If you don't mind my asking.'

There was a silence as the lantern light swung from Bill and Kal to the group huddled on the rock face. After a moment, Bill relaxed and slowly tucked his gun inside his coat.

'We're stranded,' he said. 'And we need a way home. We landed in Nephia almost two weeks ago, just after Kaiber declared war. But we had no warning of it. Sailed right into the shitstorm. Then our ship was stolen.'

'So, you're looking for a new ride,' said Joe shrewdly.

'Yes,' said Lopek, stepping into the pool of light. 'We need a ship, Mr Blake. Can you help?'

Joe let out a high-pitched chuckle. 'Well, most of these are fishing boats,' he explained. 'You won't get very far in them. And nowhere near Anthar, that's for sure.'

'We're heading for Leybridge,' said Lopek. 'I have an excellent rapport with Lord Farrow from his time as the King's Commander.'

'Is that so?' Joe mused, his eyes narrowing.

'Are any of these boats yours, Joe?' asked Kal. 'You said you were coming down to collect your things.'

'Yeah, one of them's mine,' he said. 'The big one, just there, as it happens. And I'm headed to Leybridge myself. Do you need a lift, Ambassador?'

The team let out a collective laugh, sagging in relief.

'That would be incredibly kind of you, Mr Blake. Thank you,' said Lopek.

Joe sucked air loudly through his teeth with a grimace, his head drawn back to one side.

'It's going to cost you, mind,' he said, setting down the lamp on the slab of rock between his feet.

The team's smiles waned. There was silence.

'Or we could just take it,' said Bill, stony-faced.

'We have Gilda,' said Lopek, glowering at the security officer. 'How much do you want for safe passage to Leybridge?'

'Oh, no, I don't need Gilda.' said Joe. 'To tell the truth, Ambassador, I swiped one of those old printing machines from New Antra. So, I can produce as many faux Gilda as I need! Why do you think none of the locals has turned me in!'

'That's illegal!' Lopek thundered, bristling like a sparrow in a birdbath. For the first time, Adam saw a glimmer of authority in the ex-Ambassador. But Joe just shrugged, holding all the cards.

'You're trying to steal a boat whilst on the run with a firearm, Ambassador … and after all the protocol lectures you gave! Do you really want to argue about the rules?'

'What do you want?' asked Bill.

'What I want,' said Joe harshly, looking around at each of them in turn, 'is some of your food!' His face softened into a grin. 'Anything from a packet! Please! Everything in Nephia is organic and natural and whatever – and that's great – but … I miss the processed stuff from home. I really do. And I'm willing to bet that you've got a stash of powdered flavour tucked away in those bags. Am I right? Yes? So, if you want a ride to Leybridge, that's my price, the bad stuff! Gimme, gimme.'

*

Joe's boat was a wide skiff shaped like tightly cupped hands. A single triangle of sail reached into the night sky, patched in many places. And several litres of brown water sloshed around the bottom planks, like a separated calf yearning to rejoin the sea.

Despite its shabby appearance, the team had climbed aboard without a word of protest. With some assistance from Kal, Joe had pushed off immediately, making expert use of the coastal wind.

Adam and Lynn had nestled into somewhat comfortable positions amid the lumpy rucksacks in the bow. They clutched themselves for warmth, lying back-to-back, and tried to find any sleep in the dipping and rising of the boat. Bill, Lopek, and DeVenus sat quietly near the mast, each looking in a different direction. At the same time, Kal and Joe talked behind them at the stern, taking turns at the tiller.

A thin sleep washed over Adam. His mind drifted, but he remained aware of the sharp gusts, the flapping canvas, and the rolling waves beneath his head. When he finally sat up in defeat, however, he was surprised to see the red light of dawn far out across the sea. His left ear, which he had slept on, was a hot flap of agony. He tried to rub the feeling away, but as he moved, his legs cramped up, forcing him to snap back into the rucksacks and flex them rigidly until the pain eased. Lynn had moved across to the stern to sit with Kal, and Lopek had taken her place next to Adam. Bill sat with his arms folded across his chest, his head lolling in sleep against the gunwale. Opposite him sat Joe, with his knees drawn up, tucking into a cold packet of beans in delight, a collection of chocolate wrappers lay around him. DeVenus sat bolt upright beside Joe on a fishing crate, wide awake and fresh as the morning sea spray. Exactly as Adam had left him.

'Where are we?' Adam asked groggily.

'Very close,' said Joe around a mouthful of beans. He peered across his shoulder at the mass of land to Adam's right. 'We passed Sanport around two hours ago, so we should be able to see the mouth of the Ley once the sun's up.'

'We're almost there?' said Adam incredulously.

'Yup. The wind was good to us,' said Kal with a grin, his arm resting on the tiller.

'Here, have some water,' said Lynn, tossing Adam a bottle. 'It'll ease the cramping.'

Adam took a long draught and then wiped his chin with the back of his hand.

'Should we wake Bill?' he asked. 'He'll probably want to send up his drone before we get too close to the shore.'

Joe choked. 'You guys have a drone? That's wild! Ambassador Lopek banned pens in New Antra. We had to write with feather quills.'

'Have you heard anything about New Antra since it was attacked?' asked Lynn.

Joe shook his head solemnly. 'I wouldn't worry too much about anyone in the settlement,' he said. 'New Antra's got a huge bunker underneath it, full of tech. If anyone saw the attack coming, they probably hunkered down. We used to run drills every week.'

'We heard … we heard that Kaiber slaughtered everyone inside,' said Lynn quietly.

'Yeah, I heard the same.' Joe nodded. 'But if the protocols haven't changed, then she might've only killed the service blanks.' He turned to

DeVenus and added a hasty, 'No offence.' He scraped out a final mouthful of beans and went on. 'I mean, how would she know the difference?'

'You're saying everyone in the colony may be alive?' said Adam. 'That they're just hiding underground?'

'More than possible,' said Joe. 'There was a whole procedure in place for exactly this scenario. But, like I said, it depends on how strictly they follow the guidelines these days. Old Lopek over there was a real stickler. If I remember rightly, his replacement was a little laxer, but no, I'm sure the colonists are just fine. We're the ones in real danger. People out in the open, like us.'

'What? Are there more Antharians living here, like you?' said Kal.

'Oh, yeah. Not many, but there are a few. Most of them live north of the plains because the people up here don't mind us so much. Or they didn't before the attack on King Markos. But yeah, I'm aware of at least six Elves in Berrund.'

Lynn raised her eyebrows at Adam.

'What do you think happened to Markos?' said Kal. 'Do you believe that someone really tried to murder him? An Antharian, I mean?'

'Oh, it's definitely possible,' Joe mused. 'When I worked in New Antra, there were all sorts of dodgy things going on. Secret meetings between Elves and the King's Augur. Stuff like that. Real cloak and dagger. I know at least two people who gifted him forbidden items in return for favours. But there was always a catch. And once they were in the Augur's pocket, he never let them go. So, yes. I think it's possible that someone got into deep trouble and got desperate. But that's just a guess. It could just as easily be bullshit.'

'Where are we?' Lopek suddenly demanded from his elbows, his face severe. Adam hadn't heard him stir.

Joe looked a little alarmed at the sight of his scowl. 'No more than two hours away, Ambassador, if the wind holds.' He twisted against the gunwale and pointed. 'That's the mouth of the Ley.'

*

Once Bill had launched the dragonfly, Joe and Kal manoeuvred the skiff westward toward the river's mouth. The surface churned in a haphazard wave where the fresh- and saltwater collided. Soon enough, the little boat had left the ocean behind and began pushing its way upriver.

Trees laden with hanging moss drooped inward from the banks, their canopies almost touching in the narrower straits, and the sea noise slowly faded. The wind disappeared in the shelter of the trees, and Joe began to row against the current while Lynn and Kal furled the patchy sail.

'This is the Urden Forest,' said Lopek, his frown burning a hole in the map. 'We're about five miles away from Leybridge. Almost there.'

'There's a lotta boats up ahead,' said Bill, his eyes on his wrist screen. 'At least five of them, from what I can see. Just around the bend.'

'They'll be here for the Lordship Trial,' said Joe, pulling the oars smoothly against the current. 'There'll be thousands of people coming to see it. From all over. Though I daresay, you lot have come the furthest.'

'Colton is hosting a Lordship Trial?' asked Lopek, his eyes wide with excitement.

Bill looked up uncertainly. 'You still sure about this, Doc?'

'Yes,' said Lopek. 'Leybridge is the safest place we can be.'

CHAPTER 43

The Hanging of the Cape

Colton shifted uncomfortably on the high-backed seat, his hair whipping across his eyes in the wind. He sat raised on a small wooden platform under a white sky, and in front of him, down a set of wooden steps, lay the flat, brown expanse of the newly formed battle mound in the centre of the North Field. Flaming torches marked the mound's corners, and all the people of Berrund, or so it seemed, had gathered to witness his holy oath. The ceremonial opening of the Lordship Trial. Volsgaard stood in the centre of the mound, wearing his finest robe over his chainmail, his voice thundering over the gathering.

'– this truth we hold sacred above all mortal laws,' bellowed the Augur. 'That God alone shall elect our rulers, by cutting down the weak and raising only the strong; to bring forth, by trial and blood, those with the courage to lead us against the forces of darkness. And it is for this purpose that we are gathered here today under the watchful eye of Ohrak. To discover whom among us He wills to wear the ancient Cape of Berrund. Noblest of Realms. And so, I call upon its current bearer, Lord Colton Farrow. Step forth and declare yourself in the eyes of God.'

Colton stood and ambled down the steps toward the Augur. He felt the heavy Cape of Berrund pull at his shoulders as it unfurled behind him. The cape was wildly impractical. Twenty feet of burgundy velvet edged with the pristine-white fur of a winterfox, bearing the image of the Bannebar in golden thread. All eyes followed Colton as he walked, and Volsgaard winked as he drew near. Colton lowered himself with difficulty to his knees at the Augur's feet, and Volsgaard pulled the God Stone from around his neck and held it high for all to see. The crowd hushed in awe at the sight of it. The Augur placed the stone gently in Colton's cupped hands. Then, he backed away and raised his voice for the crowd.

'Who has come to kneel before God?' said the Augur. 'State your name, son of Ohrak.'

'I am Colton Farrow, the Lord of Berrund.'

Colton fixed his eyes on the middle distance, feeling the weight of the stone in his hands. He hoped not to ruin the recitation. The Augur paced before his eyes.

'And why do you kneel, Lord Colton Farrow?' he asked.

'To demonstrate my subservience to Ohrak. To yield my fate to His will. And to seek His champion as my successor.'

The wall of faces surrounding him swam into a blur.

'You seek to initiate a Lordship Trial,' said Volsgaard, 'as is your wont and of your own free will? In the full knowledge that your mantle as the Lord of Berrund will be stripped from you, should a worthier champion arise?'

The flames at the corners of the mound flickered in the wind.

'Yes,' said Colton.

He felt but did not see the Augur shake his head as he continued to pace. And perhaps his old friend was right. After all, Colton's preferred champion was still delirious with a fever in the ward. But it was too late to abandon the trial now. If Gadryon would not compete, and someone less worthy won the contest, Colton would have no choice but to defend the ridiculous cape flapping at his back.

'Then, as the highest Augur in this Realm,' said Volsgaard wearily, 'I declare, in the presence of those gathered here today, that the Lordship Trial for the Realm of Berrund … has begun!'

The Augur strode to stand before Colton and took the God Stone from his hands.

'Commit your sword to the earth!' he said.

Colton drew his gleaming sword and thrust it, two-handed, deep into the mound. A roar of applause thundered from the crowd at each side. Under the blaze of noise, two servants hurried forward to unbuckle the pins from Colton's shoulders, lifting away the cape. Two more servants had collected the tail, and the four folded it carefully and carried it away in ritual sobriety.

Colton looked at Volsgaard. The Augur sighed but bowed.

*

'How many have put their names forward so far?' asked Colton as he pushed through the door to his chamber a few minutes later, pulling off his gauntlets.

'Not as many as I feared, my lord,' said Volsgaard, closing the door behind him. 'Two captains from neighbouring towns, a nobleman from West Reon, our own shithead Commander, of course, and, well … me.'

Colton froze in the act of pouring himself a cup of wine. He straightened up, beaming.

'Erik, my dear old friend,' he said. 'I had no idea you aspired to be a lord. I always felt like you came along reluctantly.'

'I do, my lord,' said Volsgaard, frowning as he took the proffered cup. 'But someone has to look out for you. Take out some of the lesser competitors. It's the least I can do.'

Colton laughed and said, 'Well, now there are two men before whom I would gladly lay my sword in surrender.' He toasted his Augur and drank.

Volsgaard's eyes widened. 'Don't you dare,' he said. 'I'm only doing it so Maldon doesn't win the Realm. He would make a disastrous lord.'

'Are you sure you could manage Maldon so easily?'

Volsgaard scoffed and took a sip of wine. 'Oh, I've dreamt of the opportunity for a long time.'

'Well,' said Colton, taking his seat and stretching his leg, 'if I can't bow to you, and I won't bow to Maldon, I'll just have to keep praying that Gadryon recovers overnight. And hope he agrees to fight the winner as my champion.'

Volsgaard sighed. 'I'm afraid your great plan is somewhat in tatters, my lord,' he said. 'Gadryon remains half-dead with fever. It would take a miracle for him to recover by tomorrow night.'

A soft knocking issued from the door.

'Enter,' said Colton.

A liveried servant entered and bowed deeply. When he stood, Colton saw that his face was pinched in confusion. 'There are some … people in the library downstairs, my lord,' he said stiffly, not meeting Colton's eye. 'They say they must meet with you. Urgently.'

Colton waited for the servant to say more. When it became evident that he was finished, Colton and Volsgaard swapped a look of amusement.

'What people?' Volsgaard demanded angrily.

The servant cleared his throat. 'I believe they are Elves, my lord.'

*

Colton and Volsgaard followed the servant down the spiral staircase in half-hurried silence. Whoever awaited them in the library could not be Elves. And even if they were, what business could they have in

Leybridge? But as the servant leading them opened the library doors, half a dozen faces turned toward Colton. Smooth, well-nourished faces. Elvish faces. To say nothing of their strange attire. Two stood near the stained-glass window that looked out onto the courtyard, while the other four sat on their bags in a ragtag cluster. One of the Elves near the window took a step forward.

A void opened in Colton's chest as his stomach dropped away. His heart catapulted into his throat to pound at his larynx.

Dimitri?

'Lord Farrow,' he said with a bow, holding Colton's eyes, 'I'm sorry to intrude like this, but I need your help.'

Colton remained rooted to the spot, staring at the Elf, nonplussed. The library lurched horribly. It could not be Dimitri. And yet, there he was. Standing before him. In the flesh. With those green eyes and black curls, now spun with threads of silver.

Dimitri …

'Ambassador?' said Volsgaard from a thousand miles away. 'What a surprise. We are honoured to see you again.'

The Augur brushed past Colton deliberately, knocking him out of his trance, then bowed to the Elf.

'What help may we offer you, Ambassador?' he said.

The larger, silver-haired Elf spoke briefly in Elvish. Dimitri nodded.

'We need a ship,' he said, 'one that can carry our party back to Anthar. And enough supplies for the voyage if you can spare them.'

Colton surveyed the four Elves standing over their bags. One was a stout female with blonde hair. The others were male; one was bronze skinned with a long braid, another bespectacled and rosy cheeked. The third was an oddly featureless Elf who stared vacantly. And, except for this oddity, they all looked thoroughly exhausted.

'A ship?' said Volsgaard, glancing back at Colton with a raised eyebrow. He scratched the back of his neck. 'Well. Erm. That might be possible … What say you, my lord?'

Colton turned to face Dimitri.

'What are you doing here, Ambassador?' he asked. 'I thought you'd fled from Nephia for good ten years ago. Why have you returned?'

Each man searched the other's eyes. Dimitri's face betrayed no sorrow, but his chest heaved.

'We came, among other reasons, to make contact with the Krae,' he said.

'The Krae are animals,' said Volsgaard. 'Our enemy. Why do you hope to make contact?'

Dimitri held Colton's eyes significantly.

'I campaigned to return to Nephia ten years ago. As soon as the Krae emerged in Berrund,' he said. 'But I was denied again and again. I only received permission a few months ago. Now I'm here to broker peace.'

Colton's own chest began to heave. Was Dimitri saying what he thought he was saying? Had he been forced to flee Nephia all those years ago? Had Dimitri tried to return ever since?

Colton felt the old wound, buried by time, rise to the surface afresh. But it dissolved into new hope as Dimitri – who had not abandoned him – spoke.

'While we were at sea, Kaiber declared war,' Dimitri went on, 'and we became fugitives. Our ship was taken by pirates off the Ealee coast. We escaped ashore and set out across the plains. We have no means of getting home unaided, my lord. And with New Antra destroyed, we cannot communicate our survival to Anthar either. We need your help.'

Colton's mind reeled. Had Dimitri arrived at this moment intentionally? Did he hope that Colton would come with him, like last time?

'How soon do you intend to set sail?' was all he could think to ask.

Dimitri hesitated for a fraction of a second, not taking his eyes away. 'As soon as we can, Lord Farrow.'

Dimitri's eyes had widened at the word *we*.

Did Colton imagine all this? Was he awake? He needed to get Dimitri alone.

'Well, you've arrived just in time, Ambassador,' he said, trying to keep his voice steady. 'These next few days may be my last as the Lord of Berrund. After which I will retire … and it would be my honour to grant you safe passage home.'

Tears filled Dimitri's green eyes. 'Thank you, my lord,' he said, blinking them away.

The silver-haired Elf behind Dimitri watched their exchange intently, his eyes swivelling, arms folded across his chest. Colton glanced at the man before addressing the servant at the door.

'Send word to the dock master,' he said. 'Tell him I want a ship prepared at once. Any vessel we can afford to lose. A brigantine or sloop. It should be loaded with three casks of water and enough food for two weeks. And I want it ready by tomorrow night.'

The servant bowed. But the Elves broke into a heated conversation. After almost a minute, Dimitri spoke again, indicating the silver-haired Elf.

'Our security officer would like to know,' he said, 'whether we could stow our belongings aboard your ship tonight and set sail at first light?'

Colton understood the hesitancy in Dimitri's look. He addressed the security officer directly.

'The dock is busy with arrivals for the Lordship Trial,' he said commandingly. 'Once a suitable ship is found, you are welcome to stow your belongings aboard and use it as your accommodation. But I doubt it can be readied by tomorrow morning. We will work as quickly as possible.'

Dimitri translated for the larger Elf, who gave an awkward bow in thanks. As he did so, Colton saw the line of a bandage across his collarbone. His heart quickened.

Everything was turning on its head.

'Is there a doctor in your party, Ambassador?' he asked fervently.

Dimitri frowned. 'Perhaps,' he said. 'Why?'

Colton had forgotten his secrecy concerning Elvish magic. But the Elves behind him, those who had understood Colton's question, betrayed the doctor's presence by turning to look at the female. She looked back at them in confusion, evidently unable to speak Phrenaelia.

'One of my soldiers is sick with fever,' said Colton, keeping his eyes on Dimitri. 'A young boy. Ambassador, I know your laws do not permit you to interfere, but this boy is a special case. His recovery is paramount.'

While Dimitri translated stiffly for the doctor and security officer, Volsgaard caught Colton's eye. He knew, as Colton did, that if the Elves could heal Gadryon, there was still a chance the boy could claim his destiny.

And suddenly, Ohrak's plan became clear before Colton's eyes; the boy would succeed him as Lord of Berrund. He would defeat Kaiber and become King, setting Colton free to sail away with Dimitri.

It was miraculous. Beautiful. God truly worked in mysterious ways.

The Elves had finished their discourse. Dimitri had turned back to face him.

'Doctor Carson has consented to see your soldier, Lord Farrow,' he said. 'She will do whatever she can. In the meantime, we would like to take our belongings aboard the ship. Mr Conrad here fears for our safety.'

'Thank you, Doctor,' said Colton, speaking to the female in his best Antharian Plain. She smiled awkwardly and lifted her fists, thrusting up her thumbs. Colton mirrored the odd gesture, then turned to the security officer. 'You may follow my servants to your boat immediately. But please, feel free to explore the city without fear. You shall have my best soldiers at your disposal. Acting as your personal escorts, of course.'

Dimitri relayed this to the security officer.

The doctor, Carson, asked a question.

'Doctor Carson would like to see your patient now, Lord Farrow,' said Dimitri.

Volsgaard led the doctor to Gadryon while the remaining Elves gathered their belongings. The servant at the door bid the Elves to follow him to the dock. The security officer went first, and the others took after him. Dimitri loitered near the back, and once the vacant Elf had squeezed through the door after the others, he closed it and turned to Colton.

'I'm sorry,' he whispered.

Colton strode toward him and pinned him to the door with a kiss. Dimitri met his advance with equal passion but pulled away quickly.

'I've come back for you,' he said, his hands in Colton's hair, their foreheads together. 'I'm not leaving without you this time.'

'I would not let you,' said Colton, laughing in a whisper. 'But is it possible for me to come with you?'

'Yes. If we travel to the Freelands of Anthar, where no one will keep us apart.'

They kissed again, pulling their bodies together, through time, back to those stolen months before Colton's defeat by Markos. They broke apart reluctantly, still afire, recognising the need for caution. Colton put his hand on the door to follow the others, but Dimitri stopped him.

'I need to tell you something,' he said, and a shadow crossed his face.

'Tell me later, my love,' Colton whispered, cupping Dimitri's wet cheek. 'I cannot let anything distract me from the trial. Not even you. But once it's over, I promise I will be free as never before. And this time, I will come wherever you go.'

He pulled open the door, and Dimitri sidled through quickly with a sigh of burning agitation. Colton followed a few paces behind. They quickly caught up to the others, who had not noticed their brief absence.

For the first time in years, Colton walked with an ease that even his limp could not hinder.

CHAPTER 44

Cranial Shift

Fyvern pressed himself flat against the wall, holding his breath. The servants would see him if they glanced sideways as they passed, but a suit of armour obscured him from their oncoming view. Fyvern caught their hushed conversation as they passed.

'I've put every Gilda I own on Victor Maldon to win,' whispered one. 'I 'eard some o' the nurses talkin', and, apparently, that Gadryon boy is half-dead wi' fever. And with him out of the way, who's left to stop the Commander, eh?'

'Lord Farrow,' supplied the other confidently. 'He won't let the likes of Victor Maldon win 'is cape!'

'Gettoff it! Lord Farrow's an old man! A good fighter in his day, I'll grant ye that. But Maldon'll kill him if it comes to a fight. Mark my words.'

'Care to put some money on that?'

'Didn't I just say that I've already put every Gilda –'

They rounded a corner. Fyvern exhaled. He climbed out from his hiding place, careful not to disturb the suit of armour. He paused at the corner where the servants had disappeared and peered around it. It would ruin everything to be spotted now. Twenty New Colours would testify on their lives that he, Fyvern, was presently on patrol in the Urden. He found the door he was looking for and lifted the catch quietly.

The ward was silent, serene. Only three of the twenty beds were occupied, and all were sleeping. The boy lay in the penultimate bed at the far end of the room. Fyvern tiptoed forward, keeping half an eye on the other sleeping patients, and drew out his knife.

This would reset everything. After this, nobody could claim to have bested him in combat. Not in the long run. He knew, as did his mother, that he was the Ulmar of Ohrak.

As he drew closer, he saw that the boy's arm, which lay outside his bedcover alongside his body, was slick with sweat, his hair drenched into ringlets. But his lips were parched and cracked, and his eyes half-open in delirium. Fyvern waved a palm a few inches above the boy's face, and the eyes did not move. Perhaps he truly was dying.

Better to make sure.

As he put his blade to the boy's throat, ready to slice, the catch on the door behind him clicked like a thunderclap in the silence. He dropped to the floor instinctively, pocketing his knife with shaking hands, his heart hammering, then shimmied under the boy's bed. He rolled on his shoulder to look sidelong through the forest of bedposts.

Whoever had entered hadn't seen him. There was no hesitation or urgency in the three sets of feet approaching the boy's bedside. But he was trapped. And if the owners of those feet discovered him like this, it would take little acuity to divine his intention. He scrambled around quickly for a way out. *Think!* If he could roll beneath the furthest bed before they surrounded him, he might be able to crawl from the ward unseen.

*

Volsgaard stopped at Gadryon's bedside and turned to speak slowly to the Elvish doctor.

'This is Gadryon,' he said. 'He collapsed three days ago with a fever. But he seems to be getting worse each day.'

The doctor surveyed the boy gravely. She looked at her grizzled companion, who said something in Elvish. The doctor mimed wiping sweat from her forehead, and the Augur nodded enthusiastically at both of them.

With resolution, the doctor placed her medical case on the neighbouring bed and clicked open the tiny clasps. Inside, the box was a veritable trove of strange objects arranged into neat slots. Volsgaard watched in wonder as the doctor pulled on a set of stretchy blue gloves. She opened a container and carefully pulled out a cylindrical vial of luminous green liquid. She held the vial close to her face vertically, examined it cross-eyed, flicked it twice, and squeezed its base. A tiny drop of the liquid spurted from the tip of its long needle. The security officer said something that sounded like an urgent question. But the doctor waved away his inquiry with a shrugged retort.

Volsgaard watched closely as the Elf bent over Gadryon and gently rolled his head to the side with a gloved hand. She traced the line of his jugular vein with the needle point, then carefully pierced it, plunging the liquid inside his body.

Colton had told Volsgaard that Elvish magic was not like the stories. There were no spells or incantations. They simply had better knowledge and acted with precision. But still, Volsgaard felt a little … underwhelmed. He didn't know what he had expected, but as he watched the doctor discard the needle and gloves into a transparent bag, he couldn't shake his disappointment. The doctor said something, and the security officer fumbled out a translation.

'He should be … all good … tomorrow,' he said. 'All good.'

'Tomorrow?' Volsgaard exclaimed. 'You mean he'll be back to full strength?'

The Elves did not understand.

Feeling very excited but more than a little foolish, Volsgaard repeated the word 'tomorrow' and clenched his fists, making crude gestures of power. The doctor almost laughed but managed to control herself. She nodded politely. The security officer had glanced at something over Volsgaard's shoulder. The Augur spun to see what had drawn his attention.

Almys Fyvern stood in the doorway. Volsgaard had not heard him enter during his little performance. He felt the colour rising in his cheeks.

'Fyvern?' he blundered. 'W-what are you doing here?'

'I came to check on the boy, my lord,' he said. 'Brigg's orders. The captain wanted to know how he's faring.'

Volsgaard channelled his embarrassment into anger. 'Well, you can forget Brigg's orders! Because I've got a task for you. I want you to escort Lord Farrow's guests here to their ship. You'll find it in the dock. And I want you to stay with them as their personal guard while they're in Leybridge. Do you understand?'

Fyvern's face fell, but he straightened up. 'Yes, my lord.'

*

Adam slowly unburdened DeVenus of the heavy bags. He lowered them one by one through the open hatch to Lopek, who pivoted to take each of them, standing in the depths of the ship's hold. The supplied sloop was minuscule compared to *The Alliance*. Its interior was an open, spacious cavity – complete with a dozen mouldy hammocks – and a single box room covered most of the squashed deck. But Kaldor was absolutely thrilled with it. He held the dock master hostage for several minutes, asking about its speed and handling while Adam and Lopek did all the work.

'Well … it's going to be a long few weeks with all six of us crammed in here together,' said Adam, peering down into the dark hold. 'But a ship's a ship, I suppose.'

'We should be very grateful,' was all Lopek said.

'Hey, hey!' called Kal with a wave.

Adam turned to see Bill and Lynn climbing the steep gangplank with a surly, armed Nephian in tow. Behind them, the narrow city dock was alive with activity, and nobody seemed to pay them any attention. Lopek reached through the hatch with his hands, and Bill slid his rucksack from his back.

'I have to say, Doc,' said Bill, handing down his bag, 'I wasn't sure when you agreed to stay here for a few days. But nobody seems to care that we're here, and it might be useful to rest before we journey home. So … good call.'

Bill took Lynn's bag and lowered it into Lopek's hand.

'It's a bit … cosy, isn't it?' said Lynn, looking both concerned and appalled.

'It's free,' said Lopek. 'And Kal says it'll get us home. Right, Kal?'

Kal patted the gunwale and nodded. He squinted at the furled sail and grinned as though it had said something funny. Lynn looked unconvinced. A loud clap sounded as Bill took Lopek's hand and heaved him from the ship's interior. All six stood together on the deck.

'Who's that?' asked Adam, cocking his head at the tall, curtain-haired Nephian loitering behind him on the gangplank.

'His name's Fievel or something,' said Bill in a low voice. 'That bloke, Volsgaard, put him on to us. Told him to act as our guard while we're here.'

'I said Lord Farrow would keep us safe,' said Lopek.

'Yeah,' said Bill uncertainly. 'But your old friend won't be in charge anymore if someone beats him at the Lordship Trial tomorrow, will he? And his successor might not take as kindly to our presence here. So, I think we should aim to leave before the trial ends. Just in case. What do you think?'

'Surely it depends on whether we've found a God Stone by then?' Adam interjected. 'Because I can't leave until I've secured a replacement power. I won't. Even if you lot have to leave without me.'

Bill sighed in exasperation.

'Come on, let's stay for a few more days, Bill,' said Lynn. 'We've got a ship now – a way home. And I'm still exhausted from the plains.'

'It would be nice to spend a few days in Nephia as honoured guests instead of wanted fugitives,' said Kal.

Bill scowled at them but failed to conceal the faint smile playing on his lips. Adam could see that he was torn between his duty to keep them safe and his desire to witness a fight to the death.

'Fine,' he said. 'But if we're staying, this ship needs to be ready to sail at a moment's notice. And one of us has gotta stay aboard, ready at all times. And we stick together as much as possible. While it's safer to pass unnoticed in a big crowd like this, it's also easier to get lost. So, none of us is to venture out alone. Agreed?'

'Agreed,' said the others in unison.

'All right then,' said Bill. 'Looks like we're staying in Leybridge for a few days. Kaldor, why don't you show us the ropes on this old thing.'

Leybridge bustled with energy as the night drew in. The crowds squeezed indoors, taking their noise inside the taverns and inns, their communal laughter and lamplight spilling out onto the deserted, dusky streets. A small part of Adam longed to sneak off the ship and join in the revelry. But mostly he wanted to sleep. However, his fusty hammock was damp, reeked of fish, and swayed at odds with the ship's subtle movements, like a gyroscope. The counteractive motions should have cancelled one another out. But Adam felt the dreaded motion sickness creeping in again, enhanced by the toxic stench of fish wafting from the ship's planking.

Bill was first to rise the following morning. Despite his misgivings about their prolonged stay in Leybridge, he was plainly thrilled by the prospect of imminent ritual combat. The city's population seemed to have doubled while they slept, and the streets thronged with heaving masses.

Six travelling cloaks and a breakfast feast were brought to their ship by the servants of Lord Farrow. Quail's eggs, goat's milk, cheese, ham, and freshly baked bread, all served in ornate silver tureens. It was more food than Adam had eaten in weeks, and he found that his appetite had diminished substantially. The team breakfasted together in the box room on the deck. The shutters were thrown open, and they watched the endless crowd pass on the dock below as they ate. The box room was wide and squat, with a circular table nailed down at its centre, large enough to seat the whole team. Outside the ship, merchants had parked their carts all along the roadsides and had climbed astride them, shouting down and exchanging crates of edibles for small chips of gold. Within minutes, each carriage was picked clean and trundled away, replaced by another fully laden wagon.

'We'll need to keep our wits about us today,' said Bill. 'It'll be easy to get separated in that lot.'

'Who's staying with the ship?' said Kal.

'I don't mind,' said Lynn. 'Watching people murder one another doesn't sound like my cup of tea. Although, there is a forest nearby, which could be interesting.'

'I'm sorry, Lynn, but no,' said Bill. 'I can't risk you staying here on your own.'

'DeVenus could guard the ship,' Adam suggested. 'He'd make a good scarecrow if anyone thinks about stealing it.'

'Oh, I don't think we need to worry about our ship being taken,' said Bill. 'Everyone's attention will be fixed on the trial today,' he said. 'But all the same, I think Adam's right. Let's leave the blank somewhere visible, out on the deck.'

Half an hour later, with their new cloaks over their hiking gear, the team descended the gangplank and melted into the jostling crowd. They left DeVenus on the ship's deck with instructions to turn every few minutes. The soldier, Fyvern, followed them at a loose distance, glowering miserably. The tide of trampling feet led them to an expansive field where a crowd had gathered around a rectangular mound of mud. Bill took them to the farthest side, nearer the line of trees where the crowd was thinnest. He said they had a decent view of the mound and an escape route at their rear.

'Can I head into the forest?' asked Lynn, looking back at the line of trees. 'It would be crazy to miss an opportunity like this.'

Bill's head swivelled from Lynn to the mound, his mouth working silently. Adam came to his rescue.

'I'll go with her,' he said. He couldn't see much over the rows of heads anyway.

'Me too,' said Kal.

Bill nodded at all three of them.

'Okay,' he said, 'but stay within a stone's throw of the field. And take old surly-chops with you. The doc and I will be fine on our own. If anything happens, come and find me. And if you can't, we'll meet back at the ship.'

Kal approached their surly guard. 'Erm …' he said, 'we'd like to go into the forest. If you don't mind?'

Fyvern looked down at him dispassionately. Kal looked at Adam for support.

'Could you please escort us?' he said.

The soldier's face seemed to brighten as though something important had dawned on him. He glanced back at the trees, then turned to face them avidly. He gave a half-nod, half-bow.

The three thanked him, and together they set off into the Urden.

The trees were tall and broad-leaved with thick trunks. Between them, the forest floor had been swept clean of any undergrowth. Almost instantly, the noise of the crowd fell away.

'What are we looking for?' asked Kal.

'Anything that moves, really,' Lynn replied. 'I've got plenty of flora samples but not many bugs or insects. Ideally, I'd like to find a queen ant and build a new colony.'

Their escort watched in bewilderment as Kal and Lynn began walking in different directions, hunched over, scouring the forest floor.

'Have they dropped something?' asked Fyvern.

Adam fought against the powerful instinct to lie. 'Oh, no,' he said. 'They're looking for ...' he lost the Phrenaelian word for *bugs*, 'tiny animals?'

Fyvern stepped back a little, glowering at Adam as though fearful that his insanity might be contagious. Adam shrugged apologetically, not wishing to do any more damage when a noise from Kal made them both spin in his direction.

'Oh! That stinks! That is rancid!' he said, touching his knuckles to his nose.

He had stopped a few feet from a dead animal impaled on a wooden spike. Adam and Lynn closed in, wrinkling up their noses as they entered the stench. Closer up, Adam saw the rotting lump of meat was a severed human head with a pale and twisted face, drained of blood, wearing the skull of another creature.

'What is that?' said Lynn.

Adam turned away, feeling queasy. He called over to their guard. 'Excuse me? What is this?'

Fyvern walked forward casually, smirking at their discomfort. 'That is the head of a Kraeling warrior,' he said. 'When we kill them, we put their bodies on pikes as a warning to their kind.'

There was a note of pride in Fyvern's voice, so Adam ventured an odd question to break the ice. 'Did you kill this one, Fyvern?'

The muscles in Fyvern's jaw jumped. Adam backed away.

'Okay, I accept the head is a Kraeling's, but what is *that*?' asked Lynn, pointing. 'The skull it's wearing?'

Adam translated her question for Fyvern, who was looking into the forest in agitation.

'The Krae can only work metal into crude weapons,' he said. 'Some have swords or axes, but most carry clubs and stones. They are savage people. This one used the skull of a bull as a helmet.'

Lynn shook her head as Adam explained. 'That's definitely not a bull,' she said, leaning closer. Her repulsion had vanished in the face of her curiosity. 'Unless there's a breed of giant, carnivorous bull I'm not aware of!'

Adam leaned closer too, forcing himself to see past the gormless, dead expression on the rotting face and focus on the white skull framing it. It fit snugly around the dead man's head – which was not small in itself – and Lynn was right. The skull had curved horns, like a bull, but five-inch canine teeth framed the dead man's eyes as though the Kraeling face peered from its maw.

'What do you suppose it is?' asked Kal.

Lynn straightened up, scratching her head. 'I have no idea,' she said. 'I can't think of any creature with a rounded cranium, horns, and fangs. So, unless this thing has been modified in some way, this could be … well … this could be very interesting. Could you please ask if we're allowed to take it?'

Fyvern huffed impatiently at the request.

'Will you go no further into the Urden?' he demanded. When Adam shook his head, he spoke directly to Lynn. 'Don't touch it. Leave it where it is!'

And without another word, their guard stormed off inexplicably, but purposefully, into the woods. Adam shrugged at the others.

'What did you say to him?' asked Lynn.

'I dunno. Nothing offensive, I don't think.'

'What do you want to do about this?' asked Kal, indicating the strange skull with his thumb. 'Do you think it's a new species?'

'I never said that!' said Lynn reflexively, as though Kal's words might have jinxed the find. She bit her lip. 'Oh, I'd love to study it properly and find out! Did that man say we couldn't take it?'

'Yep,' said Adam, 'but Kal and I won't say a word if you want to take it anyway.'

Kal looked away conspicuously and pretended to whistle.

Lynn bit her lip harder. 'Maybe I'll just take some photographs and a sample,' she said, kneeling to rummage in her bag. She pulled out her camera, one of her surgical lasers, and a zip bag. She took photos of the severed head while Kal and Adam grinned at each other behind her back.

When the moment came to cut a sample, Lynn aimed her laser at the base of the right horn. But as the red beam struck the white bone, the skull helmet shivered, rippled, and transformed before their eyes. It morphed into a dense black cloud that hovered upwards, collapsing and expanding like a living thing as it rose slowly from the severed head. Lynn shut off the laser in fright, and the second she did so, the black cloud re-formed into the white skull and landed on the floor between them with a heavy thud.

Adam, Lynn, and Kal stared at it for several seconds, their mouths hanging open.

When they finally raised their heads to look at one another, they each recognised the hint of fear in their collective wonderment.

'What the fuck was that?' said Kal.

'I don't know,' said Lynn. 'But if I wasn't convinced before, I am now. That is definitely not a bull.'

*

The moment the laser touched the skull, in the tiny, infinitesimal space of time that separated the moment of non-contact from the moment of contact, a beacon surged outwards from the exact location where the first atom of the skull was struck by a photon of red light. The beacon expanded outward in a perfect sphere, intangible and unstoppable, moving at the speed of light. It sped through the severed Kraeling head, through Adam, Kaldor, and Lynn, through the Urden Forest, the Bannebar, and all of Berrund and Ithea, escaping, unnoticed, into the depths of space.

Hours later, it found billions of its kin swirling around a small planetoid in a seething black mass.

The beacon relayed its message. The colossal cloud rippled.

CHAPTER 45

The Champion

Elchora walked swiftly along the empty hall, careful not to spill the hot bowl of soup she had carried from the kitchens. Clutching the bowl in both hands, she lifted the catch to the ward with her elbow and barged the door open with her hip. Gadryon was sitting up in his bed, just as she had left him. There was a little more colour in his face, and he looked around through half-lidded eyes as though trying to figure out where – or who – he was. He rasped like a frog when he saw Elchora approaching.

'What happened?'

'You collapsed from your injuries,' she said. 'Then you developed scorch fever. Eurace said it was the worst case he's ever seen. But then, praise Ohrak, a band of Elves arrived in time to heal you.'

She offered him the bowl, but he didn't glance at it. There was fear in his eyes as he touched the yellow bruise on his neck. He licked his cracked lips, breathing heavily, and swallowed. 'How long have I been here?' he asked.

Elchora withdrew the bowl and perched on the bed near his knees. She met his gaze and answered truthfully. 'Three days.'

Gadryon's eyes widened further, his bare chest rising in fits. With a grunt, he tried to throw off the bed covers but spasmed abruptly and jerked them close to his body. Elchora felt her cheeks turn pink at his nakedness. Gadryon averted his eyes, then found his bearskin clothes folded in a neat pile on the adjacent bed. He glanced back at her pointedly until she looked away. The next second, however, he fell back on the bed, one hand gripping the bedframe, the other massaging his forehead.

Elchora risked turning and saw the thin, angry welts along his back. They had healed remarkably well.

'Your strength has not yet returned,' she said. 'Your body needs more time to rest.'

Gadryon shook his head like a dog emerging from a river. Whether this was in response or to shake clear his addled thoughts, Elchora didn't know. She lowered her voice and leaned closer to his ear. 'I understand what you must do, Gadryon. But eat this first, and you'll be stronger for the journey.'

Without looking, Elchora extended the bowl before him and felt his weakened hands take the weight of it. Gadryon lifted a spoonful to his mouth.

'Orla will be fine,' she said consolingly. 'As long as she's got access to water, she'll be fine.'

Gadryon tossed aside the spoon and drank the bowl's contents in one. Elchora couldn't help but notice his muscular form as he stood and began to dress.

She watched him longer than she knew was decent.

*

Volsgaard watched the elderly blacksmith slide his blade across the spinning grindstone. The man was hunch-backed from his years of toil, but there was no finer smith in Berrund. He worked all four sides of the sword, keeping an even pressure as he slid it back and forth across the turning stone with a flourish of the wrist. Satisfied, he inspected the blade, turned it in his hands, and blew the metal. He handed it hilt-first back to the Augur.

'Thank you, Master Igniss,' said Volsgaard, feeling the sword glide smoothly back into its sheath. 'The usual price?'

The blacksmith flapped an arthritic hand. 'No charge today, milord,' he said, then he lowered his voice conspiratorially. 'Just make sure you use it well. The Commander will ruin us if he wins the cape.'

Volsgaard put his hand on the man's shoulder. It was surprisingly solid. 'You leave him to me.'

The crush of spectators on the North Field had grown impatient as the Lordship Trial unfolded before them, and Lord Farrow's expression had soured. Few contestants had actually fought thus far. Because Victor Maldon had acted precisely as Volsgaard had foreseen. The Commander had coerced his cronies into entering the trial, each laying their weapons at his feet in surrender. The tactic ensured Maldon's unharmed passage into the latter rounds. It also disadvantaged any actual competitors, whose progress was hard-fought and exhaustive. Volsgaard had duelled two of Maldon's puppets so far and had dispatched both without difficulty, conserving himself for their leader, whom he wanted with a lustful intensity.

Finally, once the sun had passed its zenith and only four contestants remained, Eurace drew the correct pairing of tokens from the chalice.

The Augur stood on the mound, face-to-face with Victor Maldon.

Both smiled cruelly, and the blood-starved crowd grew excited, sensing the palpable hatred from the combatants.

This fight, they knew, would be to the death.

'Now we will see,' said Maldon, pulling out his hammer for the first time.

Volsgaard nodded in agreement. 'Now we will see.'

Both men thrust their weapons into the ground, eyes locked. A cheer rippled through the tense crowd, cut short by Eurace, who raised his hand for ceremonial silence.

'Lord Volsgaard,' said the Obediant, 'speak the n-name of your bearer.'

'Captain Jolyon Brigg,' said Volsgaard mechanically.

Behind him, Brigg plucked a flaming torch from a corner, lifted it high, and turned on the spot for all to see.

'C-commander Maldon,' said Eurace, 'speak the name of your bearer.'

'Ableman Saul Pyke,' growled Maldon with a smirk.

It was no surprise that Maldon had selected a lowly Ableman. All his higher-ranking cronies had entered the trial, and no doubt this man, Saul Pyke, had been bullied into the position. Volsgaard walked back to face Brigg, who stabbed the torch back into the ground. The Augur lifted his arms like a bird. The captain surveyed his armour, pulling roughly at random plates until he stood back, nodded, and picked up the torch. Volsgaard turned and marched back to his waiting sword. From the corner of his eye, he saw Lord Farrow shift in his chair up on the platform. Maldon was cracking his neck behind his hammer.

'May Ohrak bear w-witness to this contest through these holy flames,' said Eurace, 'and bring forth His ch-ch-chosen victor. The field is yours, my lords.'

The Obediant scurried away, keeping the hem of his best robe above the dirt. He cast a single, fretful glance at his master as he passed, and Volsgaard winked at him, waiting until Eurace was clear of the mound. But Maldon gave no such courtesy. He plucked his hammer from the earth and spun it in his hands, flinging out wet chunks of mud. The Augur knelt behind his sword and rested his forehead against the pommel.

Ohrak, ever watchful, my God, my saviour, and my eternal guide. Please watch over me and protect me in this hour, and grant me swift victory over your enemies, that I may continue to serve you faithfully with all my heart. This, I pray.

Volsgaard stood and wrenched his sword from the ground. The crowd roared as the two men flew at one another with the ferocity of lions.

The Lordship Trial had begun.

*

'Erik! Erik! Stay awake! Stay with me!' Colton bellowed desperately into his friend's mutilated, bloody face.

The four servants staggered under his weight, carrying the mangled body with difficulty. The Augur's breath rattled through his split helmet, his one visible eyelid drifting shut, then flying open in succession, fighting the lure of death.

A trail of dark-red spots dotted the flagstones from the direction they had come. But Colton refused to look at it because it did not matter. They were almost at the ward now. Where the healers would save Erik's life.

Colton raced ahead of the servants at the last second to throw open the ward door. The harried-looking men staggered to the nearest bed and lowered the Augur as carefully as they could. As they did so, Colton saw that Erik's backplate had been punctured near the base of his crooked spine, and blood oozed from the hole. The visible portion of Erik's face was as pale as a Kraeling.

'Get him on his front!' Colton roared.

Sweating, the servants obeyed at once, rolling the limp Augur away from his wound with a clatter of bloodstained armour.

'Get his helmet off!' said Colton.

Eurace, whom Colton had not seen in the frenzy, knelt at his master's head and fumbled with the chinstrap, sobbing. After two seconds of his ineptitude, Colton strode around the bed and shoved the useless Obediant to the floor. He slowly freed the helmet from the Augur's head, revealing the deep, dark gash across the pulverised left eye socket.

'We need to stop the bleeding,' Colton commanded of the terrified assembly, pointing at the Augur's back. 'Take off his armour. Now!'

'No, wait!' came a voice from the direction of the doorway.

Colton whipped around to see Dimitri jogging toward him in anguish, followed closely by the larger Elf, who looked calm and alert. Pure relief washed over him at the sight of them. The security officer spoke through Dimitri.

'We should not remove his armour until we know what damage lies beneath,' he said. 'It may be that his armour is currently holding him together.'

Colton squeezed the helmet and felt it buckle slightly in his hands. Dimitri went on.

'Someone needs to fetch Doctor Carson right away,' he said. 'She went into the forest but will not have gone very far. Mister Conrad will do what he can before she gets here, but he needs room to work.'

Colton barked orders at the servants, and they scarpered from the ward to track down the Elvish doctor. Eurace knelt at Volsgaard's head, bent low over his master, clutching his God Stone, muttering into it in prayer. The security officer rolled his sleeves beyond his elbows and examined the broken man's wounds. For some reason, he kept stealing glances at the Obediant as though irked by another healer's presence.

Volsgaard's rattling breaths had steadied into quick, shallow gulps. Dry blood had misshapen his beard, which now stuck out at odd, clotted angles.

His duel with the Commander had been nothing short of a battering. And sickening images replayed in Colton's memory; Maldon's hammer crunching into Volsgaard's lower back; the Augur snapping like a twig, howling at the sky before he collapsed. He recalled Brigg dousing Volsgaard's flame quickly in surrender and Maldon glancing at it before delivering the final blow to the Augur's helmet.

A warm hand on his forearm pulled Colton back to the ward. He turned to see his daughter's apprehensive profile standing beside him, looking down at the man who had been with them since she was a baby.

'Will he die?' Elchora asked quietly.

'I don't know,' Colton replied, squeezing her fingers at his wrist.

A movement behind Elchora made Colton look across the ward. He found Gadryon staring back at him, fully dressed in his black bearskin furs.

Fury rose inside him like lava. The boy was not to blame for this, he knew. But Colton would no longer tolerate his reticence. If Gadryon did not embrace his destiny willingly, Colton would force him to meet it. He tore his arm from Elchora's pincerlike grip and strode at Gadryon until their noses almost touched. The boy glowered up at him uncertainly but did not back away. Colton studied his face closely, taking his measure, then stepped aside and pointed at his dying friend.

'Look at this!' Colton said. 'Look!'

The boy's dark eyes followed the path of Colton's finger. The Elvish security officer had stuffed a blood-saturated wadding of bandages into the hole at the Augur's back, pressing down on it with all his weight.

'That man over there is my friend,' said Colton, swallowing the lump in his throat. 'He entered the Lordship Trial, not for glory, but because he believed it was the right thing to do. He fought to protect the people of this Realm from the brute who disfigured him. The same brute who almost killed you, Gadryon. My friend may have lost to Victor Maldon, but at least he fought. And unless you do the same, Berrund may be lost to a madman. So, I ask you plainly, will you fight so that others need not suffer, Gadryon? Will you use the gifts that Ohrak has given you and fight Maldon as my champion?'

*

The ward was silent. All heads had turned to regard him. Gadryon took in the wounded man, the hopeful Obediant, an expectant Elchora, and the solemn faces of both Elves. Finally, his eyes returned to Lord Farrow, whose chin was thrust out daringly. Gadryon felt a bodily desire to say yes. To act as the Ulmar they mistook him for. And for a shining moment, he pictured himself as the lord of Berrund, then seated on the throne of Nephia as King, with Elchora at his side.

He wanted that future. He burned for it. But he knew his path and had sworn, long ago, to follow it to its end. Orla had been without him for three days now. The longest period she had spent alone in all her life. And his duty was to her. His sister. If Ohrak wanted Gadryon to be King, He would not have made the circumstances impossible.

Gadryon lowered his eyes from Lord Farrow's scrutiny and said nothing. But his silence spoke his refusal. Lord Farrow shook his head slowly, eyes darting over Gadryon's face in hopeless disgust. Over her father's shoulder, Elchora sighed but shot Gadryon a weak smile of understanding while Eurace twitched dejectedly. The Elves spoke in their language, filling the silence, and then the tall, curly-haired Elf addressed Lord Farrow, causing him to turn his back on Gadryon.

'My companion is confident that your Augur should live, my lord,' said the Elf. 'He's managed to staunch the bleeding, for now, and the wound is not as deep as we feared.'

Lord Farrow's shoulders dropped. 'Thank you,' he said absently. 'And what … what manner of recovery can we expect, Ambassador? In your doctor's opinion?'

The Elves spoke again, for longer this time, and Gadryon used the noise of their conversation to peel quietly towards the back door.

'The Augur's eye is badly injured,' came the voice of the lanky Elf, 'but we should be able to restore his vision, given enough time. However, there's a good chance that he won't be able to walk anymore, my lord. The damage to the base of his spine is too acute, and we don't have the equipment to repair it.'

Gadryon froze a few paces from the door, his arm in mid-air. His heart pounded in his chest. Slowly, he revolved to face the room again and looked down at the broken man sprawled on the bed. Gadryon stepped forward, entranced, and cut across Lord Farrow's half-uttered question with a more urgent request. 'You can fix his eye and make him walk again?' he asked.

All eyes turned on him once more.

'Yes. It is possible to restore his vision,' said the lanky Elf soothingly. 'But without the proper tools, our doctor – skilled though she is – won't be able to heal the wound on his back, I'm afraid. And it's unlikely he will have the same mobility he had before.'

'But it is possible to fix such an injury? To make this man walk again, I mean?' Gadryon pressed.

The Elf's brow furrowed, and he glanced at his companion. But the larger Elf was still staring sideways at the Obediant. From the corner of his eye, Gadryon saw Elchora's lips part in dawning comprehension, her confusion melting away.

'Yes,' said the fluent Elf tentatively, 'such miracles are *possible* … but it would mean taking the Augur with us back to our homeland –'

Gadryon's heart skipped a beat.

This was it! *This* was Ohrak's plan. There was no contradiction; he could do both! He could save Orla and follow his destiny! He stole a glance at Elchora. Her mouth was still partly open, but now, one of its corners was curling upward imperceptibly. Lord Farrow eyed the air between them and was about to demand answers when the Elves broke into something that sounded like a heated argument. The larger Elf, who had finished tending to the Augur's wounds, stood and folded his arms. Reluctantly, the other turned to address the Obediant.

'Master Eurace,' he began, 'forgive me, but might we be permitted to … *borrow* your God Stone?'

The Obediant frowned at the Elf, then looked down at the little purple light in his hand. He closed his fist around it and clutched it to his chest.

'It's all right, Master Eurace,' said Lord Farrow. 'The ambassador doesn't mean to take it. Though, why the sudden interest, may I ask?'

The security officer spoke in patchy Phrenaelia. 'We want to study it,' he said. 'We only need to borrow it for a few hours.'

The Obediant backed away, looking alarmed. He stashed the glowing stone inside his robes and turned to Lord Farrow for help. Lord Farrow frowned at the ambassador thoughtfully. But before he could speak, an idea formed in Gadryon's head, and he suddenly knew what to do.

'When is the final duel in the Lordship Trial?' he blurted out.

Elchora answered quickest. 'Tomorrow at noon,' she said.

Gadryon spun to face Lord Farrow. 'I shall fight as your champion.'

CHAPTER 46

The Bargain

Adam, Lynn, and Kal stepped quickly from the forest, giving the crowd of backs a wide berth, and aimed for the city wall. They half-skipped as they walked, glancing furtively at one another in excitement. The left horn of the mysterious skull jabbed painfully into Adam's armpit under his cloak, while the right horn dug into his opposite kidney. But he didn't dare adjust it now that they were in the open. If any of the surrounding Nephians were to catch a glimpse of what they were smuggling, they might be forced to put it back.

They had pointed Lynn's laser at the skull repeatedly, confident they had hallucinated the strange phenomenon. But every time, the skull had collapsed into the shifting black cloud, morphing back into the horned and fanged head when the beam lost contact. At each transformation, the three witnesses had laughed with nervous delight until Adam stuffed their discovery inside his cloak.

They had almost made it through the unguarded gate to the city when a pair of guards came hurtling around the corner up ahead and ran straight at the trio. In a panic, Adam made to unwrap the stolen contraband and hand it over, but he stopped himself when he heard what the guards were saying.

'Master Doctor! Master Elves!' they said, skidding to a breathless halt. 'Lord Farrow bade us come find you! Lord Volsgaard, the Augur, is gravely wounded and needs your magic urgently! Please, follow us!'

Kal and Adam looked at Lynn, who blinked back at them, utterly terrified. Kal translated what the guards had said, and Lynn's horrified expression resolved. She stepped forward, nodding at the guards.

'Should we come with you?' said Adam.

Lynn flashed a glance at his cloak. 'No! No, I'll be fine,' she said. And then quietly, 'Just get that thing back to the ship.'

She winked at Adam, gestured for the guards to lead the way, and

339

marched off quickly behind them, leaving Adam and Kal alone under the portcullis. Adam shifted the skull into a more bearable position in the crook of his arm, and Kal grinned at him. They sped off toward the dock. The streets were practically empty within the city walls, and, despite taking two wrong turns, they found their way back to their ship unseen. The only soul they encountered was a drunken transient fast asleep in a pile of coiled ropes at the foot of their ship's gangplank. They tiptoed up the steep plank to the ship's swaying deck, where DeVenus waited for them, staring in the opposite direction.

The blank turned in a fluid motion to regard them as they came aboard. Suddenly, like a viper spotting prey, its attention snapped to the bulge in Adam's cloak.

Adam was too distracted to notice the sudden movement. He strode past DeVenus into the shadows of the dim boxroom, withdrew the heavy skull from under his cloak with a flourish, and placed it carefully, horns-up, in the centre of the round table. Kal moved past him to the far side of the room and threw open the shutter, letting an oblong of grey daylight fall inside. Both men leaned on their elbows to look closer at their prize.

'So,' said Kal after a full minute, 'what do you suppose it is?'

Adam blew out his cheeks, shaking his head. 'How should I know?' He shrugged. 'I mean, if Lynn hasn't got a clue, what chance do we have?'

'Yeah, I suppose …' said Kal, rubbing his stubbled chin. He straightened up, wagging his finger at the table. 'But let's forget for a minute that it's in the shape of a skull. Have you ever seen a solid turn into gas like that? And then become solid again?'

Adam frowned, thinking. Something about the skull's trick seemed oddly familiar.

Before he could formulate his reply, a movement made him jump halfway across the room. DeVenus had followed them without instruction and stood at the table, staring into the empty eye sockets of the skull.

A palpable tension filled the little cabin, and the hairs on Adam's neck stood on end. Kal backed away from the table, watching the odd staring contest in alarm. It was as though both objects were about to explode. 'What's he doing?' asked Kal shakily.

Adam swallowed and took a step closer to DeVenus. 'I think the skull has triggered his threat response,' he said. 'Maybe it's the fangs.' Then he cleared his throat. 'Don't worry, DeVenus. It's dead. It can't hurt us anymore.'

The blank didn't move. Or blink.

'DeVenus?' Adam tried again.

Nothing.

Kal caught Adam's eye and shrugged.

With a jolt, Adam heard footsteps climbing up the gangplank outside. He ripped off his cloak and tossed it in a loose bundle on the table, burying all but one horn of the skull.

DeVenus relaxed imperceptibly.

Adam sighed in relief as the figures of Bill and Lopek filled the cabin's doorway. Bill's hairy forearms were covered in brownish blood.

'Ah, good, you are here,' said Lopek, ducking as he stepped inside. 'We've got some exciting news.'

'So have we,' said Kal with a grin. Then he added hastily, 'But, sorry, you go first.'

'How was the trial?' Adam cut in quickly, assuming Lopek would admonish their seizure of the skull.

'Brutal,' said Bill casually, pulling a chair from under the table. 'But I didn't think we'd be called upon to scrape the losers off the floor.' He sat heavily, glowering at Lopek.

'Well, it's a good thing we did,' Lopek countered. 'Otherwise, we might never have known they've got one.' He turned to look at Adam. 'There's a God Stone here. The Obediant has it.'

This was the only thing that could have driven the skull from Adam's mind.

'You're joking,' he said, 'what, really?'

'Yep,' said Bill, rolling down one of his sleeves. 'But the doc's right, mate. I don't think they'll want to give it up. Even in exchange for another one. The kid holding it seemed pretty attached.'

'Well, we've got to try, surely?' said Adam. 'If you're worried about offending them, Lopek, just think of the alternative – war. We've got to at least ask!'

Bill sucked air through gritted teeth.

'I wouldn't advise that strategy,' he said. 'It would be much safer to sneak in at night and swap them without asking. They could take ours by force if they learn we've got one. It's what I'd do in their shoes.'

'We're not doing that, Bill,' said Lopek firmly. 'And our hosts won't become hostile because we've got a God Stone.'

'We just watched a man get beaten within an inch of his life over a cape,' Bill retorted. 'We've got to be realistic, Doc. And time isn't really on our side. Do you really think you can convince that lad to lend us his sacred treasure in the next twenty-four hours?'

Lopek tore his glasses from his face and wiped them on his jumper, huffing. He deflected his attention to Kal. 'Well, what's *your* exciting news?' he asked bitterly.

'We, erm … we found something unusual,' said Kal, leaning on the table with his palms. His posture brought the newcomers' attention to the bundle. Just as Kal was about to reveal what lay underneath, Adam threw out a hand to stop him.

'Wait!'

A movement from DeVenus had alerted him. The blank had shifted its gaze from the covered skull to the cabin door.

Sure enough, as Kal stood frozen with his hands on the cloak, Adam heard barely audible footsteps crossing the ship's deck. A second later, a Nephian boy, with wild hair and dark eyes, filled the doorway, wearing black fur. Bill leaned forward to hide his arms beneath the table, and Adam heard a click.

'Master Gadryon?' said Lopek with a hasty bow, switching quickly to Phrenaelia. 'What brings you here?'

The boy hesitated on the threshold, eyeing them in turn. When he found DeVenus, the boy and the blank stared at one another for a moment, and the same mounting tension mushroomed between them.

Something's gone awry in DeVenus, Adam thought. His threat recognition is all over the place. The boy could not be more dangerous than the gun under the table. And that business with the skull was just weird.

He quietly resolved to reset their guardian.

'Master Gadryon?' Lopek prompted.

The boy squeezed his balled fists even tighter. 'I must speak with you,' he said, his voice quavering slightly. 'I must know if … if what you said about your healing is true.'

Lopek glanced back at Bill before replying. 'What did we say about our healing?' he asked.

The boy's eyes hardened. 'You said it was possible to make the Augur see and walk again.'

Lopek took a breath, held it, opened and closed his mouth a few times, then sighed, looking piteous. 'Yes,' he said. 'It is possible. But we don't have the right tools.'

'But it is possible to fix such injuries?' Gadryon pressed.

'If we could take him back to Anthar, then yes. It would be possible to heal him fully.'

The boy swallowed and nodded. 'There is someone who needs such help,' he said, his voice almost breaking. 'If I brought them here … would you take them with you and make them better?' Tears rolled down the boy's cheeks.

Lopek sighed again and shook his head.

'I'm sorry. We cannot take the Augur with us,' he said. 'Our laws do not permit –'

'No. Not the Augur,' said Gadryon. 'Someone else.'

'It doesn't matter who the person is,' said Lopek. 'We cannot take any man home with us.'

'But she's not a man,' said Gadryon, as though Lopek had missed the obvious. 'She's my sister. Please …'

Lopek scratched the back of his head and glanced around the cabin for assistance in explaining this hard truth. Gadryon looked at each of them, and his hope dwindled visibly in their awkward reluctance.

'I know where to find a God Stone,' he said desperately. 'A God Stone bigger than this ship.'

All eyes turned slowly in Adam's direction. But the boy was clearly mistaken. The largest Inficore fragment was presently powering the Central Quarter in Anthar and was no bigger than a melon.

'Well, I don't want to call him a liar,' said Adam in Plain, 'but it's doubtful. If any Inficore that big existed, our satellites would have detected it years ago. And if he's not lying, he's mistaken. I'm guessing his stone is just a fancy geode or a slab of volcanic glass.'

Lopek tapped his bottom lip thoughtfully with a finger and turned to the boy. 'Can you describe this … giant God Stone?' he asked.

Gadryon spoke to all of them at once, his hope rekindled. 'Ohrak watches over us from within,' he said. 'It spans the length of the cave ceiling, smooth and warm to the touch. It glows purple whenever we light a fire, and it disappears into the mountain.'

'Wait … it's inside a mountain?' Adam asked.

Gadryon shut his mouth tight, afraid he had said too much. But he nodded. 'If you promise to take my sister with you … to mend her,' he said, 'I will take you to it. Tonight.'

*

'We can't take some random girl to the Hive with us,' said Bill. 'The Algorithm would never allow it. And it's impossible to sneak someone in. Trust me.'

'There's always the Freelands,' Kal offered. 'We could take her there. I know at least three surgeons in Liberty who can fix eyesight. Not so sure about spinal injuries, though. But it's definitely possible.'

The boy's shadow swept back and forth across the light under the door.

'The Freelanders don't have the equipment,' said Bill. But Kal grinned.

'Ehhhhh, you'd be surprised,' he said in a high voice. 'Some of the Hive border guards are more … *flexible* than others. And some pretty incredible stuff has been smuggled out over the years.'

Bill folded his thick arms, affronted.

'We're getting ahead of ourselves,' said Adam. 'There's almost no chance that a God Stone as big as this ship is Inficore. And I don't think we should promise anything to this boy until we know for sure.'

'Okay,' said Lopek decisively. 'Let's offer to look at this God Stone. If it turns out to be Inficore, and Adam can transfer its energy – safely – we'll promise to take this girl to the Freelands of Anthar.'

'And what if *they* reject her?' asked Bill. 'What are we going to do, abandon her on their doorstep? We can't drag a blind cripple to Anthar and just *assume* the Freelanders will take care of her.'

'If the Freelanders can't help her, then *I* will take care of her,' said Lopek.

Adam and Kal turned to regard Lopek in surprise. Bill looked utterly bewildered.

'What are you talking about, Doc?' he said. 'I've just told you it's impossible to sneak someone into the Hive.'

Lopek's cheeks flushed. 'I'm not going back to the Hive,' he declared crisply. 'When we return to Anthar, I plan on retiring to the Freelands.'

'Whoa!' exhaled Kaldor.

Adam gawped at the ex-ambassador as though seeing him for the first time. Despite himself, he was impressed that the meek, lawful, rule-obsessed Lopek could have such daring aspirations. Bill scowled, however, dumbfounded and furious.

'And when did you decide *that*?' he asked.

'It has been my intention for a while, actually,' said Lopek in a dignified voice, his cheeks flushing a deeper crimson. But when he saw the storm on Bill's face, he elaborated. 'It's a private matter that doesn't impact the mission.'

Bill barked a laugh, making the boy's shadow pause in its pacing under the door.

'Except,' Bill growled, 'that you're now asking us to drop you off on the peninsula, adding *days* to our time at sea, after we've sailed for six weeks, in this box of a ship, with a foreign dependant!'

Adam found himself, for the first time, on Lopek's side of an argument. It made him uncomfortable, but he took a deep breath and turned to face the security officer.

'Bill,' he said calmly, 'I know you don't like *changing the plan*, but this seems like a win-win. If this stone turns out to be Inficore, we have an opportunity to restore the Hive to its full capacity, avoid war, save Genevieve from banishment, and help a young girl at the same time. Yes, some of those things will be easier said than done, and yes, there will probably be additional risk involved. But we have to try. I understand that *your* mission is to get us home safely. But *my* mission is to find replacement Inficore. And a chance has landed in our lap.'

Bill raised his hands and let them slap onto his thighs in a gesture of surrender to the apparent lunacy around him.

A silence descended among the men.

'So, we're all in agreement?' Lopek ventured.

Kal, who seemed equally impressed with Lopek, winked at him and nodded. Adam followed suit. The three of them turned to Bill.

The Security Officer, looking away, cracked his knuckles. Adam understood his conflict. They were asking him to relinquish control.

'Fine,' he said at last, the word drawn out like a poisonous confession. 'We'll check out this other stone and make a new plan from there.'

Without looking at the others, Bill stood up and opened the door.

*

Adam stopped running to lean against a damp tree, clutching the stitch in his abdomen. His heart pounded like a jackhammer, and each inhale was like swallowing a cold knife. He thought he might be sick.

A second pair of feet entered his blurry field of vision, and Bill's voice spoke to him, breathless himself.

'This kid is an absolute machine,' he said. 'It's like he can fly!'

Adam nodded, unable to speak. A salty bead of sweat fell from his chin. He looked up and saw that Bill was sweating too. The security officer had removed his jumper and tied it around his waist. His white shirt was slick against his skin. Behind him, DeVenus stared vacantly into the woods in the direction the boy had gone, fresh as a daisy. Adam shook his head and gripped the stitch tighter.

'I can't keep going like this,' he puffed. 'I think I'm dying.'

'Here, take some water,' said Bill, handing him a metal flask.

Adam unscrewed it and drank clumsily, letting the water splash onto his chest. He wiped his face in the crook of his salty elbow and stood up. The boy was stomping back towards them, looking stern. DeVenus bristled as he drew near.

'We must hurry,' Gadryon urged. 'The forest is unsafe at night. And I must get back to my sister as quickly as possible.'

Adam laughed dryly, shaking his head.

'Ask him to give us a general direction,' said Bill. 'If he wants to run on, that's fine. He can leave markers for us to follow. And it would be useful to know which mountain we're heading for or any specific landmarks. I don't fancy getting lost in here.'

Adam translated this, and Gadryon took a moment to weigh both men once Adam had finished.

'Home Cave is inside the tallest mountain in the Bannebar, furthest to the east,' he said. 'I will run ahead and cut sheets of bark from tree trunks every half-mile. Once the trees have grown thinner and the floor becomes rock, you'll see rain-carved stones, like a wall of spikes with no way through. I will wait for you at that place and bring you into the caves beyond. The God Stone and my sister will be within.'

Adam did his best to translate this but stumbled over the more complicated words. Bill made him recite the plan again, miming actions to Gadryon. Satisfied they understood one another, Gadryon gave them a cautious bow, then sped off into the growing darkness. DeVenus deflated in his sudden absence.

Once he was sure the boy had gone, Bill reached inside his pocket and withdrew the dragonfly. He held it at arm's length and turned it over in his hands, frowning at it in the twilight. His left wrist was pale without the drone's controller.

'We've just gotta hope the battery on this thing lasts,' he said. 'Let's see … I've disabled the wings and turned off the camera – which is out of range anyway – but the beacon is still broadcasting. If that conks out and we get lost, we're in trouble. It's our only connection to the others if anything goes sideways.'

Adam pushed off from the tree. 'DeVenus, hand me the briefcase,' he said. The blank obliged. Adam knelt on the cold, earthy ground and flicked open the catches. The drained Inficore fragment inside glowed a very faint purple.

'How likely is it that you'll be able to transfer energy to that thing?' asked Bill.

'Well, if there really is Inficore in the mountain, then it shouldn't be a problem,' said Adam. 'The problem will be the fallout. The mountain should contain most of it, but we'll need to plug entrances to absorb any overspill. Luckily, the lining of this case is packed with kirrion. So, we should be able to block a medium-sized hole.'

'And what if we can't? What if you don't have enough kirrion to contain the fallout?'

'I can only make a judgment call once I've seen what we're working with. But it might be worth the risk if we can stand clear from the transfer beam. There are no cities here, and it might not decimate the whole forest.'

Bill put his fists on his hips. 'Be straight with me for a second,' he said. 'How dangerous is this? Really?'

Adam closed the briefcase and stood.   'Don't ask me,' he said. 'Ask Genevieve LePlass.'

CHAPTER 47

The Kraeling

Orla dug her raw, shaking fists into the ground. She dragged her useless legs another few inches through the rough tangle of brush, grunting with the effort. She sobbed, no longer caring whether she was overheard, unaware of how far she had come or in which direction she was going. She had lost the ability to calm her mind, just as she had lost everything else, and she welcomed the return of her blindness; the only place left where nothing could betray her.

Outside her mind, she felt dirty. Soiled by her disgusting Kraeling skin. And her only thought was to keep moving. To get as far away as she could. To outrun her own flesh. Because if she stopped, the unbearable truth might catch up with her. That she was a monster. A freak! And the heart-breaking fact would rip her guts out again; that her brother, whom she loved and trusted so completely, who had been her sole companion in this life, had lied to her all along.

It made Orla question everything she knew. Was Gadryon her brother at all? Or had he simply found her as a baby and taken her in? Or taken her captive? Had he stolen her from the arms of her Kraeling mother? Then blinded and crippled her to keep her from learning the truth?

She had no answers to these questions. And in the end, they all led her to the same place. To the most brutal question of all.

Why?

Why hadn't he told her?

Orla begged inwardly for the questions and doubt to stop swirling. For the world to resolidify.

But it would not.

She stopped and collapsed to the forest floor, giving in to her grief. Her sobs came in fits of anger and despair. She wanted to die. She wanted to go home. She wanted Gadryon to find her, lift her up, and tell her that it was only a dream.

The minutes passed like hours, until she heard a rustling in the distance. Footsteps.

She sat up and listened with every ounce of concentration she could muster.

The footsteps quickened, getting closer.

'Gadryon?' she whimpered.

She screamed as a pair of rough hands ripped her from the floor and threw her sideways into a nearby tree. Her right shoulder popped from its socket, and she felt the weight of the bones in her arm dragging the burning limb away from her body. The hands were back again, lifting, pressing her into the tree, and she screamed even louder.

'Stop! Please!'

The hands released her. She smashed into the floor, sending a surge of heat through her detached arm.

'Who are you?' said the man's voice. 'How do you know our language? Filthy scum!'

Orla couldn't move. She couldn't speak. Or breathe.

'Answer me!' roared the voice.

A thousand needles pierced her scalp as the man lifted her off the ground by the hair. She screamed louder still, flailing feebly at her unknown attacker with her one remaining arm. But she froze in terror when she felt the cold, hard sharpness pressing into her throat.

'Who are you!' the voice demanded.

'I … I don't know …' Orla whimpered. And the truth of her statement struck her harder than the stranger had. Tears rolled down her face. She lifted her chin.

'Do it …' she said. 'Kill me.'

She felt the knife slice.

But then, suddenly, more footsteps came charging from the forest beyond the man, and the hands dropped Orla to the floor. She clutched her wet throat.

*

'Orla!' Gadryon cried. He heaved himself over the ridge and bounded across the platform. He threw aside the raft-like door and ducked inside Home Cave. 'Orla! *Orla!*'

The cave was almost pitch black within, save for the dim glow from the God Stone ceiling, but he knew every inch of it perfectly, just as his sister did. She wasn't answering because she was sulking. But all would be forgiven when she found out who he had brought to see her, and what they could do. He ripped the cover off her bed and groped around blindly. But the bed was empty.

And cold.

'Orla?'

He stood in the dark for a moment, listening as his eyes adjusted to the darkness. A creeping dread stole over him in the absolute stillness and quiet. All the food he had left for Orla was gone, as was his bow, his knife, and his arrows. There was no warmth in the firepit either.

His heart skipped several beats.

No. Nothing terrible has happened, he thought. *She's just gone deeper inside to get water.*

With difficulty, he climbed horizontally into the long, narrow, crushing gap that was just big enough to admit him. As he struggled through it, he felt a rising panic that had nothing to do with the enclosed space. He could hear the rush of water up ahead.

'Orla?' he called.

He tried to angle his ear toward the noise, but his head was too big to turn, and for a moment, he feared he might be stuck.

No reply.

She wouldn't ignore him down here. No matter how angry she was. He wormed his way deeper until the rock became slimy beneath his palms. He reached out with his arms and stretched them in both directions as though swimming a breast stroke and prayed to Ohrak that his fingers would feel Orla's bearskin.

But all they found was wet rock.

She wasn't there.

He felt winded. He lay there, choking with fear, blood fizzing, trapped between two compressing halves of a mountain.

Orla!

He scraped his head and chin several times on the reverse crawl to the cavern. When he finally flopped out, he darted around the cave. He plunged his hands into every nook, hoping without hope that he would find her asleep or unconscious.

But the cave was cold, empty, and silent.

His fear boiled into rage. He glared up at the ceiling accusingly.

'Where is she?' he demanded.

The enormous God Stone glowed softly, indifferent to his plight.

Gadryon let out a primal scream until his neck, jaw, and lungs burned. He darted from the cave into the cool night breeze and scampered down the cliff face. The second his feet hit the ground, he zig-zagged through the maze of sharpened rocks and pushed his way through the vines into the forest.

If Orla was not in the cave, she must be out here; this was the only way out. But what could have possessed her to leave? Unless she'd been taken …

He cast around wildly for any signs of footprints. The snap of a twig made him look down the slope toward the forest.

The three Elves had caught up with him. They stopped short, shining eerily in the moonlight. Two of them were panting.

'We found you!' said the fattest of the three with a smile. 'Good. So … where is this giant God Stone, Master Gadryon?'

'My sister is not here,' he said, resuming his search for tracks. 'I must find her.'

'She's missing?' said the same Elf.

Gadryon ignored him and crouched low to the rocky floor. He had spotted two faint, parallel lines in the superficial dust. When he put his eye along their trajectory, he saw that they ran loosely between the concealed entrance of the labyrinth and a vague disturbance in the forest shrub. He pictured Orla dragging her legs, and the image fit the pattern. But equally, he could see someone – or something – dragging her by the arms or hair. If she was alone, she couldn't have gone far. And if she'd been captured, he would find her captor and make them suffer. He followed the tracks toward the forest but remembered the Elves at the last second and turned to address them. The oldest Elf was looking at the curtain of vines, which still swayed from Gadryon's emergence.

'Wait here a moment,' he said, trying to sound casual. 'I will return shortly.'

He stared at the Elves for a moment, hoping they would wait, and then he melted into the forest at a jog, following Orla's distinctive tracks.

*

'You sneaky little bitch!' said the man, backing away quickly. And Orla heard fear in his voice.

The approaching footsteps had grown in number until Orla could feel the tree at her back trembling. She swallowed painfully but without difficulty and found that she could breathe. The man had not slit her throat completely.

'*Ekra-fey yest dah minrah!*' came a much harsher voice.   A Kraeling voice.

The man's feet turned in all directions, and Orla heard a sword sliding from a sheath.

'*Makra yamma eft erren hoss!*' came a third voice.

'*Kolto yamma,*' replied a fourth. And several people shrieked with laughter.

The human was surrounded.

'Brave in numbers, are you, scum?' said the man. 'Yes, very brave in numbers! But which of you will dare fight me alone?'

A soft thud and a slicing sound came as a sword was thrust into the ground.

'Come on! Which of you will dare?'

Many noises burst quickly: whooshes, a strangled cry, a loud clatter, gurgling, a crunch. And then silence.

Someone walked towards Orla and tried to lift her to her feet using her dislocated arm. She yelped in agony and fell face forward on her withered legs, crying for it all to end.

The voices took up urgently, and then another set of hands rolled Orla gently onto her back.

She was rigid with fear, clutching her shoulder. She flinched as fingertips caressed her face and closed her eyelids. Then the fingers moved to her good hand and gently prised it from her shoulder. And a soft voice tutted in pity. A female voice. A fingertip traced the cut on Orla's neck, and a warm palm came up to wipe the tears from her hot cheeks.

'*Erda, erda, malina. Lanthraa emmen yarra.*'

Orla had no idea what this meant, but the voice was soft and peaceful.

'*Erda …*' said the voice. '*Wolnin traveil sotti?*'

Orla could tell by the inflection that the voice had asked her something, and she could feel many other Krae close by, watching.

She swallowed again, then whispered the only thing that came to her mind.

'*Wahnei.*'

CHAPTER 48

The Cape of Berrund

In the hour after dawn, Leybridge was a frenzy of activity. Its population had more than quadrupled in the last few days. Two grubby cities of canvas tents had been erected haphazardly to the east and west of the battle mound. Children ran in groups between the tents, their shrieks of laughter piercing the rumble of chatter from the waking masses. Dozens of people swam or waded in the city moat, and the Ley's northern riverbank was crowded by those who had ventured out to collect water.

Elchora stood facing the battle mound with her back to the Urden, a spear resting against her shoulder. Her fellow Ablemen nearby whispered to one another, laying bets on the imminent trial or bemoaning their duty to guard a rectangle of mud. But at least, said one, they would have the best view.

A plume of white smoke from an extinguished fire drifted laterally across the ground like a phantom. Elchora shivered, cold and agitated. She kept glancing back at the forest, hoping to catch an early glimpse of a figure coming to her father's rescue. It wasn't that she doubted Colton's ability; his prowess among the elite in Laudria had been her suit of armour growing up. But he was ten years older, in a distant Realm, out of practice – and shape. If Gadryon didn't turn up to fight in his stead, Colton would have to face a wildly strong opponent who was bent on killing him.

The hours raced by as the milling spectators coalesced gradually into a solid mass, jostling for position. Elchora could no longer see the forest through the packed bodies behind her. She knew, however, that Gadryon had not yet emerged. For his appearance would surely cause a wave of excitement.

But he was cutting it very close. The sun was almost directly overhead. *Where are you?* she thought, willing his appearance.

Just then, the people on the far side of the mound began craning their

353

necks, and a ripple of laughter swept through them. A few seconds later, the crowd parted, allowing a bedraggled and tragic-looking figure onto the mound. And at first, Elchora didn't recognise the man.

Eurace, the Obediant, must have stumbled face-first into the mud. The front of his finest robe was lost under a slick covering, while the back remained gold and pristine white. Half his face was caked in mud too, and he was twitching like a dying animal. The laughter only grew as he made his way to the centre of the mound, crushing any remnants of his dignity.

Elchora had never felt so sorry for anyone.

Eurace unfurled a scroll with shaking hands and began to read aloud. But his voice was drowned by the fading laughter. Gradually, when it became evident that the Obediant would not wait for silence, the crowd hushed itself until the speaker could be heard.

'– to b-b-bear w-w-w-witness to this holy c-c-c-contest. Therefore, before almighty Ohrak, I c-c-c-call up-p-pon those who w-w-w-would seek to win this honour and c-claim lordship over this R-realm of Berrund … The ch-challenger, Commander V-victor Maldon –'

The temperature seemed to drop as Maldon, clad in formidable armour, ascended the mound with his entourage of cronies.

'– and the d-d-defending lord, Colton Farrow.'

The crowd broke out into whispered gasps as a tall, lean man leapt onto the mound with the agility of a cat. Elchora's lord father, wearing not a scrap of armour, his chin clean-shaven, his hair tied back in a ponytail, and a gleaming sword dangling neatly at his side. He was ten years younger. Fit, deadly, and radiating composure.

Every inch the warrior who had almost toppled the King.

A hesitant cheer swept through the crowd – why would he not wear armour? And Maldon's cronies sneered openly. The Commander himself, however, looked uncertain.

'C-c-combatants!' called Eurace. 'Announce your bearers!'

'Captain Luis Trapp,' Maldon bellowed, and one of the men behind him held a flaming torch aloft while his fellows descended the mound.

'Ableman Elchora Farrow,' said Colton.

Only after all heads had turned in her direction did these words register with Elchora. Heart hammering, she handed her spear to her neighbouring Ableman and climbed onto the battle mound. The sea of faces expanded in every direction. She swallowed and walked to her father, who handed her his torch calmly.

'What do I do?' she asked in a whisper.

'Hold it up high,' he said. 'And don't drop it for anything, do you hear me? No matter what happens.'

The little girl inside her shook with terror. But her father's unwavering stare gave her courage.

She looked into his eyes and nodded. Maldon's second was adjusting the straps on the Commander's armour.

'If I die,' said Colton, 'run to the Elves. The ambassador will keep you safe.'

'But you won't die?' she said. She had not meant it as a question.

Colton cupped her cheek in his warm hand and looked at her for a long time. 'Don't lower the torch,' he said. Then he turned and walked towards Maldon.

*

Maldon stared across at him, then buried his hammer deep in the mud. Colton dipped the tip of his sword into the ground and bowed. Maldon slammed his visor shut, wrenched his weapon free, and marched at him like a battle horse.

Colton evaded the first wild swipe of the hammer, then the second, feeling the rush of wind as the beak-like anvil cut through the air. Maldon could move faster than he had anticipated in his armour.

But not fast enough.

Colton lunged inside the third swing and brought his sword down on Maldon's head. The blade crunched through the seam of the helmet, and when Colton withdrew the sword, the helmet came away. Maldon blinked in surprise and swayed, looking sick. A deep red line ran the length of his scalp, dripping blood into his eyes and beard.

The crowd erupted.

A younger Colton would have backed off to give his opponent a reprieve. But he was wiser now. He slammed his pommel into Maldon's face and sent him sprawling.

Maldon's bearer looked stunned but kept his Flame of Oath aloft. Colton kicked Maldon's hammer from his slackened grip and crouched over his enemy. 'Yield,' he said.

Maldon tried to spit blood into Colton's eyes, but Colton yanked his head aside by the beard and held it firm.

'Finish me!' Maldon growled. 'Do it!'

Years of suppressed hatred boiled over in Colton's gut. Hatred of Markos for defeating him and showing mercy. Hatred for his failure. And hatred for the vile man underneath him. The man who had almost killed

355

Erik. He leaned in close and spoke into Maldon's ear. 'No,' he said. 'I'm not going to kill you, Victor … because I want you to remember this. I want you to remember.'

Maldon's visible eye widened beneath him like a skittish horse. He tried to buck free, but Colton kept him pinned to the ground with his restored strength.

'Kill me!' Maldon grunted. He tried to raise his voice above the cheering from the crowd. 'I do not yield! I do not yield! Kill me! Kill me, you fucking coward!'

Colton twisted the beard in his fist, and the bleeding man brayed pitifully. 'Remember this moment, Victor. Take it inside and remember it always. I want you to feel the shame and humiliation in this defeat. Everyone can see you, Victor. Beneath me in the dirt. Do you hear them cheering? They will always remember this. As you will. I want it to haunt you in your sleep, Victor. I want you to remember how you begged me to kill you.'

Colton felt a surge of cathartic euphoria as he expunged his venom. Maldon writhed weakly in apparent madness. But after a moment, Colton realised that he was laughing. Maldon managed to gain an inch and twisted to look up at Colton with both eyes, grinning insanely.

'But I've already won, Farrow!' he cackled. 'Because I took your daughter! That's right! I shoved my cock inside your daughter's little cunt! And she wanted it, Colton! She moaned like a whore and begged me to go deeper! And I did… I pumped my seed into your daughter's cunt. Your little princess was my little bitch! I want you to remember that!'

It was Colton's turn to laugh. To deliver his ultimate cruelty. He put all his weight on Maldon's head, pressing it into the mud.

'I know, Victor,' he said. 'I've always known. But your account of the deed is not the whole truth, is it? Because, in your own twisted way, you love Elchora, don't you? You love her more than anything you have ever loved in your mediocre life. And she rejected your love, Victor. She used you then discarded you. And now you follow her around, hoping for any morsel of affection. But you were only her plaything, as you are mine. A repulsive little dog, sick with love, owned by a better man.'

With immense satisfaction, through the blood, Colton saw tears forming in Maldon's eyes. Maldon gritted his teeth and howled in broken hatred. He mustered all his remaining power in a final attempt to throw off his tormentor. But Colton slammed an elbow hard into the rising face, and Maldon slumped to the dirt, unconscious.

The crowd cheered as Colton rose in victory. But the noise seemed oddly subdued, marred by a growing murmur. Movement rippled through the crowd to Colton's left, and, at first, Colton thought Gadryon had returned, at last, to claim his destiny. But then, Colton saw the five dark figures suspended above the crowd, swaying gently on horseback. And with a plummeting sense of dread, he recognised their sneering, sharp-cheeked leader.

Kaiber Almanfier had grown in the ten years since Colton had last set eyes on her. She was broad-shouldered, as tall as her father, with a face like a bony diamond. The huge figure of Braemond Almanfier rode to Kaiber's left, and a bald woman rode to her right. Both were flanked by slimy, grinning men with identical faces.

The crowd scattered in earnest before the five advancing horses. But the riders drew up, keeping their distance, except Kaiber, who kicked her mount onto the battle mound.

Colton stepped toward her, sheathing his sword, and bowed, thinking fast.

How had she marched around the city without warning? Why hadn't anyone sounded the bell?

It doesn't matter. Don't let her see that she's caught you unprepared!

'Queen Regent?' he said, drawing up. 'What brings you to Berrund so soon, Your Grace? I was told not to expect you for several weeks yet.'

Kaiber's thin, colourless lips curled in a sneer. 'Lord Scratch,' she said. 'I'd forgotten that you were alive up here.'

Colton ignored the jibe. 'You honour us with your presence, my Queen,' he said. 'Please, you must allow me some time to make ready my chambers. They shall, of course, be yours while the Throne Trial is in progress.'

'I'm not here for the Throne Trial,' she snapped. 'Not yet …' She turned her horse in a circle, glowering down at the crowd. 'I am here by God's will,' she announced. 'A party of Elves has fled here to hide among you. They carry something of great importance. And I bid them, step forth and kneel before me, now, or be found and suffer my displeasure.'

The crowd babbled quietly at this odd pronouncement. And from his viewpoint on the mound, Colton saw Kaiber's forces spreading out to encircle the gathering.

Dimitri! he thought, his heart pounding.

Suddenly, a wordless, desperate cry erupted from somewhere close behind him, making Colton turn his head. Elchora was reaching toward him, torch in hand, eyes wide, her lips drawn back in horror.

It was the last thing Colton saw as the hammer ripped through his skull.

CHAPTER 49

The Elf and the Witch

The crack from the skull made Kaiber's mount rear and whinny. Lord Scratch flew sideways, leaving a cloud of red mist where his head had been, his limp body dead before it hit the mud.

Many things happened at once.

The killer roared at the dead body in savage triumph as an outcry of fury burst from the crowd, who hurled stones at the victor. At the same time, two figures dashed across the mound; one ran straight at the bald killer, clubbing him with her flaming torch, shrieking through the uproar like a banshee. The other figure – smaller and hooded – threw itself theatrically across the twitching corpse of Lord Farrow, clawing in despair at the dead man's back.

Kaiber steadied her horse amid the chaos. The bald killer, caught unaware by the torchbearer, defended his exposed head from the attack.

'Braemond!' Kaiber called, whirling around in her saddle.

The giant dismounted from his horse with surprising agility. He jogged to Kaiber's side, his head almost level with hers.

'Break them up!' she ordered.

Braemond marched into the hail of stones and kicked the woman to the floor like a disobedient dog. Inexplicably, the bald man seemed incensed by this. He picked up his hammer and raised it, ready to swing at Braemond. But the giant was too quick and too powerful. He grabbed the bald man by the throat at the height of his backswing and lifted him bodily into the air. The bald man dropped his hammer again, his face turning red, then puce, his veins and eyes bulging in terror.

The barrage of projectiles subsided, and pockets of the crowd began to shout their approval as the bald man choked.

Kaiber pounced on the lull to regain control.   'Men of Iron!' she thundered.

From all directions came the sound of swords scraping from their sheaths. Heads in the crowd pivoted fearfully at the noise. Those nearest to the outer circle of armed soldiers backed inward, corralling the crowd into a denser mass.

A silence fell, except for the gargling of the airborne killer.

'Release him, Commander,' Kaiber called. 'You are throttling the new lord of Berrund.'

Braemond let his victim crumple to the floor. He coughed and gasped, clutching his throat for air beneath a ginger beard. The crowd murmured, and the woman holding the torch shrieked, 'He is not the lord of Berrund! He's a murderer!'

Several others among the townsfolk voiced their agreement, and Kaiber saw one or two people dip out of sight to gather more stones.

Kaiber slid from her horse and strode toward the woman but stopped suddenly in her tracks. An image of a pretty, sly, spoiled little girl had stirred in her memory. A girl with blonde curls and impeccable manners, who batted her long lashes whenever she wanted something, and whom everyone had called *princess* ...

Kaiber tilted her head to one side in amusement.

'I remember you,' she said with a crooked smile, glancing from the now-familiar woman to the sprawled, haemorrhaging remains of Lord Scratch. 'You're the Farrow *girl*, aren't you? Elchora!'

The blonde woman took a step forward and defiantly thrust out her trembling chin. Braemond mirrored her advance, but Kaiber stayed him with a lazy hand.

'I am Elchora Farrow,' she said, quivering. 'And I remember you well, Queen Kaiber.' Unexpectedly, she lowered herself onto one knee. 'And I humbly beg that you deliver justice for the murder of my father.'

Kaiber glanced over at the bald man, who had staggered back to his feet. His ginger, bloodstained beard twitched as his jaw muscles flexed in rage, but he averted his gaze, nonetheless.

Kaiber turned back to the livid, pretty face and smiled. 'Murder?' she asked. 'Was this duel not the conclusion of the Lordship Trial for Berrund?'

Elchora's head drew back a little in confusion. 'It ... was, Your Grace. But ... you saw yourself how Commander Maldon–'

'I saw a foolish old man killed lawfully by his opponent,' Kaiber supplied. 'Your father should not have turned his back. And *you* were acting as his bearer, were you not? Holding his flame aloft faithfully while he stood unprotected?'

Elchora's eyes darted from side to side inwardly as she replayed the fatal moment. Her chest began to heave, her mouth slack in horror.

Kaiber crouched down to recapture her attention, chuckling derisively. 'You stupid little girl,' she whispered. 'I always knew that you would pay for your lack of discipline. Coasting through life on your looks. Now, your self-obsession has cost your traitor father his life. And I will take great pleasure in anointing his killer as his successor.'

Kaiber stood, leaving the girl to drown in her grief, and turned to address the battered champion. 'You. What is your name?' she asked.

The man slipped his hammer into a loop at his side. 'Victor Maldon, Your Grace,' he growled, ducking his gashed head.

'*Lord* Victor Maldon,' Kaiber corrected, looking him up and down. 'Allow me to be the first to offer my congratulations on your … worthy ascension. But,' she took a step closer, 'if you interrupt my business in Berrund again, I shall slice open your fat belly and fill the wound with maggots. Do you hear me?'

The visible patches of Lord Maldon's face – those not covered in blood – went pale. He flashed his bloodied scalp once more in a gesture of submission.

A movement in the crowd behind Lord Maldon seized Kaiber's attention. Those close enough to have heard their exchange were shifting in agitation. A fresh spate of murmuring broke out among the disgruntled faces.

Kaiber almost laughed aloud. Surely these wretched northerners were accustomed to dishonour in their lords? She began to pace the width of the mound, intending to address the seething masses, when she spotted the profile of the thin, curly-haired man weeping over Lord Farrow's body.

Her eyes rounded in excitement. 'Bring Ambassador Lopek to me, Braemond,' she said quietly, pointing.

The giant obeyed, plucking the Elf from Lord Farrow's body like a kitten, and threw him at Kaiber's feet. The ambassador yelped. He skidded to a halt on his knees, his palms splayed on the floor as though in worship. He sobbed at the ground, and Kaiber was forced to wrench his head upward by the chin. Tear tracks cut clean paths through the mud on his cheeks, and his glasses were cracked and lopsided. Unmistakably, however, beneath the years and grime was the pedantic diplomat she remembered.

Kaiber smiled into the haggard face.

'Where is it, Ambassador?' she asked softly in Elvish Plain. 'Where is the Flash Weapon?'

Lopek's eyes bulged, but he set his jaw firm and said nothing. Kaiber tousled his curly locks with a sigh of mock impatience. Artan and Elden would have no trouble loosening his tongue. But a more expedient solution was required.

'Subei!' she called, making the Elf flinch.

She heard the witch ascend the mound and felt her kneel close by.

'Allow me, my Queen,' she said, cutting in. 'If he knows the truth, I will find it.'

Kaiber backed away as Subei locked eyes with the Elf. Lopek shrivelled under the penetrating, white stare but did not look away. Silent seconds ticked by until the witch's eyebrows came together.

Kaiber had never seen anything tarnish the masklike face before. What had the witch found?

Subei lowered her eyes at something in the Elf's lap. Tenderly, she lifted one of the Elf's arms and rolled back the sleeve. A wide, metal bracelet hung loosely around Lopek's hairy forearm. The Elf made to snatch his arm back, but the witch held him firm, and on his second attempt, she slapped him, whipping the glasses from his face. She unfastened the bracelet and stood slowly, inspecting it. After another few moments, her eyes widened in wonder before she shuffled over to Kaiber. But the shadow of doubt still lingered in her expression.

'What is it?' said Kaiber, spotting a faint glow from the object.

'An Elvish map, my Queen,' said the witch, handing it over.

Kaiber took the bracelet reluctantly and turned it in her hands at arm's length. There, on the far side, etched magically into the curved pane of dark glass, was a precise map of northern Berrund. Jagged, thin blue lines shone very faintly, detailing the city behind her, the forest ahead, and the mountains far beyond. Elvish words annotated the map, and a pair of distinct red shapes stood out clearest against the black background.

A solid triangle revolved like a compass needle as Kaiber manipulated the bracelet, and a circle flashed far to the north, near the mountain furthest to the east.

Kaiber marvelled at the object in her hands. It possessed magic she had never seen, yet she instinctively understood its symbols' meaning. She supposed the triangle must represent the bracelet itself, and the pulsating red dot must signal the location of the thing she sought most dearly.

The Flash Weapon.

Kaiber looked up at Subei and saw that something still bothered the witch. And it suddenly occurred to Kaiber that Subei might desire the Elvish weapon herself.

'What is wrong, dear Augur?' Kaiber probed.

Subei seemed to awaken from her daze. 'It's nothing, my Queen. Just … something I saw …' She glanced over her shoulder at the Elf.

'What did you see?'

'I'm … uncertain,' said the witch, who looked deeply uncomfortable at the utterance of such words.

'Something to do with your prophecy?' said Kaiber, pressing the bracelet firmly into the witch's breast. 'Do you still swear your loyalty unto me?'

The half-threat cleared Subei's troublesome thoughts away at once. She took the bracelet gently in her fingers and bowed.

'Until my death, my Queen.'

'Good,' said Kaiber. 'Commander Braemond.' The giant straightened. 'I want you to escort Lady Subei into the forest. Follow her wherever she may go. And take fifty of your best riders with you.' She turned back to the witch. 'I will have my Elvish prize before this day has ended. Do not come back without it.'

The witch bowed stiffly and swept from the mound with a billow of her cape toward her mare. Braemond glanced down at Kaiber.

'Keep close,' Kaiber whispered. 'If she does anything out of the ordinary … you know what to do.'

Kaiber heard the leather of the giant's glove creak as he gripped the hilt of his sword. He caught up with Subei and launched himself deftly into the saddle of his much larger stallion. Kaiber watched as they cut a path through the wary mass of townsfolk. Braemond followed closely at the witch's shoulder, pointing at fellow riders as they passed. Once they had gathered enough men in their wake, the double file of horses peeled north and trotted into the trees.

As soon as the party of riders had disappeared, the sea of heads turned slowly back in Kaiber's direction. Thousands upon thousands of faces. And she suddenly felt exposed, standing alone at the centre of this hostile mob.

Though the crowd was mainly composed of townsfolk, young and old alike, it dawned on Kaiber that they now outnumbered her soldiers by ten to one. And she had sacrificed nearly half of her best riders. A handful of townspeople glanced around, perhaps drawing the same conclusion. And a cold gleam of sweat began to prickle at her skin.

Assert your dominance, came her father's voice. *Quickly! Show them you're in control.*

'Good people of Berrund,' she bellowed. 'Ohrak has witnessed your Lordship Trial and summoned forth a new champion! To protest this outcome further will be treated as an act of heresy unto God! And I, Queen Kaiber Almanfier, shall smite you down in His name!'

A few of the sterner faces softened.

'Now …' Kaiber went on, 'step forth and kneel before me, Lord Victor Maldon … and be adorned with the Cape of Berrund!'

A stone sailed past Kaiber's head, missing her by an inch. She whirled around to see the Farrow girl back on her feet, snarling like a snared wolf, her fists clenched tight.

The moment protracted horribly.

Kaiber was about to brush the incident aside, but her soldiers fanned the girl's flame. One of her generals shouted, 'Protect the Queen!' as the twins kicked their horses onto the mound. Lord Maldon drew his hammer and backed away.

The crowd responded. They stormed the muddy slope as one mass, roaring in anger.

Kaiber drew her sword as the bedlam of bodies approached.

Screams rent the air. The riot of Leybridge had begun.

CHAPTER 50

Tracking

Gadryon ran, eyes darting across the forest floor. Orla's tracks meandered in odd directions, popping in and out of existence. A flattened patch of weeds bent southward, but a hundred yards later, he found the faint imprint of a fist heading due west.

As he came upon each tiny clue, a mounting sense of unease grew in the back of his mind. Wherever Orla was going, she was not being dragged against her will.

There were no other tracks to follow.

But why had she abandoned Home Cave? What could have possessed her to venture into the forest alone? Had someone discovered their sanctuary, forcing her to flee? Had a bear or wolves come sniffing around?

He pushed these questions to the back of his mind, determined to find her at all costs. Orla didn't know it, but with her Krae-like skin, she would stand out to predators from a mile away.

Another painful hour passed, and the trail went cold more times than Gadryon could count. Then, he found something that made him freeze with a crippling dread.

Many footprints converged around a blood-spattered tree. A few feet away, a sword that Gadryon knew well was thrust into the ground, the name FYVERN etched along the blade.

Gadryon's blood ran cold. The challenge from Fyvern was clear.

Gadryon saw the truth in his mind. Orla had fled Home Cave because someone had come too close. And without her brother to protect her, she tried to escape into the forest.

But Fyvern had caught her. Had perhaps already killed her …

No! Fyvern would want to humiliate him. To discredit him publicly. To destroy him.

And everyone would see Orla as a Kraeling. They would burn her on a pike.

Gadryon ripped Fyvern's challenge from the ground, turned to face downhill, and pelted southward as fast as his feet would carry him. To Leybridge.

*

The red triangle and the flashing red dot converged slowly on the black glass. Subei split her focus between the map and the forest ahead, trying to lead the column of horses directly to the Flash Weapon. But the terrain forced her to detour more than once. And Braemond drew up beside her every time they deviated, watching her every move.

On any other occasion, this paranoid behaviour from her mistress might have alarmed her. But Subei was too distracted by the images she had seen in the Elf's mind.

A vivid memory had floated to the surface of his thoughts through his grief and pain. A memory of the Elf handing a garment to the King's Augur.

'It's a type of armour,' the Elf had said. 'It will harden if the King is struck but otherwise appear to be an ordinary tunic.'

Lord Malcifer inspected the material warily. He drew a dagger from his belt and tried to pierce the fabric several times. When he withdrew the blade, tiny, hard lumps had formed wherever the point had failed to penetrate the tunic. The Augur eyed the Elf suspiciously, disguising his astonishment.

'And why do you seek to secure victory for Markos Almanfier?' he asked.

Because if Colton dies, the Elf had thought, *then I lose him forever. And if he beats Markos and wins the throne, then I will lose him all the same.* But he uttered not a word of this, saying instead, 'Anthar would like to prolong the prosperity that Nephia has enjoyed under King Markos. All we want in return is your assurance that Commander Farrow will not be killed in the trial. We would like him to come to Anthar, indefinitely, to act as a conduit between nations.'

'Banishment?' said the Augur thoughtfully. 'Yes. I might be able to persuade Markos of that. You have a deal, Ambassador.'

The implications of this memory were very troubling indeed. It was no great shock that Rowel Malcifer had cheated, but Commander Farrow had famously struck a blow to the King's midriff. A blow that had merely scratched his tunic.

What if that blow, under fair circumstances, had proven fatal? What if Ohrak had intended for Colton Farrow to rule Nephia? Only for the Elves to intervene and scupper His plan. Or did Ohrak hold equal dominion over the actions of Elves, making Markos the rightful King?

This seed of doubt worried Subei greatly. And she was unaccustomed to uncertainty. Silently, she recited the prophecy that God had entrusted to her. *When the true King falls, his champion shall be reborn as the Ulmar of Ohrak, and made immortal, for all time.*

But if *Colton Farrow* was God's *true* King, had she completely misinterpreted the prophecy's meaning? Was Kaiber Almanfier not the Ulmar?

But if not, then who?

The land sloped upward, and the horses' hooves began to clop on the rocky terrain.

Subei shook the doubt from her head and regained her composure. After all, the prophecy was redundant now that she was within reach of the Flash Weapon. She looked down at the map.

The red shapes were almost touching.

CHAPTER 51

The Queen and the Boy

The north field was a brawl.

Bodies collided, pushing and grappling all around. Voices shouted. Horses ran here and there, some riderless, while black-clad soldiers tried to fight their way inward to the battle mound. Those who were cut off from their allies were quickly overpowered and engulfed by the mob, their swords ripped from their hands, their bodies trampled underfoot. In every direction she spun, Lynn saw gruesome acts of violence. She gripped Kaldor's sweaty hand as they pushed and pulled each other from harm's way, dodging their way through the clamour.

'We need to get to the ship!' Kal yelled, pulling Lynn from the path of a rogue horse.

He tried to drag her again, but she dug her heels into the ground.

'Lopek!' Lynn cried, pulling Kal in the opposite direction. 'We have to get Lopek!'

A soldier nearby pulled his bloodied sword from the back of an elderly man and marched straight for them, grim-faced. Lynn felt her fingers crunch in Kal's hand. She jerked him aside, and the soldier passed them, heading, like the others, to protect his Queen.

Crouching low, Lynn and Kal wheeled around to chase the soldier, following the path he cleaved towards the battle mound. The soldier came up against an immovable wall of flesh and began hacking. Lynn and Kal broke away and pushed through a gap further along.

They scrambled up onto the mound, where the ugly Queen was fighting many people at once. The air around her was filled with dust, and the floor at her feet was littered with the dead. Among the bodies, far to the left, Lynn spotted Lopek, still clutching the body of his dead friend. She pulled Kaldor towards him, and together they scooped Lopek under his armpits and stumbled to the wooden platform.

*

The pounding of feet on the wood above made Eurace flinch. He squirmed into the shadows, clutching his knees to his chest. On the platform overheard, through all the screaming, he heard voices shouting in a language he did not understand.

Elves.

Deciding upon something, the group of feet sped from the platform, and Eurace twisted to peer through a pinhole gap in the planking to see which way they had gone. Through the distortion, he saw Elchora Farrow, sword in hand, her blonde curls swishing as she ducked and slashed, leading a cluster of Berrundish soldiers against Kaiber and Maldon.

*

Elchora's fury pumped strength into her every sinew. Rage and bile swirling. One-handed, she slammed one of Kaiber's guards to the dirt and killed or wounded at least two others in the pandemonium. But the black-armoured soldiers were beginning to rally, regaining pockets of control, and Elchora was determined to avenge her father before they quelled the riot.

She could see Maldon swinging his great hammer only a few paces away. But he was ensconced by his faithful cronies, who fought off the dwindling crowd in a frenzy of iron.

Wait for a gap! Then kill him! she commanded herself.

From nowhere, a wiry madman flew at her horizontally like a spear, knocking the air from her lungs. He landed on top of her, writhing powerfully, yammering spittle through gritted teeth while wrestling her limbs to the ground.

With her arms pinned, Elchora tried to twist her body free. From snatches of the man's face, she realised that the aggressor was one of Kaiber's greasy-haired twins. Slowly, with unnerving strength, he pulled Elchora's hands together and pinned them with one of his own, leaving his spare hand free to draw a knife.

He raised it high, shrieking.

*

Maldon headbutted the New Colour in the cheek and watched him go

369

limp. He snatched up the boy's sword and spun to find his next opponent when he saw the muddied blonde hair of Elchora Farrow struggling beneath one of Kaiber's men.

No!

He barged through his circle of protectors in her direction. When the man atop Elchora raised a dagger, Maldon hurled the acquired sword like an axe.

It spun twice before hitting the man in the temple, pommel-first. He swayed off balance on his knees, dropping the dagger, which pierced the ground inches from Elchora's face. She rolled the man over in the direction he was toppling and collected the knife as they righted. In the same motion, she pushed the blade mercilessly into the man's neck until it came out the other side.

Relief flooded Maldon's whole body. But in the next instant, Elchora was back on her feet, limping straight at him, armed with a sword, a dagger, and all the hatred in the world.

'Stop!' he roared, backing away. 'Don't make me kill you!'

Elchora's dagger dented his breastplate and dropped harmlessly to the floor. Maldon glanced down at it in shock, but she was already upon him, screaming, her sword raised in both hands, aiming to kill. Maldon met her wild lunge with a deft swipe of his hammer, knocking her weapon from her grasp.

But still, she came.

Maldon was running out of room to retreat. And running out of patience. He let Elchora grab his hammer and used it to pull her in close. She thrashed, spat, and flailed in his arms, but he had her.

*

The Iron Company had swarmed the mound, pushing the rebels to the lower ground. Inside their protection, all around her, Kaiber saw the trapped Berrund soldiers throwing down their weapons.

Then she saw him, lying face-up in a pool of blood, pale and dead but still grinning at the world.

Artan, her beloved.

She knelt beside him to touch his hair. He could not be gone.

'Please, my Queen, we must get you to safety!' said one of Kaiber's officers, offering her a hand unseen.

Without looking, Kaiber pivoted as she rose and cut the man's head clean from his shoulders. The decapitated body stood there for five seconds, arm still outstretched before it toppled like a felled tree.

'Stand down!' Kaiber barked at the men shielding her. 'Let me through!'

Those who heard her – or witnessed her expression – jumped quickly aside, clearing her path to the baying crowd. But some continued to fight, their backs turned.

Kaiber's temper broke. She ran her sword through one of her defenders. Straight through his armour and out his chest plate. The man gasped as the point emerged, clutching at the sopping blade as Kaiber steered him into the stunned crowd like a living shield.

The nearest cluster of the mob retreated in the face of Kaiber's aggression.

Using the space she had won, Kaiber scraped her sword from the impaled soldier and slammed it into the ground until the entire blade was buried.

'All eyes on me!' she thundered at the top of her lungs. 'And bear witness to my challenge!' She began to pace behind her sword, keeping it within arm's reach. All eyes had indeed found her, and silence had descended. 'Let us end this madness!' she went on. 'Let us end this needless bloodshed!' She shoved the man she had skewered to the floor, and the crowd stepped back another pace. 'I challenge any man among you to single combat! Any man! For peace and dominion over all the Realms of Nephia! For the throne itself!'

She stopped, letting her words reverberate across the field.

'Choose any champion you desire, people of Berrund! Let the bravest among you step forth and accept!'

The crowd's attention fractured as they searched hurriedly among their ranks for their best fighter.

'Who will it be!' Kaiber called impatiently.

*

Up on the mound, Elchora struggled against Maldon's steely hold. But her chin was locked in the crook of his armoured elbow, and he choked her into semi-consciousness every time she attempted to spasm free.

'Hold still!' he growled, his beard tickling her scorching-hot ear.

Elchora aimed a hopeless fist at where she supposed Maldon's face must be. But she couldn't work an angle to generate any power. Maldon punished her by squeezing harder, and her vision blurred horribly at the edges, the pressure in her head threatening to rupture as her limbs became weak and heavy.

G. G. ROSS

The sounds of their tussle had attracted the attention of Queen Kaiber in the relative silence. She strode toward them like a shadow, drifting in and out of focus.

*

The Farrow girl was red-faced and drooling in Lord Maldon's snare, her chin raised high, all dignity and beauty suffocated. Kaiber clutched a fistful of the blonde curls and prised the girl's head from Lord Maldon's arms. He released her reluctantly, and Elchora came forward on her knees. Kaiber put her sword to the girl's throat and turned her to face the crowd.

'You have one minute to select your champion!' she said. 'If no man steps forward, then your ringleader shall pay the penalty for your treason!'

As the crowd's muttering intensified, Lord Maldon hissed urgently into Kaiber's ear, 'Forgive me, Your Grace. But Elchora Farrow cannot come to any harm. She is betrothed to your brother, Prince Henrik!'

Kaiber's fist tightened in Elchora's hair.

A savage urge to slit the usurper's little throat came upon her, which intensified as Elden suddenly shrieked, 'She's the one that did for Artan! With his own knife! I saw it!'

*

Elchora screamed as Kaiber hoisted her by the hair and swung her at Elden's feet. Kaiber excelled at combat, but Elden was unequalled in making a mess.

'Don't kill her,' Kaiber commanded as Elden drew his dagger hungrily. 'I want you to ruin her. Slowly. I want you to change her face until she envies the gargoyles of High Castle! And then we shall see her worth! When I present my brother a deformed sculpture!'

*

Maldon gripped his hammer as the greasy man mounted Elchora and set to work. He sawed at Elchora's scalp, wrenching off clumps of hair and skin as she screamed.

*

372

Eurace clutched the God Stone and shut his eyes against the screaming. He could have seen what was happening outside his shelter, but he dared not look. The monstrous crime was feet away from his hiding place, and nobody knew he was there.

A dreadful, familiar battle raged inside him as two opposing instincts clashed within his soul; his cowardly instinct to hide, against his longing to save the helpless Elchora.

But what could he do?

Please, God, he prayed. *Give me courage. Please!* He gripped the stone until it burned in his fist.

Elchora's screams altered pitch, horribly.

Eurace tried to emerge from beneath the planking. To burst forth and cry out with Ohrak's wrath. But his legs refused to move.

Then he heard it above the screaming. A distant voice. Calling out in primal rage. Without thought, Eurace squirmed from his shelter as the distant voice roared again.

'*Where is she?*'

Kaiber's devil stopped his butchery, and all heads swivelled to locate the speaker.

But Eurace found him first, behind the crowd. And his skin prickled into gooseflesh as Gadryon burst from the forest to claim his destiny.

'*Where is she?*' he bellowed.

The crowd broke into wild cheers, Eurace loudest of all.

The prophesied Ulmar had come.

*

'*Where is she?*' Gadryon roared.

He marched through the scene, stepping between fallen bodies, barely registering the strangeness of it all. His only thought was to find Orla. And the man who had taken her, whose sword he held in his grip.

The crowd parted as he advanced, pumping their fists.

'*Ulmar! Ulmar! Ulmar!*'

A knot of black-armoured soldiers came into view on the battle mound.

Gadryon kept moving, unsure what horror he would find. Had Fyvern brought Orla here to execute her publicly?

Someone spoke from inside the wall of soldiers, and they parted to let Gadryon through.

More bodies littered the mound, but a few people stood in an uneven

373

group, watching him as he entered, including Victor Maldon, bloodied and broken.

'Where is she?' Gadryon demanded over the incessant cheering.

A tall, bony-faced woman stepped forward. She looked him up and down.

'What is your name, brave challenger?' she said.

Gadryon ignored her and continued to scan the faces surrounding him for Fyvern's beak-like nose.

He would fight them all if it came to it.

'Look at me!' screamed the unknown woman suddenly. 'You have accepted my challenge, boy! Now name yourself and declare your bearer!'

Gadryon ignored her again and looked at Maldon. 'Where is Almys Fyvern?' he demanded.

Maldon wheezed out a chuckle. 'Almys Fyvern would never act as your second!' he scoffed. 'Even if he *had* returned from the forest!'

Gadryon felt an icicle plummet through every vertebra of his spine. He spun back to face the Urden, the terrible truth dawning on him.

Fyvern had not left his sword in the forest as a challenge … He was dead. And Orla had been taken by those who had killed him.

The Krae.

'Name yourself!' cried the tall woman at his back.

The soldiers had closed the circle. He would have to fight his way through them to get to Orla.

Then, a voice spoke his name very softly. 'Gadryon …'

He turned.

Were it not for the familiarity of her voice, Gadryon would not have recognised the speaker. Elchora's head was a patchwork of gashes. Both her ears had been hacked off, and her upper lip was split in half.

The man keeping her upright grinned at Gadryon's horror, then licked his teeth obscenely.

*

Faster than a fork of lightning, something silver flashed through the air. The next second, Kaiber looked across to see a sword buried deep into Elden's face, the name FYVERN on the blade that jutted out the back of his skull, dripping blood.

Kaiber screamed as Elden toppled backwards.

She wrenched the hammer from Lord Maldon's hands and flew at the boy with every scrap of strength she possessed, wielding the heavy hammer as though it were a stick.

But the boy was fast. And equal to her strength. He met each of her blows with the sword from his waist, stopping the hammer dead with each parry.

It was like striking a boulder.

Kaiber retreated to catch her breath, and the crowd chanted louder. The boy did not advance. He merely stared at her with those dark-blue eyes.

Kaiber threw herself at him again, swiping, cleaving, crushing. But the boy remained resolute in his defence. Eerily steady, calm.

Make him attack, came her father's voice.

She glanced over at Elden's grotesque handiwork and marched at the disfigured girl.

It worked. The boy launched himself forward with breath-taking speed to intercept her.

Kaiber had no time to think of a counter. The hammer was too unwieldy, and she barely kept up with the boy's ferocious attack. Each of his blows numbed her hands until, at last, he left an opening.

Kaiber brought the hammer down with all her remaining might, catching the boy off-guard.

Except she hadn't.

Somehow the boy had anticipated her move – had left the opening intentionally. He pivoted aside, letting the hammer slam into the mud at his toes.

The hammer became light as a feather as Kaiber pulled it from the ground. She stumbled backwards in giddy surprise, barely keeping her feet.

But the hammer had not come with her at all. It remained in the mud several feet away, a familiar, severed forearm clutching its handle.

Slowly, Kaiber looked down at the blood-pumping stump as the agony seared through the adrenaline.

She collapsed to an explosion of cheers, clutching her half-arm to her chest.

It could not be real.

It could not be real.

'Kill him!' she shrieked, crawling away from the advancing boy. 'Kill him, now!'

But the black-armoured men around her were watching her flap around with odd, hesitant expressions. Some had joined the cheering outright, while others looked torn, glancing at one another for guidance.

'Ulmar! Ulmar! Ulmar!' cried the jubilant crowd.

*

Eurace's throat was on fire. But he did not care. He pushed his way through the swarming throng, desperate to put his hand on Ohrak's fabled warrior.

The ecstatic mass, a mixture of Berrundish townsfolk and Kaiber's own men, had engulfed the fallen Queen. They lifted her above their heads as she cursed them, vowing retribution.

Maldon, too, was fending off the rush of hands that threatened to seize him, and Eurace almost laughed. But in the blink of an eye, Maldon had wrestled a crossbow from one of his assailants and aimed it at Gadryon, who was busy helping Elchora to her feet.

Eurace stepped forward and felt the bolt break his ribs and pierce his heart.

'Oh,' he said, as a warmth and cold spread out from the puncture.

*

A scream made Gadryon turn on the spot. He took up his guard, expecting to see the woman returned to her feet, somehow whole again. But instead, he found the Obediant smiling at him serenely. A bolt jutted from his chest, a red rose blossoming at its base.

Gadryon rushed over to support the man as many hands engulfed Maldon.

Gadryon lowered Eurace gently to the floor. He was smiling toothlessly and looking straight into Gadryon's eyes.

'Thank God,' he said softly, placing something warm in Gadryon's hand. 'You're all right.'

Then his face slackened, and his head lolled to one side, his eyes still open.

Gadryon looked at the purple God Stone in his palm and felt a lump wedge his throat shut. He did not understand it. He had hated this man for as long as he could remember. And yet the grief was overwhelming.

His last brother from Fairwater was dead.

He closed the Obediant's eyes so that he might be sleeping.

Gadryon felt a pair of strong hands lifting him gently to his feet.

The people all around were kneeling, staring up at him with quiet reverence. He turned to look at the person who had raised him. The new colour, Tom Cloyn, whose nose was mushy from battle, smiled at him in astonishment. He lifted one of Gadryon's arms and declared, 'All hail the King of Nephia!'

'*All hail the King*!'

As the cheers rent the air, Gadryon yanked his arm from Tom's grasp and turned to address him over the noise.

'I'm not the King!' he spat, causing Tom to pull back in fright.

Gadryon strode to the miserable, sobbing figure of Elchora, who had slumped back to the floor, hiding her head under her arms. Gadryon prised her arms apart and pulled her back to her knees, kneeling opposite her.

She lifted her mutilated face reluctantly, and Gadryon twisted to address Tom Cloyn. 'Get her to the infirmary,' he said.

Elchora gripped his hands, unable to speak through her lacerated lip.

'I must go,' Gadryon consoled. 'But I will return. I promise.'

Elchora shook her head pleadingly. Gadryon drew her carefully into an embrace.

'The Krae have taken Orla,' he whispered, unsure whether she could still hear him. 'I must find her.'

Gadryon felt Elchora's grip tighten briefly. Then she released him, looked into his eyes, nodded, and got shakily to her feet, keeping her face averted from the onlookers.

Tom Cloyn put her arm around his shoulder. He led her toward the city wall, encouraging her every step with softly spoken words that Gadryon could not hear. He watched them walk until Elchora looked back at him for the last time and disappeared across the drawbridge.

The remaining crowd took up the chant once more. But Gadryon returned his attention to the forest.

Orla was still alive in there. He knew it.

He kissed his father's God Stone, swallowed his exhaustion, and took off again, praying that Ohrak would lead him to the Kraeling tracks.

The crowd chanted his false glory as he sped by.

CHAPTER 52

The Protector

Bill's head popped over the ridge, grinning down at Adam in astonishment.

'You'd better get up here, mate!' he called. 'You're not gonna believe it!'

Adam glanced up at the sheer rockface.

'I'm, err … I'm not sure I'll be able to climb this thing, Bill,' he called back.

'Just do what I did,' said Bill's head unhelpfully. 'Move one limb at a time and always maintain three points of contact. Easy-peasy.'

'Oh, okay, sure!' Adam replied. He rolled his eyes at DeVenus. 'What do you think?'

The blank said nothing.

'Cheers,' said Adam, rubbing his palms together as he approached the wall. It rose higher as he got nearer.

Carefully, he put his hands into jagged crevices above his head and tested their firmness. 'Here goes.'

He began to climb, inching his way up the cliff face with all the haste of a snail. But the floor receded beneath his feet.

Ten minutes later, sweating profusely, Adam found himself within arm's reach of the summit. Bill gripped his forearm, leaned back, and hauled him onto the ledge. Before the two men could steady themselves, DeVenus landed beside them, having crawled up the wall with Adam's case.

'Show-off,' Adam panted.

'Come take a look,' said Bill excitedly.

He led Adam across the ledge to a small opening in the rockface. Bill ducked inside, almost at a crawl, and Adam followed him into the darkness.

After several feet, Bill stood up, and Adam felt, rather than saw, the cave walls open all around him. He stood up cautiously, keeping a blind hand above his head. But, feeling nothing, he allowed himself to stand at his full height in the pitch black. The cave was dry, silent, and very still. The air was close and suffocating, though there was a sweet scent on it, and the floor was solid and mostly even.

As Adam's eyes adjusted, he saw a ring of stones surrounding a blackened firepit at his feet. On either side were two brownish beds of woven palm fronds covered loosely in some black material he could not identify in the dark. The smaller of the beds was laced with white flowers.

Bill turned to grin at him, just visible, his eyebrows raised, and pointed upwards with a finger. Adam lifted his chin and gasped.

The entire ceiling glowed a soft, electric purple. And Adam could do nothing but gape in wonder. Lost for words. It was like standing beneath a silent, rolling storm.

'Oh my God …' he whispered.

'So, it is Inficore?' said Bill. 'Not some weird trick of the light?'

'Oh, no, that's Inficore all right,' Adam replied. 'But it's … it's almost too much! That thing probably has enough energy to power a galaxy of stars.'

He wanted to reach up and touch it and run away in equal measure.

'How does that work, though?' asked Bill. 'Surely, if all Inficore has an infinite capacity, then its size doesn't matter, right?'

'From what I understand, it's about aperture,' said Adam. 'If the surface area of that ceiling is a thousand times greater than the fragment in my case, it has absorbed a thousand times the amount of photon energy.'

'But it's inside a cave. How much light could it have absorbed in the dark?'

Adam's laugh came out like a scoff. 'It doesn't matter,' he said. 'Inficore is as old as the universe itself. Maybe older – we don't know. But at the very least, it's billions of years old. On a cosmic scale, this giant piece has been in this cave for the blink of an eye. And its potential energy content is terrifying.'

'Right …' said Bill uncomfortably, frowning at the purple light. 'So … do you think you can transfer what we need into the smaller stone? Safely, I mean?'

Adam took a deep breath. 'Yeah,' he said, looking around, an idea forming quickly in his mind. 'This place is weirdly perfect. A natural chamber. I could place our fragment in this firepit and wedge the kirrion case into the cave's narrow entrance. I doubt it'll fit exactly, but it should capture most of the radiation.'

Bill let out a long sigh through his nose, scratching his beard.

'And you're sure about this?' he said, sounding a little afraid. 'You're positive that it's safe? And it won't, like, blow up or anything?'

'There's no reason it should,' Adam said. It was the best he could offer. But instinct told him it would work.

Bill huffed out another sigh. 'All right,' he conceded, rubbing the back of his neck. 'I'm gonna trust you on this one. But, please, I'm begging you, don't fuck it up, okay?'

A few minutes later, Adam was wedging the opened briefcase into the cave's entrance, using the stones from the firepit to plug any gaps. Satisfied, he stepped away, clapping the soot from his hands.

Bill crouched to inspect his work. 'What happens if the radiation leaks through?' he asked.

'Oh, some will definitely leak through,' said Adam. 'But a trace amount. Inficore *wants* to absorb the energy. If you and I stayed up here, we might experience some wild hallucinations, but that's about it.'

At that moment, a deep, rushing suction issued from beyond the flared briefcase and the crude pile of stones.

The transfer had begun.

At Bill's insistence, Adam descended the cliff first, followed by DeVenus. All three were safely back on the ground in no time.

'Is this far enough away?' said Bill, looking tentatively up at the ridge.

Sensing his apprehension, Adam said, 'No, let's keep moving, we should –'

Adam stopped abruptly as DeVenus pivoted to face the forest. 'What is it?' Adam asked, following the blank's line of sight through the labyrinth of sharp pillars.

Bill bowed his head, listening. 'Sounds like horses,' he said.

Adam heard them too. The distant clopping of many hooves. He looked back at the security officer. 'Who would be all the way out here?' he whispered.

'I dunno,' said Bill. 'Maybe a search party? I'll go take a look. You stay here.'

Adam ignored Bill and followed him quietly through the narrow maze. He could hear voices now. A woman and a man. Speaking Phrenaelia.

Bill edged close to the curtain of vines, careful not to disturb them, and peered through.

'Soldiers,' he whispered, barely audible. 'Wearing black.'

Adam tiptoed beside him and leaned his head toward a thin gap in the vines. Outside, some thirty armed soldiers on horseback, or possibly more, were milling around the sloping, stony clearing. Only two riders moved with any purpose: a massive man with an offset jaw, and a bald woman, holding something at arm's length as though scanning the rocks.

With a jolt, Adam recognised the cylindrical object the woman was holding.

Bill must have recognised it at the same moment. He took the dragonfly from his pocket and fumbled to switch it off.

But it was too late.

The woman outside was pointing Bill's wrist controller directly at them. She said something, and two men dismounted and drew their swords.

'Fuck, *fuck*,' Bill hissed.

He pulled the gun from his belt, cocked it, and stepped through the vines, hiding it behind his back.

The advancing men stopped, and all eyes turned on Bill.

The tall bald woman rode forward a few steps. Her eyes were completely white.

'*I know what you carry, Elf*,' she said. '*The Flash Weapon. Hand it over, and you shall not be harmed.*'

Flash weapon? thought Adam, his breath coming fast and shallow. What did that mean? Had he misheard or mistranslated? The woman's white eyes stared fixedly at Bill, as though seeing right through him.

Bill cocked his head a little to one side, and Adam realised that he hadn't understood what the woman had said. Adam took a deep breath and stepped out into the clearing. All eyes shifted in his direction.

He swallowed.

'Greetings, erm … My … companion does not speak Phrenaelia. He means no insult by his silence.'

The woman's white stare was like a laser, cutting straight into Adam's brain. Her full lips curled in a smile of satisfaction.

'Ask her what she did to Lopek,' Bill growled from the corner of his mouth.

'Your companion holds a weapon of great power behind his back,' the woman said, addressing Adam. 'A Flash Weapon that we require. Hand it over peacefully, and you shall live. Resist and die.'

Stammering, Adam translated for Bill.

The security officer showed no sign of distress. He stared back at the woman for several seconds, then aimed the gun into the air and pulled the trigger.

The gunshot blasted through the clearing and echoed from the rocks, causing several horses to rear and dart around skittishly. One rider was thrown off completely, and many had to wrestle their mounts into submission. The two soldiers on foot had flinched and backed away, as had Adam.

Only the woman seemed unmoved by the gun's power. If anything, her smile widened as Bill pointed it at her.

The giant man rode forward beside the woman, looking grim.

If this escalated, Bill had fewer bullets than there were soldiers.

Adam could smell the musky resin from the gunshot. His ears rang. But a rustling sound behind him made him turn in alarm.

DeVenus emerged through the vines.

The woman turned her icy gaze on the blank and her smile faltered for the first time. As her eyes met the blank's, her smile crumpled and her mouth fell open. Her eyes bulged. She let out a terrible scream.

'Kill them!' she screeched, her features inhuman with dread. 'Kill them *now*!'

The two soldiers on foot dashed forward, one aiming for Bill, the other for Adam. Another gunshot rent the air. The man running at Bill hit the floor with a clatter, and Bill swivelled to aim the gun at the second.

But there was no need to discharge.

DeVenus had stepped in front of Adam, taken the soldier's sword and impaled him with it.

The riders drew their swords and charged, led by the giant.

Nothing Adam had ever seen or dreamt could have prepared him for what happened next.

With one hand, DeVenus stopped the charging horse dead in its tracks. The huge rider flew over its neck like a crash-test dummy. Then the blank shoved the horse backwards, straight into the onrushing riders, scattering them like bowling pins.

The riders who had gone for Bill were unaffected. But the security officer fired several more rounds in rapid succession, killing at least three.

The giant got to his feet in a roaring daze, his enormous broadsword gripped tight in both hands. He lumbered toward Adam, forcing him back into the rocks. But then, something silver slipped through the giant's throat and retracted instantly, like a cuckoo bursting from a clock at a thousand times the speed.

The giant halted, his face went slack, his eyes rolled. Then he fell forward with a boom into a halo of dust, revealing DeVenus, who stood vacantly behind him, holding a blood-tipped sword at his side.

The other riders who had been knocked from their horses were staggering to their feet. They ran at the blank in horrible misjudgement.

It was too brutal to watch. And yet Adam could not look away.

The blank did not swirl or dance. He simply dipped his sword into the heart or brain of each man with unbelievable speed and sickening precision as though it were a needle.

Kill. Kill. Kill. Kill. Kill.

Dozens crumpled exactly as the giant had, falling in slow motion. And before each hit the ground, more had been killed.

Behind the carnage, the screeching woman had turned her horse's tail. She galloped into the trees, abandoning her remaining men to the slaughter.

The rapid volley of gunshots had ended, replaced by a clicking. Bill had run out of ammunition. But a single soldier continued to advance on him, sword held aloft.

The two men rutted viciously in a grapple.

The Nephian soldier, taller than Bill by a full head, overpowered the security officer and wrestled him to the ground in a tangle of limbs.

The blank was still on his killing spree.

Why isn't DeVenus protecting Bill? Adam's head screamed.

He raced across to help the security officer himself, but the two men were rolling as one. When they finally settled, each throttling the other – with the Nephian on top, Adam dived at them.

A rogue elbow hit him in the neck as he landed amid them. Adam's throat closed. He rolled away, clawing at it, unable to breathe.

Bill clubbed his attacker on the forehead with the butt of his gun, and the Nephian fell away, briefly stunned. By the time he had recovered himself, Bill had slid a second magazine into the handle and pulled back the hammer.

Bang!

The soldier's head twitched as the round flew through it.

Bill got to his knee and scanned the clearing with his weapon for his next enemy. No soldiers were left standing, but Bill's face was still hard, staring at something over Adam's shoulder.

Adam felt the first merciful, painful gulp of air fill his lungs.

'Call him off!' said Bill, backing away with his gun still raised.

Adam whipped around. DeVenus, drenched in blood, was advancing on Bill with a sword.

'Adam! Call him off!' Bill roared. 'Call him off, or I'll fucking shoot!'

Adam scrambled to his elbows and tried to yell. But the words wouldn't come.

DeVenus, stop! he gargled. *No! Don't shoot!*

Bang!

As the bullet left the barrel, DeVenus surged forward, faster than the metal charge. He skewered the security officer straight through the heart.

Bill's chin dropped to his chest. His arms flopped to his sides. The gun slipped from his hand.

'No!' Adam screamed, apoplectic terror overriding his pain.

DeVenus retracted the blade, and the security officer crumpled like all the others.

Adam crested the wave of nausea and got unsteadily to his feet. He staggered over to Bill's body across the collapsing world. He fell beside it on his knees, conjuring all his disbelief to fight this impossible, vivid reality.

Bill's grey hair wavered gently in the breeze, and it struck Adam how very different the man looked, lying there. There was no trace of Bill left in the muscular frame. All his components remained, but the pilot was simply … gone.

Adam's throat closed anew, and his breath came in ragged sobs. He looked up at the murderous blank and felt revulsion for his monster.

The landscape was littered with corpses. And all of them, Bill included, were Adam's fault.

Adam reached over Bill's warm body and snatched up the sweaty gun, not caring what DeVenus might do. He aimed the barrel point-blank and cried out in catharsis as he unloaded the cartridge.

Seven grey, stone-like spots appeared on the blank's torso. Bullet shells tinkled on the rocky floor.

DeVenus stared down at Adam without expression. The grey spots reformed into flesh.

'I'll kill you!' Adam whimpered, casting around for another weapon.

He made to grab a nearby sword, but DeVenus blocked his hand.

And again.

And again.

'DeVenus, reset to base mode and forget all primary commands!' Adam cried. 'Do you understand?'

The blank did not comply.

Adam repeated the command, slowly, clearly, keeping all traces of emotion from his voice. But the blank did not comply.

With a jolt, Adam saw that DeVenus's ears had turned stone grey.

Shit! He's protecting himself from my commands. *He's recognised* me *as a* threat.

The blank began to advance slowly.

Shit!

Adam stumbled to his feet and backed away over Bill's body. Panic boiled his veins as the blood-drenched blank walked at him directly.

'DeVenus, *stop!*' Adam shrieked. He changed direction and backed away quicker, his hands splayed innocently.

DeVenus pivoted to follow him, matching Adam's speed.

What can I do? What can I do? Think! Adam pleaded of himself. He picked his way through the bodies of horses and men with DeVenus three paces in tow, dripping blood.

Why did I try to kill it? How could I be so stupid?

But through his dread, Adam registered that the blank had not killed him instantly. Not like those on the ground.

Why? he thought furiously, almost slipping in a pool of blood. *Stay calm. And think. Why am I not yet dead?*

Adam trod carefully between limbs and viscera, trying to keep his retreat at an even pace. Intuition told him that sudden movements might encourage the blank to attack. Sweat dripped from his chin with the effort of maintaining steadiness against the will of his flight instinct.

On his third lap of the bloodbath, an idea came to Adam at last. *He's still protecting me,* he thought. *His threat response is at odds with his command to protect me. I am both a threat and the one he must protect.*

But if that were true, what did that mean? Would DeVenus harm him if he stopped retreating? Adam didn't feel like finding out. But he could not keep walking forever.

Against all his instincts, Adam turned his back on DeVenus but kept walking away. He winced for a second, half expecting a sword tip to emerge through his chest. But none came. He opened his eyes and exhaled, still walking. He heard DeVenus close on his heels. It was easier to walk forwards, but his panic ratcheted terribly without sight of his cold pursuer.

Keep walking, he urged himself. *Keep walking and don't look back.*

He circled the clearing again, careful not to stumble or change his speed.

But what next?

He couldn't risk walking back to Leybridge. He didn't think he could make it. And if the blank followed him, it might kill everyone who crossed its path.

Adam couldn't call it off anymore.

Nothing can stop it now, he thought.

Adam's heart sank under the weight of stupidity. He trudged helplessly from his abomination. From his imminent killer. The manifestation of death he had brought to life.

The minutes stretched into hours with no change in the stalemate pursuit.

Perhaps it would be easier to stop, Adam thought wearily. *To turn and face what I have made and let it kill me.*

Yes. Yes, there was honour in that. To accept his end and die facing it. Like Bill.

He looked over to where the security officer lay and felt his courage return.

No! Adam thought defiantly, careful not to alter his speed. *Bill would never give up. He was our true protector, not the thing behind me. It was Bill who saved our lives on the ship, while DeVenus was … was …*

Adam roared in triumph as hope rekindled in his every fibre.

He had a plan. A way to survive.

'This is for you, Bill,' he shouted, diverging from his orbit. He looked over his shoulder at the blank. 'That's right. Follow *me*, you son-of-a-bitch.'

Adam steered a path towards the curtain of vines and pushed his way through without slowing.

Two seconds later, he heard DeVenus follow but did not turn to look. He picked his way through the winding maze of stalagmites until he saw the cliff up ahead.

I'll have to climb without speeding or slowing, he thought. *If I slow down, he'll catch me. If I speed up, he might charge.*

He scanned the cliff face for handholds as it came at him fast. He gripped the wall and began to climb. Up. Up. Up.

He missed the fourth handhold and sped up in a panic.

DeVenus closed the gap, and Adam made the mistake of looking down.

A dripping red face chased him up the wall like a human spider, and Adam almost lost his footing.

Keep going! he willed.

Miraculously, dizzyingly, he reached the top without pause. But the blank's hands were mere inches behind his feet now. With an almighty effort, Adam heaved himself onto the ledge and sped toward the cave on his hands and knees.

But the increase in speed was his mistake.

As he grabbed the solidified briefcase, a hand crushed his left ankle to powder.

He howled in agony as he tore the kirrion briefcase from the pile of stones.

The sound of deep suction intensified. And when Adam rolled aside to look back, he found the point of a sword millimetres from his eye.

But the hand holding it had turned grey.

DeVenus withdrew the sword and looked at his hand as though assessing this new threat.

The grey stone spread quickly over the blank's body. Patches absorbing patches.

Unable to fend off this anomaly, DeVenus adopted a neutral stance. Gradually, in the flow of radiation, he morphed into a solid statue, staring into the middle distance.

Adam flopped on his back, breathing hard. After a few seconds, he bellowed out his lungs then sobbed in agony.

Colourful spots filled his vision as the Inficore radiation melted his synapses. But there was little he could do to stop it now. This was the price he must pay for his mistakes. At least he would die knowing he had stopped DeVenus.

*

Adam lay sprawled, staring at the pale blue sky, a breeze licking his sweaty brow.

It was nice up here, on the mountain. He could drift away. Just … let himself go and *drift* peacefully. Even the hot agony of his pulverised foot seemed too distant to bother him. The whole world was too remote for his concern. Through half-lidded eyes, he watched a perfect cotton cloud inch silently across the sky. Behind him – or perhaps beside or beneath him, he couldn't tell – the suction noise of the transfer beam changed frequency until it became like the static of a radio, pouring from all sides into his consciousness.

Curiously, as the sound increased, the cloud above expanded, its indistinct edges erasing the world as Adam watched in exhausted, stupefied wonder.

He blinked slowly in surprise and found himself staring into a white, endless void. The radio static had died away. Only the sounds of his breathing remained.

What's happening? he thought lethargically. *Am I dead?*

The notion didn't seem to trouble him.

He looked around, half hoping to find Bill waiting for him in death, ready to brief him on the rules of this afterlife. But all he could see was a featureless expanse of white in all directions.

He made to rise but suddenly realised that he had no *weight*. He could see and feel his body, which was painless and whole, but he couldn't feel anything else. He was neither lying down nor standing up, for there was nothing against which to orient himself.

Adam, said a voice from all directions at once.

He turned, if such motion were possible, and his weightless heart almost ruptured at the sight he beheld.

Genevieve LePlass, skinny and pale, wearing a grey hospital gown, stared at him through the suspended window of her room in Felix Primary, otherwise surrounded by the void.

'Genevieve!' Adam called. He tried to run to her but his feet simply paddled through emptiness. He waved absurdly. 'Genevieve! I'm here!'

But Genevieve gave no sign of acknowledgement. She continued to stare through the window. Through Adam. She was ten feet away, as clear as *he* was, but apparently unable to hear or see him.

Where am I? he thought. *Is this real?*

The moment these questions arose, he felt clarity and reason seep back into his mind. Of course this wasn't real. He wasn't floating in a white void. He was dying on a mountainside. And his brain, under the influence of Inficore radiation, sensing its final moments, had conjured the last thing it wished to see before it died.

'Genevieve,' Adam said aloud. 'I'm sorry.'

Adam, replied the void.

And this time, Adam heard her voice in the word. Her lips had not moved – because the voice had not come from her body – yet, unmistakably, Genevieve had spoken.

'I hear you!' he said, his voice thick with suppressed tears. 'Can you hear me?'

She spoke again, disembodied. *Yes.*

Despite his knowledge that this was a dying dream, Adam yelped with cathartic joy. He had found her.

'Where are you?' he asked, looking at her face through the window, if only for a point of reference.

Everywhere, she said. *Always.*

'I don't understand,' said Adam.

Look, said Genevieve.

Adam leaned forward to look more closely at her face. As he did so, he glided several inches closer to the window.

He could move.

Clumsily, he piloted himself around the window to float beside her.

Look, Genevieve repeated.

Adam, not daring to touch her physical body, followed her gaze to the window. And through it, he saw himself, sitting in profile in a cramped room, at the control desk of the Inficore chamber. It was like watching a play, a reenactment of a memory.

The Adam inside the window pushed a button on the desk and spoke into a microphone. 'Control is green,' he said.

'Copy that!' came Genevieve's voice from the reenactment. 'Initiating Chronosphere test.'

Adam watched from the void, marvelling at the power of his unconscious mind, as the window shifted its vantage point to show Genevieve, clad in the kirrion suit, crouching to press a button on her prototype.

A familiar, electric-blue sphere popped into existence above the machine, its speckled light collapsing inward. Genevieve squealed and punched the air as muffled noises of elation erupted from beyond the blast shield.

After a moment of frenzy, Adam's voice came clearly through Genevieve's helmet.

'Gen, the power has spiked a little. I need you to perform another motion test before we proceed. Please confirm.'

'Confirmed!' said Genevieve, practically dancing with excitement. 'Motion remains nominal. Wow! This is the most beautiful thing I've ever seen!'

'Copy that,' came Adam's voice. 'Begin test phase two on your mark.'

'Beginning test phase two,' said Genevieve, removing the wooden cup from her harness as though she were underwater. She held it directly above the blue sphere of light. 'Test asset in position.'

Both Adams, past and present, watched in rapt awe.

'Make history,' they said.

'Releasing the asset in three … two … one!'

Adam drifted away from the window, braced for the explosion, as Genevieve opened her hand.

The cup fell into the ball of light.

Instantly, the scene inside the window blinked into non-existence, save for the cup, which remained suspended in the void beyond, in the exact position it had fallen. Adam looked at Genevieve's emaciated profile.

'What happened?' he asked.

Standing on a surface that Adam couldn't see, Genevieve stepped through the empty window frame and collected the cup gently in her hands, her movements graceful and precise. Slowly, she returned through the window to Adam's side, her eyes fixed absently on the cup, holding it like a precious relic. The instant she stepped clear of the window, another scene formed inside it.

It was as though a door had been opened to a snow-covered landscape in the pitch dark. The bottom third of the window was filled with powdery whiteness, sliced vertically by the invisible pane of glass.

Adam peered inside the dark at the deep layer of snow. It was absurdly vivid. Real.

Genevieve knelt and reached inside the window, resting the cup delicately upon the snow. The moment she withdrew her hand, the entire scene disappeared, replaced again by the immaculate white void.

Adam watched as Genevieve stood and resumed staring into the empty window.

'What is this?' he asked his unconscious manifestation. 'Why am I seeing all this?'

We must prepare, said the disembodied voice.

Adam frowned but decided to humour his delusion. 'Prepare for what?'

Genevieve lifted her chin to stare at something high over Adam's shoulder. *They are coming*, she said.

Adam scanned the direction Genevieve had indicated. At first, he saw nothing but total, endless white. But then, just *there*, almost imperceptible, hung a minuscule black dot. A single dark pixel on a perfect white screen.

Adam reached for it, unable to gauge its size or distance. Evidently, whatever it was, it was too far to touch.

'What is it?' he asked Genevieve's profile.

Behind her, a new scene assembled inside the window.

Again, Adam saw himself, in a dark shed beside Kal's Nightfinder telescope. He folded a chair and laid it neatly against a wall. Genevieve stepped inside the scene once more, apparently invisible to Adam's past self. Delicately, with one hand, she turned the Nightfinder in the direction of the speck.

Adam watched himself react, saw himself move hesitantly toward the telescope. A dreadful unease formed in his gut like the shifting of tectonic plates. He *remembered* standing in Kal's observatory when the Nightfinder had moved on its own.

Only it hadn't. Genevieve had moved it. Adam had just watched her do it in exactly the manner it had happened.

Abruptly, the scene winked from existence, leaving only Genevieve and the Nightfinder in the void. She stared directly at Adam now, suddenly able to see him, waiting for him to move, inviting him inside.

Adam swallowed. He drifted tentatively through the window to the telescope, Genevieve's eyes following him intently. He put his eye to the viewport.

A sphere of swirling darkness came sharply into focus against the white. A seething, churning storm of dense black clouds, overlapping and consuming itself, its movements unnatural.

The hairs on Adam's neck stood on end. He looked up at Genevieve, breathing hard. 'What is it?' he asked, looking out at the speck.

When he turned back to Genevieve, he found a familiar table holding up a large, horned skull between them. At once, the skull twitched, then tremored, then rattled, as grotesque flesh formed around its features. The table collapsed into a broiling black cloud. The cloud formed a dark body, then arms, legs, claws, fangs, and wings, until a nightmarish, primeval demon, ten feet tall and terrible to behold, stood towering over Adam in the void.

Adam stared up in paralysed horror, too petrified to move or speak. The demon stared back with inky, black, comprehending eyes. The eyes blinked and the creature vanished.

Adam waited for his heart to stop hammering. When enough of his composure had returned, he looked over at Genevieve, whose expression remained masklike.

'Genevieve,' said Adam in a small voice, 'where are we? Is this real? Please tell me this isn't real.'

We must prepare, said the voice. *They are coming.*

Adam willed his brain to stop torturing itself. It was connecting random puzzle pieces and forming absurd pictures. But the images were impossible and incomplete. He tried to force his thoughts in order. To think logically.

'Okay,' he said finally, as much to himself as Genevieve, 'if I'm not dying from Inficore radiation and a planet of demons – as you insist – *is coming* … then I will do whatever I can. I will program an army of blanks to defend us. Like DeVenus.'

For the first time, Genevieve's expression changed. Her eyes widened, her lips parted, her whole face crumpled in dread. She let out a scream that split Adam's head apart and shattered the void itself.

With a gasp, Adam sat up panting on the mountainside.

The sun had long since set, and the sky glittered with stars.

CHAPTER 53

A King, Restored

Rowel Malcifer clutched the Elvish communicator hard to his ear, pacing along a hedgerow, a ringed finger buried in his opposite ear. He could barely hear the voice on the other end of the communicator over the chanting.

Ulmar! Ulmar! Ulmar!

'It's chaos up here, Rowel,' bellowed the voice. 'Colton Farrow is dead. But the new lord of Berrund was dragged away somewhere with Kaiber. I think they've been taken to the city dungeons. From what I could make out, her fight against the boy looked more like a brawl than a formal duel. So, I don't know what it means that she lost… but the people here are celebrating a new King, and Kaiber's Iron Company contingent has defected.'

Ulmar! Ulmar! Ulmar!

The Augur swallowed. Reeling. The Queen Regent was supposed to be in Emeron, not Berrund. What was going on?

'Is Kaiber alive?' he asked, trying to keep his voice low.

'Sorry?'

He stopped pacing and glanced around the immaculate gardens. 'Is Kaiber unharmed?'

A brief shuffling sound issued through the communicator, and the crowd's noise dimmed. The informant was on the move.

'She's alive, I think, but she's in bad shape, Rowel. Lost her arm, from what I could see, among other injuries from the duel. I don't know if she'll survive long without a Healer. And that's if the mob doesn't string her up first. It's bad, Rowel.'

Bad? No, no. This was fathoms deeper than bad. This was bedrock catastrophe. Rowel shuddered to think how Markos would react; Kaiber defeated and imprisoned. Mutilated.

He cast around for any driftwood in the whirlpool.

'You said the duel wasn't formal?'

'No. There were no proclamations, no torchbearers, no Augur. Kaiber did issue a challenge, but the boy never accepted it. They just started fighting. But nobody seems to care about formalities. Kaiber challenged and lost. Like I said, it's chaos.'

Rowel tore at a protruding branch from the hedgerow, cutting his hand on a thorn as he yanked it free. Who was this unknown boy who could so easily defeat Kaiber Almanfier?

Apparently, Rowel must have spoken this thought aloud, for the voice inside the communicator answered. 'Gadryon something… Phalhurst. Gadryon Phalhurst.'

'You said the lord of Berrund was dragged away. Was this Gadryon not the anointed lord?'

'No, some other fighter killed Colton Farrow in the trial.'

'Then why did Kaiber consent to duel him?'

The informant explained the strange sequence of events. How Lord Farrow had been murdered while his back was turned after Kaiber's arrival. How Kaiber had anointed the murderer and incited a riot. And how Gadryon had appeared from the forest amid the melee, forcing Kaiber to challenge him to avoid losing the skirmish.

'So, the duel took place amid a riot?' Rowel interjected, an idea forming quickly. 'Yes. Then it was a brawl, not a duel. Yes. I can use that. The Queen Regent was attacked by a mob and betrayed by her protectors. She was cut down in cold blood. Yes. Yes! Commit that truth to your memory, Mr Blake. Spread it wherever you can. Forget the boy's name too. Confusion and doubt shall free us from this mistake. Yes. Any news of a duel will not filter south of Reon for at least a week. So, there is time. Tell me again what happened.'

Mr Blake's voice sharpened with certainty. 'Kaiber has been cut down in cold blood, my lord,' he said. 'Her turncoat soldiers betrayed her and joined the Berrund mob.'

'Perfect, Mr Blake,' said Rowel. 'I shall inform the King. Your payment will be sent to the usual place.'

'Thank you, my lord. But there's more. And I think this information is worth double the usual price. I came across the old hive ambassador, Mr Lopek, on my journey to Berrund. He was travelling on foot with a party of Elves, but I brought him to Berrund by boat. He's stranded up here, in Leybridge, ripe for the plucking, my lord. I would have killed him, but the opportunity never presented itself.'

'Dimitri Lopek is in Leybridge?'

Rowel processed the problem as quickly as he could. If Lopek was in Leybridge, he might have confessed his part in Markos's victory over Lord Farrow. But to whom? Lord Farrow was dead. And with him gone, who was left to believe the story of an Elf? Still, better to cut this irksome loose end once and for all.

'Thank you, Mr Blake.'

The life in the communicator died.

It was time to face the King.

*

Markos regarded Rowel with cold sobriety as he relayed the news of Kaiber's defeat. Prince Henrik was not so adept at masking his fear and kept glancing at his father. The Augur framed the events in Leybridge delicately but spoke in quiet fury, just as he had rehearsed it on his walk to the Throne Hall; Kaiber had been injured in a brawl, he'd said. Taken prisoner by Berrundish dissidents, who claim to have won the throne in her capture. The King must act quickly before their lies spread to other Realms. He must summon the full might of the Iron Company at once and crush the rogue defectors.

When Rowel was done speaking, Markos stood from his throne and walked toward him. No trace of weakness. Rowel almost smiled. Here, at last, was his King, restored. And he knew that all the chaos threatening Ohrak's great plan would soon be remedied into order.

Rowel felt his windpipe close as the King seized him by the throat, lifting him bodily from the floor. *No! Stop!* He couldn't breathe. *No!* He couldn't breathe. Boiling panic flared in sickly waves as every vein in his head threatened to burst under the pressure. He clawed wildly at the rock-hard forearm and tried to wriggle his neck free. But the King's grip was vicelike. Restored to full strength. And there was no air. No air! He flailed like a salmon, pounding his knees at the King's scarred chest. But Markos only stared into his bulging eyes, tightening his grip. No! Something popped loudly in Rowel's neck, and his whole body quivered into warm, fuzzy paralysis. He looked over the King's shoulder at the young prince as his vision began to blacken at the edges. He reached out a hand for him. Henrik would save him, for Henrik would be King. Henrik must be King. Ohrak had shown him. Ohrak had a plan. And he thought *God would not discard me like this.*

Then, he thought nothing.

Markos let the corpse dangle in his grip. When he felt sure its weight had slackened completely, he let it flop to the floor. He turned to look at his son, who had taken a step back in terror.

'You are now the Commander of the Iron Company, Henrik,' he said. 'Assemble your men, Commander. We march on Berrund tonight.'

Less than three hours later, a silver serpent of men uncoiled itself through the gates of High Castle, with Markos and Henrik at its head. They had marched a full mile before the snake's tail had cleared the threshold, and pennants cracked in the wind all along its length. Markos looked ahead into the night.

All those responsible for Kaiber's mutilation and imprisonment would suffer at his hands. He was coming for all of them. To burn the North to ashes.

CHAPTER 54

People of the Bannebar

Gadryon clung to the sheer rockface, each breath lacerating his lungs. Both his feet and left hand were planted firmly into crags on the wall while his numb right hand groped overhead for the next solid hold. His bearskin was doing little to keep out the icy wind, which washed over him in vicious, biting avalanches, stabbing icicles into the wounds on his back. There was precious little exposed rock left to grab, and as he craned his neck to look higher up, resting his chin on the mountain, he could see the rockface disappear beneath solid sheets of ice. He had reached the foot of the Bannebar Ridge, a vertical glacier that formed a blade-like wall between mountains. Despite his determination to find Orla, Gadryon knew he could not climb an ice wall without tools. He held his body close to the outcrop of rock, trying not to imagine the warm safety of Home Cave deep in the mountain's belly. But then, Home Cave would never be his home again. He had returned to it after the duel to locate Orla's tracks, hoping she would simply be there, alive and well. But all Gadryon found was terrible evidence of Ohrak's anger at his failure. The mutilated bodies of men and horses littered the ground outside the maze, sprawled in twisted heaps, with crows feasting on their innards. At first, he did not understand what could have happened. But when he entered the cave and saw the black ceiling, he knew that Ohrak had burst from the mountain to smite every living thing in His path. The only detail that remained unclear to Gadryon was the presence of a stone statue outside the cave's entrance. But he dared not linger to discover its meaning. He had gathered up what remained of his belongings and set out to track Orla's captors. He begged for her life and for Ohrak's mercy.

He found the place where Fyvern's sword had stood in the ground. This time, Gadryon examined the area with greater attention, eventually finding the footprints of the Kraelings that had taken Orla hostage. Gadryon could almost see what had happened; Fyvern must have discovered Orla at Home Cave and tried to drag her toward Leybridge. But a band of Krae had stumbled upon them in the forest, mistaking Orla for one of their own. They rescued her and took Fyvern's body for food. Gadryon could only pray that Orla would not meet the same end.

He had followed the Kraeling tracks for a full day and night. They disappeared for long stretches, and each time, Gadryon retraced his steps and widened his search. In the end, the tracks had vanished completely, and he was forced to guess which way they had gone based on their trajectory. And the tracks pointed squarely at the Bannebar.

The Krae were taking Orla with them back to the darkness of Kininumbra.

A thought occurred to Gadryon as he shivered on the rock face. If he could not climb the ice ledge to cross the ridge, the Krae could not either. This was simply another dead-end.

As he looked down for a foothold, he saw a dim light emanating weakly from a patch of ice nearly thirty feet beneath him to his left. He twisted on the rock to get a better look, thinking that the ice must be reflecting the light of the setting sun to the west. But the glowing patch of ice lay in shadow.

The light shone from within.

Gadryon climbed toward the glimmer and found a large, oval-shaped hole in the ice sheet, tall enough to stand inside and wide enough to reach out with both arms without touching the walls. Carefully, he lowered himself into the oval mouth and peered further in. He found a long tunnel, smooth on all sides, stretching away into the glacier. A flickering golden light glistened on the wall of a distant bend. Gadryon began to walk through the bowel of the ridge.

So, this is how they cross the mountains, he thought.

The wind whistled through the tunnel as Gadryon advanced cautiously.

Before he knew it, the far end of the tunnel came into view around the bend, and Gadryon had walked clean through the blade of the Bannebar, from Nephia into the Darklands of Kininumbra, which were aptly named.

The sun could not have set in the scant minutes it had taken him to cross the ridge. But the sky on the far side was thick with clouds, and pitch darkness expanded away from the mountain without end. The only source of light was a fire near the opposite entrance. And as Gadryon drew closer, still concealed inside the mouth of the icy tunnel, he began to hear voices speaking in a familiar language he did not understand. He edged toward the exit and peered down.

Here, the ridge was not a vertical blade of ice. It was an enormous drift of compacted snow, sloping down and away from the mountain like a slide, its brilliant whiteness swallowed gradually into the dark oblivion below. Twenty or so Kraelings had dug out a circular shelf in the drift, ten feet from the tunnel's entrance. They huddled beneath blankets around a fire, and a cooking pot bubbled away over the flames. Even against the pure white snow, the exposed Kraeling faces shone brightly, emitting soft light.

They were eating.

One of the wrapped figures leant inward to turn the skewered meat. As it did so, the blanket it clutched slipped, parting like curtains, revealing Orla's face in profile. She clung to the bosom of the female Kraeling, sound asleep.

What's wrong with her? What have they done to her?

His heart hammering against his ribcage, Gadryon drew his sword as quietly as he could. Only a dozen of the twenty figures were armed, but two had longbows. He would have to kill the archers first, and fight off the others as quickly as he could. There could be many more in the darkness beyond the firelight. He took a breath and adjusted his grip on the sword.

Just as he was about to leap from the tunnel, Gadryon froze. The female Kraeling holding Orla had torn a strip of meat, put it to her lips, then gently roused Orla and offered her the morsel. Orla accepted it freely, then snuggled back into the warm folds of the blanket. The female Kraeling brushed Orla's hair behind her ear and began to rock back and forth, humming softly.

Hot tears rolled down Gadryon's cheeks. He watched for several long minutes as his sister was simply held.

The other Kraelings paid Orla no attention. They ate and drank and spoke and laughed in contentment. Not ignoring her, merely accepting her at their fireside. All at once, Gadryon was caught in a crosswind. Rage boiled in his stomach at the sight of her with their enemy. While, at the same time, a cold relief washed over him. She was safe. And she would be safe without him forever now.

Orla belonged with these people.

As Gadryon stood separated from her in the mouth of the icy tunnel, he felt a surge of loneliness that threatened to unman him from what he must do. He sheathed his father's sword with a soft thud and took a final, heart-wrenching look at Orla. His beloved sister. And as though she could sense him, she raised her head from the blanket and turned her face in his direction.

Orla blinked her blind eyes, and then her hand shot through the curtain of blankets, pointing in Gadryon's direction. The Kraelings spotted him at once and took up their weapons. Gadryon turned to run.

An arrow pierced his side, thrusting up inside his ribcage, causing him to stagger into the tunnel wall.

The air wheezed out from his lungs. He put his back to the wall and tried to pull the arrow free when a second arrow slammed into his gut.

Orla.

His vision blurred in and out of focus.

He keeled sideways and fell.

Suddenly, the orange glow of the Krae fire was flying away as Gadryon tobogganed down the drift into the darkness, gathering speed, the rushing snow setting his back on fire. He tried to roll and dig his arms into the frozen powder, but the arrow in his side snapped, and he felt the arrowhead inch further inside his chest. No scream came from his mouth as he slammed headlong into a pile of rocks in the pitch dark.

He could feel the wet blood pumping out from the top of his head and felt his death as the numbness took hold.

A jumble of memories swam through his head all at once. The smell of his father's head as he sat on his shoulders. The infectious sound of his mother's laugh. The first time one of his traps had caught a rabbit in the Urden. Feeding goat milk to his baby sister. And Elchora's touch on his skin …

All gone, forever.

But Orla is safe, he consoled himself drunkenly. *You kept her safe.*

Absently, as the blood and heat seeped from his body, he realised that his left hand was warming up somehow. He let his head loll to the side to face it but could see nothing in the complete darkness. He moved his fingers and felt the gentle stir of water.

Strange, he thought. *Warmth in the frozen dark.*

But he was glad for the water's company as he drifted away. As his fingers stirred the water, something hard brushed against his knuckles. An object.

Gadryon clutched for it with a final effort and brought it before his eyes.

A wooden cup.

Feeling some of the water sloshing inside, Gadryon brought the warmth to his lips and drank.

ABOUT THE AUTHOR

G. G. Ross was born in Cardiff in 1987. He lives in South Wales with his partner and their two sons. His written work to date includes a few short stories on a misplaced memory stick and a handful of modestly successful plays. *The God Stone – Book One* is his debut novel. He is quietly but willfully completing the trilogy. His future works include:

The God Stone – Book Two

The God Stone – Book Three

FROM THE AUTHOR

Hello, dear reader.

Thank you for taking the time to read my book. If you enjoyed it, please consider sharing it, or leaving a review online so that other readers, like you – though less intelligent and attractive – might also find it. If you like, you can also contact me directly at thegodstone@outlook.com, where I will endeavor to answer as many emails as possible. In the meantime, wherever you are and whatever you're doing, have a brilliant day, and remember to do that thing you've been putting off.

G.G. Ross.

Printed in Great Britain
by Amazon